Valerie's Verdict

Dixon Brothers Book 2

A novel by

HALLEE BRIDGEMAN

To: Kim

Live a life of love.
Ephesians 5:2

Hallee
Bridgeman

Copyright Notice

PUBLISHED BY: Olivia Kimbrell Press™*, P.O. Box 470, Fort Knox, KY 40121-0470. The Olivia Kimbrell Press™ colophon and open book logo are trademarks of Olivia Kimbrell Press™.

**Olivia Kimbrell Press™ is a publisher offering true to life, meaningful fiction from a Christian worldview intended to uplift the heart and engage the mind.*

Original Cover Art by Amanda Gail Smith (amandagailstudio.com).

Library Cataloging Data

Names: Bridgeman, Hallee (Bridgeman Hallee) 1972-

Title: Valerie's Verdict; The Dixon Brothers Series book 2 / Hallee Bridgeman

406 p. 5 in. × 8 in. (12.70 cm × 20.32 cm)

Description: Olivia Kimbrell Press™ digital eBook edition | Olivia Kimbrell Press™ Trade paperback edition | Kentucky: Olivia Kimbrell Press™, 2019.

Summary: Broken and battered, Valerie comes home and finds a lifetime of love waiting for her.

Identifiers: ePCN: 2019952627 | ISBN-13: 978-1-68190-151-0 (ebk.) | 978-1-68190-160-2 (POD) | 978-1-68190-160-2 (trade) | 978-1-68190-161-9 (hardcover)

1. clean romance love story 2. women's inspirational 3. man woman relationships 4. Christian living 5. physical abuse 6. forgiveness redemption 7. secrets and lies

Valerie's Verdict

Dixon Brothers Book 2

A novel by

HALLEE BRIDGEMAN

Published by
Olivia Kimbrell Press™

Olivia Kimbrell Press™

Table of
Contents

This book is dedicated to every abused spouse who had the courage to get out and make a new life for yourself. God bless you.

If you are in the United States and suffer from domestic violence, the domestic violence hotline is: 1-800-799-7233. I urge you to seek help.

Bradford Dixon stood on the little stone bridge that spanned the koi pond in his parents' back yard. His bare feet gripped the stone as he punched forward, pivoted on the ball of his foot, and kicked high in the air with his left foot. With his leg still raised, he angled his body, turned his foot, and kicked two more times, ending the sequence with a loud, "Hi-ya!"

The white cotton material of his *dobok*, his uniform, nearly clapped with the force of his kicks. His red and black cloth *dhee*, his belt, moved along with him as if accentuating the ironic grace of his powerful motions. Then, as he did a half-turn, he fumbled and paused, his face flooding with heat when he spotted Valerie Flynn sitting on the ledge of the gazebo, watching him with a silent smile that simultaneously teased and warmed him.

She had skin the color of rich milk chocolate, light brown eyes that reminded him of buttery caramel, and a face he dreamed of at night. That beautiful face. Tonight, she wore denim shorts that made her legs look impossibly long and a white T-shirt with a glittery flying unicorn on it. She'd kicked her sandals off and they lay on the grass next to her. She had painted her toenails the same rich glossy burgundy as her fingernails.

Losing his form, unable to concentrate, Brad stopped working and padded toward her on his bare feet.

"Black belt test tonight?" she asked, her smile growing wider.

"Yeah. We have to leave in a few minutes." He would normally sit next to her—he really wanted any excuse to get closer to her—but he didn't want to risk getting his gleaming white Tae Kwon Do uniform dirty. He stood just a few feet away and caught her eyes.

"You'll get it. I have faith in you." The sweltering Georgia summer sun beat down on their heads, making her black hair shine as if lit by a halo.

"I said I'd get it before high school. Kind of have to since school starts tomorrow." He shrugged and tried his best to look confident and self-assured. "Besides, since Ken and Jon got theirs last time we tested, I kinda have to get it this time." Being the middle son of three identical triplet fourteen-year-old brothers born minutes apart led to some serious competition in his family.

"It's not your fault you had the flu. You'd have your

black belt if you hadn't gotten sick." She ran her painted bare toe over a loose rock on the path leading to the gazebo. "Anyway, don't talk about school starting tomorrow. I don't even want to think about it."

Brad knew her apprehension had nothing to do with the imminent first day of ninth grade, and everything to do with the fact that, just as soon as her Uncle Buddy got home from work tonight, she'd leave the Dixon home forever. Valerie and Buddy had lived in the little cottage on the property for the past eleven years, ever since her parents had been taken from this world far too soon. Brad's mom had insisted on helping her husband's best friend raise his orphaned niece. Buddy had determined that after this summer, Valerie didn't need the "babysitting" anymore, and had bought his own house in another part of Atlanta miles from here.

They'd spent the last week moving the two of them. Brad and his brothers had hauled boxes, furniture, and suitcases. With every load, Brad felt his heart break a little more.

When Brad returned from his black belt test tonight, Valerie would not greet him and congratulate him. Tomorrow morning, Valerie would not join the family at the breakfast table. They would not make their way to school together. Brad knew these facts shouldn't make him angry or sad, or make him feel some unexplained longing, so he tried not to think too much about his emotions.

Valerie stood and pulled a small metal box from her pocket. "Did you bring it?" When Valerie stood, her eyes were level with his chin. He had to incline his gaze to stare down into her caramel brown eyes. He did gaze, wondering what she would do if he leaned closer and kissed her right on those amazing lips. As he gazed into her eyes, he noticed once again the fascinating gold flecks in her eyes that sparkled whenever she giggled. "Brad? Hello? Did you bring it?"

"Yes." Trying to play it cool, he casually broke his gaze, licked his dry lips, and walked over to the gazebo where he picked up the sealed envelope from the bench.

"Your brothers gave me each of theirs at the house." She opened the box, and Brad saw three envelopes inside. Valerie had written her name on the top one. He handed her his envelope. "This box contains our hopes and dreams." She smiled up at him, and her large mischievous eyes shone with excitement. "Where should we hide it?"

He looked up at the rafters of the gazebo. "Give it here." Putting the box between his lips, flinching a little at the feel of the cold metal against his tongue, he stood on the bench and, using a beam for support, climbed to the top of the back of the bench. His bare toes gripped the wood of the bench like little fists and stabilized him. He could just barely brush the top of the beam with his fingertips, so he aimed, flexed, jumped, and grabbed the beam with both hands. Executing an easy pull-up, he held himself aloft at the top and investigated the area until he saw a spot tucked away at one of the corners of the roof, where the roof and a wall beam came together near one of the gables. After slipping the box onto the little shelf there, he lowered himself back down, dropping the last few feet to the bench.

"There you go."

Valerie clapped her hands. "It is going to be so much fun to open them!"

"Fifteen years from now."

"We should have made the pact for fifty years."

"Fifteen years from now, we'll be thirty. That's pretty old. Fifty years would be too long to wait. I don't think I'd want to wait that long." Thinking about what he'd written down on his note card, he prayed it would come true. If it did, the next fifty years would go by like a dream. "Did you talk to Buddy last night about you switching schools?"

Valerie shrugged and leaned over to pluck at a piece of grass. When she stood again, the movement of her body and limbs looked just as lithe and supple as any intentional movement a *prima ballerina* might perform on some grand stage. Every time she moved, she exhibited this natural economy of motion, poise, and grace. She even walked as if she were gliding from place to place, hovering above the earth upon which these heavy mortals trod.

"He wants me in a high school that's more 'diverse.'" She said the word like it tasted bad in her mouth and accented it with air quotes.

"I guess." He looked down at his bare foot next to hers and wished he didn't have such stark white skin in comparison. Maybe then Buddy wouldn't have an objection and they could just stay. "Doesn't seem right, though."

"Doesn't *seem* right because it's *not* right." A sharp whistle sounded from the house. Without hesitation, the two of them started walking in that direction. Brad slowed his long, loping strides to match Valerie's easy, feminine footfalls. "But it's the world we live in. So, I'll do what he wants and miss you guys every day. With the three of you, I always had at least one of you guys in class with me. Now, I'll be all alone."

He grit his teeth and his lips tightened. Even at fourteen,

Brad recognized that Valerie always lumped him together with his brothers. He'd spent the last two years wishing and praying that she would see him as an individual, an eligible man, a man who cared more for her than any other man could, and not just an even third of some nebulous triplet whole.

Right before they stepped out from the tree line, he impulsively reached out and took her hand. "Valerie...," What should he say? Was it too late to kiss her? How could he possibly convey his thoughts and feelings when he didn't know how to satisfactorily categorize them for his own understanding? He cleared his throat as she looked up at him with those clover honey eyes. "I... if you ever need anything, ever, anything at all, call me. I'll be there."

Her smile vanished and she nodded exactly once. Right before she turned and dashed toward the house, he could have sworn he saw her eyes fill with tears.

Slowly, wanting to delay his departure for as long as possible, he walked the same direction she ran, watching her grow smaller and smaller in the distance.

Ten Years Later

Moving just as fast as she could, Valerie Flynn raced into the walk-in closet and pulled the suitcase off the top shelf. Opening it right there on the floor, she grabbed clothes and tossed them into it without bothering to fold a single thing. A few skirts, some blouses, a couple pair of pants. Check. Now, shoes.

She wore a navy skirt with matching heels and a white silk blouse. Her outfit would go with most of what she'd thrown into the suitcase and make a few more outfits.

She looked at her shoe rack, at the dozens of pairs there. The idea of leaving them hurt some feminine part of her. No choice, though. If she wanted to get out, she had mere minutes left to do it. Grabbing a pair of black flats and a pair of tan heels, she tossed them on top of the clothes. She'd already gotten cash out of the bank. She could buy a toothbrush and new underwear when she got to Atlanta. As she snapped the suitcase shut, she heard the front door slam.

Feeling her stomach turn to water, she quietly turned off the closet light and pulled the door closed. Maybe he'd leave. She fisted her hand and held it to her mouth, realizing how cold her fingers felt. Eyes closed, holding her breath, wishing the floor would dissolve under her feet and envelope her, she waited, listening to him tear through the apartment looking for her. She tried very hard not to make a single sound.

"I know you're here!" he bellowed, storming into the bedroom.

She gave a startled cry when he kicked the closet door open. Holding her hands up in front of her face, she tried to evade his grasp, but he managed to grab hold of her hair and pull her out of the closet. She moved her feet as fast as she could to keep up with him, trying to alleviate the pull on her scalp. Reflexive tears streamed down her face and she started talking.

"I'm sorry. I'm sorry," she said over and over again.

He stopped in front of the full-length mirror next to the closet. "Look!" he screamed in her ear.

She hated when he did this. But, years of conditioning had her opening her eyes. She saw her lip curl up in disgust as she stared at herself. Mascara had mixed with tears and ran in black streaks down her brown face. Her shirt had shifted and she could see bruising on her shoulder from two nights ago, the dark purpling barely showing against her chocolate skin.

Tyrone's eyes had a frenzied look to them, and she could smell cheap blended whiskey on his breath. Her stomach turned at the smell. He was well beyond reasoning right now. If she just endured it, it would eventually end. He would eventually sleep it off. Then she'd leave, for good, with or without the suitcase.

"You see this?" he said, no longer screaming. He grabbed her chin from behind and squeezed hard enough to make her whimper. "This is mine. You think I'll let you just leave?"

Without warning, he let go of her chin and smashed her forehead against the mirror. She felt the glass cut into her skin and screamed more in fear than pain.

"The only way you'll leave me is in a coffin," he declared, spinning her around to face him. As soon as he let go, she stepped backward, holding her hands up in front of her. She could feel the blood dripping down her face. "Do you understand me?" he screamed, spittle flying from his mouth, emphasizing each word.

"Yes, yes, yes," she whispered over and over again. "I'm sorry. Yes. Please, just don't hurt me."

"Hurt you?" Hurling an obscenity at her, he reached back and punched her with his closed fist. She felt her knees buckle at the pain that exploded in her cheek. Stunned, she fell, clutching out to try to stop her fall. She couldn't end up on the floor. He'd start kicking her if she fell. She had to stay on her feet.

Somehow, she managed to grab the edge of the dresser and pull herself up. Before she could step away, he had her by the neck. "I don't think you're really sorry," he said.

As soon as she realized he had started to drag her to the glass doors, she started fighting him, screaming, clawing, scratching, kicking. But he was bigger, stronger, angry, and drunk. He threw the door open so hard she heard the glass shatter. With a roar, he pushed her up against the balcony and screamed at her. "You want it over? Then I'll end it!"

Crying, clawing at the hands around her neck, she kicked out and managed to jam the heel of her shoe into the flesh of his thigh. He roared in pain and grabbed her shin.

She could feel the metal railing of the balcony digging into her shoulder blades seconds before he flipped her over it. Suddenly, Valerie felt nothing, nothing at all. She didn't even feel the air rushing past her the entire way to the ground.

Then she felt everything for exactly as long as it took for her vision to flash red like lightning at sunset. She felt glass shattering all around her, and saw it fly up into her flesh like a thousand razor blades and all around her like a million glittering diamonds the instant before she felt unforgiving cement welcome her back to earth. She felt more pain than she had ever felt before in her life for less than one heartbeat before the world completely vanished in that bright red flash.

Bradford "Brad" Dixon closed his eyes and took a deep breath as the commercial jet completed its descent. It bumped up, then settled back down on the runway, the wheels chirping loudly as the rubber met the asphalt.

Realizing that he gripped the arms of the seat so tightly in his hands that his fingertips had turned bone white, he intentionally relaxed his hands and let out the breath he had held, slowly trying to force his body to relax again. After hours and hours of flight, they had survived and landed back home in Atlanta. As much as he enjoyed the work on the mission field where he spent the last ten days building a medical clinic in rural Alaska, the flight home always made him think he'd never go again. Maybe next time he would donate his vacation for a mission in Georgia. Surely, Atlanta could use a new medical clinic, or perhaps housing for the homeless.

He glanced over at the next row of seats. Ken and Jon sat side-by-side. Ken looked a little pale. Brad knew he feared flying on a level that even he couldn't fully appreciate. The fact that he still got on a plane once a year to serve on the mission field impressed Brad. Especially when he was involved in a local charity that built houses in Atlanta. He could easily consider his job done from that alone.

Jon flipped the page in the book he read, as if completely unaware of the fact that the steel tube they found themselves in just plummeted thousands of feet to the ground. Jon's steadfast faith and level business head had always impressed Brad. He strove to be like his older by seven minutes brother. It appeared that everything came easily to him and nothing ever seemed to bother him. Brad felt like he personally worried about everything to the Nth degree. He would love to have some of Jon's confidence and assurance in God's plans and his part in them.

The obnoxious loudspeaker welcoming him to Atlanta interrupted his thoughts and he shut his eyes and grit his teeth. Even his headphones couldn't cancel out the noise as superfluous offers for airline credit cards and memberships to exclusive clubs assaulted him.

Finally, the plane came to a complete stop. He unbuckled his seatbelt and pushed himself carefully to his feet. At six-five, he had to duck beneath the overhead bins. His brothers stood with him, and he watched the two of them also stand in slightly bent-down positions.

"It would be nice to occasionally go someplace that didn't require any flights on airplanes," his brother Ken mused.

Jon laughed as he slipped his backpack strap over his shoulder. "I thought the exact same thing. And, judging by the way Brad almost ripped the arms off his seat when we landed, I think he was, too."

"You know what I really think would be nice? I think it would be nice to occasionally have my own thoughts," Brad remarked to his identical brothers.

They all had close-cropped brown hair, strong features, and gray eyes. All of them worked with their hands and regularly played sports, giving them long and lean muscle tone and well-developed chests. They had gone on this trip for their annual birthday celebration mission trip, this year celebrating twenty-five years. "Though I confess it's a little nice that at least someone understands me." He said that in a mocking tone, putting his hand to his heart.

"No one understands you, Brad." Ken laughed.

"I don't think we share thoughts, bro," Jon offered doubtfully. "I don't even want to know what kind of sick things go on in that noggin of yours."

They moved forward when the first-class cabin door

opened. Brad scowled at his brothers as they made their way out of the gate. "You know, dad is doing the thing with the straws tonight."

Jon's lips thinned. "I wish he wouldn't do that."

Ken shrugged. "Has to do something. Only one can be in charge, right?"

"I just hope it's one of you. Maybe I can just abstain." Brad rolled his head on his neck, thinking of his father's idea to have the brothers draw straws to see who would become the next president of Dixon Contracting, one of the largest contractors in the southeast. "I cannot imagine sitting in the office all day, wearing a suit."

"I can see it," Jon said with a grin. "You'd clean up real good. You're nearly as good lookin' as me."

"Dad feels like it's up to God this way." Ken gestured at the sign that pointed toward the train that would take them to baggage claim. "I told him we should cast lots. You know, keep it Biblical." He laughed in his dry humor way. "But he thought drawing straws would be easier."

"You did not." Brad narrowed his eyes. "Seriously? Why would you encourage this?"

Ken shrugged. "Someone has to take over."

"He should just divide it up." Jon nodded at his own idea as if his brothers automatically understood his logic. "Then we'd each have an even share."

Brad narrowed his eyes at Jon. "Then we'd all be stuck in an office wearing suits."

Jon mocked a shudder. "I'd change the rules for my company. No ties."

After a few stops, they got off the train and worked their way to baggage claim. "Don't know about you two," Ken said, "But I could use a steak."

Immediately, Brad's mouth started to water. "You know mom's going to have some big birthday feast waiting on us. You trying to get us killed?"

"Oh, yeah. She'll have cake," Jon said, always the sweetest tooth. "Steak and cake. Perfect welcome home meal."

"I'm just ready for a shower," Brad said, thinking about the amenities, or lack thereof, of their trip. He and his brothers had gone on their first mission trip on their fifteenth birthday, and every single year, he came home humbled and broken by the wealth and luxuries he enjoyed.

He'd spent the last two nights writing plans in his journal—plans to make changes in his life so he could help benefit his community. He wanted to sit down with his mother and see what she thought about his ideas. He wished he had someone like his dad had in his mom—someone to encourage and support him as he maneuvered through life. How long had he prayed for God to reveal his wife to him? Since he had turned thirteen? He thought God had once, yet here he stood, a quarter of a century old, still single, still waiting.

Without encouraging it, Valerie Flynn's face floated through his mind, but he shoved it aside. Valerie had made her own decisions regarding any future they might enjoy.

"I may skip the shower and settle straight for the hot tub," Jon said. "Every muscle in my body hurts. Obviously, I've not spent enough time this year with a hammer in my hand."

"If you're looking for opportunity, I always have an in on charitable building work," Ken said. "Just ask and I'll send you out, hammer in hand."

Brad closed his eyes in exhaustion, leaning his shoulder against the wall of the train, and listened to Ken and Jon talk about the details of Ken's upcoming projects. His phone vibrated with a text message.

WE ARE IN SAVANNAH. VALERIE FLYNN IS IN THE HOSPITAL. DAD LEFT THE CAR IN THE PARKING GARAGE FOR YOU THIRD LEVEL. TEXTING YOU A PHOTO OF THE LOCATION. WELCOME HOME! BIRTHDAY CAKE IN FRIDGE.

Brad looked up and saw Jon and Ken looking at their phones, too. Ken met his eyes, his own worry reflecting back at him just as the train came to a stop.

Valerie Flynn sat in the witness stand. She wore a forest green skirt and an ivory silk blouse. She'd pulled her hair up and twisted it into a simple bun on the back of her head. On the outside, she looked calm, collected, and professional. However, her mouth felt like someone had stuffed it with cotton balls seconds before blow drying it. Sweat trickled down her back, making her want to fidget and tug at her blouse.

The prosecuting attorney stood in front of her, half facing her, half facing the jury on her left. She glanced at the water sitting on the table near her. Her stomach started rolling and she swallowed. That just made it worse. If her hands would stop shaking, she'd risk pouring a glass. She cleared her throat.

"Miss Flynn, can you please tell me about your relationship with Tyrone Baker?"

She couldn't look at Tyrone or she would lose her nerve. Instead of making eye contact with him, she stared directly at the prosecutor. "He was an architect in the firm I work for. I'm an architect, too. We were working together on the design of a new hotel here in Savannah down on River Street. It was my first big project out of college. During the months we worked together on the project, our relationship formed and grew."

She thought back to those days and the attraction she'd felt for him. She wondered when the manipulation began. In the beginning? Or later? How could she have been so naive and gullible?

"Mr. Baker was married at that time, wasn't he?"

Shame heated her cheeks. Nervous, guilty, she licked her lips. "Yes," she whispered, then sat forward, closer to the mic, and said it again. "Yes. At the beginning of the project, he was married. By the end, his divorce had started, but I'm ashamed to say we did not wait for it to be final before our romance began." She shot a look at the judge, who stared stoically at her from his bench. "I can look back and see where I went wrong at every turn."

Wanting to believe she saw some semblance of understanding and possibly even sympathy in his eyes, she sat back in her chair and answered the questions as they came. So far, the defense attorney sitting next to Tyrone hadn't said a word. Sooner than she hoped, the questioning turned to that horrible night in September.

"You've said that Tyrone had assaulted you before that night."

The defense attorney didn't even look up from his legal pad and in a bored voice, he interrupted, "Objection. Facts not in evidence."

The prosecuting attorney raised his eyebrows then addressed the judge. "Your honor, I'm not sure it would help the defense one iota to open that can of worms, but if he insists, we can enter all kinds of those facts into evidence."

The judge smirked and gestured toward the defense attorney with his gavel. "What say you, Esquire?"

"Withdrawn, your honor."

The prosecuting attorney gave a significant look to each of the members of the jury. He then turned back to Valerie and asked, "What was different about what happened that afternoon of September eighteenth?"

Like a slide show on super speed, images flew through her mind; snapshots of that horrible afternoon. "I'd decided that I didn't want to be involved with Tyrone anymore. The abuse had long since gone beyond verbal, and he'd started hitting me. Especially when he drank."

She licked impossibly dry lips and cleared her throat. "I had enough of myself left to see what was happening to me, and I decided to get out. I applied for a transfer inside my company and accepted a job, a promotion actually, that would move me to Atlanta. I thought I'd leave without Tyrone ever knowing my plans. But an interoffice memo email went out congratulating me on my transfer. As soon as I saw it, I rushed home to pack and leave, but he'd already read it. He'd been waiting for me in the parking lot of our apartment building and followed me inside. He was very drunk."

She paused, her voice shaking. Oh, what she wouldn't give for a sip of water! The prosecuting attorney put his hand on the divider in front of her and leaned in. "What happened?"

"He told me that the only way I could leave him was in a coffin. He slammed my head into a mirror and broke it, then punched me. I tried not to fall down because then I knew he would start kicking me. So, I stayed up. I think if I'd just fallen, he wouldn't have—" She barely realized the tears that streaked down her face.

"Your honor," Tyrone's attorney interjected. "She 'knew' he would start kicking her? Did Miss Flynn have a crystal ball?"

"No!" Valerie nearly shouted. She cleared her throat and took a deep breath. "No. I didn't need a crystal ball. I had past experience."

The judge didn't even look up. "I'll allow it."

The prosecuting attorney asked, "Why didn't you just leave or resist when he started hitting you?"

Valerie looked back at the prosecuting attorney. "I'd learned not to fight back. To just take it. But when he started dragging me through the apartment, somehow, I knew what would happen, and I started fighting him."

"Objection. 'Somehow' she knew? I didn't realize we were in the presence of Madam Zohrah the tea-leaf reader, Your Honor. Would the witness like to offer any stock tips or perhaps some lottery number picks under oath?"

The judge sighed. "Redirect, counsel."

The prosecuting attorney nodded and asked, "Miss Flynn, you said somehow you knew what would happen. Are you saying that because of the violence Tyrone had committed to that point and his verbal threat to put you in a coffin, you had an instinct that he intended to attempt to take your life?"

The defense attorney was on his feet. "Your Honor. Leading the witness."

"You opened this can of worms and you'll have your opportunity to cross. I'll allow it. Take a seat."

The prosecuting attorney made eye contact with the jury members again before resuming his questioning. "So, you knew he was going to try to take your life—to kill you. You tried to fight back. What happened next?"

Valerie looked her hands. "I wasn't strong enough. He had me on the balcony, pushed against the railing. For a minute, my legs held me. I could barely breathe because he had both of his hands around my neck. He screamed in my face about how he would be the one to end our relationship, then he grabbed my legs and flipped me off the balcony."

A woman in the jury box gasped. Valerie's heart pounded until she could barely breathe. Finally, unable to avoid it any longer, she looked at Tyrone. He glared at her with such hatred in his eyes that she wanted to hold her hands up in front of her for protection and slink away. "How far did you fall, Miss Flynn?"

"Seventeen feet. I landed on a table on the porch below ours. I think it broke my fall enough that I survived."

She could still hear the breaking glass from the tabletop. "Go on Miss Flynn," the attorney prompted.

"I don't remember a lot after that. My neighbors were outside. They heard the fight and saw me fall. I woke up once in the ambulance, and once in the hospital. Then I was out for a couple of days."

"Can you tell us what was medically wrong with you?"

"Tyrone had broken my nose on the mirror and my left cheekbone when he punched me. I had hundreds of stitches from the glass table. My left elbow was broken. My left hip was broken. My lung had collapsed."

The prosecuting attorney pulled out a file. "Your Honor, at this time I would like to show the jury the medical forms, photographs, and X-rays from people's exhibit sixteen."

More murmurs ran through the jury box. She wished her testimony would end here; however, she knew that she had to face Tyrone's attorney now. She hoped she had the wherewithal to maintain her courage.

Valerie sat in the courtroom and watched as the judge looked over his notes. The trial had taken a long and exhausting two days. The jury returned with a guilty verdict for the violence but did not find him guilty of attempted murder. Now the judge would render the sentence, and she would find out how long she could breathe without fear.

"Mr. Baker," the judge said, looking at him over the rims of his glasses. "You have been tried and found guilty of aggravated battery. That can come with a twenty-year sentence in prison. However, because you have no other charges on your record, I'm going to sentence you to ten years, mandate anger management classes, and place a protective order on Miss Flynn effective on your release date. If, after you are released from prison, you in any way, shape, or form break that protective order, then I will personally see to it that you get the maximum sentence." He sat back and slipped his glasses off his face with his left hand while picking up the gavel with his right. "You are hereby remanded into the custody of the state of Georgia to begin your sentence of incarceration at an appropriate penal institution. Court dismissed." After he pounded the gavel, he stood and left the room through the door behind him.

Valerie's breath escaped her lungs in a rush. Ten years? Anger rushed through her heart; bitterness filled her mouth. So much for justice.

She stood. Using her cane, she slowly and carefully hobbled out of the courtroom. In the hall, she leaned against the wall and took long slow breaths. She couldn't stay in Savannah. Where could she go? Where could she run?

"Valerie."

Startled, she turned to see Philip and Rosaline Dixon. The sight of Auntie Rose, in her smart plum-colored suit, her frosted hair swept up in a simple twist, brought back a flood of memories of playing in her backyard with the Dixon boys. Nostalgia for home poured into her heart. Rosaline had stayed by her bedside in the hospital and took care of her at home. She and Uncle Phil had sat in the courtroom every day.

With a sob, she fell into Rosaline's arms. "This seems remarkably unfair," she cried.

"I'm so furious right now," Rosaline said, running her hand down Valérie's back. "I think I'm even angrier than when the jury's verdict came back."

Phillip patted her back. "What can I do?"

She had worked for him since graduating from college. Through all her hospital stays, surgeries, and rehabilitation, he'd kept her on the payroll.

"You've done so much," she sniffled, straightening. Rosaline handed her a tissue and she used it to wipe her eyes and nose.

Rosaline stepped forward and took Valerie's hand. "You're our family. What do you need?"

"I don't know," she whispered, "but I can't stay here."

"That job in Atlanta at the main office is waiting for you," Philip said, slipping his hands into the pockets of his slacks. "We would love to have you there. One word is all I need."

Rosaline studied her face then reached out and took her hand. "You take your time deciding. Talk it over with Buddy. Let him help you make the decision."

As if on cue, Buddy walked through the courtroom doors. He had barely aged over the years. His brown skin stayed smooth, not marred by wrinkles or lines. White hairs scattered among his black curls gave the only indication that he very quickly approached his sixtieth birthday. He looked around, saw them, and approached. "Got caught by that prosecutor. He's concerned for you. Wanted me to assure him that you'd be okay." He held his hand out to Philip. "My brother."

"Buddy. Whatever you two need," Philip said. "Day or night." He looked at his wife. "Ready, love?"

Valerie watched them walk away, feeling less scared, less trapped. "He still has a job for me in Atlanta."

"He'd probably give you a job anywhere in the country," Buddy said. "You do what you have to do. You were ready to move there in September."

"Lots happened since September." She straightened from the wall and they started walking down the wide hallway. She braced herself with the cane more than she wanted to and hated every step she took. "I can take my time moving there, right? No rash decisions. I have five years, if I understand the parole process."

"I'm praying for you, girl," he said in an untypical moment of softness.

"I know you are," she said. "I just wish I had the faith you have that someone is listening. Would be nice to think of some loving deity up there helping us make decisions."

Buddy's lips thinned but he simply said, "There was a time you knew it to be true."

"There was a time I believed in woodland fairies, too. I grew up. My worldview changed." She looked at her watch. "Do you want to get lunch?"

"Nah. You go on, girl. I have to get back to Atlanta." He put a hand on her shoulder and looked at her, his brown eyes kind. "I'm sorry for not stopping what happened to you. I ignored the signs until it was too late. Please forgive me."

Overwhelmed, she put her arms around him. "Uncle Buddy! You have nothing to be sorry for. I never said a word to you."

"Nevertheless." He cleared his throat and stepped away. "This chapter in your life is over. Don't let it define you. Garner strength from it, take the lessons God would have you learn, and move forward. Not backward." He put a hand on her shoulder and squeezed. "Whatever that means for you, you have my support and blessing."

He turned and walked away from her. She mulled over his words, dissected them, and believed him. She knew he encouraged her to come back to Atlanta so she'd live closer to him.

That aside, did she want to go back to Atlanta? Or maybe farther away? The idea of leaving Georgia, the only home she'd ever known, overwhelmed her. Maybe Atlanta would offer a good fresh start. If she felt the need to go further after she settled there, she certainly had the freedom to do so. Her stomach rumbled as she looked at her watch. She'd give it until Monday to decide. She had a window of five years to make a good decision.

Four years later

Brad Dixon sat back in his chair and looked out at the bright Atlanta sun. He had always loved the early spring season, as the days became longer and warmer. Working outside in the Georgia clay, watching progress as buildings climbed toward the sky, layer by layer, the hot sun beating down on heads covered by hard hats, making the evenings spent cooling off in the lake something he could look forward to.

Instead, here he sat, in a perfectly contained environment, the air discreetly cooled by air conditioning. No noises, no beeping of trucks, no grinding of machines, no voices raised over the cacophony of the jobsite. Just a contained little world of peace and quiet and comfort.

With a sigh, he closed his laptop lid and pushed away from the desk. How would he stand it? For most of his life, he'd spent the majority of his time outside. Now, with the luck of the draw, he had to take over the company his father had built. That meant he had to run it from the inside.

What he wouldn't give to go back to that fateful night four years ago and pick a different straw.

He shoved his hands in his pants pockets and fisted them. He knew he fought with the Holy Spirit as much as he fought with himself. Everyone else, his father included, felt like the results of the whole straw thing had worked out perfectly. He thought differently than his brothers, had a more organized brain, operated more systematically. Phillip had told him privately that he'd prayed Brad would pull the short straw and had wondered to himself what he would have done had the results been any different.

That didn't make him feel any better about his current situation. In fact, in a way, it made him feel worse.

Pulling his mind away from spring fever that made him want to leave for the day and hit his favorite fishing spot, he intentionally turned his mind to thoughts of his upcoming morning meeting. Valerie Flynn would arrive at any moment. He felt a little acceleration of his pulse at the thought.

He hadn't seen her in a few years—not since the Thanksgiving after her attack. She'd been withdrawn and unsocial at the time, and Brad had instinctively not pushed. He'd felt such intense anger at Tyrone Baker, and had the completely unexpected urge to inflict violence on the man, that he had left the celebration early and spent the rest of the weekend contemplating his thoughts and reactions. She had not returned for any other holidays. His mother had told him she needed time to heal, emotionally and spiritually, and that she'd come home eventually.

She had moved here to take a promotion in Dixon Contracting's architectural division. He knew his father wanted her groomed to take over the interior design department. Brad had looked over her portfolio and certifications and started monitoring her work output from the Savannah office. He could find nothing that would make him disagree with Phillip's desire. He didn't look at her as a favored daughter of his best friend as Brad had feared, but as a fully qualified and highly skilled architect. She just needed to show Brad leadership skills and he wouldn't hesitate to hand her that position.

Valerie—the woman around which all his hopes and dreams had centered. Once high school started, he'd rarely seen her. She'd played such an integral part of his childhood and one day she was just gone. But only physically.

Mentally, he kept her right beside him. Any time he'd dated in high school and college, he'd found her in the back of his mind and, right or wrong, he often found himself comparing other women to her. When she moved in with Tyrone, it had broken Brad's heart and he had intentionally turned off any thoughts of her.

Today she would begin her new job in his building, working for him, technically, and some part of his brain perked up at the thought of seeing her and interacting with her on a regular basis again.

How much of her personality changed with maturity,

and how much had Tyrone crushed? What aspects of her personality shifted to accommodate the trauma?

Before he could go any deeper into his head, the quiet tone of his intercom interrupted his thoughts. "Brad, Valerie Flynn is here."

A smile teased the corners of his lips. "Have her come in." He walked around his desk just as she came through the door.

The last time he'd seen her, she had walked with a cane. Today, though, she walked unaided, with just a slight limp. She wore a suit the color of daffodils, a beautifully sharp contrast to her dark brown skin. A thick chunky gold necklace hung from her neck and a matching bracelet graced her wrist. Her curly black hair brushed her shoulders, and she had gold hoops in her ears.

Despite his thoughts before her arrival, he found himself surprised at how his breath caught in his chest at the sight of her. It almost stopped him in his tracks. Her beauty filled the room and overwhelmed him.

Finding some rational thought in the cloud descending on his brain, he held out his hand and grinned. "How good to see you again," he said.

She smiled back and took his one hand with both of hers. "Likewise. It feels good to be home."

Had Brad detected something else in her casual gaze? Had she held his hand a few seconds longer than strictly necessary, perhaps caressing the back of his hand with her fingertips? Was her smile the private smile of his childhood? Or had that all merely been wishful thinking on his part?

Valerie looked around, obviously looking at the furniture and decorations. "Last time I was in this office, it was your dad's. I think I was twelve." She walked over to the black bookshelf and ran her finger over a wooden giraffe. "I love the décor."

She loved his taste in his chosen décor. Could that mean she loved him? Even a little? He determined to get a grip on himself before he said or did something embarrassing.

He looked around, forcing himself to remain objective, seeing the space through the caramel-colored eyes of an interior designer. Black and white furniture, items collected from his international missions work, clean lines, minimalist style. "Thanks. I didn't like dad's heavy wood look. Felt claustrophobic. Wanted something more open with a cleaner feel."

She pursed her lips and nodded. He tried not to stare at her lips. "I get clean. And efficient. It suits you." She used her chin to point toward the tall, thin elephant statues that stood sentry on either side of a credenza. "Very African in the décor."

"Well, I've spent a lot of time in Africa. It's where my heart and mind are, usually." He gestured toward the small sitting area and she chose the white leather couch. He sat across from her in a black leather wingback chair. "Welcome home."

"I hope so." She settled back and crossed her long legs. "I haven't called Atlanta home since the day I graduated from high school."

"Dad's been trying to get you here for ages. He's excited." He gestured with his hand in the general direction of his father's office. "He has a year left before retirement. Having you here, he's claimed, will make his last year a joy."

"Uncle Phil has always been a smooth charmer."

A pause in conversation felt awkward. She met his eyes without flinching or looking away. He couldn't fully interpret everything her eyes said, but he could see the pain behind her expression. Brad didn't think he should broach certain topics, but he believed they both felt the presence of the proverbial elephant in the room. "You settling in okay?"

"I am. I rented a small house on a short lease. Once I feel settled, I'll start looking for a house to buy." As she spoke, she moved her hands, and her bracelets clinked on her arms. "It was time to leave Savannah. I contemplated moving, well, anywhere, but Atlanta just felt right."

"We're certainly happy about that," he said warmly. "You'll find the architectural division here a little larger than the one you're coming from."

"I toured here during some training a couple of years ago, remember?" No. He didn't remember. He wasn't even in the country, and when he heard she had come by the office, he felt angry and frustrated for weeks afterward. He knew he would have to process the concept that she just assumed he had been here and would surely remember her visit. She was here now. That's what mattered. Valerie continued, "To think that you have an entire floor dedicated just to the architectural division is amazing. As you know, in Savannah, I shared a large office with three other people."

"We've spoken of enlarging Savannah's operation several times. But we always have nine other projects with higher priority." Brad had wanted to go to Savannah to head up that proposed expansion personally and, if he just happened to run into Valerie Flynn while down there, well, all the better.

She smiled brightly, showing even, white teeth and

dimples on either side of her mouth. "Uncle Phil took a little home building operation and turned it into a multi-state design, build, commercial and residential contracting company in just thirty years. I imagine there are more than nine projects in front of Savannah's little office complex."

Brad laughed. "You're probably right." Far more than nine. More like forty-nine, much to his frustration. He settled back comfortably in the chair, forcing himself to relax the tension in his shoulders and neck, and he watched as she relaxed, too. "Mom been in touch with you yet?"

"Oh, yes," Valerie said with a warm smile, her southern drawl pouring forth like smooth sweet honey, effortlessly elongating those two little syllables. "She met me at my house the day I got here. She acted like I was a long-lost child come home."

"Well, to her, you are." In that moment, they were fourteen again. An awkward boy trying to act cool and a coy girl trying to act distant. He could almost smell the swimming pool out back and feel the planks of the gazebo beneath his bare feet as he stared into this woman's eyes. She had changed. She had grown up. But the Valerie he loved with all his heart still lived inside this grown-up woman in his office. He suddenly wondered, what would his mother say about his attraction toward Valerie? Would she approve? He could not imagine that she would disapprove.

A thought suddenly occurred to him. "Hey. You do know they're building that church library and dedicating it to your parents? That's not new information, I hope."

Her lips thinned and she lifted her chin in a very subtly defensive manner. "Yes. I do know that." After clearing her throat, she said, "I'd love to see where I'll be working."

Understanding that the shared personal history moment had passed and the professional relationship now took over, Brad stood. Obviously, her parents were a hot-button topic. That confused him.

Valerie's parents had died when she was three, so she didn't have a real memory of them. She told him one summer when they were eleven or twelve that all her memories consisted of her and Buddy; that she only knew what her parents looked like because of pictures. When he asked her if that bothered her, she shrugged and said that she didn't know anything different.

"I'll have Bentley come up here. He's expecting you. You'll be working directly for him, but really, we want to do a lot of knowledge transfer. As of today, you're training to take over his position when he retires in a few months. That hasn't been announced but it's kind of an open secret."

When she stood, Brad extended his hand. He watched her hesitate ever so slightly before placing her fingers once again into his grip. When she took his hand, her grip was feminine but firm. "I am really happy you're here, Valerie. Looking forward to seeing you around."

She pulled her hand away before she replied, "I really look forward to whatever is next."

Valerie shut her office door and leaned her back against it. She closed her eyes, exhausted—both mentally and emotionally. She thought of her little corner of a shared office in Savannah and her total understanding and comfort in the job and the expectations for the job. Now they had her training to head a team, working on the seventh floor of a ten-story building dedicated entirely to Dixon Contracting.

It overwhelmed her. How could she possibly run a team? What made her more qualified than the people who had been working with Bentley in this office all along? She, a young black woman, coming into this office thinking she could take over just because of her relationship with the Dixons?

Her meeting with Brad this morning – she'd hoped that since so many years had gone by since she had even seen him, the silly attraction she felt for him would have dissipated. But it hadn't.

Instead, the light in his eyes as he smiled and welcomed her this morning had caused the breath to catch in the back of her throat. His eyes had crinkled in the corners, his sun-streaked hair catching the light from his windows.

She'd wanted to hug him, kiss his cheek, see what he felt like as a man. Her attraction for him had always been very one-sided, though, and, as a teenager, she'd never had the courage to make the first move.

Now, she came back as a broken shell compared to her previous existence. Nothing about her made her available, even if he was interested. Which he couldn't possibly be.

As doubts plagued her mind and she started to sink inside her head, she ran her finger over the scar on her right wrist that ran from her wrist bone up to the bottom of her pinkie. Suddenly, she realized she didn't hear her own voice, but his. Tyrone's. Even after all this time, the doubts he'd fed into her subconscious still surfaced and took over.

Intentionally straightening and moving away from the door, she pushed thoughts of Brad and Tyrone out of her mind and walked into the middle of the room and took a slow turn.

She had a drafting table on one side of the room, right under the window, and on the wall facing that, a long counter stretched across most of the wall. A whiteboard hung above it at one end, and a smart screen above it at the other. A tablet connected to the smart screen sat on the counter, plugged into its port.

Where the counter ended, she could see a rack that would hold building plans. At the end opposite the door sat an L-shaped glass desk with metal legs. A phone and a black desk pad sat on the surface across from her. A keyboard and mouse sat on the short arm of the L, facing a wall filled with four large screens. She knew the screens could be combined to show one image or four different images, allowing her to work with her design and engineering software.

A white leather desk chair sat behind the desk and in front of a wall filled with built-in shelves. A company policy binder sat on the otherwise empty shelf.

Boxes sat near the counter and in front of her desk. She recognized the boxes she'd had delivered from Savannah. Deciding to go ahead and unpack, she opened the first box and found her leather-bound books on design, a college graduation gift from Uncle Phillip. Inspecting the shelving, she strategically placed the books sporadically around the shelves, then filled the gaps with some knickknacks, photos, and awards.

An hour later, her hip twinging with a dull ache, she stood in the middle of the room and inspected the shelves. Using her artist's eye, she made a few changes, shifted some things around, then set the empty boxes by the door.

She walked to her desk and slid into the chair. The leather arms felt smooth under her hands. She brushed her palm over the empty desk pad and smiled. This move felt right. It felt good. As the years had gone by, she'd watched Tyrone's parole date move closer and closer, and knew she'd have to leave Savannah. The idea of running into him on the street or in the grocery store or anywhere else filled her with terror. Everywhere she looked for a job, either within Dixon Contracting or without, no city felt right except Atlanta.

Using her ID, she logged into the computer system and synced the new tablet with her laptop and the desktop, making sure all the screens worked, separately and together. She felt a sense of giddy excitement at all the new and shiny electronics and technology around her. She noticed that the IT department had already transferred her internal files to this location, and she worked her way through her calendar to make sure all the meetings and conferences that had been set up in Savannah before her decision to move had been canceled or reassigned to the architects who had taken over her projects.

Just as she closed everything down in preparation to leave for lunch, she heard a tap on her door. "Come in," she called loudly enough for her voice to carry to the door at the other end of the room.

The door opened and in walked...Jon? Maybe Ken? Either way, a grin crossed her face. "Hello!"

"Hi, sunshine," her greeter said. Definitely Jon, ever the charmer. "Aren't you a sight?"

"Jon!" With a laugh, she accepted his friendly hug. "What a treat. I guess I knew I'd be working with Brad, but some part of my mind assumed you and Ken would be out and about."

"Sometimes we are. Right now, we're both in town. I'm just recently back, actually." He slipped his hands into the pockets of his khaki pants. She couldn't help but compare his black collared shirt stitched with the red Dixon Contracting logo to Brad, three floors above her, who had on a gray suit with a sharp red tie. "Mom sent me here to invite you to dinner tonight. She said she'd call you, but she didn't know your new office number."

Valerie pulled her phone out of her pocket to make sure she hadn't missed any calls. "She could have called my cell."

"Uh, we're talking about my mother," Jon said dryly. "She doesn't call cells if you're anywhere near, and I quote, a 'real phone.'"

Valerie laughed comfortably, feeling the years melt away. "I will definitely be there for dinner. What time?"

"She's working around a meeting dad and Brad have tonight, so it will be a little later. Maybe seven?"

Later worked better for her, for no reason other than she wouldn't have to contend with the Atlanta traffic right after work. "That sounds great. I'll be able to get a lot done between now and then."

"Great. I'll see you there." He stepped backward and put his hand on the door. "Let me know if you need to follow me or anything. I know it's been a while since you came out to the house."

After he left, she gathered her purse and keys, and went to find the best place to grab lunch. She hoped to find something in easy walking distance. She ignored the stares of the people on her floor. Curiosity about the new girl prompted the glances, she knew. She also knew that some of them knew her from Savannah and had some idea about what had happened. Perhaps some of the stares were people trying to see a scar, or a limp, or some other sign of distress that would give them an opening to whisper behind their hands while they relived her personal terror from four years ago.

Determined not to let any of those thoughts show, she put a smile on her face, waved a few times, and made it to the elevator without totally collapsing.

Ever since she moved out of Tyrone's apartment and into her own, she had a hard time with change. A disruption in her schedule or plans threw her out of whack. It caused anxiety that manifested with scattered thoughts, dizziness, pounding heart. She knew she would feel out of sorts until she got used to the routine here, until the new became normal. The intellectual knowledge helped a little bit, but it didn't stop the anxiety attack from manifesting. She closed her eyes and took deep breaths through her nose, let them out slowly through her mouth, envisioning herself standing in the doorway of a grass hut looking out onto the warm sand and gently rolling surf.

By the time she reached the ground floor, she felt more centered. She entered the moderately busy lobby with confidence. As she started toward the front doors, she smelled grilled bread. Her stomach rumbled in response and she glanced around, seeing the sign pointing to the café. Instead of heading out onto the street, she turned and walked past the guard desk and through the glass doors into the café area.

At lunchtime, the place bustled with traffic and noise. She maneuvered her way around little round tables and fellow Dixon Contracting employees and made her way to the back of the line. As she inched forward, she glanced through the menu hanging above the cashier. Everything sounded good and was made with local, fresh ingredients. By the time she made it to the front of the line, she'd settled on a sweet potato hash with a poached egg and fresh spring greens tossed with a light vinaigrette.

Once she placed her order, she stepped to the side to wait for it to come to the counter.

"Fancy meeting you here," a deep voice said in her ear.

Her heart froze in panic a split second before she turned and saw Ken. He had on a black T-shirt with the red Dixon Contracting logo over the pocket. He looked like he could have used a haircut about two weeks ago. Putting a hand on her heart, she laughed and nudged his shoulder. "Goodness. Don't sneak up on me like that, Ken."

"Sorry to scare you, Val." She could see the contrite look in his eyes and immediately felt bad for overreacting.

"It's okay. I think I was lost in my own head." She gestured at the counter. "When did y'all put a restaurant in?"

He pursed his lips. "Three years ago, I think. It's just easier for everyone. We bought the building across the road on this side of the building and installed the IT department there, which freed up this entire area."

She thought of the massive amount of equipment that they would have had to move across the street. "Did you have to dig the street up for the cabling?"

He laughed, and his eyes wrinkled with laugh lines. "It's so much fun to work here and to talk to people who think like me."

Ken nodded to the woman on the other side of the counter who held out a paper bag to him. He took it but kept talking to Valerie. “Yeah. We dug up the road and ran the cables. Actually created an underground culvert that would even allow us to send someone in there if we have to. It was stupidly expensive, but it beats having to get a backhoe every time we need to repair a cable or update the system.”

He pulled his phone out of his jeans pocket and fielded a text. “Ah. Have to run. Got a meeting.” He started to turn away but stopped and looked at her again. “Mom said you’re coming tonight?”

“Yes. Dinner. Seven.”

“Awesome. See you then, Val. You look amazing, by the way.”

Waving him off and laughing, she accepted her tray of food and found an empty table. As she sat down, it occurred to her that she’d greeted Brad with a polite handshake and business talk. Jon and Ken had come to her with hugs and lifelong friendship. Would she ever relax around him, or would she always feel clumsy and foolish, flushed with a crush that he did not reciprocate?

Determined to try to work it out later, she picked up her fork and took a bite of the hash, enjoying the flavors, glad for her choice of meal.

Valerie stepped into the grand hall and felt an overwhelming sense of coming home flood her heart.

She looked at the floor, thrilled to find the giant vintage compass rose on the cream tile floor exactly where she remembered. The dark blue compass bordered with glittery gold shone in the light of the chandelier. A round table that held a huge vase of white roses and greenery sat on the center of the compass. She knew the flowers came directly from Rosaline Dixon's rose garden, and she walked forward to put her face close to the blooms and breathe in the fragrance. The smell of roses always reminded her of Auntie Rose. Nostalgic tears threatened to fall. When she heard footsteps on the tile, she took a moment to compose herself before raising her head.

"Mama picked those this morning," a grinning and very male baritone voice said. As she came around the table, Valerie spotted Ken.

She smiled and said, "Hello again, Ken."

His tight grin suddenly showed some teeth. "Only you and my parents have ever been able to do that consistently. Other than my brothers, of course."

She approached him with confidence and hugged him. "It's great to be here."

"Of course, it is," he said, hugging her back. "This is your home."

He led the way to the sitting room on the west side of the hall. In a house full of men, Rosaline had claimed this one room as hers and made it entirely feminine. Cream-colored couches with a mauve rose pattern and gleaming mahogany wood tables formed a comfortable sitting area. A piano sat near the window and framed art showcasing dried flowers graced the walls. The patio doors opened onto Rosaline's rose garden, and Valerie knew from experience that if she stepped out onto that patio, the sweet fragrance of flowers would fill the spring night.

Rosaline, dressed in a white blouse tucked into a purple skirt accented with a purple and pink scarf tied around her waist, rushed toward Valerie, her arms outstretched. "I'm so happy you're here!" she exclaimed, throwing her arms around her. "Welcome home!"

Valerie couldn't help but grin as she embraced her pseudo-mother. "No one is happier than I am," she said. "I didn't realize how much I missed this place until I smelled the roses in the hall."

Jon came into the room, typing into his phone as he walked. When he looked up, the distracted, concentrated look on his face evaporated and he smiled at Valerie. "Hello again," he greeted, "welcome home."

After hugging Jon with the same enthusiasm she'd given his brother, she settled onto one of the couches and felt every muscle in her body release tension she didn't even realize she carried around with her. "I can't believe how much is still the same," she said, looking around and recognizing so many of the furnishings and pictures. "I'd have redecorated a dozen times by now. This is such a great room with great light."

Rosaline laughed. "You're the interior designer. You'd consider this room a blank canvas. I couldn't wait to get this home furnished and decorated so I could be done with it. It was all such a chore."

"I think growing up here really inspired me to be a designer." She looked around. "I love every room, and they're all different."

"That's what happens when you tackle each room, taking advice and ideas from a different month's home decorating magazine."

Valerie chuckled. "I don't think you're giving yourself enough credit."

"Possibly." She stood. "I just heard the front door."

As she left the room, Valerie looked at Jon, who stood near the patio doors. "I heard you were just in Egypt."

He nodded. "Just got in a couple of days ago. Quite an incredible and inspiring journey. My time there changed everything about me. Have you ever been to that area of the world?"

Thinking of all her dreams and desires that somehow got swallowed up by college and career and a very bad relationship decision, she shook her head. "I've still only ever been to Georgia and Florida."

She watched the look of shock cross his face. "What?"

"I know! I need to take a trip!" She looked out the window at the mostly familiar view. "What were you doing there?"

He gave a slight shrug of his shoulders. "Dad met a guy. He was looking for someone to teach project management at a school over there. I was a guest speaker for a couple weeks, then a mentor to two PMPs for a couple more."

"That's wonderful. Did you enjoy it?"

His face tightened. "Some. I'd been there before, when I was sixteen. Different culture. I had a lot to learn about it before I left, and I'm glad I did. I'm a Georgia boy through and through, but I think the years I've spent going on mission trips helped me survive being so far out of my element."

Brad and Phillip entered the room just as she started to reply. Phillip stood just an inch shorter than his sons. He had the same color chestnut brown hair, though he now had a sprinkling of gray. He still had a wide chest and thin waist and he walked into the room with the confidence of a man who knew exactly his own position in the world.

She grinned as she stood and let Phillip embrace her. "Valerie. Girl, I am so glad to see you back home."

The Dixons kept suggesting that this castle was her home. She should object, she knew, because as many hours of her early life as she spent playing here, sleeping here, *living* here, when she thought of home, she pictured the house Buddy bought right before her high school years began. Yet, her heart disagreed. "I can't tell you how happy I felt when I walked across that compass rose on the floor. Such a feeling of nostalgia."

"I feel the same way whenever I walk through that front door." He stepped aside and she greeted Brad with a smile. He looked just as fresh as he'd looked that morning, even though she knew he'd had a twelve-hour day. Did he have a girlfriend who helped ease the transition from work to downtime? Why did she wonder that?

Phillip kept his arm over her shoulder and turned toward his wife. "Rosie, my love, what is for dinner?"

"Jon went fishing this morning. He caught a twenty-pound bass. You'll be tired of eating it before it's gone."

"Fishing?" Phillip narrowed his eyes with exaggeration toward Jon. "So, I'm paying you to fish in the middle of a workday, is it?"

Jon's lips formed into a smirk. "Thought I might use one of those two-hundred eleven personal days I've accrued but never taken." Jon slapped his father on the back. "It's amazing what six hours in a boat on the Chattahoochee can do to a jet-lagged soul."

Phillip laughed and released her to guide everyone out of the room. Valerie smiled as she walked behind them, remembering Phillip teaching all of them how to fish years ago. Brad walked next to her. "You always looked right at home in that room," he observed.

She stole a glance at him out of the corner of her eye and caught him staring down at her with a contemplative look in his gray eyes. "I, uh, have always loved that room. It's so peaceful."

"It's very feminine." He paused and let her precede him through the doorway. "You looked just as relaxed and content in there as my mother does." They followed the crowd into the dining room. A wall of windows looked out onto the same flower garden as Rosaline's sitting room. Gleaming hardwood floors shone under the giant chandelier that hung suspended above a long rectangular table that could easily seat ten people.

Phillip took the spot at the head of the table, and Rosaline sat to his right. Next to her, Brad held out the chair for Valerie to sit, and he took the chair next to her. Across the table from them, Ken and Jon sat. Valerie ran her finger around the silver-rimmed plate and leaned in toward Brad. "Remember when we threw that Frisbee in here and it broke the glass door of the china cabinet?"

She giggled as his cheeks turned bright red. "I don't think that was me."

"Yeah, right. I know the triplet game." She cut her eyes over to his brothers, who were laughing. "I remember. And if you told your mom one of them did it, you fibbed."

Rosaline mock glared at Brad. "Oh, he admitted it. Don't you remember?" She raised her eyebrow. "I'm sure he regretted the act, too."

Remembering her own punishment of having to work with the gardener until she and Brad had finished paying for the replacement door, Valerie laughed. "He wasn't the only one." She tapped the plate with her fingernail. "At least you were able to replace the plates that got broken."

"And you two learned a hard lesson."

"I actually learned a lot about landscaping and plants native to Georgia," she admitted, remembering the gardener who loved teaching his trapped audience. "It was really inspiring for me in college when I studied landscape design." She looked out the window at the gardens lit by the setting sun. "I still love working with plants."

Brad's laugh erupted around the table as Phillip lifted the cover on the platter piled with flaky white fish. "There you go, Mom. Your punishment inspired an entire career."

Rosaline winked. "Best kind." She held out her hands, and Valerie, remembering family tradition, took her hand in her left and Brad's with her right. Holding hands, the entire family collectively bowed their heads, and Phillip issued a prayer thanking God for the food and Valerie's special homecoming.

Touched, she raised her head and pulled her hands free, rubbing the hand that Brad had held. Somewhere along her adolescence, her faith in God had crumbled. She believed in a Creator, but just didn't quite grasp the concept that He cared about her or anyone else on earth. But she knew the love this family had for the being they called Jehovah and respected their beliefs.

They passed the platters in a clockwise motion, and soon she had fish, hush puppies, coleslaw, bright green sweet peas, and wild rice on her plate. Recognizing one of her favorite meals, she broke off a flaky bite of bass and put it in her mouth, closing her eyes as she tasted lemon and garlic.

"This looks wonderful, my love," Phillip said to Rosaline. "Thank you." He turned his head and looked at her. As he picked up his knife and fork, he asked, "You settled in?"

She gave a small shrug. "I didn't bring much. I rented a furnished house. I had a few boxes of some kitchen stuff and then mostly books and clothes." She cut off another bite of fish. "Clean start."

Brad leaned toward her. "You know the guest house is available. You didn't need to rent a place."

She looked at him in his tie and suit and thought about how much he loved the outdoors, and how much he must hate sitting in an office all day. "Do you still live here?"

He shrugged. "I do now. My brothers and I buy apartments or townhouse communities, then refurbish them. I typically live in a unit until they sell. We closed last month, so I've been back home since then."

"Your way to get your hands dirty even though you're in a suit, huh?"

"He realized he had soft hands." Ken chuckled. "He came to me about doing this apartment flip thing. If he can get home before midnight, it works out."

"At least we don't have a deadline when we start," Brad said. "We can afford to take our time." He looked at Valerie. "It feels good to take the suit off and pick up a hammer, especially after a day like today."

She stared into his gray eyes. They glowed in the soft light of the chandelier. "I imagine it's hard for you."

Phillip said, "God has plans for us all. Doesn't mean we have to agree with Him."

She watched a muscle clench in Brad's jaw and his eyes harden. "I've never disagreed."

Jon chortled. "Yeah. You've just suffered. In silence, maybe, but some attitudes are louder than words."

"You're welcome to take over any time, brother," Brad said in a steely voice. "I'd trade places in a second."

Phillip pointed his fork at Brad. "That's the problem,

son. Need to just go with it. Let God work. You continue to resent how He positions you, you're going to miss out on the blessings of obedience."

If she hadn't been sitting so close to him, she might have missed the tension that suddenly radiated off Brad and his quiet intake of breath. After a long, silent second, he nodded and placed his napkin next to his plate. Pushing his chair back, he stood. "Mama, dinner was great. Thank you." He looked around the table. "Goodnight."

Rosaline raised an eyebrow and looked at Phillip. "Time and place, dear?"

"Clearly." He took a bite of fish and looked at Valerie with a pointed look and immediately changed the subject as Brad left the room. Valerie watched his retreating back. "I should have offered the guest house. For some reason, it didn't occur to me."

She thought of the little two-bedroom cottage on the other side of the koi pond. The Dixon family had lived there until the boys were three, while Phillip and Rosaline built the castle. Just as they moved out, she and Buddy moved in, and for the next eleven years, that little cottage had been her home. "It's okay. My new place is closer to work. The traffic in Atlanta is so bad that I'd be leaving at six in the morning every day just to try to get in front of it."

"That's what the boys and I do. Best way. Then you stay past seven at night, and you're golden."

Jon and Ken burst out laughing. "Now you know why he's late every night, Mama. It's a traffic avoidance ploy."

She chuckled. "At least there's a reason."

An hour later, after Ken and Jon had excused themselves, and Valerie had hugged Phillip and Rosaline goodbye, she left by the front door. As she stepped on the walkway to go to her car, she felt compelled to turn and walk around the house instead.

The early spring air had cooled slightly, and she rubbed her bare arms, wishing she hadn't left her jacket in her car. When she entered the rose garden, though, she forgot the chill and slowly walked, letting the fragrance float up to her and take over her senses. She ran her fingertips over the open blossoms of the roses and listened to the crunch of gravel as she slowly walked.

When she reached the end of the rose garden, she noticed the shadow of a man in the gazebo. Knowing without needing confirmation that Brad sat on the bench, she stepped onto the bridge and walked across it, listening to her shoes echo on the cedar bridge. She could tell when he heard her or sensed her presence because he raised his head and stared in her direction.

"Permission to come aboard?" she called out, using the line required to enter the occupied gazebo from their childhood.

He chuckled. "Aye."

Without hesitation, she made the short leap from the bottom of the bridge to the top step of the gazebo, jumping over the imagined alligator filled moat. It surprised her that she could still make the leap. When she landed, she felt the twinge in her hip and wondered if she'd regret that in the morning.

"Your mom saved your plate."

"She would." He scooted over on the bench, and she sat

next to him, turning her body to face him.

After a few moments of silence, she asked, "Is everything okay here?"

Brad shrugged. "I thought so, but then my dad speaks a little bit of truth, and I storm out in the middle of dinner like a spoiled child. So, maybe not. Spent the last hour trying to analyze that."

"I don't think spoiled child is the right description. You're in the position. You're doing your duty. Nothing like wishing you were doing something else. What other choice do you have?"

She could see the glow of his eyes in the moonlight. "I'm a twenty-nine-year-old man with a decent education and a lot of really specialized training. My choices are limitless. It isn't obligation that has me running Dixon Contracting. It's love. I love my family, and I love the company." He rubbed the back of his neck and stared at the floor. "The question should be, what do I want to do about it?"

"Fair enough." She put her arm along the back of the bench and leaned toward him. "What do you want to do about it, Brad?"

His laugh echoed out in the night. "I want to be happy in my position and not have spent the last four years longing to be somewhere else." He turned his head to look at her again. "But I can't go back. Going forward, I want to feel content in my job, knowing it's important and exactly what I need to do right now."

With a slow nod, she said, "That sounds doable. Target set, sights fixed. Now, execute." Her hip aching, she slowly got to her feet, needing to stretch it out. "I loved it here. I hated moving from you guys."

She tried very surreptitiously to rub her hip. "Uncle Buddy told me about six months after we moved that I'd wasted most of my high school freshman year feeling sorry for myself. He asked me if I planned to spend the next three years making both of us miserable, or if I wanted to decide to be happy and content and go with the flow of life."

Brad grunted then said, "You never struck me as a Pollyanna. Your personality is much more down to earth."

"My personality?" She walked the perimeter of the gazebo, running her finger over the back of the bench, remembering so many memories she hadn't thought of in more than a decade. "A lot of times, our attitude about our current position has everything to do with a choice we make and little to do with our circumstances or personality." She made her way back to him and put a knee on the bench, shifting her body to stretch her hip, trying to make the motion look natural. "I may not be able to alter my personality, but I can always adjust my attitude."

Brad smiled at her, and she could see his teeth in the night. "Why do I feel like I've just been schooled?"

"Probably because I just schooled you." She leaned closer to him. "You must have forgotten how very wise I can be."

For several seconds, Brad stared at her. She could almost feel the heat from his face and her eyes glanced over his lips. Finally, he said, "Actually, I haven't forgotten a single thing about you." He carefully stood and extended his elbow. "How about I walk you to your car?"

Brad Dixon stood in the driveway and watched Valerie Flynn's taillights until he couldn't see them anymore, then went back into the house. Instead of heading to the staircase, he strolled into his father's study. As expected, his mother sat on the small sofa next to his father's desk, crocheting, while his father worked through the stack of papers that sat in the briefcase he had open on his desk.

He cleared his throat. Both his parents looked up at him. His father raised an eyebrow. "It was a hard day and I brought it to the table with me. My mistake. I apologize for leaving dinner."

After several seconds, Phillip nodded. "Apology accepted."

Rosaline set her crocheting down and slipped off her glasses as she looked up at him. "It was good to have Valerie at the table again."

He smiled. "I agree. Glad you had all your little chicks in the same roost tonight."

"It made my mama heart happy." She put her glasses back on and picked her crochet hook back up. "I saved your plate. Make sure you eat before bed."

Brad bent to kiss her cheek. "I will. Goodnight."

They both bid him goodnight as he left the room. He made his way to the kitchen and pulled his plate out of the refrigerator. While it heated up in the microwave, he took his phone out of his pocket but didn't turn it on. Instead, he plugged it in and intentionally left it sitting on the kitchen counter before taking his plate up to his room.

After setting the plate on his desk, he pulled off his tie and unbuttoned his shirt, untucking it from his pants so it hung loose. He pulled a bottle of water from his mini fridge and sat at his desk. While he ate his reheated dinner, he thought about what Valerie had said, appreciating the wisdom of her words and the simple way she shared them.

As he searched his heart, he realized that he truly served as the only remaining barrier blocking his contentment with his current position. He really should find joy in the evening work as he refurbished a building instead of resenting his brothers for the work they did every day during daylight hours. He really should have put his whole heart and mind into his job instead of withholding this little part that just clung to resentment like he had clung to the short straw when he pulled it.

He pushed his half-eaten plate away and closed his eyes,

taking a deep cleansing breath and letting it out. He honestly felt like he needed to repent. As he chuckled out loud, the thought became more focused.

"I'm sorry, God," he said audibly. "I should have looked at the opportunity you gave me as a blessing and taken into responsible stewardship. I'll go forward with a clean heart, with ready willingness, and with gratitude."

The simple two-sentence prayer ended with a burden releasing itself from his heart. He took his water bottle and walked over to the window, opening the sliding door and stepping out onto the small, semi-circular balcony. He sat in the comfortable lounge chair and took a sip of water while he stared at the gazebo in the moonlight.

Often, he'd start to think about Valerie and childhood, but he pushed the memories back, keeping them distant and vague. Tonight, though, they crowded his mind and he closed his eyes, remembering summers in the pool, fishing from the dock, exploring the hidden passageways his father had built into the plans of the house. He vividly remembered the last time he saw her before Tyrone—the day she had graduated from college.

He'd wanted to tell her how he felt then and there, about the love he'd carried inside for so many years. However, he didn't feel like she would take him seriously.

Instead, he played the brother role that Ken and Jon easily fell into and just celebrated with everyone as a group, never singling her out, never pouring his heart out to her. Finding out that she'd moved in with a man a couple months later—a married man who worked for their father—didn't make his decision to keep his mouth shut any easier. That experience taught him never to hesitate, not with important matters.

Yet, today he'd seen her twice in one day, once professionally and once personally, and still hadn't said anything beyond normal conversation. Both his brothers had hugged her. He had given her his elbow for a stroll to her car. How long would he have to hold out until confessing his lifetime of love for her?

He leaned his head back and looked up at the night sky. The temperature had dropped significantly since the morning. In late February, the weather tended to act a little erratic. A seventy-degree high could turn into fifty overnight.

Thinking about the ongoing local jobs, and what severe weather could mean, he mentally made a note to discuss spring weather forecasts with the team in tomorrow's weekly project management meeting. Then he shook his head. He'd left his phone downstairs on purpose, intending not to think about work at all tonight. Instead, he looked at the gazebo again.

Then he remembered. The metal box. The cards with their hopes and dreams in them. They had made a pact to open them in fifteen years. That would mean this September. Thinking of the words he'd written, his heart skipped a beat and his throat went dry. What would Valerie say if she knew that Brad had summed up all his hopes and dreams?

Wondering if he should even remind his brothers and Valerie about the box, he finished his water and stood. Maybe he'd wait to see if even one of them remembered.

Going back inside, he slid the door shut behind him and grabbed the dinner plate to take down to the kitchen.

Valerie drove home from the Dixon castle, immersed in thoughts about the family and their unique closeness. She had grown up with them, so nothing felt wrong. She had realized halfway through high school what a unique family they were and how blessed she'd been to be a part of them. She realized how much she missed them and longed to be back with them.

By the first semester of college, she'd found an entirely different world and the Dixons became an adored family "back home" whom she rarely saw and rarely gave a second's thought. She knew it had a lot to do with the way her faith had shifted, but it also had a lot to do with the friends she made in college, her attitude about Buddy moving them, and a freedom of movement she gained living independently for the first time in her life.

Intentionally shutting down the happy thoughts about college, she pulled into the driveway of her little house and got out of her car, listening to the chirp of the horn to confirm she had, in fact, locked the doors. At the end of the driveway, she checked her empty mailbox, then walked up the path to the front door, listening intently, looking all around her, her senses heightened.

After she opened the door and turned off the alarm, she shut it behind her, making sure to lock the deadbolt and attach the security chain. Securely inside, she started turning on lights—first the little entryway, then the overhead light in the living room, the light above the small table in the dining area space, and the kitchen light. She set her purse on the table but kept her keys and phone in her hand while she walked back through the living room, checking that the sliding lock was still secure on the coat closet. She turned on the hall light and did a quick check of the bathroom, the spare bedroom, and finally her bedroom. All the closets remained bolted shut. She didn't actually get on the floor and look under the bed, but she did check the base of the full-length mirror she'd strategically placed next to the bed and made sure she could see the reflection all the way through to the other side of the bed.

Believing herself alone in the house and sure that no one had broken in and hidden anywhere, she relaxed fully, slipping her shoes off and pulling her earrings out of her ears. She set them on the tray on top of her dresser and rolled her head on her neck.

After she slipped her clothes off, she pulled on a nightgown covered in coffee cups and Eiffel Towers, then went into the bathroom to wash her face. As she dried off, she stared at her reflection, running her finger over the scar under her jawline caused by the flying debris of the table she'd landed on. Closing her eyes, she shook her head to clear the image then left the bathroom.

She walked back down the hall and stopped to look into the empty second bedroom. Did she want to invest in a desk for here, to turn this into an office? Or did she want to make it into a spare bedroom for any guests who might stay overnight?

Right, she snorted, *what guests?*

Tyrone had separated her from any college friends years ago, and he was her only approved work friend. Lying in the hospital bed, broken, cut up, and bruised, no one came to visit her until Uncle Buddy arrived followed by Rosaline and

Phillip Dixon. Tyrone had worked everything until she had no world left but him.

Thankfully, she'd kept Buddy away from their relationship, in the dark about everything until she just couldn't hide it all anymore. Buddy's personality kept him from interfering too much, though, which gave Tyrone the idea that he didn't serve in any way as a support system for her, and that caused Tyrone to leave their relationship alone.

If she believed God would hear her, she'd thank Him. Instead, she just felt general gratitude over the way she still had a support system in place, a family in Atlanta that still loved her. Until those lonely days of healing, she had no idea how much she needed people to care about her.

Once Auntie Rose, as Valerie had called her since toddlerhood, had come to visit, the maternal love flowed from her and Valerie felt herself getting better in response. She stayed for three weeks, sitting next to her hospital bed, then sleeping on her couch and driving her to therapies and doctor visits. Valerie honestly didn't know what she'd have done without her.

She imagined her mother would have done the same thing—provided Tyrone hadn't managed to destroy that relationship, of course. Aunt Rose's presence resettled her and started her healing emotionally more than anything else could have.

She rubbed her stomach, as if she could rub away the ball of shame that came from knowing how easily Tyrone had manipulated and used her. How, oh how, could she have let that happen? What hole in her life had Tyrone filled that convinced her to allow him to treat her the way he had, without ever stopping him or confiding in someone? How could she ever trust herself to fall in love again?

With a sound of disgust, she shut the bedroom door and walked back to the entryway to make sure she had actually dead bolted the lock and secured the chain. Her mind at ease about the task, she went into the kitchen. She needed to get to the point that she didn't think someone hid under her bed every night before she could get to the point of thinking about a future relationship that probably wouldn't ever materialize anyway.

She could see it now. "Hi, I'm Valerie. Nice to meet you. My last boyfriend threw me off a second-story balcony and broke my hip. But don't worry, no baggage here. I do have a lovely scar, though, from my hip replacement surgery."

Without meaning to, she slammed the kettle onto the stove so that the sound cracked through the room. Realizing what she'd done, she covered the handle with her palm, as if trying to calm it down instead of herself, and took a deep breath. Feeling less crazy, she turned the knob for the burner, listening to the ticking sound of the gas igniting. While the water in the kettle heated, she put a bag of spearmint tea and a squirt of honey into a mug. She leaned against the counter and waited for the water to boil, thinking back to dinner tonight.

It had been so wonderful to sit at that table again, surrounded by the Dixon family. She didn't even realize how much she'd missed being there for the last thirteen years. Walking through the gardens, pretending to jump over alligators, chatting with the boys, looking into Brad's eyes and wishing he'd see her as something other than a sister, it all felt good and right and normal. It felt as if the rest of her life had just existed as this out-of-place event that happened to her peripherally, and the Dixon estate and family had all paused and waited for her to put her life back where it belonged.

Silly, though. She'd lived away from Atlanta almost the same amount of time as she'd lived in Atlanta.

After pouring boiling water over her tea bag, she checked the sliding glass door again, made sure that metal bar security lock was tightly in place, then went back to the front door and double-checked the locks. Leaving the lights on, she moved back through the house and to her bedroom. She plugged her phone in next to the bed, set the five o'clock alarm, and slipped between the covers.

Phillip Dixon looked up from the job schedule he examined and saw Rosaline staring off into the distance. "He's going to work it out," he said.

Her lips curved in a soft smile. "Eventually. Doesn't mean I can't worry about his heart right now."

He raised an eyebrow. "We can't control his heart. That's up to someone else."

His wife of forty years set her crochet hook into her yarn basket and stood, lifting her arms above her head and stretching left and right. "She's back now. Maybe, just maybe, he'll find peace and contentment."

"Rosie," Phillip said on a sigh, "it's been a long time. They were just fifteen. It's been almost fifteen years. Tell me something. What makes you think he still feels the same way?"

She walked around to his side of the desk and sat on the edge of it, leaning forward so she could put a hand on each of his shoulders. "Did you see his face tonight, love? Did you see how he looked at her? I did."

Phillip's jaw clenched. "I saw him walk out of dinner."

Rosaline closed her eyes and nodded. "I know, dear. You have a year before retirement. I'm sure he's overwhelmed, overworked, and now Valerie Flynn is back. Let's see if things settle with him."

"He's the right man for the job, Rosie. I know it. You know it. His brothers know it. What's more, he's very good at it."

"Of course, he is. He's your son. He has the benefit of your wisdom and hard-earned experience." She kissed his cheek and he inhaled the smell of her perfume. "He'll know it when it's time. God's called many people who took some kicking and screaming before they settled in. We'll just continue to pray for him and be here for him. Just like with Jon."

Phillip felt a rush of anger mixed with sorrow. "That boy. What are we going to do about him?"

"We've done it, love. We've trained him up. Whether he returns isn't up to us. We just love him." She straightened and pushed off the desk. "I'm heading up. I have a women's club tea in the morning. Don't stay up too late."

He stared at the open doorway to his office for a long time after Rosaline left. Pushing thoughts of Jon and his newly declared rejection of a life of Christian faith aside, he focused his mind on Brad. Each of his sons had different strengths. Before he'd promoted Brad to the presidency, he'd contemplated splitting the company up between the three brothers. But that never felt right.

In his early twenties, he'd partnered with Jeremiah Mason and created Mason-Dixon Contracting. They'd grown faster than either could hope for, but a disagreement over a single building contract caused a split between the two men and a division of the company. Jeremiah had gone into massive real estate building and city planning, and Phillip had concentrated on home building and smaller commercial projects. After Jeremiah's untimely death, Phillip found himself in a position to buy out the company, finishing up the current projects Mason had started, and growing his bonding capacity with the profits.

The higher his insurance company would set his bond limit—the insurance that would protect investors if the builder pulled out of a contract for some reason—the more expensive the projects he could bid and win. Soon, he had his own architects and engineers, in-house legal teams, and accounting teams, and had split the residential from the commercial contracting in terms of project managers and superintendents.

By the time his boys entered his workforce, he owned one of the largest general contracting and architectural firms in the southeast. They had hundreds of jobs spanning six states going on at one time and satellite offices throughout Georgia, Alabama, Florida, and the Carolinas.

If Brad didn't want to continue as president of his company, he'd have to split it up. He didn't have another option. Neither Ken nor Jon had the skills to run the entire thing the way Brad ran it. If only Brad would come to see that.

As if his thoughts conjured his son, Phillip heard a

footstep in the outer hall and watched Brad come into his office. He wanted to put on the hard outer shell of a disappointed father, but his heart hurt too much for his son to pretend.

"Hey."

"Hey, Daddy."

"It's late," Phillip remarked, looking at the clock and noticing the midnight hour approaching.

"I wanted to talk to you alone, before the workday starts."

Brad still wore his clothes from the day, but he'd lost the tie, unbuttoned his shirt, and now walked around barefoot. "Sure." Phillip gestured at the love seat where Rosaline normally sat.

Brad perched on the edge of the cushion and rested his elbows on his knees, lacing his fingers together. "I want to apologize. I realized, talking to Valerie before she left, that I've had a really bad attitude. And, that attitude is entirely under my control. Please accept my apology and know that I will enter the building tomorrow morning with a fresh look at the opportunities God has placed in front of me."

Phillip felt his chest swell with emotion. He pushed his chair back and stood, walking around to sit next to Brad. "Son, I want you to know that God has you there. This is you giving in to His will, not mine."

Brad's lips curved in a smile. "Yes, sir. I understand. I've already had a talk with Him about it."

Phillip laughed and slapped Brad on the shoulder. "Fair enough, son." He stood and gestured toward the door. As they walked out together, he turned the light out behind them. "I look forward to tomorrow."

Brad took the stairs twice as fast as his father, stopping halfway up them to smile down at him. “Me, too,” he said, before finishing the climb and going to his room.

Valerie's eyes burned with fatigue as she parked in the gym parking lot. She closed them as she yawned and rested her head on her steering wheel for just a second before turning the car off and grabbing her bag off the seat.

She should have skipped yoga this morning and gotten that extra hour of sleep instead. She could have done the workouts from her living room, but she tended to want to hide away in her home. Once she started skipping workouts, she'd just never go back. Over the last four years, she'd learned to force herself to come and go from her home, go out more, stay in less, training her brain to accept that as much as she loved the comfort and security of her locked house, she could not make it her default.

Which meant that even though she went to bed at midnight, that five o'clock alarm still rang, and she still got out of bed and prepared for yoga class, packing her makeup bag and clothes for the day so she could go straight to work from there.

She entered the gym and swiped her membership card at the desk. The young girl behind the counter gave her a very bubbly welcome, and Valerie smiled back, more at the girl's enthusiasm than anything else. She stopped off in the locker room and set her bag on the foot of the locker and hung her garment bag on the hook.

Even though she'd only attended class here a couple times, this gym felt very comfortable to her. She had attended another gym in this chain when she lived in Savannah, and so much of it had the same feel. Most of that had to do with the identical décor and the same music piping through the speakers, but it still made her feel less like a stranger in a new town and more like someone who belonged here.

She found her classroom and went inside, stopping at the back table to initial next to her name on the roster. She slipped her flip-flops off and walked to the front of the room, finding a spot to unroll her yoga mat.

"Good morning, Valerie," Brooklyn, the instructor greeted. "How is your Tuesday treating you?"

Valerie sat cross-legged on the mat and leaned back on her hands. "Late dinner party. It's going to be a long day."

"We'll set you up for your day," Brooklyn said with a laugh. She moved to the next person who had just come into the room.

"Valerie Flynn?"

Surprised to hear her name, she looked behind her and saw Sami Jones sitting on a fuchsia-colored mat. If she hadn't said something to Valerie, she never would have recognized her as Brad's secretary. Normally, the dark-haired woman wore bright colors and patterns, always with bold makeup and a hat or a head scarf or some other eccentric accessory. Right now, though, she wore a pair of black yoga pants and a gray T-shirt. She'd pulled her blue streaked black hair back into a ponytail and wore no makeup.

"Sami," Valerie said with a smile, turning around to face her. "I didn't even recognize you."

Sami made a sweeping gesture over her face. "Nakedness. I've tried dressing up for yoga, but it feels wrong to leave a makeup mark on my mat." She laughed and jumped up, picking up her mat and moving to the spot next to Valerie. "It's so good to see you here."

"Thanks. You, too."

"I remember you coming for the first time last week. I just didn't know who you were then."

Valerie chose this particular location because of its proximity to the office. "Do other Dixon employees come here?"

Sami shrugged. "Probably. Not in this class, though, and this is about all I do. Sometimes I can do the spin class at night. Most days, I work from seven to seven. Brad, bless him, works long, hard hours. This five-thirty class is my mental prep for the day. I've never been out in the gym area, and I don't take any other classes."

"I have exercises I use for my hip. So, I'll do yoga three

days a week and the gym area for three days."

"Your hip?"

Surprised, Valerie's eyes widened. "You don't know? Haven't heard the gossip?"

"No time for gossip. Not much patience for it either, really. Just heard a few things."

Valerie tried not to scowl. "What have you heard?"

Sami pursed her lips. "I know you're coming from the Savannah office. And I know Buddy is your uncle and that you're a childhood friend of the Dixon brothers. That's about it."

Valerie looked up at the fluorescent lighting and felt some hidden weight of stress suddenly leave. "I guess the gossip isn't as bad as I thought. Maybe I'll relax a little more."

"You keep saying that. What gossip?"

"I, uh, had an ex-boyfriend who wasn't a nice man. Since we were both architects with Dixon, I just assumed everyone knew what happened four years ago."

"Hmmm." She ran a finger over her bottom lip. "Let me think. Yes, I remember. I knew about it, but I didn't know names." She reached over and put a hand on Valerie's forearm. "I'm so sorry you experienced something like that."

Memories flashed through her mind's eye. Shaking her head to bring herself into the present, she smiled. "I am way better these days than I was four years ago. This move was the final step in reclaiming myself. I'm happy to be home."

Sami grinned and settled herself to face the front as Brooklyn called the class to order. "I'm happy you're here, too," she whispered.

Despite the lack of sleep, Brad entered the building whistling, ready to start his future with a new attitude. Something about right now signaled the beginning of the beginning. Usually, he got here before seven. This morning, though, he'd left later than usual and hit heavier traffic than normal, so he came into the lobby at the peak of the morning rush. Several people stopped him to briefly say good morning, to ask a question, or to simply confirm this meeting or that telephone call. By the time he made it to his private elevator, it was nearly eight o'clock.

As he stepped into his office, the overhead LED lights automatically came on. He set his backpack on top of his desk and pulled his laptop out of it. Just as he attached it to the docking station, his door opened and Sami walked in, a cup of coffee in one hand, her tablet in the other. She wore a blue and green flowered silk style dress that fell to her knees. She had her hair pulled up and blue chopsticks sticking out of the bun. She could no longer surprise him with her outfits.

"Good morning. I'm so glad to see you here and healthy. I was about to call you. Or, you know, the hospitals." She set the coffee in front of him and brought her tablet to the ready. The steam rising from the cup caught the morning light shining through the window behind him.

He smiled. "I slept in, if you can believe it. Late night."

"Your dad called about twenty minutes ago."

Brad sipped the coffee and nodded. "He caught me on my cell."

"And you have the meeting with the design team for the Nashville mall in fifteen minutes."

"Right. Who's the interior designer on that?"

Using the tablet, she pulled up the meeting information. "Blank. I'm guessing Owen hasn't assigned one yet."

Thinking of Owen Wakefield, the lead architect for this project and his personality and character, he nodded. "Okay. What else?"

"Nothing pressing." She tapped on her screen then shut the cover on her tablet and turned toward the door but paused and turned back around. "Oh, one thing. How many in your reservation for Calla Jones' restaurant opening? There's an email requesting confirmation. Your brothers have all responded separately, so this is just you."

He started just to say one but changed his mind. He had a few weeks to see what the future held. "Two. Thanks."

"Two?" Sami smiled. "Got it." She looked up at the clock on the wall. "Don't forget the design team. Conference room two. This floor."

"Thanks, Sami." As the door shut behind her, he slipped out of his suit jacket, inverted it, and draped it over the back of the chair while he used his cell phone to call the architect. When Owen answered, Brad greeted, "Owen, Brad. Good morning."

"Morning. What's up, boss?"

"Have you selected a design architect for the Nashville mall yet?"

"I have. I just haven't updated the meeting notice yet. Your dad asked me to bring on Flynn, Buddy's niece, the one who came up from the Savannah office. She did some preliminary consultation on it way back when, so I've added her to the team. May I ask why you ask?"

"Nothing. I just noticed the hole and wanted to make

sure that the team was complete. Thanks."

"Sure. I'll update the documents this morning."

Brad set his phone on his desk and took another sip of hot coffee. He'd watched Valerie's work from a distance for the last couple years, but he felt a little excited at the thought of getting to see her work up close, to sit in meetings with her and watch her interact on a professional level.

After fielding a couple time-sensitive emails, he grabbed his tablet and made sure he had the right project pulled up. Leaving his jacket off, he walked out of his office and into Sami's. She took the empty coffee cup from him and refilled it from the carafe behind her desk. "Thanks," he said, looking at his watch. "I think I have a lunch meeting today."

Sami tapped the computer screen with the eraser of her pencil. "Chamber of Commerce. Twelve-fifteen."

"Right. Thanks." He pushed open her office door and stepped out into the busy office.

Interns, assistants, business analysts, and junior project managers worked in the maze of cubicles in the center of the floor. The offices of the senior project managers lined the walls all around the floor. Right off the bank of elevators were two glass-walled conference rooms that could have the center dividing wall removed to become one very large conference room. Projection screens and smart boards covered the rear wall.

Brad and his father both had corner offices with internal offices for their assistants. The elevators took up another corner, and the restroom area the last.

Cutting through the sea of cubicles, Brad walked from his corner office to the back door of the conference room.

"Bro," he heard. Looking up, he spotted Jon coming from another direction. "Morning."

"Hey. Glad you got my note."

"Nashville, huh? Why do I feel like you're always trying to get rid of me?"

"Not this time. This one goes to a different team. We just haven't assigned it yet. Don't worry. You're stuck here for a little bit at least."

Jon snorted. "Right. Maybe I should start doing residential houses like Ken. Then I could just keep building Atlanta. I hear it hasn't sprawled out enough yet."

"Working on something less than twenty million dollars? You'd be bored out of your mind in a week." Brad opened the back door of the conference room and they entered to find the rest of the team present.

He walked straight to Owen and held out his hand. "Good morning."

"Morning." They shook hands and Brad took a seat in the center of the table. Owen would run this meeting. Along with him and Jon, Brad saw Ian Jones, the mechanical engineer, and Al Carpenter, the electrical engineer. The door opened and Valerie walked in, wearing a lilac-colored pantsuit with a lime green and lilac scarf around her neck. He noticed a very slight limp in her step, but only because he knew to look for it.

He said good morning to her, then turned to Ian. "How's the restaurant opening going?"

Ian grinned. "Been lots of fun so far. Never seen my wife so stressed. I'll be glad when the opening night is a smashing success so she can relax a little bit."

Brad smiled. "Congratulations."

"Thanks. You gonna make it?"

"Definitely. I've had your wife's cooking."

Owen stood at the head of the table. "Okay, welcome to everyone. Obviously, if you're here, you know we won the design-build for this mall. The process for competition for the contract started eighteen months ago, so it's nice to finally start rolling up our sleeves and getting down to it. Remember. This entire area was flooded and under up to twenty feet of water not too long ago."

He pressed a button on the table in front of him. The screen behind him lowered and the lights dimmed. To emphasize his point, Owen started his presentation with a few aerial shots of the flood on the overhead.

"What we're looking at is an eight hundred thousand square feet shopping experience in a suburb of Nashville. This project is worth almost $400 million, so we're also planning on adding personnel to our Nashville office, which right now is just staffed with a couple project managers and a secretary who works remotely part-time."

The computer model of the mall appeared on the screen. "Everything we've done to this point is a shell of a preliminary concept designed to give us something from which to pull bids and give the owners an idea of what our conception of the project looks like. We're going to use that as the base to truly design it. Senior Mr. Dixon handpicked this team, so I know what we're looking at is the best team our company can put forward."

Ian spoke up. "Is the environmental cleanup on the site complete yet?"

Owen nodded. "Right. For those of you coming in new, this mall is being built on the site of an old steel mill. The mill never recovered after the flood. It has been a massive cleanup for another company on another contract and has taken three years. Their projected completion date is in six months, which gives us time to finalize all of our plans and specifications and solicit bids from subcontractors."

Valerie raised her hand slightly. "How much input is the owner going to have on the interior design?"

Owen tapped a thin folder in front of him. "They've given us some input and asked us to give them three different approaches. They'll look those over and choose one of the three." He slid the folder toward her. "I know you did some preliminary stuff a year ago. I also know they really liked what you came up with. I'd definitely stick with that as the base for all three."

He pushed a button and the image on the screen changed to an overhead view of the site. "I want to talk about access now."

Nearly two hours later, the meeting broke up. Brad sat at the table for another minute, making notes in his tablet while the thoughts were fresh in his mind. When he shut the cover, he looked up and saw Owen stacking notebooks. "Phenomenal job, Owen. You've clearly made this project your own."

"Thank you, Brad. I will admit that I wanted it." He laughed. "A lot. I have ideas on top of ideas, and these owners are so open to new and innovative."

"I know that's up your alley." He shook his hand. "I have a thing. I'll see you next meeting."

"Sir."

Brad slowly walked out of the conference room, going through the back door, which brought him out into a cubicle aisle. He tried to concentrate on the information handed out in the two-hour-long meeting, but he could only remember what Valerie had talked about, the questions she asked. He wondered now if he should have given her that promotion. Maybe he needed more distance from her in order to function properly.

"Brad!" He turned and saw Al Carpenter, who'd had to leave the meeting to see to an issue on a jobsite. "Hey. Sorry about that."

"No problem. Current projects need to take precedence. Everything okay?"

"Oh, yes. It's resolved."

"Good." He looked at his watch. "I have a Chamber meeting in forty-five minutes."

"Your dad relinquishing the hobnobbing, too?"

"Apparently." He laughed. "I remember the first time he invited me to go with him. I was so excited. I think I was sixteen."

"Would be nice if we could find some of that young excitement again occasionally, eh?" He paused outside Jon's office door. "I'm heading into Jon's office. See you later."

"Bye, Al."

Back in his own office, he pulled up his email program, but paused and said out loud, "I hear you, God. Being thankful, finding excitement, not dragging my feet and wishing I was doing something else. Thanks for the confirmation from last night's revelation."

He glanced at the clock in the corner of his laptop screen. He could spend about thirty minutes catching up on emails before he absolutely had to leave to make it to the Chamber lunch on time.

Valerie stood and shifted a stack of paint samples off her desk as Buddy set the two cardboard containers on top of the desk. She could smell tangy barbecue sauce and her mouth started watering.

"Is this Mama Robinson's brisket?" she asked, setting the samples on the floor and grabbing one of the boxes.

"Surprised you had to ask. I wouldn't get barbecue from anywhere else in Atlanta." Buddy laughed.

"How'd you get it?"

"I was on that side of town this morning and placed my order an hour ahead of time."

She opened the lid and put her nose close to the meat, breathing in through her nose and inhaling the spices. "Oh, heaven."

"Speaking of," Buddy said, holding out his hand.

Reluctantly, Valerie placed her fingers in his and bowed her head. As soon as he finished the declaration of thankfulness for the food and the company, he said, "Amen," giving her the opening to pick up her plastic fork.

After taking a bite of creamy potato salad, she picked up a pepper packet and sprinkled black pepper over the potato salad and coleslaw. "I had dinner with the Dixons last night. I missed you there."

"Rosaline invited me, but I had a working dinner with some people wanting us to build their house."

Valerie raised an eyebrow. "Since when are you working residential?"

He pulled a bottle of hot sauce out of his backpack and sprinkled his beef liberally with it. "Oh, 'bout a year now. Philip and I reworked a few things a couple years ago. I'm VP of residential now, directly under Ken. I pretty much handle the front part of the high-end houses."

She dipped a slice of meat into the tangy barbecue sauce and took a bite. Her taste buds exploded in delight with the burst of flavor. After chewing and swallowing, she said, "Why? Are you okay?"

"Val, my lovely niece, I'm simply almost sixty-five years old. Your mama was my baby sister. I don't want to be out there in the Georgia sun, breathing red clay and listening to the clutter of the jobsite. I want to sit in my air-conditioned office and appease millionaires who are building showcase homes."

How did she not know this? As she pondered that thought for a minute, it occurred to her that she simply hadn't asked. Looking at Buddy with narrowed eyes, she realized he wore khaki pants and a black golf shirt with the red Dixon Brothers logo emblazoned on the chest. Throughout her young life, he wore blue jeans and Dixon Brothers T-shirts. She hadn't even noticed his clothing difference.

Now she examined him closely. He'd had salt-and-pepper gray hair for as long as she could remember but had white temples now. His chocolate skin looked smooth and healthy, but his fingers had a slight curve instead of straightening all the way, and his left hand had a faint tremor.

"I've not been a very doting niece, have I?" She picked up her drink and took a long pull of the syrupy sweet iced tea.

"Never have done. You was always closer to Rosaline. I think, looking back, taking you away from there for your high school years wasn't the right decision." He shoved meat into his mouth and chewed.

While he savored his meal, she thought about his words, knowing he spoke the truth but feeling like she needed to defend his actions at the time. When she opened her mouth, he held his hand up to stop her. "Ain't no arguing it, girl. You knew it then, but I was so concerned about you growing up so sheltered and wanted you to have some diversity in your life. Putting you into a different school and taking you away from your family, no matter what color they were, that was wrong. But I think maybe I was a little jealous of your relationship with Rosaline. Decided to remove you from her so I could have that love and attention you gave her."

Sharp tears stung her eyes. She reached out and gripped Buddy's wrist. "I love you. I'm sorry if I didn't properly show it. You're my blood. She's just...."

"... your Auntie Rose. I know. I know that now. Took me facing myself after what happened to you to realize what I'd done and why. Wasn't nothing against them. Just was for me. Wrong decisions all around. God worked it out in me."

They ate in silence for a few minutes before Valerie replied, "My last couple years of high school were great, and I made friends and had experiences I never would have had. Don't feel like it was all wrong, even if you wish you'd done something different. We, uh, all make bad decisions."

"We do, girl. Life is full of 'em. Thank God there is redemption, or I'd be a hurting soul."

She took a few more bites, trying to word what she wanted to say. "Uncle Buddy, I'm thankful for everything you've ever done for me. I feel like you gave up your life for me, and that is not anything I'll ever forget."

He barked a loud laugh. "Gave up my life? What are you talking about?"

"You never married. I don't even remember you ever dating."

"Bah, dating ain't for me. Never was. Never met a woman I'd want to marry. I was content in my bachelorhood before I got you, and I'm content in it now." He pointed at her with his fork. "What your mama and daddy did leaving you to me, that saved my life. You gave me a purpose, something to work for, someone to provide for. Who knows what would have happened without you. You didn't make me give up my life; you gave me a life."

Feeling overwhelmed with sentimental emotion, tears stung Valerie's eyes—tears she would not let fall. She blinked them back and shut the lid on her empty container, her mouth still singing with spices and flavor, her stomach full of good barbecue. "Alright, then," she laughed, "that's enough seriousness for one lunch. You still got Braves season tickets?"

"Yup." He shoveled potato salad into his mouth and talked around it. "Same seats I always had. Right next to Philip and Rosaline's. You want to go to the opening game?"

Her eyes widened. "Of course!"

"Been too long since we sat in the stadium together. Will do us both good." He tossed his fork into the empty container and shut the lid. "I enjoyed this, girl. Want to make it a habit?"

"More than you know." She grinned as she gathered their food containers and put them into the bag in which he'd brought them. "I'll toss these in the break room trash so the smell of barbecue doesn't haunt me all day."

They started out of her office, but Buddy stopped with his hand on the door. "By the way, Sweetwater Church is dedicating its new library building to your parents. The memorial service is next month. I expect you can come."

Her stomach clenched in response, but she didn't immediately tell him no. Instead, she smiled and leaned over and kissed his cheek. "Shoot me the information. I'll look at my calendar."

"Do that." He stared at her for several seconds. "Opening game for the Braves is the last Thursday of next month."

"I'll check my schedule for that, too." She opened the door and stepped out onto the main floor. "We doing this next Tuesday?"

"That's a great idea." He pulled his phone out of his

pocket and swiped to his calendar. "It's going in firmly. Tuesday lunches with Val. Perfect." He put a hand on her upper arm. "I love you, girl. I've missed you for years. Glad you're home."

"I've missed you, too." He left her to go in one direction, and she went in the other to throw the garbage away. After stopping in the restroom to wash her hands, she went back to her office. For several minutes after she returned to her desk, she stared at the empty screen of the Smartboard.

She had no desire to go to her parents' church to let them dedicate a building in honor of their going on a mission trip and getting killed. She harbored a lot of anger at her parents for leaving her when she was just three years old. She felt like they should have waited a few more years before getting back into inner-city missions. But they just handed her to Buddy, a bachelor who had never had kids, and used their vacation to go on a mission trip in South Central Los Angeles, as if they couldn't have found something charitable to do in the inner city of Atlanta. A gang shooting left both her parents dead on the street in California and left her and Buddy with just each other.

No, she would not go see them honored. They deserved no honor. They put an imaginary deity ahead of her well-being, and she would not let go of that.

The question remained, though, how to convey that to Buddy? All her life, he took her to church, prayed with her, prayed for her. He and Philip Dixon met weekly to discuss Bible studies over breakfast, and until the day she left for college, he required her regular attendance at youth group events. His relationship with his god consumed his entire life, as it had her parents'. Simply telling him she stopped believing in what he believed sometime during her college freshman Philosophy class would do no good. He wouldn't hear it.

Taking a deep breath through her nose and slowly releasing it, she let it go. She'd just have to take one day at a time with Buddy and let him see her, really see her, so he understood.

Valerie stood in front of the Smartboard and rolled the remote control around in her hand while she looked at the interior of the main entrance of the proposed shopping mall. Several catalogs showing fountain designs lay open on the floor in front of her and swatches of fabric samples draped over every available surface. Frowning, she stepped forward and double-tapped the screen, allowing her to access the object on the screen so she could select a different color for the tile accent lining the fountain.

Not liking that one, either, she finally hit the button and turned off the board. She had reached the point of overthinking it. Time to step away for a few minutes.

She grabbed her empty water bottle and stepped out of her office. The hum of conversation and work-related noise from all the cubicles and open office doors made her thankful for good sound dampening in the design of the interior offices. She'd realized the first week here that with her door shut, she could forget anyone else even worked in the same building with her. In Savannah, she'd heard every telephone chirp, every text message notification and, unfortunately, most conversations. Here, though, she only heard other people when she had her door was open. At first, she had a hard time concentrating in silence. But after a couple days, she realized how much better she could think and how much more efficiently she worked without constant interruptions.

She walked through the cubicles to the other side of the floor and into the break room. She saw Sami Jones sitting at one of the round tables with two women she recognized from the staff meeting Monday morning, a receptionist from the top floor, and a mechanical engineer.

Sami hopped up from the table. "Valerie! Just in time. We're talking about our meeting that's during lunch today. We'd love for you to join us."

Valerie unscrewed the lid to her water bottle and leaned down over the water cooler to fill it. "Lunch today?"

The mechanical engineer spoke. Valerie recognized a slight northern tone to her voice. "National Association of Women in Construction. We meet the third Thursday of every month."

The smile crossed her face before she could stop it. "NAWIC? Oh, my goodness, I used to be a member in Savannah." Used to, meaning, until she started dating Tyrone and he took that away from her like everything else. How had she forgotten about it? The time spent with other women in her city who worked in the construction industry had, frequently, been the highlight of her week. She'd started to forge some close friendships; at least, until they went away. "I'd love to come. When and where?"

Sami clapped. "Awesome. Eleven-thirty today. I'll email you an invite. It will have all the details."

Valerie slipped her phone out of her pocket and checked

her schedule. "I can do that. Thank you so much!"

As she walked back to her office, she rearranged her afternoon plans. She'd originally intended to have a quick sandwich at her desk. Now, she knew, she'd lose a couple hours in the middle of the day between driving to and from and the meeting itself.

Back in her office, she took an extra five minutes and pulled up the NAWIC website. Memories of friendships, dinners, and local meetings flooded her mind when she looked at the logo. Intentionally closing her browser, she opened her email. She sent Owen an update on the main lobby of the mall and the color schemes for the second and third-floor handrails and elevator frames. Putting that project to the side, she replied to emails for two other current projects and sent Ken the information for a new wallpaper supplier for a 6,000 square foot home he had contracted. Before she left her computer, she saw the email from Sami with the information for the meeting, along with an invite to ride with her. Shooting a reply telling her she'd meet her in the lobby in ten minutes, she cleaned up the fabric samples she'd had draped all over the office and filed them in the milk crate for that project.

She ran her hands down the side of her orange pantsuit. She'd worn a necklace with large yellow flowers with orange centers, a yellow belt, and yellow heels. Taking a few minutes to refresh her lipstick, make sure she had enough cash in her purse for lunch, and check email one more time, she walked out of her office.

After two weeks here, she had started to get to know people. She waved, smiled, and stopped briefly to say a thing or two to different people as she worked her way to the elevators. Somehow, despite the closeness to lunch, she had the elevator to herself and it went straight to the lobby. Glancing through the sparse crowd, she didn't see Sami, so she wandered along the walls, looking at the different construction projects Dixon Contracting had built back to the days when the company was called Mason-Dixon Contracting. She stopped at a newspaper article with a photo of Philip Dixon and country music star Melody Mason Montgomery at the thirtieth anniversary of the company's first groundbreaking. She read the caption:

Melody Mason Montgomery charmed the crowd at the thirtieth anniversary of the Mason-Dixon Contracting first groundbreaking, telling stories of her father's passion for building in Atlanta.

Valerie thought back and tried to remember if she knew that the Mason who had once partnered with Philip Dixon was Melody Mason Montgomery's father, but nothing about that sounded familiar.

"Valerie!"

Turning, she spotted a Dixon brother headed her way. Her eyes scanned his blue jeans and worn leather boots and she identified him. He must have gotten a haircut. "Hi, Ken."

He laughed. "You are one of the few people in the world to do that consistently."

She smiled. "You have tells."

"Well, keep them to yourself. I'll be subconscious." He checked the time. "Do you have lunch plans? I wanted to talk about this new estate house we're building. The owner is being super picky about colors and I just don't trust her opinion."

She shook her head and pulled her phone out of her

pocket. "I do have lunch plans. I have a NAWIC meeting. Can we do something after work, maybe?"

"No." He frowned. "Coffee in the morning?"

She smiled. "Perfect." Waving at Sami, who had just stepped out of the elevator, she added coffee with Ken to the calendar on her phone. "Want to meet here or somewhere else?"

"Here's good. Seven?"

"Perfect."

Sami joined them. "Hi, Mr. Dixon," she said.

"Ken," he casually clarified, then stepped away from them. "Enjoy your meeting, ladies. Represent us well."

As they walked toward the parking garage, Sami quietly said, "I can only ever tell Brad, because he wears a suit. I swear they should all have different facial hair or something."

Valerie laughed. "I've always been able to tell them apart. I can see the differences in their faces and their walks."

Sami glanced at her and shook her head. "That's not normal. Must be the artist in you."

"Maybe." She followed Sami to her convertible VW Bug painted the brightest yellow Valerie had ever seen. She noticed the door was unlocked, so she slipped into the passenger's side, automatically assessing the back seat. "I've also known them my entire life. Grew up with them. That probably helps."

"True." Sami started the car. The daisies on the dashboard danced with the vibration of the car engine.

"Jon has a chicken pox scar on his right temple," Valerie said. "Of course, you have to be close enough to see it."

Sami laughed and darted out of the parking garage. "I think I'll just stick with Mr. Dixon." Valerie held onto her seatbelt as Sami took a corner a little faster than comfort allowed. "Much safer that way."

Trying not to react to Sami's chaotic and aggressive driving, Valerie nodded and swallowed. "Safety first," she whispered, then laughed.

Brad wandered into the kitchen and found his father at the stove. "Smells good," he said, walking up behind him and looking into the pot of bubbling soup. "Tomato?"

"Buddy was trying out a greenhouse this year. I don't think he gave enough credit to how well he could possibly grow produce in the late winter." He gestured to the crate half full of tomatoes. "I told him we'd do soup after church today."

"Looks like you have enough to feed the congregation." Brad laughed, grabbing two coffee cups out of the cupboard. "That's a big pot."

"Yeah. Your mom will want to can the leftovers." He

gestured with the knife. "You should call Valerie. See if she wants to come eat, too. She always did like my tomato soup."

"Sure." He poured coffee into the cups and grabbed a banana out of the fruit bowl then glanced at the clock on the stove. "I'll call when it's not five-fifteen."

Phillip chuckled. "Guess we're weird."

"Guess so." As he walked out of the kitchen, he looked back at his father. "Enjoy your tomatoes."

On his way out the front door, he stopped and grabbed a fleece jacket out of the coat closet. He stepped out into the cold morning, feeling the chill of the sidewalk on his bare feet. He quickly dashed to the pool house, letting the lighted path guide his way in the dark, careful not to spill any coffee. The humid air greeted him as he slipped into the room.

In the summer, they would retract the ceiling and remove the walls. In the winter, though, they heated the water and covered the pool. That's where he found Jon.

He walked over to the table where Jon had left his clothes. On top of his towel, Brad found Jon's watch and saw the timer counting down. He had ninety seconds left of his thirty-minute timer.

Jon had come home from Egypt a changed person, angry, impatient, anxious. He'd snapped at Brad over little things that would never have bothered him before, and Brad worried something had happened during his trip.

Two laps later, the alarm went off and Brad watched Jon slow his pace and lift his head up out of the water. He held up a cup of coffee and waited for his brother to climb out of the pool.

Jon slipped off the goggles and took out the earplugs. He

accepted the towel Brad offered and wiped his face. "Coffee smells good. Is it still hot?"

"Yeah. I poured it just now."

"Beautiful." Jon sat on one of the patio chairs and took a sip. Water pooled at his feet and under the chair. "Thanks."

Brad noticed the tattoo on Jon's shoulder, a geometric shape that made him think of ancient pottery. He'd never seen it before, and he often brought his brother coffee to the pool house. That meant he got it in the last three months when he was out of the country.

"Nice ink," he remarked.

Jon looked at his shoulder as if surprised to see it there. "Right. Forgot about that."

Brad chuckled. "Mom see it yet?"

With a sigh, his brother said, "I'm twenty-nine. I hardly need my mother's permission to get a tattoo."

Brad took a sip of his coffee before he very dryly said, "Nevertheless." He set the coffee cup down and peeled his banana. "You already give her enough reasons to pray for you. That might send her over an edge."

"We can't all be the perfect and highly favored son, can we, Bradford? Some of us need our own identity."

Brad raised an eyebrow. "Is that right?" As triplets, they all craved and sought individual identity. He took a bite of banana and chewed and swallowed before he said, "You think I don't have my own identity?"

"I think you're doing exactly what dad wants you to do in exactly the way he wants you to do it. Follow the rules. That's always been your M.O. Strictly. You've never even stood close enough to see the line, much less toe it or cross over it."

Irritation clawed at the back of his throat. "Just because you hope to break every possible rule before your thirtieth birthday doesn't mean those of us who choose to abide by them are doing something wrong."

"Every rule?" Jon chuckled. "One tattoo and two missed church services now constitute every rule?" He picked up the mug of coffee. "You need to get out more, Brad."

"Maybe."

"I had high hopes for you the other night at dinner. I thought you'd finally speak your mind. Instead, you chickened out, clammed up, and left. Then you found the gumption to get up the next morning and put on that tie."

Brad's lips thinned. "Actually, I'm at peace with my position now. I came to an inner understanding. It's a relief."

Jon nodded and rubbed at his wet hair with a towel. After taking another bite of banana and washing it down with coffee, Brad decided to change the topic of conversation before something got said that ought not get said. He surprised himself by saying, "I'm thinking of asking Valerie to be my date for Calla Jones' restaurant opening."

Jon raised an eyebrow. "Date date? Or, an old family friend come as my desperation guest date?"

"Date date. Like I should have asked from the moment dad allowed us to date. That kind of date."

Jon stared at him for several seconds before he asked, "Why didn't you ever have the guts to ask, bro? Because she's practically your sister? Or because she has darker skin pigmentation than you? Afraid folks would think the rich white boy was dating the help?"

Taken aback by the question, Brad visibly flinched.

"Seriously? You jump to bigot in front of all the other reasons I may have?"

"You're saying her skin color, or your lack of skin color, had nothing to do with your hesitation back then?"

The question shocked him to his very heart. How could Jon even think the color of their skin had ever been a factor? It had honestly never even occurred to him. Not once. "Of course not."

"Then what?"

It embarrassed him to say it out loud. "A few reasons. First of all, I didn't want her to think I asked her out as a last resort. I didn't want her to agree out of some sort of pity."

Jon nodded and drank some more coffee before asking, "And number two?"

Heat that had nothing to do with the coffee he just swallowed flushed his face. He shrugged, almost defensively. "What if...?" His voice trailed off, as if he refused to voice his fear.

Jon, however, went ahead and said it out loud. "What if she turned you down? What if your feelings were one-sided after all? Better to pine from a distance for fifteen years than have all your hopes and dreams trampled under her little feet, eh?"

The spark of irritation he'd felt earlier at his brother slowly burned to anger. He grabbed his banana peel and his coffee cup and stood. "You know what? You've been a real jerk lately. Not sure what's up with you. I came out here to try to talk to you. See if you needed me. But I'm not going to be a target just because you're in one of your moods."

He left without another word. Outside the humid pool house, the morning air felt cooler than before. Instead of going inside, he wandered along the path and found himself in the gazebo. So many memories that normally lay in the back of his mind had come forward in the days since Valerie returned. Memories and feelings. How much of the past had he projected onto the present? Did it even matter?

His coffee had long cooled, so he tossed it into some bushes and put the banana peel in the empty cup. Jon was just in a bad mood and pushing Brad's buttons. Intellectually, he knew that. No one could do that better than Jon. Later today, he'd come to Brad with a hand outstretched and say something like, "Sorry, bro. Bad mood and took it out on you." Brad would forgive him, because he ought to, and because he always did.

However, it didn't make the hint of truth in his words affect him any less. He had pined from a distance to keep from discovering how Valerie felt. He'd stayed safe. He'd guarded his heart. Look where it got her. If he had only... but, no.

No matter what, he would not allow himself to shoulder the blame of what happened to her. She made choices. Tyrone was a bad man, a perfect storm of terribleness surrounded her. She got out, though. Finally safe. Home. Time to quit doing anything from a distance at all.

Pulling the phone out of his pocket, he checked the time. Six in the morning. He could probably go ahead and send a text. If she still slept, she'd sleep through an incoming text.

DAD IS MAKING TOMATO SOUP FROM BUDDY'S BOUNTY. LUNCH AT THE CASTLE AFTER CHURCH?

He slipped the phone back into his pocket and headed back to the house. As he walked, he felt the vibration of an incoming text.

LOVE YOUR DAD'S SOUP. SEE YOU AROUND ONE.

He couldn't stop the smile that covered his face.

Valerie settled more comfortably against the arm of the couch and cradled the cup of tea in her hands. She'd worn a simple, ankle-length dress the color of light coffee that she adjusted as she folded her legs under her. Alone for the first time in a couple hours, she took a moment to inspect the room around her. A painting of the three brothers playing in the sprinkler hung on the wall across from her. They must have been five. The artist had captured the summer heat, the cool water, the joy on the boys' faces. She imagined that Rosaline could capture infinite memories just with a glance at it.

"Here we are," Rosaline said, coming back into the room. She wore a tan skirt with a white shirt tucked into the waist and a thick black belt and a beaded black necklace. She'd piled her hair on top of her head, and Valerie could see the small gray roots among the frosted curls. She carried a pink gift bag that had white tissue paper covered in shiny pink polka-dots sticking out of the top of it. "I found this last year, cleaning out one of my cabinets. I put it away to save for you. I'm sorry it's taken so long to get it to you." She held out the bag. "We'll call it a housewarming gift."

Valerie straightened her legs, feeling the twinge in her hip, and set the cup on the little table next to the couch. Curiosity warred with almost childlike excitement as she reached for the gift. "Thank you," she said. She took the bag from Rosaline and reached into the tissue paper, pulling out a framed photograph.

Immediately, emotion filled her chest and brought tears to her eyes. She and the boys must have been about thirteen. They'd gone to a wedding for someone at the church. The bride had taken a silly photo with the groomsmen, laying on her side across their arms. Valerie and the Dixon brothers had mocked it, lifting Valerie into their arms and holding her on her side while she posed with her head in her hands as if resting her elbow on the floor. They all could barely hold the pose, though, because they were laughing so hard. Brad, in the middle, did not look at the camera. He looked at her, and she could almost hear his laughter.

Buddy had bought her a dress special for the wedding; a bright, lime green one with spaghetti straps and eyelet lace on the hem. She'd felt bold and beautiful and more sophisticated than this picture revealed. The boys all had on summer suits, light blue, light tan, and light gray, with white shirts and matching ties.

"This is amazing," Valerie said, running her fingertip over the black wood frame. "We were so young!"

"Doesn't seem like that long ago to me," Rosaline said. "That year was special. That year I saw my boys as men and you as the wonderful woman you are today."

Valerie didn't know what to say. "Thank you."

"I'd forgotten all about that picture until I found it. Funny what memories get set to the background and how easy it is to bring them back." Rosaline picked up her teacup and sat in the wingback chair across from her. "I set about cleaning out that cupboard and ended up bawling my way through boxes of pictures, remembering times when my house was full of the kind of joy only four kids can bring."

One by one, doors in her mind opened in a domino effect. "You were a good mom," Valerie said quietly.

"I loved being a mom. We didn't think it would happen. We'd lost three before the boys. I stayed in bed for weeks with them. Talk about stir-crazy. And poor Phillip was working so hard. The company had just gotten off the ground and there was too much work and not enough immediate revenue to pay salaries for help, so he and your uncle were doing the brunt of it. I declare, if it weren't for your mama, I think I would have gone insane."

Surprised, Valerie asked, "My mama?"

"Oh, yes. Your mama and I met through Buddy and Phillip and became such good friends. She had just found out she was pregnant with you about the time the doctor sent me to bed. She came over every day and kept me company. We made baby clothes, worked on scrapbooks, and talked about these babies of ours. She loved you so much, honey."

Valerie felt the pang of knowing she should miss something she'd never known. "I don't remember a thing about her."

"I know." She set her cup and saucer on the table. "I wish you could remember. She was an incredible woman who loved the people in this world with such grace that it practically shone out of her. I look at pictures, sometimes surprised I don't see the aura glowing around her like a halo."

Valerie pulled her legs up onto the couch and leaned against the arm. "It feels unfair at times. I know so much in my life would be different if she'd lived. However, the things that would change like growing up here, with you and Uncle

Phil, the boys..." her voice trailed off. "But I wouldn't have made the same decisions I made if I'd grown up with my parents, with brothers or sisters." She looked at the picture again. "Maybe."

"Child, if 'ifs and buts' were fruits and nuts we'd all have a merry Christmas. You can't live like that. 'What if' is a dangerous game to play. Think of King David. The result of his sin with Bathsheba was a child. A son. God took that son as a punishment. The whole time the baby was sick, David fasted and prayed and cried out to God. After the baby died, David cleaned himself up and ate. Why?"

Rosaline paused and waited. Valerie might have felt annoyed at the Biblical analogy, but she knew better than to just shrug it off and refuse to answer. Instead, she pulled her education from the back of her mind and said, "Because he couldn't change what God had done."

Rosaline raised an eyebrow, clearly reading Valerie's tone. "Because he couldn't change what had happened. There was no sense continuing to fast and mourn. What was done was done." She stood and crossed over to Valerie, sitting on the table in front of her and taking her hand. "You can't change the mistakes you made, the decisions you made, the things you're not proud of in your past. You don't have that power. You do have the power to get up, clean yourself off, and resume life. You've done a really good job of that. I'm so proud of you."

"Thanks, Auntie Rose," she whispered, using the name she'd called her all her childhood.

A noise at the door made Rosaline look over her shoulder. Brad stood there, leaning against the door frame, his hands in his pockets. He had untucked his shirt and taken off his tie. Valerie noticed he also wore no shoes. “Am I intruding?”

“We were just walking down memory lane,” Rosaline said, squeezing Valerie’s hand before she stood. “I have to get dinner going.”

Valerie slowly stood up from the couch and raised her hands above her head, stretching her body from side to side, loosening muscles that had tightened while she sat. “Your mom found the neatest picture,” she said, grabbing the photo and the bag off the table. “Look. Remember this?”

She walked toward him and held out the photo frame. He had a quiet, contemplative look on his face and his gray eyes had darkened and looked like a stormy sky. When he blinked and smiled, his features softened. He took the photo from her and after a second, laughed. “I remember this.” Still smiling, he handed it back to her. “You looked so beautiful in that dress.”

“I felt very grown up in that dress.” She put the photo back into the pink bag. “Looking at it now, though, I was so very young. What made me think I was in any way mature?”

“Oh, I don’t know. I think we were all on the cusp of a new maturity. What were we? Thirteen?”

“Yeah. Full-blown puberty times four in that picture,” she laughed. “Lord, how did your mama do it?”

“It was certainly a gift.” He straightened and gestured with his head. “Want to walk?”

“No. Actually, I brought my suit. I thought I might swim a few laps. I think that would feel really great on my hip.”

With a raised eyebrow, he asked, “Mind if I join you?”

“I kind of assumed you’d want to. Never could keep you out of the pool.” She picked up the bag she’d set by the door.

"I'll go change in the pool house. Meet you there in ten minutes?"

"Sounds good."

Brad slipped a short-sleeved shirt on but did not button it up. On his way out of his room, he put his watch on the charger on his dresser and slid his feet into a pair of slide sandals. In the hall, he ran into Jon coming up the stairs.

They'd made up as soon as Brad had come home from church. Never one to hold a grudge against his brothers, Brad had gladly accepted Jon's apology and offered his own.

"Valerie and I are going for a swim. Want to join?"

Jon glanced at his watch. "Sure. Yeah. I have about an hour." He paused with his hand on his bedroom door handle. "It's nice enough out you could probably open the roof."

"I was thinking that, too. See you down there."

He didn't encounter anyone else as he walked through the house and down the path to the pool room. When he went inside, he saw Valerie swimming laps. Instead of announcing himself, he went to the control panel and activated the motors that would retract the part of the roof above the swimming pool. Knowing that next week, the temperatures would cool off slightly, he didn't want to go through the effort of retracting the entire roof and pushing the walls back. This would give them some sun and make it easier to put everything back in place when they finished swimming.

He went to the little bar area against the side wall and

pulled two bottles of water out of the mini fridge, then grabbed a towel and walked over to the table where Valerie had set her things.

He remembered the day his father finished building the pool house around the pool and installed the pool heater. Suddenly, swimming became a year-round activity for them instead of just something they enjoyed in the summer months. The four of them would barely finish homework before the race to the pool house began. Phillip had experimented with his own home to help launch a special section of Dixon Brothers Contracting and Design that specialized in pools, pool houses, glass walls, and mechanical roofs.

Once he'd kicked his shoes off and slipped the shirt off his shoulders, he walked over to the deep end and executed a smooth dive into the tepid water. Already he looked forward to the days when the sun warmed the water instead of the heater. Smoothly cutting across the surface, he swam to the end and rolled and turned in the water, using the wall to kick off and start stroking back to the other side.

After swimming ten laps, he paused in the middle of the pool, letting the water lap up to his chest. He saw Valerie sitting in the chair and drinking from the water he'd left out. She had a towel draped over her shoulders. When she saw him looking at her, she lifted her face to the sun and smiled. "I can't wait for summer," she exclaimed. "When it's hot all the time and not alternating with cold."

He floated to the edge of the pool and crossed his arms on the edge, letting his body float. "It's the most wonderful time of the year."

She screwed the cap into place and set the bottle on the

table. "What are your plans this summer?"

"Ken and I close on a townhouse complex next month. It has thirty-nine units plus an office. I think that will tie us up quite well."

Valerie raised a perfectly manicured eyebrow. "Your mom told me you do that regularly. But, don't you guys usually do that in the fall? Hole away all winter with it?"

He thought about the buildings. "Usually. But this one is going to take a lot of exterior renovation. They look like they were built with a low budget in 1975. Seriously. I don't know why Ken doesn't just plan to bulldoze them to the ground and start fresh. I think he must be bored with simple interior renovations."

Her laughter filled the room. "I'd be curious to see what your definition of 1975 low budget means."

He couldn't help but grin in reply. "I'll be sure to show you as soon as we close."

"Do they have people living there?"

Bracing his hands on the side of the pool, he pushed himself out of the water. As he reached for a towel, he said, "No. They've been vacant for a couple of months. We got a really good deal on them. If we can renovate without bulldozing, we should make a good profit." Wrapping the towel around his waist, he reached for a water bottle and sat across from her. "We'll know more when we dig into them next week. Ought to be interesting."

"You got your dad's mind for things like that, that's for sure." Valerie stood and the towel slipped off her shoulders. Brad liked the hot pink swimsuit. The color flattered her skin tone. He didn't know where else his mind would have gone because as she turned around, he saw the scars along her exposed back and shoulders. As she took a step, he saw the scar on the side of her thigh running up to her hip.

Intellectually, he'd known what happened to Valerie. He'd seen her with a cane and noticed her limp. When Tyrone threw her off a balcony and she crashed onto a glass table, the desire to physically hurt the man had overwhelmed him. If he'd gone to Savannah with his mother and had come across him, Brad might be the one in prison right now instead of Tyrone. He didn't visit her, didn't seek to experience sitting next to her while she lay bruised and broken in a hospital bed because he didn't think he had the self-control to keep from reacting.

But, honestly, four years had passed. How could he possibly still harbor so much venom for a man who had spent the last four years in prison?

Because, witnessing these scars, seeing the remnants of the pain another man had inflicted on someone he had loved since childhood, suddenly his hands fisted, and he found himself clenching his jaw so tightly it started to ache. He could find no rational thought as a roaring started in his ears and fury took hold of his mind. The edges of his vision started to turn red and he gradually stood.

The slamming of the pool house door pulled him out of his rage. It startled him and he looked up, seeing Jon come strolling in. Slowly, the roaring faded, the red haze retreated, and his hands gradually relaxed from fists.

As he came aware, he caught the end of Valerie's sentence. "...and this estate is like an architectural marvel because he had so many amazing influences and talented colleagues. Don't you think?"

Brad took a deep breath, but the warm, humid air did

not do anything to help him. Instead, he grabbed his shirt and slipped his feet into his slides. "Got to go take care of some things. See you at work tomorrow."

He almost reached the door when he heard Jon ask, "What happened? He looked furious."

Valerie's voice reached him as he put a hand on the door. "I don't think anything happened. Maybe something at work—"

The door shut on her words. Instead of going to the big house, Brad slipped the shirt on and walked along the path until he reached the end of the garden. He crossed the moat, passed by the gazebo, and kept walking. A dozen yards later, he entered his dad's fruit tree grove and passed by the little cottage where Buddy and Valerie had lived. He stopped beyond the cottage, at the black iron fence that backed up to the woods. There, he gripped the fence with both hands and shook it, pulled it, tried to rip it open, until his arms ached and his fingers hurt. His throat burned with the need to scream out loud and sweat mixed with tears ran down his face.

Finally in control, he pulled the towel from around his waist and used it to wipe his face, then put it around his neck. Slower, exhausted, feeling slightly weak, he walked back to the big house. When he glanced into the pool house, he saw Valerie and his mom sitting at a table with a deck of cards between them and Jon diving off the diving board. Not wanting to talk to anyone, he moved quickly past and went into the house.

Valerie walked into Sami's office and said, "Good morning."

Sami's fingers hit the save button on her computer as she looked up. "Hi there. How has your morning gone?"

"Quiet for a Monday," she said, then gestured at the closed door behind Sami. "Is Brad free?"

"Sure. Go on in."

Valerie tilted her head and looked at her. "Just go on in? You don't need to let him know or anything?"

"Not for you." Her phone started to ring, so she put a hand on it and said, "You, his mom, his dad, his brothers, y'all are on the, 'If I'm not in a meeting, send them in,' list."

She held up a finger and lifted the receiver. "Brad Dixon's office, please hold." After hitting the hold button, she shrugged. "So, go on in. He's available for you."

Leaving Sami engaged in her phone call, she put her hand on the handle of the door and paused just for a moment before walking in. As the door opened, Brad looked up from his computer. His face immediately relaxed into a smile that made her heart skip a beat. "Good morning," he said, standing and walking around the desk. "What a surprise."

"Good morning." He gestured at his sitting area, so she perched on the edge of the couch as he took the chair across from her. "I just wanted to make sure I didn't offend you in some way yesterday. You were relaxed and chatty, and suddenly angry and gone."

He stared at her for several seconds before replying. "Something occurred to me. I had to go sort it out."

She pursed her lips. "Occurred? What could have occurred to you to form such a negative reaction as I talked about architecture and what helped inspire me in my career as it pertains to your home?"

"It had nothing to do with the conversation." He straightened an already perfectly straight arm cuff.

She waited but he did not elaborate. Impatiently she asked, "Something to do with me then?"

Brad closed his eyes and took a long breath. Finally, he said, "You did not do or say anything that upset me. I am sincerely sorry if you got that impression."

She waited a few moments in silence. Finally, she stood. "Okay. Thanks for clearing that up." She stepped backward and lifted a hand in a clumsy wave. "I'll just see you later then."

She turned and took two steps when Brad's voice stopped her. "Valerie, wait." When she turned, she saw him standing by the chair, his hands in his pockets. His face looked strained. "May I ask you a question?"

"Sure."

"I hesitate to even bring this up." He took two long strides toward her. Another step and he'd completely invade her space. It took willpower not to take another step back. "I couldn't help but notice. I've watched your, ah, well, your ease, I guess, with Jon and Ken. Yet you appear to be uncomfortable and nervous around me. Why is that?"

She could think of a dozen different questions she expected from him, but not that. She couldn't possibly tell him that he made her nervous and fluttery and all she wanted in the world was for him to see her as something other than some pseudo-sister. So, she lied. "Uh, hmmm," she stammered, frowning. "I don't know. Maybe because you're the boss, which changes our dynamic. Maybe because our first meeting in years was in this office about business instead of casually in the café like with Jon. Maybe because they both came to me smiling and arms outstretched, and you frowned and barely shook my hand." Lifting her chin, she said, "It could be any one of those things. Why do you ask?"

"Not sure. Curiosity, I guess. Maybe wondering what my brothers have that I don't. Perhaps a desire to get back to the way we once were."

"Brad, the way we were was fifteen years ago. We need to focus on the way we are, not the way we were."

His smile covered his face and lightened his eyes.

"You're absolutely right." He took another step toward her, and she had to lift her head to keep eye contact with him. He suddenly felt a little too close for her comfort. She started to shift her feet but stopped.

"I'd rather you didn't think of me with the boss title. I know it's hard, since it's what I am, but I'd rather be a friend first." He stepped back. "I'll talk to you later."

More than a little confused, she walked to the door of the office and put her hand on the handle. When she looked back at him, he was back at his desk and had the laptop open and appeared engrossed in whatever occupied the screen. Instead of saying anything else, she walked through the door and into Sami's office.

"Hey," Sami said with a smile, "I just confirmed dinner tonight with my friend, Calla. She's a chef. Do you want to join us?"

She really liked Sami and felt like they could become good friends. Despite the internal knee-jerk reaction to say no so she could get home and lock all her doors, she smiled and said, "I'd like that."

"Great! I'll text you the details. Calla knows where all the best spots to eat are. As soon as she gets with me, I'll get with you."

"Thanks." She looked at her watch. "I'm going to head down and grab a sandwich before I go back to work. Can I get you anything?"

"Nah. Thanks, though." She tapped her desk drawer. "I brown-bagged it. Brad's usually nonstop on Mondays, so it's better to be prepared than wishing I'd brought something around three this afternoon."

Valerie lifted her chin toward his office. "Is he good to

work for?"

Sami grinned. "Best boss I've ever had. Seriously. I hope I have this job for the rest of my life."

"That's awesome." As she started to leave, she paused. "Oh. What time tonight?"

"It'll be seven or later. Is that still okay?"

Thinking through her afternoon, she nodded. "Sure. That's better, anyway. Okay, see you later!"

Brad pulled his tie off the second he got into his car. Another long Monday lay behind him. He felt mentally burned out and physically exhausted. The idea of driving home held absolutely no appeal.

Instead, he turned left instead of right and worked through the evening traffic. He stopped right off his exit and bought takeout fried fish and french fries with a big bowl of cold coleslaw and a bag of hush puppies. Back on the road, the smell of the fried batter filling the car, he made three more turns and pulled up in front of the first house at the entrance of a dirt road.

Ken's truck sat backed up to the side of the house. Brad grabbed the bag of food and walked along the red dirt path to the truck. The twangy tones of country music filled the air. He found Ken in the back, pouring dry concrete mix into a wheelbarrow. Floodlights filled the back yard with artificial light and cast long shadows. Dozens of bugs attacked the hot lenses of the lights.

Ken glanced up as Brad's shadow fell across him. Brad held up the bag. "Dinner."

His brother wore a denim baseball cap and a gray T-shirt. He set down the half-empty bag and took the cap off, using his shoulder to wipe the sweat off his forehead. "You here to help, too?"

"Yeah. After we eat. Mind if I change?"

Ken typically built a house, lived in it while he finished the interior work, then put it on the market, moving out of one project and into his next project. This one he bought from a guy who'd run out of money while building it. He'd liked the layout, and since the shell of the house had already been built, and the plumbing and wiring installed, he basically had to finish the interior work. "First bedroom on the left." He wiped his hands together. "I'll eat before I mix this water."

The inside of the house smelled like freshly cut lumber and wet paint. Ken had installed the wood floors, but they lay smooth and bare. Cans of varnish sat stacked near the stone fireplace hearth.

Since he'd been there last, Ken had installed the kitchen counters and cabinets. The appliances still had stickers and plastic on them. He walked along the line of throw rugs Ken had thrown down to protect sanded flooring and entered the first bedroom on the left. Ken's single bed sat on top of a concrete floor. Rolls of padding and carpet lay propped against the wall. In a cardboard box, he found jeans and a T-shirt. On the floor next to the bathroom door, he found Ken's spare work boots.

He changed quickly, then went back outside. Ken had set up the meal on the end of a wire spool the size of a bar table. Two camp chairs sat side-by-side, and obviously cold water bottles sat perched inside the chairs' cup-holders, sweating in the evening air.

"Thanks for the food. Your text was a welcome blessing."

"Wasn't ready to get home." He piled fish and fries on a paper plate, then the two brothers bowed their heads to seek God's blessing on the meal. He bit into a salty fry. "How much more do you have to do here?"

Ken looked around, surveying beyond the lit space. "Need to finish the flooring, paint the back bedrooms, and do some interior trim work. I have offers in for four more lots down the road. I think they'll sell better when there's more than one house here." He used his teeth to rip open a packet of malt vinegar and liberally sprinkled it on a piece of fish. "To answer the original question, maybe two weeks, less if I take a couple days off work."

Brad knew Ken did most of the work himself. Other than certified electrical and mechanical contractors, he could do it all. It gave him a bigger profit margin when it came time to sell the house. "Floors look great."

Ken looked back toward the house. "Yeah. Buddy helped me with them last week. I need to varnish them before they get too scuffed up by my boots."

"I can do that tonight."

"I could use help with getting the structure of this deck set, honestly."

The rumbling of a truck engine interrupted the evening sounds. Brad saw the flash of headlights seconds before the engine shut off, followed by the sound of a door slamming. Seconds later, Jon came around the side of the house. Like the two of them, he wore jeans and a T-shirt and a pair of brown leather work boots. Unlike the two of them, he carried a six-pack of beer from a local brewery.

"House looks good," he said, setting the beer on the makeshift table. He pulled one out and offered it to Ken, who held a hand up and shook his head.

"When have I ever?" Ken asked rhetorically.

"Pretend it's a near beer."

"I. Don't. Want. It."

Brad took it from Jon, twisting the top off and tossing it onto the table.

Jon looked at the house. "I haven't seen it since I left. You were buying it then."

"'Bout done. It was different coming in and starting with an already set frame. Usually, I put it together in my head as I'm building it and know the flooring and trim work. This one, I had to sleep in for a few nights and let it speak to me."

Jon grabbed a camp chair out of the back of Ken's truck and set it up then fixed himself a plate. "I've missed good fish and chips." He doused his fish and french fries with malted vinegar. "I could get fish and I could get fries, but they never tasted like this."

Brad looked at his brother as he took a sip of the cold beer. The sharp hops flavor filled his mouth, the perfect flavor to accent the fish. "I'm jealous of that trip you took. I almost offered to do a twin switch with you."

"Dad would have figured it out by the third day I was in a tie." Jon laughed. He ate for a few minutes before adding, "I didn't want to go, but I'm glad I did. Things became clear to me there."

Ken laughed and tossed his paper plate and empty water bottle into the trash can. "You say that with every mission trip, too. You never want to go but you're always glad you did." Brad watched Jon's face as Ken spoke and noted the thinned mouth and narrowed eyes. By the time Ken looked at him again, his face had relaxed.

Ken walked back over to the bag of concrete mix laying by the wheelbarrow. "I just want to set the posts tonight."

Brad took another sip of beer and finished his last two fries. "You have us both tonight. Might as well get it built."

"Then quit loafing."

Brad chuckled and set his half-finished beer on the table, tossed his trash, and pulled on a pair of work gloves. The three of them had spent their entire lives building together, and worked as a unified team, barely having to speak directions. Instead, they worked in silence, the air filling with the sound of saws, hammers, and the scrape of tools against wood.

As he worked, he thought about what Jon said, about things becoming clear to him in Egypt. Should he just ask outright or let him come to them when he felt ready? Brad was torn. He wanted to talk to Ken about it but didn't want to gossip. What should he do?

A few hours later, they sat on the newly built deck. Brad's shoulders ached from the physical labor, but his spirit felt amazing. "Feels good to work. I was getting slack the last couple of weeks."

Ken smirked. "Not quite pencil-pushing."

"Yeah." Brad stretched and rubbed his face. "Except I'm not sure where a pencil is. It's more like mouse clicking these days."

Jon pushed himself to his feet. "As much as I'd rather hang with you two ladies, I am headed home. I have a long day tomorrow and it's closer to midnight than I'm willing to admit."

Brad stood, too. "I'll follow you." He did a quick visual sweep of the area and made sure he hadn't left any garbage out. "See you tomorrow, bro."

Ken lifted a hand as he unplugged the lights and immediately cast the area into darkness. Brad blinked a few times before he went inside and grabbed his clothes. When he came out of the bedroom, Ken leaned against the back door, pulling his boots off. "'Night," he said, and left through the front door.

Valerie pulled into her driveway at ten minutes past ten. She had not anticipated spending the evening with Sami and Calla, of having so much fun that the time just flew by, of letting the sun set around her and darkness fall over the city on a night she forgot to leave her porch light on.

She distinctly remembered turning it off that morning, knowing she'd come home about six and settle in for the night. When she'd accepted Sami's invitation, the porch light never once crossed her mind.

Now she sat in her car contemplating driving to a hotel instead of walking up the dark drive into the dark house.

She closed her eyes and took a deep breath. Her heart pounded in her chest, and she couldn't think about anything but that stretch of path between her porch and the car with bushes on either side. Between the bushes and the dark, someone could hide so easily. Lie in wait until she had her back to them while she unlocked her door. They could attack from behind and get her into the house, and she'd have no way to escape.

Sweat beaded her forehead. The sound of a whimper escaping her throat startled her. She gathered her purse and clutched it to her chest. With keys in one hand and the other gripping her cell phone so tightly her palms ached, she pushed open her car door and got out. The dark path loomed in front of her.

Suddenly inspired, she ripped the car door open again and reached in, flipping the headlights on. Suddenly, the path lit up. Mouth so dry she thought she would choke, she ran to her front door, lunging forward with the key. It barely found its way home before she turned the lock and ripped the door open. Once inside, she shut the door behind her and leaned against it, panting, sweating, glancing wildly around the room as she fumbled for the light switch.

With the foyer illuminated, she gripped the door handle with her hand. She had to go out there and turn the lights off. She couldn't just leave them on. Her battery would die and then what would she do?

Replace it in the morning light.

No. No. She would go outside like a normal person and turn the lights off. She'd turned the porch light on and all the reasons for her fears would vanish in the glow.

Putting a shaking hand on the doorknob, she closed her eyes, took three deep breaths, then pulled the door open. She started to race to the car but stopped and locked the door, making sure no one could sneak in behind her while she had her back turned. Keys in hand, she raced to the car and pulled the door open. Reaching in, looking all around her, she turned the car lights off and ran back to her door.

Safely back inside, she rested with her back against the

door, staring into the darkened house. She would never, ever leave the lights off again. Wanting to just curl up into a ball in her foyer, she licked her dry lips with her dry tongue and said out loud, "Do the search. Make sure no one is here. Then relax."

Turning lights on as she went into each room, she checked corners, closet locks, behind furniture, inside cupboards, under her bed, inside the bathtub. Once she made her way into the kitchen, she thought she ought to check one more time and did another run through the house.

Finally, she sat in her living room, her back pressed against the corner wall, able to see the kitchen in one direction and the bedroom hall in another. She strained to listen, to hear the sound of another person breathing, of another heart beating. Sweat rolled down her back and her hip ached and protested sitting on the hard floor. Instead of moving, she pulled her legs up, trying to find a more comfortable position.

An hour went by, then two. Her heart finally stopped pounding, and the sweat cooled on her body. She felt foolish, stupid, more than a little insane. With shaking limbs, she pushed herself to her feet, stumbling as her hip didn't immediately respond.

She couldn't possibly shower. Maybe tomorrow morning, when the sun came up and the world came back into light. Maybe then. For now, she kept her keys and cell phone in her hands and went to her bedroom. After checking under the bed one more time and double-checking the lock on the closet door, she crawled onto her bed and collapsed, still fully dressed, and closed her eyes.

Brad pushed away from his desk, restless and edgy. He didn't feel overcome by spring fever like before. He had reconciled those feelings and embraced his job like never before. But he'd arrived at work at six and had worked solidly for five-and-a-half hours. He needed to move his body.

He slipped out the door and saw Sami's empty office chair. He figured she had gotten up for a break, too. Just as he started out her door, he ran into her coming in.

"Hi," she said, startled. He noticed she wore glittery purple eyeshadow and wondered how that didn't affect her vision. "Do you need anything?"

He shook his head. "No. Just going to stretch a bit. I'll be right back."

She set a bottle of water on her desk pad. "Sure thing, boss."

As he wandered to the elevators, he looked out and saw the top floor of the empire his dad built. Here on the executive floor, project managers oversaw multiple projects, and the executives handled the background details. He went to the elevator and hit the button for the sixth floor. In the front of his mind, he headed to his friend Ian's office. In the back of his mind, he hoped he had an opportunity to run into Valerie.

When he stepped off the elevator, he found the noise level elevated on this floor compared to his own. Architects and engineers lined the offices, and assistants, interns, and junior architects and engineers filled the cubicles in the center of the floor. Telephones rang, people talked over cubicle walls, and a meeting was taking place in the glass conference room in the center of the floor. An engineer rushed by him, an arm full of building plans, a cell phone held up to her ear.

He loved the energy on this floor, the creativity and logic that came from the brains who worked here.

Casually strolling along the wall of offices, he glanced around, not really looking for Valerie, but hoping maybe he'd see her. When he got to Ian Jones' office, he felt slightly let down that he hadn't come across her. At his light tap on the door, Ian bid him enter.

He found his friend perched on a stool at his drafting table, one hand on the mouse pad of his laptop, the other holding a pencil. He looked up at the monitors on his wall. Brad followed the direction of his gaze and saw the intricate design of a truss system.

"Yes?" Ian hadn't looked his way.

"Free for lunch?"

At the sound of his voice, Ian's head whipped around. "Hey, Brad. Sorry, was in the middle of two things when you came in."

He slid off the stool and held his hand out. Brad shook it and slipped his hands into his pockets. "No worries. I could have called, but I've been sitting all morning. I wanted to move."

"Understood." He looked at his watch. "Yeah, I can do lunch. I have a one o'clock three blocks down. Let me grab my stuff and we can hit this place I usually go to after church on Sundays. They should have room for us, and it's near where I need to be."

Within minutes, Ian had a bag slung over his shoulder and stood next to Brad in the elevator. Brad used the ride down to send a text to Sami to let her know he'd left early. Ian took the time to send two texts, then looked over at Brad as he slipped his phone into his pocket. "Sorry. It's been a little crazy."

Brad lifted an eyebrow. "My father suggested I might want to look into increasing the staff in your department. Do you need it?"

They exited the building. The bright sun felt warm. Brad slipped on sunglasses. "If we keep the same work burden, then yes. We definitely need help. If this is just a temporary overlap of work and it will slow down, then no."

They walked in silence for a few moments while Brad contemplated it. "I'll let you know. I think the design division is growing fast. I know Valerie Flynn remarked about how little space they had in the office in Savannah. It's almost like we've spent so much time growing and not enough time accommodating growth."

Ian gestured at the doorway to the restaurant. They walked in and the hostess immediately greeted Ian with a smile. "Mr. Jones, so good to see you today. Will your wife be joining you?"

"Just us two today, please, Rebekah. Thanks."

After she seated them at a table by the window overlooking the street, Ian picked up their conversation. "I don't think that you've neglected anything. The problem with growth, especially in this industry, is that you might be looking at a feast or famine type of scenario. You don't want to overload your staff if you're in a feast that will turn into a famine, but you also don't want to overwork those that work for you. I know it's a delicate balancing act, and from what I can see, you do a remarkable job." He didn't pick up the menu. "The rib eye sandwich is the best in town."

"Thanks. I appreciate your encouragement." When they gave their orders to the waitress, he asked, "How is Calla's restaurant coming?"

"We are very hectic right now." Ian laughed. "I should have probably taken the week off of work to help her." He fielded a text on his phone. "She has changed the menu five times, and just finished hiring the last of the staff this morning. I think it's going to be a great success."

Calla had worked for Dixon Contracting for several years before quitting to go to culinary school. "Knowing how hard she works and what a hole she left in her department when she quit Dixon, I believe she'll be a tremendous success."

The waitress returned with drinks. Brad smiled his thanks, then took a small sip of his tea. Ian said, "Calla told me you RSVP'd for two. Anything I should know about?"

Brad took a deep breath and released it slowly. He looked around, then spoke quietly, "I plan on asking Valerie Flynn to be my date."

"Oh really? Do tell."

"Well, there's not much to tell. She's a childhood friend. I did once propose, and she accepted."

"Are you serious?" Ian sat forward.

"Dead serious. I've never held her to it. We were maybe eight years old at the time."

Ian laughed. "Oh, I see. Well, maybe that will give you some leverage." He looked toward the entrance and his smile grew larger. "Speaking of."

Brad turned his head and watched Ian's wife Calla, Sami, and Valerie walking toward them. Ian and Brad both stood. Calla easily went into Ian's arms, giving him a quick hug and a small kiss. "Rebekah told me you were here. I thought you had to work through lunch."

"I should be, but when Mr. Dixon shows up in your office and asks you to lunch, you sort of go."

Brad chuckled. "You could have told me you had work to do."

With a smile, Ian gestured at the hostess. "You say that now." When Rebekah approached, he said, "I think we need a bigger table now."

"Of course. Right this way."

Brad picked up the menu she'd handed him and followed the group. As he pulled out a chair at the new table, across from Ian and next to Valerie, he said, "Sami, if I'd known you were out, I wouldn't have bothered you with a text."

"No worries, Mr. Dixon. Your text came in seconds after Calla asked if I wanted to go to lunch. So, the timing was perfect."

After the table ordered food, Brad looked over at Valerie. Even though she laughed at something Calla said, he noticed a tired look in her eyes. From this angle, he could see the scar that lined her chin and went partially down her neck. His mother had once commented on how another inch and Valerie would never have survived. He internally thanked God for protecting her.

Instead of dwelling on that, he said to Calla, "Ian tells me you've finalized the menu for opening night."

She pushed her black-framed glasses further onto her face. "I have! *Bon Manje* will be a very unique experience."

"*Bon Manje*? I know you and Ian support a mission in Haiti. Does Haiti play a part in the name?"

She emphatically nodded. "Haiti plays a part in it all. *Bon Manje* means good food in Creole. I'm taking some traditional Haitian dishes and 'chefing' them up, introducing these flavor profiles to the foodie world. The interior décor, the menu, the name, it's all a result of my time cooking at the orphanage in Haiti. And, the profits will go there as well."

Ian rubbed her back. "We're very excited. She's bringing one of the regular cooks at the orphanage here to help her with the menu planning. She'll be here through opening week."

Brad knew how much Ian's family did to support the orphanage in Haiti. Dixon Contracting had contributed regularly to hurricane and earthquake relief efforts on his behalf. He appreciated the heart and thoughts behind Calla's restaurant. "We are definitely praying for a great success for you," he affirmed.

Calla nodded. "Thank you."

Valerie finished her last french fry and stood as the rest of the table stood. She looked at her watch. The quick lunch she intended to take before Sami abducted her from the lobby of the building had turned into forty-five minutes. She calculated how much time she had until her meeting with the design team for the Nashville project. She hadn't slept more than two hours last night and felt fatigue tightening the muscles in her neck, forming a headache in her temples. She had to figure out how to get through the rest of the day without crumpling in a heap.

"I have to go with Calla and look at the colors she picked for tablecloths and napkins. Do you want to ride with us?" Sami asked her as they walked away from the table.

"No, I'll walk back. I have a meeting in twenty minutes." She slipped her purse strap over her shoulder.

Brad appeared at her side. "Ian's on his way to a meeting. Want to walk with me back to the office?"

"Sure." They walked outside into the bright sunlight. She waved at Calla and Sami as they headed in a different direction and fell into step beside Brad. "Sorry for the intrusion into your office yesterday. I feel like I stepped out of line."

He let out a sigh before he spoke. "I think it's hard for a

friend to step out of line, truly. And, I really wish you didn't feel like you had to apologize to me all the time. I honestly can't think of anything you've ever done in the lifetime I've known you to merit an apology."

"I'm so—" she cut herself off and laughed. "Fair enough."

She lifted her face to the sun and felt the warmth. So many fears dissipated in the light of day. How could she transfer this feeling to the nighttime? What made the dark so scary? Tyrone had attacked her in the middle of an afternoon.

They stopped at a crosswalk. Brad slipped his hands into his pockets and looked down at her. "I'm glad we were able to walk back alone. I wanted to ask you something."

She had started to look at her phone but slipped it back into her pocket. "What something?"

Of everything she could think he would ask her, what came out of his mouth didn't even come close. "Would you be my date to Calla's restaurant opening?"

She opened her mouth, then closed it again. What did he mean? Her heart rate increased. "A date date? Like a romantic date?"

As soon as she asked, she felt foolish. Of course, he didn't mean a romantic date. He probably just didn't want to go alone. His brothers probably weren't going or something. As she thought that, though, his next words surprised her. "Yes, Valerie. A date date. A romantic date. A man and woman going out together kind of date."

Her eyebrows came together as she considered his request. What would that mean to her life? What would people think about her showing up on Brad Dixon's arm, the boss-man's date? Did it matter? Could it be that the only thing that mattered at this point was how excited the prospect made her? She looked up at him, surprised to see a sour frown on his face. When she smiled, he relaxed, and the frown faded. "I'd love to."

"Really?" She didn't realize the light had changed until someone jostled her into Brad. He put his hands on her shoulders to steady her and looked menacingly at the back of the person who'd run into her.

"Yes. Really. That would be a lot of fun." She gestured toward the crosswalk and stepped away from his hands. "Shall we?"

They walked the rest of the way in silence. When they entered the lobby of the Dixon Contracting building, she looked up at him. "Thanks for lunch. Buying for the table was very kind of you."

"That was my pleasure." They got into the elevator and Valerie selected their appropriate floors. "It was a fun lunch."

"It was." She laughed and put a hand on her stomach. "And filling. I think I'm going to have a hard time staying awake for my afternoon meetings." The elevator doors opened, and she stepped out and turned around. "See you later."

He smiled and lifted his hand in reply as the doors shut. She walked to her office, thinking about what had just transpired. Brad Dixon had asked her out, on a romantic boy-girl date. What in the world?

They weren't teens anymore. Why would he ask *her* out? He was Bradford Dixon, one of three of the most amazing men she'd ever met. He and his brothers were loyal, strong, smart... people like them didn't ask people like her out. She was what? A woman broken, wounded, scared all the time? He must not realize the scope of damage done to her by Tyrone. If he had, he'd never even look at her twice, much less ask her on a date.

Maybe, years and years ago, she would have felt worthy of Brad Dixon. When he asked her to be his date for his senior prom and she'd felt like she could fly, she was so excited. It felt right on his arm, like she fit there. They'd had a great time, and when he took her home, he hesitated before kissing her on her cheek. Oh, how she'd wished he'd forget her role as a sister-figure and realize she was a young woman. She had so wanted the lips that brushed her cheek to move just a couple inches over.

She hadn't seen him again until graduation day. He'd treated her warmly, attentively, and she barely noticed. Thoughts of the freedom that came with the diploma in her hand and a school somewhere away from Atlanta had occupied all her thoughts. He gradually became a memory of her childhood, someone she saw here and there as their paths crossed at occasional family holidays, a peripheral figure grouped with his brothers as a single unit referred to by everyone as The Dixon Boys.

Pushing aside her insecurities, she focused on the fact that he *did* ask her out – a dream come true.

In her office, she tried to quit thinking about a romantic date with Brad Dixon and focus on work. It proved a challenge, though. Every time she tried to focus on her computer screen, she saw his stormy eyes looking down at her.

"Idiot," she muttered to herself. "It's not like he

proposed. He asked you on a date. He'll probably regret it within minutes."

She closed her eyes and shook her head, trying to clear it. Her value lay in her work. She was talented, gifted, and had mad skills. Personal relationships didn't work well for her. She needed to let any flights of fancy go and focus on the one thing she knew she did well.

That downing pep talk worked in the way in which she intended it. Thoughts of Brad Dixon and any kind of date, romantic or not, fled. She could now focus on her task at hand and prep for her meeting without thinking about it again.

But as she closed her computer down and gathered her notes for the meeting, she couldn't help but think about it again.

Valerie held the red beaded necklace up to the sleeveless black turtleneck and moved her head to the left and right. No. It didn't look like casual date night. It still looked like board room ready. She unhooked the shirt from the valet and hung it back up in her closet.

Obviously, she overthought this. If she didn't have a date, a romantic boy-girl date, with Brad Dixon, what would she wear to her friend's restaurant opening? She wanted to come across as chic, casual, and light-hearted. She'd built her wardrobe around professional, woman-take-charge. How did she merge those two worlds?

Digging through her dresser drawer, she found a pair of black faux leather leggings. Inspiration struck, and she went back to the closet, digging into the back and coming out with an off-the-shoulder white shirt she'd never worn because she didn't like the longer length. It would go perfectly with the leggings. Add a pair of ankle-high black boots, and voila! Yes!

She draped the leggings over the valet and hung the shirt above them. Stepping back and looking at the whole ensemble, she nodded. Yes. This worked. She just had to keep herself from over-accessorizing it and taking it above the level of "comfortable relaxed" that she intended.

Now that she'd covered tomorrow's date outfit, she needed to focus on her work outfit. As she approached her closet, the doorbell ringing made her freeze in her tracks. Who would possibly ring her doorbell?

Mouth dry, heart pounding so loudly she could hear it, she moved as quietly as possible, leaving her room and tiptoeing down the hallway. At the edge of the hall, she put her back to the wall and quickly ducked her head around the corner to try to see through the glass in the door. As soon as she saw the crown of a very familiar head, she leaned her head back on the wall, pressed her palms flat against the wall, and closed her eyes. She intentionally took a deep breath through her nose and slowly let it out through her mouth.

Pushing away from the wall, she walked calmly toward the door, ignoring the trickle of sweat that slid down her back.

"Uncle Buddy, hi," she greeted with a smile that she hoped look casual and relaxed. When he smiled, she swung the door open wider.

"Sorry to drop by unannounced. I was inspecting a

house and realized I was only a block away."

"No, I'm glad you're here." She automatically locked the deadbolt when he came inside. "I made chili this morning. Put it in the slow cooker. Would you like some?"

His smile crinkled the corners of his eyes. "That would be wonderful. I'd love some." She led him into the kitchen where she'd already laid out her bowl and spoon. Reaching into the cupboard, she took out another bowl.

"That smells so good."

"I'd planned on just having chili, but I can make you a salad or something."

"Child, no need for all that."

Steam poured out of the cooker when she lifted the lid. She noticed she still had a slight tremor in her hand and really hoped Buddy didn't notice. "I have some cheddar in the fridge."

From behind her, she heard him open the refrigerator door and shut it again. When he came back into her line of sight, he had a bag of shredded cheese and a pitcher. "Is this tea?"

"Raspberry tea. Sweetened with honey." She pulled open a drawer, grabbed a spoon, and slid it shut with her hip. The look of confusion on his face as he stared down at the pitcher made her chuckle. "You might like it."

"I'm willing to find out."

Laughing, she carried the bowls to the table. Buddy set the pitcher and cheese down while she turned back to get glasses. Once she'd filled them with ice, she poured tea and finally sat down. Buddy started to sit, too, when she said, "I forgot napkins."

"I'll get them. Tell me where."

"Paper towel roll is hanging above the sink." While he was gone, she sprinkled cheese liberally over the chili in her bowl, watching as the finely shredded pieces immediately started to melt when they came in contact with the hot liquid. "Hot sauce is in the cupboard to the right of the stove."

Seconds later, Buddy returned. He set the paper towels on the table and set the hot pepper sauce next to his bowl. She waited, not eating yet, knowing he would want to pray for blessing over the meal.

He sat down and immediately bowed his head. "God, thanks for this chance to spend time with my niece. And bless the food. Thank you for letting this old bachelor enjoy a home-cooked meal."

She picked up her spoon when he did. "You are perfectly capable of making homemade meals, you know. You don't have to wait to get one from someone else."

"Oh, I know that. Don't let anyone else find out though." He winked at her as he liberally doused his bowl with hot sauce. "Problem is I work. I work a lot."

She raised an eyebrow. "I don't?"

"Weeeeellll," he drawled out the word, giving it an extra syllable and saying much without saying anything. "You always were more organized with this kind of thing than me. When we got our own place, it was you who did the cooking and shopping. Honestly, I was relieved not to have to worry about it anymore."

Valerie chuckled. "Are you serious? 'Anymore?' Uncle Buddy, you never one single time ever had to worry about it. First, Auntie Rose took pity on you and fed us, and then I did it because it was do it or go hungry while I waited for you to bring junk food or fast food or soul food home." She pointed her spoon at him. "That doesn't change what I said. You are perfectly capable. And I've been gone a long time. You've had plenty of time to adjust."

"Hmph." He made the noise around a mouthful of chili. After a few moments of silent eating, he set his spoon down and sat back in his seat. "I did want to talk to you about something."

Valerie raised an eyebrow. "Oh?"

"Wondered if you'd had a chance to check your calendar for the library dedication at Sweetwater Church. It's just a week away, and you haven't said a thing. Now, this is important to me."

Guilt clawed through her chest. She knew it was important to him. She should go for that reason alone. However, Valerie set her spoon down and crossed her arms on top of the table. "I checked my schedule. I'm afraid I cannot go. However, I can go to the Braves game Thursday after next. How does that sound?"

He slowly shook his head. "What could you have on a Sunday afternoon that would interfere with something I informed you about a couple weeks ago? Are you getting married?"

A slow burn of anger crept up her chest and she pushed the guilt aside. "The truth is, I don't have anything that would interfere. I simply do not want to attend."

He raised both his eyebrows as a startled look covered his face. "Don't want to? How could you not want to go see your own parents get memorialized in such a beautiful way?"

The burn moved up her neck and over her face. Before

she could keep the words inside, they spilled out of her in a bitter gush. "Why would I want to go honor two people who abandoned me at the age of three? Left me in the care of a thirty-five-year-old bachelor so they could go preach Jesus to a bunch of gangbangers. Those very same criminals ended up murdering them in a drive-by shooting, leaving me to make my way in a world with no parents? How is that worthy of my respect?"

She stood, snatching her bowl and spoon and marching them into the kitchen. She tossed them into the sink. The sound of the porcelain bowl crashing into the stainless steel sink did nothing to calm her fury. When she turned, she nearly ran into Buddy. "Calm down, girl," he said, and the words acted like fuel getting tossed on the fire.

"Calm down? Calm down?" Her voice echoed around them. "What do I have to be calm about? You know what? Forget it. You don't care about me or what happened to me. You only care about the perception of me, and I'm unwilling to let that be what defines me."

His eyebrows snapped together in a frown. "Perception of you? You best explain yourself."

"I was happy!" Hot tears streaked down her face, and she angrily wiped at them. "Do you not understand what you did to me? You started to say something about it when I first came back and I just brushed you off and lifted you up, but the fact is, I was happy. I was secure. I was loved. And you ripped me away from that so that you could get me out of my, quote, rich white school. You took me away from everything I knew and all the love I had, then left me at home alone all the time. I'd hear you leave at five-thirty in the morning and come home at ten every night. How was that better for me?"

He opened and closed his mouth several times before he finally said, "It was good for you to get out of the sheltered life and enter the real world."

"Why?" she spewed, "so that I could hook up with the first guy who smiled at me and then end up thrown off a balcony? That was very wise of you."

"That's not on me, girl!" He waved a finger at her. "I didn't make those choices for you."

Crossing her arms over her chest, as if to protect herself from the thought, she said, "So it's my fault?"

"Of course not." He took a deep breath and released it. "But decisions you made took you from A to B to C. You were an adult."

Angry words filled her mouth but she swallowed them. She knew as well as he did that she made her own choices. She didn't choose to get beaten nearly to death, but she did choose to hook up with a married man fifteen years her senior. She didn't choose to get thrown off a building, but she did choose to move in with him even though he had already begun the heavy drinking and the mental abuse. She knew she carried responsibility for her own actions, but she would not sit by and let him voice that blame. It felt like a betrayal from the one person who was supposed to love her.

"I was fifteen when you took me out of a loving home and set me in a house by myself. Auntie Rose—"

"Is not your mama!" Buddy's voice echoed around the room. "She is my best friend's wife, but she is not your mama. Your mama loved you from the second she found out about you."

"Yeah. Love," she said the word like it tasted bad on her

tongue. "Love had her leaving me and going across the country when I was so young that every single memory I have of her is from a photograph." She stretched out her arm and pointed to the side, as if pointing toward the Dixon castle. "Auntie Rose is every bit a mother to me. She did everything for me and loved me like I was her own. You taking me away from that because of skin color?" Putting her hands on the side of her head, she made an uncontrollable noise that sounded like a wounded animal. "Don't spend years raising me to believe skin pigmentation doesn't matter then rip my world apart in the name of 'diversity'. You want to know why I took off to Savannah and never looked back? Because you hurt me. You crushed me. I didn't even know how to say it to you at the time, but there it is."

Buddy stuck his hands into his pockets. "Valerie, you're almost thirty years old. Why are you just now putting this on me?"

Defeated, she looked up at the ceiling and closed her eyes. Absently, she rubbed at her hip. "Because I didn't understand the depth of my hurt until a counselor helped me uncover it last year."

"Well, ain't that just something?" He turned to leave the kitchen, but she could still hear every word. "Some quack headshrinker convinces you that every bad decision in your life is my fault 'cause I did my level darnedest to raise you when that was never the plan for my life. And because a stranger who never even met me says it out loud, you just buy it hook, line, and sinker."

She didn't speak but followed him out the kitchen and met him by the door. "I'll tell you something that won't surprise you," he said. "I ain't buying it. Now, look here. You come to your parents' memorial service. You do it for me and everything I ever sacrificed for you. You already know the time and the place. I expect you to be there." He unlocked the deadbolt and threw the door open. "I won't be asking you again."

She locked the deadbolt and the chain on the door, then stumbled into her living room, falling facedown on the couch. Sorrow washed over her like a wave, and she sobbed into the pillow.

Brad rang Valerie's doorbell then stepped back on the porch. Seconds later, he saw her through the glass in the door. A nervous anxiousness that had tickled the back of his mind all day surged forward and sweat beaded his upper lip. When she opened the door, he felt like all the air got pushed out of his lungs.

She wore tight black leather pants, high-heeled black leather boots, and a white shirt that lay off her shoulders and drifted down to somewhere beyond her hips. She'd pulled her hair to the side and secured it with a black ribbon covered in little white polka-dots. Silver hoop earrings hung from her ears.

"Hi," she said with a smile. "Ready?"

"Uh, yeah. I think so." She smiled. He took another step back and made a bow while gesturing toward his car. "Your chariot."

She used the key to bolt the door. Three steps down the walk, she said, "Wait!" He expected her to run inside and grab something, but instead she checked the door, used the key to unlock it then lock it again, and tested the door one more time.

Witnessing this, he realized he'd have to dissect that later. Right now, he didn't want anything distracting him.

As they walked down her drive, he looked down at her. "You look amazing."

Her eyes skimmed the black shirt that he'd left unbuttoned at the collar and his charcoal gray pants. "You do, too. It's like we coordinated on purpose."

"Must be some kind of telepathic communication." He'd considered wearing jeans, not wanting to overdress, but had changed clothes at the last minute. Now he was really glad he'd changed. He opened the car door for her and waited for her to get settled into the seat before closing it. As he walked around the front of the car, he took a deep, calming breath and let it out just as he got to his side.

He felt steady as he slipped into the car. Backing out of her driveway, he asked, "Have you ever been to a restaurant opening?"

"Uh, no, actually. I don't even know what to expect." He left her neighborhood as she said, "You know, I think the last time we were alone in a car was the night of your senior prom."

The smell of her filled the car. It made him think of sun-ripened strawberries. His mind flashed back twelve years.

She'd worn a bright blue, sleeveless dress with a sequined top and a long, flowing chiffon skirt. A silver clip had secured her hair in a twist on the top of her head, leaving her shoulders bare. He remembered how smooth her skin had looked and how nervous he'd felt all night long.

Refusing to let that same nervousness invade tonight, he just chuckled and glanced at her. "Did you have fun that night?"

"I'll never forget it. It felt so good to be back in the fold like that. I can't tell you what it meant to me. I know you could have asked anyone to prom, and you picked me. It meant the world at the time."

"Valerie," he said, very softly, "I didn't want to ask anyone but you." He glanced in her direction and saw her watching him. "I'd planned to ask you to prom from the moment I knew what a prom was. Maybe I was ten. I don't really remember."

"That long, huh?" Her laughter filled the car. "I think that was about the time you asked me to marry you."

His grin came quick. "So, you do remember. Actually, we were eight."

Putting a hand over her heart, she said with an exaggerated drawl, "How could I forget a marriage proposal from one of the Dixon Brothers?"

Even though he laughed, he couldn't help but think about how she still grouped him with his brothers. "I meant what I said, too, with all the seriousness that an eight-year-old could muster," he said dryly.

"I'm sure." Her laughter filled the car.

"As I recall, you accepted so I guess we've been engaged for twenty years now."

"Where's my ring?"

They chatted about childhood memories and the prom for several minutes, both of them laughing almost continuously. Valerie pressed her palms to her cheeks and leaned back against her seat. "I needed to laugh like that," she said as the conversation died down.

"Me, too." He tried to remember when he'd laughed for so long. In a way, he felt a little sad that they were almost to the restaurant. He would love to freeze this time with her smiling and relaxed.

"Brad, what did you mean by a romantic date?"

He slowed as he approached the parking lot of the restaurant, spotting the entrance for the valet. As he idled and waited in line for their turn at the valet stand, he glanced over at her. "I'm not sure I understand your question."

She toyed with the edge of her shirt, rubbing it against the leather fabric of her pants. She did not look up at him. "I mean, why did you ask me on a date?"

"Because, Valerie Flynn," he said as he pulled up to the door and put the car in park, "I wanted to take you out. I wanted to take *you* out on a date with *me*."

The valet opened her door before he could finish his thought. He slid out of the car and took the offered claim ticket, joining Valerie at her side of the car. He put a hand on her arm and stepped a little closer. "I've always wanted to date you. I've never pretended otherwise."

"You dated other girls, Brad."

Brad's eyebrows shot up. "Like who? No, I didn't. I've never went out with anyone except you."

Valerie had a puzzled searching expression for a few

minutes. "No, I guess you never did. Your brothers...."

"I'm not Jon and I'm not Ken, Valerie."

She had to crane her neck to look at him. He watched as her lips, shining from some gloss she'd applied, opened then closed. Finally, she said, "That was a lifetime ago."

"Yes, it was." He moved his hand to the small of her back and they stepped toward the door. He almost whispered, as if speaking to himself, "There's plenty of life still ahead of us."

The entire front of the restaurant was constructed of a glass wall. Wooden frames gave the glass some depth. Black scrolling words above the door formed the Creole name *Bon Manje*. Inside, they could see the glow of lights and the crowds of people.

Brad pushed open the door and let Valerie precede him inside. They stepped into the lobby where a tall, thin man in a tuxedo greeted them from the host stand. Brad supplied his name and he smiled and nodded and gestured into the main restaurant. "Please, enjoy," he said, then greeted the people coming in behind them.

The din of conversation drowned out almost any other noise. Light bulbs hung from the exposed ceiling on silver chains that matched the ductwork nestled inside dark wooden beams. Floor to ceiling curtains of thin silver ropes helped break the room up in sections. Gleaming dark wooden tables sat on top of a floor tiled with large gray squares. Black framed chairs with wooden seats and backs complemented the tables. Valerie stood and soaked in the atmosphere, loving the upscale casual theme Calla had refused to describe to her.

All around them, people made casual conversation as

they ate. Along a wall, a buffet table practically bowed under the weight of the dishes and platters of food so artistically arranged that Valerie wondered how people dared to break into it to partake.

As Brad and Valerie worked their way through the crowd, he heard his name and looked up and saw Jon across the room. He lifted his hand in acknowledgment and they headed in that direction.

"Insane turnout," Jon said when they got close enough to hear him.

"I know!" Valerie grinned and clapped her hands. "Calla is going to be so pleased. She was convinced no one would show."

Jon gestured toward the buffet. "Incredible food. You can't go wrong with any choice."

A loud tapping of metal against crystal echoed through the room. Brad instinctively turned toward it and saw a microphone set up near the doors to the kitchen. Ian stood at it, clinking a fork against a glass into the microphone.

"Hello friends. Thank you for joining us." After the crowd's murmur of greeting, he gestured toward the door. "Please say hello to my beautiful bride, and the brilliant mind behind *Bon Manje*."

The door behind him opened and Calla walked out. She had on her white chef's jacket, which had two rows of black buttons down the front, and a pair of gray pants. She wore her black hair pulled back into a ponytail, and her black-framed glasses stood out from her face.

"Hi, everyone!" she greeted with a huge smile. The building erupted with applause. People whistled, yelled, and clapped and Calla reacted by putting her hands on her hips and smiling at the crowd. "Wow, thank you," she said. "A few years ago, I spent several months cooking in an orphanage in Haiti. While there, I learned how to make do with what supplies I could get my hands on and how precious every morsel of food is, and became aware of how limited food supplies are to too many people in the world. I also got to experience a whole new palate of spices and flavor combinations. That food is what inspired the food here at *Bon Manje.*

"This restaurant, some of the proceeds from it will go back to that orphanage and to others like it. Hettie? Where are you?" Brad looked in the same direction as Calla and saw a young blonde woman raise her hand. She stood next to a tall black man who had his arm around her. Calla continued, gesturing to the couple. "My cousin-in-law, Hettie, and her husband Emmanuel run the orphanage and I am just so happy and honored that they could be here tonight."

Applause filled the room again and Calla smiled until it died down. "So, let's enjoy the food my staff and I have worked so hard to prepare, enjoy the drinks, enjoy the music, and tomorrow, tell all your friends how amazing *Bon Manje* is."

She stepped away from the mic but did not go back to the kitchen. Instead, she started working her way through the room. Brad looked at Jon. "Rather impressive."

"Ian is so proud of her he could bust. Did you see him watching her?" Jon gestured toward the food. "I'm going to get some more. There's some plantain boat-looking thing that is honestly the best thing I've ever eaten."

Brad looked at Valerie. "Want to battle the crowd for food?"

"Definitely!"

He waited until she stepped in front of him, then walked behind her while they slowly made their way to the food line. As they stood there, people in chef's jackets regularly came out of the kitchen carrying dishes, replenishing the food on the buffet line.

They chatted with each other and with people they knew around them, and slowly moved forward. As they took plates from the stack, Brad listened to the servers stationed behind the table explain the dishes. They sounded like contestants on some televised food challenge with their elaborate descriptions.

Soon, he had his plate piled with roasted chicken, polenta, the plantain dish that Jon had recommended, and some fruit pastries that looked like they should grace the cover of a magazine, and he carried a spiced tea with his other hand. He and Valerie made their way to a table, joining his father and Ken.

"Can we sit here?" Brad asked, gesturing at the empty seats.

"Sure," Phillip said, gesturing at open chairs with a chicken wing.

After setting down his plate, Brad held a chair out for Valerie. Before sitting down, he said, "Do you need anything?"

She touched the bundle of silverware rolled up in a napkin and looked up at him, smiling. "Nope."

He sat down next to her, automatically reaching for her hand and bowing his head. Because of the noise, he prayed silently, then gave her hand a gentle squeeze and looked at her. "I'm starving."

For a moment, she looked uneasy, then she smiled and unrolled her tableware. "Me, too. I've hardly eaten all day in preparation for this."

Ken leaned close so they could hear him. "Great turnout. I know how nervous Ian was before tonight. Can't imagine how Calla felt."

"She felt so nervous that she could barely chop an onion this morning," Calla said, standing at their table.

Brad smiled and stood, holding his hand out to her husband, Ian. They shook hands as Valerie and Calla hugged. "This is amazing," Valerie said, resting her hands on Calla's shoulders. "I can't believe how beautiful this all is."

Calla laughed and slipped an arm around Ian's waist. "That's his fault. He did the design. My input started and ended in the kitchen."

Ian rolled his eyes. "She told me how she wanted everything, not just the kitchen," he said, clearly proud.

Calla gestured toward their table. "Please, eat and enjoy. I'm going to keep working my way through the room." She put a hand on Valerie's shoulder. "I'd love to do breakfast Saturday, if you're free."

"Sure. Give me a call."

After sitting back down, Brad took a small bite of the plantain dish. He closed his eyes and savored the flavors of goat cheese, lamb, and plantain.

"What did I tell you?" Jon said as he slipped into the seat next to him. "I could eat these morning, noon, and night."

Brad looked at the mixture sitting in a black plantain skin that looked like a boat. "Yeah. Wow."

"I know where I'll be eating my next thousand dinners,"

Jon said. He looked at Valerie. "You didn't get the boat."

"Yeah," she said, wrinkling her nose, "I don't much like lamb. Or feta." She speared a carrot with her fork and held it up. "These roasted vegetables, though. My word. To die for."

Phillip smiled his thanks as a waiter cleared his plate. "I'm going to head out. Your mom had a meeting at church tonight that conflicted with this. I told her I'd pick her up on my way home."

Jon stood, too. "I'm out, too. I've eaten three boats. I think if I get another one, they'll make me leave."

"See you soon," Valerie said, waving and smiling.

Ken's eyes caught something across the room. "I need to go talk to someone." He stood and pushed his chair back in. "Don't worry about holding my seat. I have already eaten." He rushed off.

Brad ate half of the food on his plate before Valerie leaned toward him and said, "Calla's got herself a winner on her hands, doesn't she?"

He looked around. Happy people. Smiles, laughter, hugs. Empty plates. "Assuming the management's up to par, then yes. The food is amazing. The colors, ambiance, furniture. She has done everything right so far."

Valerie gestured toward the serving table. "The staff seems to be really on the ball. They act like they've worked together for years instead of a week."

He nodded. "They depend on the success, too."

They ate some more. Just as he took his last bite, he heard the strum of guitar strings. They both looked up at the stage as someone began tapping out a rhythm on drums. Soon, an entire band had taken up instruments and played a very lively, island sounding song. Brad watched as Hettie and Emmanuel moved to empty floor space in front of the band and started dancing rhythmically.

Valerie grinned and started clapping her hands. Remembering prom night twelve years ago and how she never left the dance floor, he gestured with his head. "Do you want to dance?"

The frown that crossed her face confused him until she spoke, then he understood. "I don't know if I can anymore. My hip..." her voice trailed off and she slowly quit clapping.

"Tell you what. Let's try, and if you can't, we'll stop. You used to love to dance." He stood and held out his hand. She hesitated about two seconds longer than he anticipated, then put her hand in his and let him pull her to her feet.

Like always when she first stood, she walked with a slightly more pronounced limp, but by the time they got to the area where couples had started coming together to dance, it had almost entirely disappeared.

He turned and held his arms out and she easily stepped into them, putting one hand in his and the other on his shoulder. He gripped her waist with one hand and smiled down at her as they slowly started moving.

Letting her set the pace, they gradually sped up until they danced in rhythm with the band and the other dancers. He watched her face fill with joy, a look he hadn't seen in over a decade. He grinned and continued dancing.

She lasted maybe twenty minutes before she held up her hand. "I can't or I'll be in a wheelchair tomorrow." Despite her words, her smile lit up her face from the inside.

"Do you need to sit?"

"No. I need to lean, really. Maybe one of those taller chairs by the bar will work."

They worked their way through the crowd. He couldn't help but closely monitor how she moved her feet, seeing the limp clearly now, searching her face for signs of pain. Thankfully, he found her an empty seat at the bar and watched as she arranged her legs so her right leg hung down, stopping a few inches off the floor. She fanned at her face with her hand.

"That was so nice. I needed that so much."

He put a hand on the back of her chair. "Good. Can't help but like dates that use phrases like, 'that was so nice.' It means I'm doing something right."

"What can I get you?" the bartender asked.

Brad immediately said, "Club soda with lime." He looked at Valerie, who pursed her lips.

"The same, but I want lemon and lime." She smiled up at him. "I worked up a thirst."

"Me, too." He watched as Sami approached. She wore a sleeveless white shirt tucked into a purple skirt with big white polka dots on it and a red belt. She'd curled and pinned her purple hair so one giant curl bounced on the front of her head and a red bow secured the bun to the back of her head.

"Nice moves, Mr. Dixon," she said, smiling with shiny red lips. "I approve."

His laughter barked out of him. "I'm sure you do."

She leaned toward Valerie. "Did you see Calla yet? Isn't she awesome?"

"Very much so. Yes, I saw her. When we first started eating." Valerie looked around, gesturing with her hand. "I'm overwhelmed at this."

"Me, too, and I knew what was coming!" She looked up

at Brad and pointed to her hair. "No panicking. It's just temporary for tonight."

With raised eyebrows, he said, "I never said a word." The bartender slid their drinks to him and looked at Sami.

She held a finger up to him, and he nodded but did not speak to her. Seconds later, he slid a tall glass filled with a bubbling amber drink. "You wouldn't. Doesn't mean you're not thinking it." She took a sip from the straw then waved. "See you two later."

Valerie frowned. "I hope she has a ride home."

Brad shook his head. "That was ginger ale. She hasn't had a drink in six years." He drank about half his club soda in three swallows. After setting his drink down, he asked, "How's the hip?"

"Not as bad as I feared." She took a small sip of her drink. "This was fun. Thank you for inviting me."

"Thank you for coming with me." Despite what she said, she absently rubbed her hip. Even though he'd rather not see an end to their evening, he leaned down and asked, "Ready to go?"

"I think so." She gingerly slid off the stool and took a long pull from her glass. He tossed a folded bill into the bartender's tip jar and put a hand on the small of Valerie's back. He let her set the pace as they worked their way through the restaurant, stopping several times to speak to people they knew from work. Across the room, he saw Ken, so he lifted his hand to tell him goodbye, and they stepped out into the cool evening.

As they waited for his car, Valerie lifted her face to the sky and took a deep breath through her nose. "I smell wisteria," she said, eyes closed. "Oh, that makes me think of your mama's garden shed." She opened her eyes again and looked up at him, a soft smile warming her eyes. "Does she still have it, with all that wisteria covering the sides? It looked like a fairy's house."

He laughed and stepped forward as his car pulled up. "She does, though she's tried to tame the vine a few times. It always takes over from her." As he opened the door, she slid inside. He handed the valet a tip and walked around to the driver's side.

The sun had not yet set but lit up the western sky with vivid streaks of bright reds and oranges. Brad headed in the direction of Valerie's house.

They chatted easily on the ride there. The topic went from wisteria-covered garden sheds to antics of summertime in the pool. Valerie laughed, smiled, snorted, and gasped as she remembered their childhood.

Too soon, he pulled into her driveway. He turned the car off before he got out and opened her door. He offered his hand to help her rise out of the car. Keeping her hand in his, he walked her to the front door, then slowly released her and slipped his hands into his pockets.

"Thanks for being my date tonight."

He watched as she checked the door before she used the key to unlock the deadbolt. "It was fun." She let the door swing open and gestured inside. "Want some tea?"

With a small smile, he said, "You talked me into it."

He followed her inside, stepping into the living room. He noticed she set her purse on the table but kept her keys and phone in her hand. He slowly followed her, watching as she tensed, her face becoming drawn. She started to set her keys on the table next to her purse but fisted them in her hand

and raised the fist to her forehead, closing her eyes. "I thought with you here I could...." Again, she trailed off, not completing the sentence.

"Could what?"

Her eyes flew open and he could see the panic in them. "I just need to check something. I'll be right back." She went into the kitchen. He watched her reach up and check the latch on the pantry door lock. She hurried past him. From his vantage point, he watched her check the coat closet, the hall closet, and the spare bedroom door lock. She went into her room and came back out seconds later, much more relaxed and at ease. By the time she made it back to him, she even had a smile on her face. She set her keys and phone down next to her purse.

"Tea!" she said, as if reminding herself. "Any preference?"

Intrigued about her behavior just now and the way she had checked the lock repeatedly when they left, he frowned but said, "Anything's fine. Whatever you're having."

He followed her into the kitchen. By the time she had the kettle heating up, she had started acting normal. No more underlying tension, no more near panicky movements. She assembled cups and tea bags with grace and ease.

"Do you take anything in it?" When she looked at him, he noticed her eyes still skirted with a little bit of panic, maybe discomfort. How he longed to have the right to pull her into his arms and soothe the fear away.

"No. Nothing. Thanks."

They carried their steaming cups into the living room. Valerie gestured at the couch and set her cup on the table in front of it. "Sit, please."

She perched on the edge of the cushion, but he settled back, cradling the hot cup between his hands. How did he approach her behavior tonight? Should he, even? A very large part of him wanted to help her fix it.

As if reading his thoughts, she said, "I just have to check, make sure I'm alone when I come home. I am able to relax once I look."

He looked at the coat closet. "So, you put locks on the outside of the closets?"

"Right. Someone can't very well be hiding in there if I have it locked, right?" She picked up her mug. "I know it's a little compulsive. But my doctor said it's not abnormal, and one day I won't even realize I forgot to do it."

He nodded as he blew on the surface of his tea. "Have you ever forgotten to check?"

"Not so far." She laughed and shrugged. "But I can sleep every night." She took a sip and flinched back from the heat. "Well, most nights. I don't know why you asked me out. I'm broken, Brad. Physically, mentally, emotionally. I don't know what you're looking for but I'm pretty sure I'm not it."

Her directness had never once surprised him. He responded just as directly. "I've had feelings for you since childhood, Valerie. I know you've been through a terrible time, and it's hurt you. Physically, mentally, spiritually. I get that." He set his cup down and leaned forward. "But I'm not in a hurry and I'm willing to go at whatever pace works for you."

She opened her mouth then closed it again. Finally, she said, "But—"

He interrupted her. "But work. Yes, I know. Boss. Employee. Propriety. Like I said, no hurry. And I also asked you to quit thinking of me as your boss. Our relationship goes beyond that. Just like my dad and me. Just like my brothers and me."

"True." She looked down at her tea and finally back up at him. Excitement lit up her eyes. "Fair enough."

He couldn't help but smile. "I'll take fair." Wishing he could stay but knowing he had to go, he slid forward, about to stand. "I am going to go now. I did want to ask if you'll go to church with me Sunday. I know you've not been going to our old home church since you've been back, so I don't know if you're going anywhere else."

She stared at him for several seconds then finally blinked and picked her mug up by the handle. "Brad, I don't go to church anymore."

His eyebrows drew together in a frown. "What do you mean?"

She took another hesitant sip of her tea before responding. "I mean, I don't go to church. I don't believe in God like that anymore. I certainly don't worship any gods."

"So, what? You suddenly think life, the universe, and everything happened by accident?" Brad asked, skeptical.

"No. I'm not stupid, Bradford." She sounded a little bit defensive as she explained. "I do believe that everything was created by a higher power. I just don't believe that creator gives a hoot about you or me, much less loves us."

Brad stared at her. For three or perhaps four long heartbeats, his mind raced as he tried to determine if she was serious, or if this was some kind of terrible joke. When he concluded that she meant it, a painful sadness gripped his heart in a tight fist. Just like that, his world collapsed around him, like a house of cards that just fell in on itself when someone in the room sneezed. She didn't believe in God anymore? How could he continue...?

Well, obviously, he couldn't. That wouldn't work, and the Bible carefully and clearly explained that. The tight ache that stabbed icy cold fingers through his chest felt eerily similar to the one that struck him when he found out she'd moved in with another man, when he heard she wore an engagement ring on her finger. He had lost her. He had lost her for once and for all.

"I see." He set his mug back down and stood. "Well, I'm going to get going. Thanks again for coming with me, Valerie. I really appreciate it."

Without waiting for her to walk him out, he made a beeline for the door, unlocking locks until he could throw the door open and leave.

Brad scrubbed at the stubble on his chin and leaned back in his chair, watching the morning sunlight dance on the surface of Lake Oconee. He shifted the bill of his cap, bringing it lower to help shield more of the glare, and glanced at the tip of his fishing pole.

"You're being awfully quiet," Ken remarked, threading fishing line through his pole. "Big date Thursday night. How'd it go?"

"It went." As the pole dipped down, he snatched it up and tightened the line. Nothing resisted. He slipped it back into the PVC pipe he'd attached to the side of the dock to use as a stand for his pole.

Ken picked a weight out of his tackle box. "That all you

got to say? You've been looking for that second date since prom."

He'd thought fishing would help relax him and quiet his mind. He'd barely slept last night and his eyes burned. "Second Corinthians six."

With the weight tied onto the line, Ken picked an orange spinnerbait for the lure. Brad watched him go through the complex knots to make sure he tied it securely to the end of his line. Once he cast it and it plopped into the water, he looked at Brad. "Afraid I don't have the entire Bible memorized like some people."

Brad sighed and pulled his pole out of the pipe again. "Do not be unequally yoked with non-believers." He reeled in his line and saw one empty hook instead of a baited hook. Maybe he needed to use a shiny lure instead of crawdads. He'd try one more time. Dipping his hand into the bait bucket, he pulled out the small crustacean and rigged the hook through the back of the tail, then stood to cast it into the water.

"Val isn't a non-believer. Or do you know something I don't?"

Before Brad could sit back down, he felt the telltale tug on his line. It vibrated through the pole to his hand as he set the hook and slowly reeled in the line, letting the fish on the end of it try to fight itself off the hook.

Once he had the fish out of the water, he used pliers to get the hook out of its mouth and put it into the cooler with the other two they'd caught that morning. Taking a break, he laid the pole down on the dock next to him and leaned against the dock rail, crossing his arms in front of him. "Valerie is apparently now an unbeliever. Despite our childhood and adolescence, she explained to me Thursday night that she no longer believes in Jehovah God."

"Hmm." Ken settled his pole into a PVC pipe and sat in his chair. "Well, I find that hard to believe."

"If only your difficulty believing me could in any way change the facts." With a heavy sigh, Brad looked at the wooded area around them. Ken had bought this property years ago, but never developed it beyond a boathouse with an indoor restroom and a small kitchenette. Every time Brad spent the day out here fishing, he offered to buy the lot from Ken, imagining how amazing it would feel to come home to this location every night. Of course, then he'd battle the traffic for the hour-long drive back into the city, and the trip nearly always changed his mind.

"Maybe you..." Ken started, but Brad interrupted him.

"Maybe I'm just going to do nothing right now." He pulled his hat over his eyes. "Maybe I'm just going to start figuring out how to finally let her go."

He heard Ken make an unintelligible noise, then heard the nearly silent clicking of the spindle of Ken's fishing pole. He let the warm sun and the gentle breeze on his skin relax him the way nothing else in the world ever had or ever could.

After about twenty minutes of silence, Ken said, "Y'all looked good dancing. Well, she looked good. You looked like day-old chewed gum." When Brad lifted the brim of his cap to glare at his brother, Ken just shrugged and said, "Just sayin'."

If he had any energy at all, he'd kick Ken into the water. Instead, he just pulled the brim of his hat back down and closed his eyes, trying to forget how he had felt while dancing with Valerie Thursday night. How she had felt moving along with him.

Valerie turned the corner and saw Calla and Sami sitting in the shade of the outdoor patio of the restaurant. She waved and went into the restaurant, then followed the directions to get to the patio. Finally, she slid into the metal-framed chair and laughed. "I had a terrible time finding parking."

"So did we. There's a music festival going on downtown today," Calla said, taking a sip of her foam-topped coffee. "If I'd remembered it, I would have suggested somewhere else."

Valerie ordered a coffee and a croissant from the waitress then looked at her friend. "I've learned that wherever you recommend, I will eat. Seriously, girl. How do you find these spots?"

"Food is what I do. It's really just that simple."

"How did you like the opening on Thursday?" Sami asked. "I mean, we had fun, but how did it go for you?" True to her word, she'd shown up for work yesterday morning with jet black hair instead of purple. Valerie understood why she'd changed the color for the workplace, but really enjoyed her friend's sense of fashion.

"We've been fully booked from four until the last reservation, which is at nine-thirty every night. I'm really praying a food critic was there, because we were totally on our game. No hitches anyone could see." She crossed her arms on the tabletop and leaned forward, "But we've been talking about my restaurant for weeks. Let's hear about something really important."

Sami chimed in, "Oh, yes. Let's!"

Calla chimed in again, "So, spill. Let's hear all about Valerie's date with Mr. Dixon."

Valerie gasped and covered her mouth with her hand while Sami laughed. "Y'all, it's not that big of a deal. I've been friends with the Dixon brothers all my life."

"Valerie," Sami said, leaning forward, "I hate to break it to you. But that man did not look at you like he looks at a friend. There's more there than you're saying, or more there than you realize."

Heat flooded her cheeks. "Well, he asked me out and his words were 'he wanted to go on a romantic date.' He did tell me that. But I don't think—"

Calla gasped and grabbed her wrist. "He's not one to just talk, Val. If he said romantic date, he meant romance."

Sami chuckled. "Did he bring you flowers?"

"No. Of course not." She narrowed her eyes. "Do guys even still do that?"

Sami pointed at Calla. "Don't ask her. She's the one who sent a giant bouquet to Ian."

Calla laughed. "Inside joke. I'll tell you the story one day."

Valerie put both hands on the table. "Listen, friends, I appreciate the interest. Especially you, Sami, because you're so close to him. If things ever go forward with Brad and me, I will tell you. But for now, I just consider him my longtime friend." Her coffee and croissant arrived. Strawberries and kiwi fruit formed a decorative flower on the edge of the plate. Picking up her cup, she took a delicate sip before adding, "Even though he once asked me to marry him."

Laughter erupted around the table and Valerie grinned and took a bite of her pastry, remembering her childhood, feeling a giddy excitement at the thought of Brad admitting he'd always wanted to date her!

Brad carried the cooler of fish into the kitchen, setting it next to the sink. His mom stood at the counter, stirring milk into a bowl of cornmeal. "All cleaned," he announced. She grabbed a handful of chopped green onions and tossed them into the batter before she reached over and paused the audiobook playing on her tablet.

"I have hush puppies here. How many fish?"

"Three. Kind of smallish to medium. Want me to freeze any?"

"No. Jon's here. With you three boys and your father, I'll be lucky to sneak a bite in."

"Buddy pulled in right behind us, too."

"Three is perfect then."

He walked over to her and kissed her cheek from behind. "Want me to help?"

She looked over her shoulder and smiled at him. "That would be lovely." The batter mixed, she set it aside and wiped her hands on her apron. "I'll get you some potatoes to peel."

She restarted her book and they listened to it together. Several minutes later, it came to an end. Brad chatted with her about it because he'd already read it. They dissected the crime uncovered in the book.

"It's hard to think of such evil in the world when I'm standing in the sunny kitchen with my son." She grabbed a cutting board out from under the cupboard and selected a knife. "It's never made sense to me."

Brad knew his mother had not had an easy adolescence, and that she did not speak from ignorance. "We both know how evil permeates society. Look at what happened to someone in our own sphere. Look at Valerie."

Rosaline stopped working and turned to fully face Brad. "Why don't you unpack that a little bit more for me, son."

He tossed the last potato into the bowl and set the knife in the sink. "I've always...." He didn't know what to say. This was his mom. How could he verbalize this?

"You've always had feelings for Valerie. Yes, Brad, I know." Brad must have looked astonished. "Bradford. I'm your mother. A mom knows."

Brad closed his eyes and took a deep breath. When he opened his eyes, he said, "When she left, I kind of held onto this childish hope that one day she'd come back. Then she and Tyrone moved in together, and I didn't know how to process that because it didn't make sense. It made no sense based on everything I knew *should* be." He leaned his hip against the counter and crossed his arms. "Then she came back and I thought, 'Okay. Everything's right again.'" Taking a deep breath, he rubbed the back of his neck.

"But it's not all right again, is it?" His mom reached out and put a hand on his arm, gently squeezing. "She's not the same person."

"Neither am I."

"No. But, you didn't suffer violent tragedy. You just grew up, matured, took on a multi-million-dollar company and pined for the girl you lost." When he opened his mouth to protest, she laughed and held up a hand. "I'm not going to argue about whether you pined. You pined. I saw it."

A sheepish smile covered his face. "Okay. Yes. But surely not this whole time."

"Only when you thought about her." She reached into the sink and grabbed his bowl of peeled potatoes. "What happened that has you pining again? Your dad told me you two were together Thursday night."

He took a deep breath through his nose and let it out of his mouth. "Well, apparently, Valerie Flynn has decided that she no longer believes in our God."

Rosaline stopped dicing potatoes and set her knife down. "Oh, Brad."

He shrugged. "I can't." He cleared his throat. "I just have to let it go. Maybe it was never meant to be."

Rosaline stared into his eyes. He could see her understanding and her hurt. "I don't know what to say to you to make you feel better."

"Well, just don't start with, 'You've wasted twenty years waiting for the wrong girl,' because I don't need the affirmation."

"You've wasted nothing." She patted his cheek and turned back to her potatoes. "Of course, I completely expected to be a grandmother by now, so you'd best be getting your head into that game."

Knowing she teased, he laughed and walked over to the refrigerator, pulling out some eggs to boil for the potato salad. "Yeah, okay. I'll get on it."

She paused and turned to him again. "You understand that even with the pining and the waiting, if the woman God had designed for you had come into your life, you'd have known it, right? Don't suddenly get all remorseful about wasted time and opportunity. When she's right, you'll not doubt."

Jon's voice startled Brad. "Says the mother of three terminally single almost thirty-year-old men." He laughed and opened the fridge to pull out a bottle of water. "You'd think one of us would have accidentally gotten married by now. Wild night in Vegas or something."

"Jon," Rosaline scolded, "leave it to you." She took the pan of eggs from Brad. "Go shower, son. You smell like your fish. And on your way upstairs, let your daddy know that dinner is in forty-five minutes. He and Buddy can set the table for me."

"Waste of time. He'll just tell me and Ken to do it," Jon said after draining the water. "Might as well just go ahead and save him the effort." He opened the cupboard and grabbed a stack of plates.

Brad chuckled as he left the kitchen. He could sense something going on with Jon, but he didn't know how to fix it. He thought maybe just their family, together like always, would go a long way. At least, that's what he prayed.

Valerie set out six freezer containers on the kitchen counter and ladled leftover chili into each one. The smell made her think of Uncle Buddy, and she felt a tug of regret for the way their conversation had gone the other night. She should just go to the dedication. He had asked her to, and she knew the level of importance it held for him in his heart.

She loved him. It should be that simple.

Once she had the containers sealed, she used a label maker and printed the date, then stuck the label onto the lid of each container. After she stacked them neatly in her freezer, she worked out the available space and pulled the family-sized package of chicken breasts out of the fridge. After putting some olive oil in a large skillet, she added the chicken and salted and peppered the meat.

She had a bad habit of eating out. Early morning yoga followed by full days of work made the concept of cooking so unappealing. However, she had no desire to continue giving in to laziness and grab a hamburger or bag of tacos on her way home.

Spending a Sunday cooking would stock her freezer full of a variety of meals. She could just grab a container out of the freezer and reheat it. She had chili, vegetable soup, and now she'd freeze chicken and rice together. She'd already prepped a salad that she'd eat from for the week.

It felt good to work and prepare and know she spent her time wisely. When she caught herself humming, she smiled. So many things in her life right now affirmed her decision to move back to Atlanta. Especially after Thursday night.

Did Brad mean what he said? Would he really wait for her to heal?

The damage Tyrone had done to her mentally might take a long time to overcome. Even after five years they overwhelmed her thoughts and actions. She didn't even know how she could see healing in her future.

What did that mean to her? What did it mean for her?

Apparently, he'd carried a flame for her for a long time. He'd waited this long. Would he wait longer? What if she couldn't ever get past what happened to her? What if she stayed truly broken always and forever?

She checked the chicken and put the lid on the boiling rice, turning down the heat. She would find a way to heal. How had she not known he felt the same way for her that she felt for him? All these years and she'd never known.

She wanted to believe that she had it inside her to love someone else again.

She'd spent hours and hours in therapy in Savannah. At first, she went a couple times a week. By the time she moved, she had graduated to just once a week. Since coming here, though, she hadn't sought out a counselor.

Maybe she still needed one, so she'd have someone to talk to, someone she could trust who would let her talk without judgment, who could guide her in healing exercises and teach her better coping skills. She made a mental note to contact her therapist in Savannah and see if she had any recommendations for someone to call here in Atlanta. It felt good to think about the future instead of just surviving the day-by-day.

After seasoning the chicken, she went to her pantry to see if she had enough canned tomato products to make a big pot of marinara sauce. She pulled out cans of crushed tomatoes but checked the freezer again. If she put the chicken in bags instead of bowls, she'd have room to add the marinara.

With her mind wandering through checklists of menus before bounding to therapists and back to Brad and over to Buddy, she stirred the rice and kept working on her upcoming meals.

Valerie checked her watch as the elevator came to a stop. Shifting the roll of plans in her arm so she could adjust the strap of the bag over her shoulder, she nodded hello to a coworker and stepped out onto the top floor. Through the glass wall, she could see most of the team already gathered.

She rushed into the room just seconds before the scheduled start time and slipped into a chair at the end of the table closest to the door. When she settled in, she looked up and caught Brad staring at her. She smiled in greeting, but he didn't smile back. He looked away and spoke to the man at his right. Valerie recognized the man as the developer of the hospital Dixon Brothers had contracted to design and build.

Since she had taken over from another architect upon coming to the Atlanta office, she'd had no interaction with the team about this project specifically, and spent the first part of the meeting making notes, catching up, garnering an understanding of the scope of the work and what tasks she would need to perform. She made a note to arrange a meeting directly with the owner to discuss color needs, design desires, and concepts. That meeting could happen much later than right now, of course. However, she hoped she could come out of this meeting with enough information to start putting together a package for bidders.

She noticed her name on the agenda right about the time Brad asked, "Valerie, do you have anything for Mr. Cooper?"

Looking at Mr. Cooper, she said, "I know there was another architect in my place before today. Did the two of you agree on any specific design needs?"

He spun his chair so he faced her directly. "We agreed that the meeting could come later in the process."

She nodded. "Very good. I want to go ahead and set that up with you. I have a lot of experience in medical facilities and understand the psychology behind the colors needed for the different rooms, etc. If you have an idea of what you want, design-wise, for the interior, I can give you preliminary concepts very quickly."

"I'll get with you before I leave."

Brad met her eyes, nodded, and turned to Jon. "What kind of time line will we need from finalized plans to breaking ground?"

"Six weeks."

“That seems optimistic,” Brad observed.

Jon cleared his throat and sat forward. “Conservative, actually. Once we have the final plans in hand, we’ll need at least two weeks to advertise the bid and prepare to receive bids, and then two more weeks before bid day. From there....”

Valerie listened to Jon speak with half an ear while she made notes in her tablet. As she finished her to-do list, the meeting ended and she stayed in her chair, waiting for the room to clear so she could corner Mr. Cooper and schedule a meeting directly with him.

While she sat there, a reminder of a meeting in fifteen minutes vibrated from her phone. She swiped the screen of her tablet to pull up the details and see what kind of mental shift she needed to make.

“How’s it going?”

She glanced up, expecting to see Brad, but instead found his brother. “Good, just a little overwhelmed. I was handed this project two days ago and didn’t realize the owner would be in this meeting today.”

Jon tapped the top of the specification book. “This isn’t even the right project.” He laughed.

“I know,” she said with a smile. “That’s the next meeting. I need to sit down and seriously organize the projects I have. I don’t want to drop any balls, but I don’t think I could be handed another one.” She gestured with her chin toward the head of the table where Brad and Mr. Cooper spoke with Philip. “What about you? I didn’t realize you were staying in Atlanta.”

He shifted so his hip propped against the table. “I have no desire to stay in Atlanta. I want to get far away and stay there as long as possible. However, until a project comes up, I'm kinda stuck. I teased Brad about trying to get rid of me. I'm afraid I gave the impression I want to stay." He picked up a paperclip from the center of the table and gradually unbent it. "I love my family like nothing else. But, after my trip to Egypt, I very much desire to create my own identity away from them."

"I'm sure there are specifics that pertain to you and not to me. But just know that I understand what you're saying so much more than you probably even realize," Valerie said. With his raised eyebrow, she laughed. "Of course, I'm not a triplet, so maybe I don't completely understand." She stood as Philip left the conference room. "Excuse me," she murmured to Jon, and made her way to the head of the table. "Mr. Cooper, do you have a minute now to schedule a meeting?"

Brad checked the time. "We're on our way to talk to the soil testing company."

He said it without emotion, and without room for any kind of argument. When she looked at his face, she watched his lips tighten and his eyes slightly narrow. Frowning, she wondered at the entirely out of character but clearly hostile attitude. Mr. Cooper kept her from having to ask. "It will only take a sec to check my calendar, Brad," he said, pulling his phone out of a clip on his belt. "Is there a day you have in mind?"

Valerie smiled, her calendar already pulled up on her phone. "I have a staff meeting Monday mornings at nine."

They worked through dates until they found one that gave them a full two hours to work together. She held out her hand and he took it in his firm grip. "Thanks, Mr.

Cooper. I look forward to meeting with you then."

"Likewise," he said with a wink, and turned back to Brad. "Ready to go find out what kind of soil we have to work with?"

When Brad left without even a goodbye, she frowned at the door. What in the world was wrong with him?

Deciding she couldn't worry about his particular mood, she gathered the set of plans and specifications she'd brought into the room with her and carried them over to the conference room next door. Even though the two conference rooms shared a media wall that retracted, she had to exit the room, enter the main floor, and then enter the adjacent room through another door. The other three walls of each room were made of glass and looked out on the cubicle work areas of the floor with hallways on either end of the rooms and the elevator area. Controls in the room would allow the walls to become opaque if needed.

When she entered the second conference room, she saw half the team there. After greeting everyone, she went to the computer and accessed her file for her time of presentation. Syncing her tablet to the presentation, she finally sat back down in her seat, ready and waiting for her turn to present.

Brad shifted his weight and lifted the granite countertop. "There," Ken said, leaning down to look directly at the bubble in the level. "Just hold that."

Instead of replying, Brad grunted. He had a good stance with this angle, so the slab didn't feel too heavy.

"Okay, good," Ken said, sliding the level into his tool

belt.

Brad very gently released his hold on the slab of granite. He ran his palm over the smooth surface. "Nice. Beautiful."

"I agree. Got it for a steal, too. Someone miscut it for another job. So, I just had to custom build the cabinets around it."

Brad stood back and looked at the kitchen. Visually, he couldn't see anything different between the cabinets on this side of the kitchen and the ones on the other side. "How far off scope are you?"

"Three-quarters of an inch. Easy fix."

Brad looked around the room. "What else?"

Ken shrugged. "Post-construction cleaning. We're done. House goes on the market as soon as the landscaper lays sod and the cleaning crew makes it shine."

The front door opened, and Jon walked in. "Hey," he said, "landscaper Billy followed me in from the highway and the sky is quickly turning black. Do you want us to help him?"

"It'll go faster."

Brad followed his brothers outside and lifted a hand in greeting to Billy. He looked up at the dark sky and felt the cool breeze against the heat of the day. In the background, he could hear the forklift removing the pallets of sod from the back of Billy's truck. "We have to hurry if this is going down," he said.

"That's why I headed over," Billy said.

Jon and Ken grabbed a roll of sod and carried it to the edge of the house. Ken picked up the heavy rake and started raking right in front of the roll. As he worked backward, Jon slowly unrolled it. Brad walked over to the pallet and he and

Billy picked up the next roll.

By the time they made it to the edge of the property, the wind had increased a good twenty miles per hour. Debris flew around them and big, heavy raindrops had started to fall. Ken gestured toward the house. "You go on in," he said. "Billy and I got this last one."

Brad followed Jon onto the porch where they watched as Billy efficiently raked the ground as Ken unrolled the sod behind him. Brad rubbed his forearm, noticing the dirt smear in the sweat. "That's harder work than I remember."

"Too busy wearing ties," Jon smirked.

"Yeah." He crossed his arms over his chest. "So, what's going on, brother?"

Jon raised an eyebrow. "What do you mean?"

"I mean, you seem a little on-edge. Almost hostile, but not quite."

Jon pursed his lips and nodded, then looked up at the sky. "Tell you the truth, Brad, inside, I kinda feel like that sky looks."

Brad followed his gaze and saw the dark clouds high in the sky, and lighter colored clouds moving fast with the wind. Trees shook and bent and twisted with the force of the gale. Thunder rumbled a little louder than the last time. As Brad watched, a sudden bolt of lightning lit up the sky, momentarily leaving an imprint on his vision when he blinked.

"Do you have some idea what it is you're seeking?"

Jon walked along the porch, stopping to look in the window. Manufacturer labels and construction dust clung to the glass. Brad couldn't tell if he looked into the living room or if he stared at his own reflection. "Meaning, I think.

Every year, we go to these places where people live in such horrible conditions, in pain, in need...." His voice trailed off and he rubbed the back of his neck. When he looked at Brad, his eyes were as stormy as the sky. "I just don't understand what's going on with the world. How can God be so removed from it?"

Brad opened his mouth to offer encouragement, but Jon held up a hand and stopped him before he could start. "I don't need platitudes, brother. I already know everything you can possibly say to me. It doesn't chill what's going on in my heart and mind. What I saw...." He let out a breath. "I just need to work it out myself."

Brad swallowed and nodded. "How can I help? What can I do?"

Jon shook his head. "Nothing. But, thanks. I mean it." He lifted his chin in Brad's direction. "Now, give. What's going on with you and Valerie?"

"Nothing."

Like a shark, Jon smelled blood in the water. "Aw, come on, now. Saw you finally went on that second date with her after prom. Only took about twenty years. Good for you. I take it you proposed. I hear spring weddings are nice. Now, I give good toasts, so obviously I'll be your best man. Ken would make an adorable ring bearer."

He didn't think he needed to burden Jon with his own inner turmoil. So, he said, "The date was great, but there's nothing going on. I think what I wanted in high school doesn't exist anymore."

Jon stared at him for a long time before he said, "Well, no kidding, Brad. I imagine a lot has changed inside both of you since high school."

"More than I can talk about now." He looked at his watch. "Did you get my email about our mission trip this year?"

"Yes, sir, boss man. When the big boss man personally sends us little peons an email, we read them right away." Jon grinned at his own wit. "Has Ken weighed in?"

Brad had researched possible projects for them to do on their annual birthday trip and found three options. An earthquake in Alaska changed his original plans, though, and he'd sent that information to his brothers with the suggestion of possibly going there.

"Ken would rather go to the panhandle of Florida. So much rebuilding needed after last year's hurricane."

"Yeah. And because Florida's a day's drive but Alaska would require a flight."

Brad nodded. "I know that. You know that. I don't know if he knows that."

With a booming laugh, Jon slapped Brad on the shoulder. "Let's give him a break this year and head down to Florida. We'll even let him drive."

Brad couldn't help but smile. "Fair enough." He looked at his watch. "I need to head home before I get caught too much in this storm." He held his hand out and Jon immediately took it. "See you, brother."

"Yeah. I'm going to hang out with Ken. Probably sleep here tonight."

He blew a sharp whistle toward Ken as he walked to his truck, pulling the keys out of his jeans pocket. Ken looked up and yelled, "Thanks! See you at church!"

Instead of fighting the wind with his voice, he just gave him a thumbs up and fought to get his door open. As he backed out of the yard, he saw Billy run to his truck and Ken dash to the porch seconds before the sky opened up and a hard rain fell, almost blinding him through his windshield.

Valerie rang the doorbell and stepped back, waiting. Within seconds, Philip opened the door. “Well,” he exclaimed, stepping back and opening the door wider, “aren’t you a sight for this old man’s sore eyes?”

“You’re hardly old.” She laughed, stepping into the foyer. “You make it sound like you’re sitting in a rocker with a blanket over your hips waiting for company.”

He laughed. “That will be me eventually, girl, if I’m blessed. You look good. The work must suit you.”

“Suits me right down to my shoes, Uncle Phillip.”

Phillip covered his heart with his hand. “Oh, that does my heart good. What can I do for you?”

She shrugged. “I got out of work with some daylight left.

I was hoping Auntie Rose was home." Actually, she knew she didn't tell the complete truth. She knew Brad had left the office early and hoped she'd catch him here, outside the work environment.

"She's in her room." He gestured toward the door to her parlor. "Go on in. She'll be happy for the company."

Valerie crossed the tiled floor, following the compass arrow telling her to head northwest. She noticed Rosaline had changed the flowers in the large vase that sat on the table in the middle of the room. Gone were the flowers from a few weeks ago, and in their place were some stunning pink orchids. She paused and touched the bloom of one of them, feeling her breath catch in her throat.

"Aren't they amazing this season?" Rosaline said from the doorway of her parlor.

"I have no words. Wow!" She kept walking until she reached Rosaline and stopped to hug her. "When did you get into orchids?"

"Oh, maybe three, four years ago. One of the boys got me one for Christmas and the bug bit me." She followed Valerie into the room. "I've started entering competitions now. It's a whole new world that one." She gestured at the couch. "Can I get you anything?"

"I'll probably get some water in a few minutes." She looked around the room then back at Rosaline. "I just didn't feel like going home on such a pretty day. Maybe I'll walk around outside for a bit."

"I'd love to show you my greenhouse," Rosaline said, immediately coming to her feet and crossing to the sliding door. "Would you like to see it?"

"Definitely." She stepped out of the cool house and into

the humid evening. Bright pink azaleas bloomed along the path. She knew in another few weeks, the heady smell of honeysuckle would fill the hot air. Now, though, she breathed in through her nose and only smelled freshly watered earth and cut grass. "I used to wish I could turn into a fairy and build a little fairy house right about there," she said, pointing to the wide patch of a flowerbed at the foot of a magnolia tree. A hummingbird feeder hung from one of the branches.

"You could always move into your old house," Rosaline said, grinning at her over her shoulder. "For now, it's only ever used when my brother comes into town. I know you'd love it."

Could she come back here? Would she feel safe here? Out of nowhere, she felt her throat start to close in on her and her hands tingled in panic. Would they find out how much damage Tyrone had done to her? Would they start looking at her differently if they understood the level of fear in which she existed every minute of every day?

Oh, but to be just a scream away from men who would protect her against any foe.

"We talked about it recently, remember? I'd rather live where I live than fight the traffic."

"Phillip and the boys worked it out," Rosaline said, stopping at the greenhouse. "It doesn't have to be a stumbling block. The time is well used by them. I know Phillip and Brad use it to listen to Bible studies or their audio Bibles. Jon was telling me the other day about a book he's listening to."

Rosaline opened the greenhouse door. When Valerie stepped in, she immediately felt like she walked into a warm cloud. The smell of rich dirt and sweet flowers filled her nose. On a low table to her right, freshly planted seedling trays sat. She could see the dampness from a recent watering. On her left, a tall table filled with pots and buckets of bushes and flowering plants built a wall, keeping her from even seeing to the other side.

"Oh, Auntie Rose, it's so beautiful in here!" She trailed her fingertip over a small tomato plant. "You must love coming out here."

Rosaline smiled. "I'm very blessed to get to."

They walked along the row, and Rosaline showed her plants, vegetable seedlings, and flowers. Along the back wall, a tiered shelf held pots of orchids. Valerie couldn't believe the array of colors and sizes.

"You did get bitten by a bug, didn't you?" She laughed.

"It's crazy. I think Phillip might make me move in here." She giggled and took a small pair of scissors off the shelf, using them to cut a dead flower from one of the plants. "But, he hasn't yet."

"He probably totally indulges you and buys you more plants."

Rosaline winked. "And takes me to shows. But he's starting not to enjoy that as much. I'm afraid the bug didn't bite him as hard." She paused as she set the scissors down. "Or at all."

They discussed flowers for several more minutes. Finally, they started out of the greenhouse. "This is wonderful," Valerie said, stopping while Rosaline secured the door.

"Thank you. I'm very pleased with it." She gestured at the house. "Stay for dinner. I'm about to make some tortillas to go with the steak I have marinating."

Should she? Her mouth watered at the tempting thought. "Sure. That'd be great."

They went into the kitchen, and Valerie washed her hands while Rosaline went into the back room and returned with a tortilla press. "Remember how to do this?" she asked, plugging it in.

"Of course." She started off a little hesitant and unsure of the kitchen just because so much time had passed since she cooked there. While Rosaline pulled marinating steak out of the refrigerator and carried it outside to place on the grill, Valerie searched for a bowl, then a wooden spoon, and then the masa corn flour. By the time she started mixing the dough, the layout of the kitchen came back to her. When Rosaline returned with an empty platter, she felt completely in her groove, mixing dough, rolling and cooking tortillas.

Rosaline stirred a pot of beans on the stove and measured water and rice. Once she had that cooking, she took a block of cheese out of the refrigerator.

The two women chatted very casually. Valerie told Rosaline about her house and how she thought about keeping it longer than originally intended and her plans for decorating it, about her office and the clean lines and simple colors there. "Brad's office is pretty impressive," she remarked.

"His years of missions work on display," Rosaline said with a smile, washing the meat platter. She left momentarily and came back in with the steak. The tang of the spices on it filled the air. Valerie lifted the lid on the press and felt the tortilla. Maybe ten more seconds on the heat. "He basically handed the interior designer everything and told her to put it together."

The timer on the stove dinged for the rice. She lifted the lid and steam billowed out. Using a wooden spoon, she fluffed the rice and put the lid back on it. "That'll do it. Time to eat." She gestured toward the cupboard with the plates. "We only need three. Jon and Brad are helping Ken finish a house tonight."

Valerie tried not to let her disappointment show as she set the table for the three of them. All her careful, hopeful plotting went out the window.

Phillip joined them, and Valerie bowed her head while he prayed, asking God's blessing on the meal. When the prayer ended and they started filling their plates, she asked, "Is Ken building a house? I thought they were refurbishing an apartment building."

Phillip piled grilled steak on the open tortilla he held in his palm. "Ken is always building a house. It's what he does. He'll build as much as code allows him to build by hand, then sell it for a huge profit. I think the apartment building is next on the list, but I wouldn't be surprised if he's already closing on a land deal to build another house." He looked at Rosaline. "This looks delicious, my love. Thank you."

Valerie felt a little glow in her chest. For as long as she could remember, Phillip said that to Rosaline at mealtime. She wondered what it would be like to have someone adore her that much.

While they ate, they chatted about little things, work things, and flowers. The sky outside darkened until the evening looked like late night. Wind picked up and tree limbs batted against the windows.

"I hope they got that sod laid before this hit," Phillip

muttered, frowning at the window.

"If they didn't, they'll have to finish it tomorrow." Rosaline stood and looked at Valerie. "I have something for you. Then I want you to get home before the storm gets worse. Either that or you should plan on spending the night. I don't like the look of the sky."

"Yes, ma'am." Valerie followed her out of the room, knowing Phillip would clear the table.

Rosaline led her into her sitting room and went to the desk in the corner of the room. She picked up a stack of leather-bound books, tied together with a ribbon. She held them out and Valerie automatically accepted them. "Those were your mama's."

The breath immediately caught in the back of Valerie's throat. "What are they?"

"Her prayer journals." Rosaline reached over and put a hand on Valerie's shoulder. "I want to ask you to read them. For me."

She started to speak but had to clear her throat. She didn't have anything personal from her mother. She had jewelry and pictures, but nothing like this. "Thank you," she whispered. "I will read them."

Rosaline hugged her, a hard, tight squeeze that conveyed support and love. "Good. I saw a flier at church the other day about a group that I think would do you some good. So, I made a copy for you and put it in one of the journals. Now, get yourself home before the sky opens up."

They walked through the foyer to the front door. When Rosaline opened the door, the wind took it out of her hands and it slammed into the frame. "You want to stay?" She asked, raising her voice above the wind.

"No. Best get home before it gets worse." She dashed out of the house and to her car, remotely unlocking it five feet away. She paused to check the back seat as she got in, wiping the water from her eyes and checking one more time as she shut the door.

She battled the wind all the way home. The storm made the usually bad Atlanta traffic even worse. As she turned onto her street, the sky let loose and water poured down, blinding her even with her slow speed and windshield wipers on high.

She turned into her driveway and turned the car off, feeling the wind rocking it. It took a few seconds for her to get up the gumption to actually get out of the car and face the weather. She had a perfectly good umbrella sitting next to her front door. Why did she never remember to leave one in her car?

It took pressing her shoulder against the door to open it against the force of the wind. She'd pulled a little too close to the edge of the driveway, and as she stepped out of the car, her left foot landed in the wet grass. Between the wind and the car door and her own unsteady feet, she suddenly found herself lying on the ground, her left hip having taken most of the brunt of the fall.

Rain poured down on her. She blinked the water out of her eyes and gingerly made her way to her feet. It didn't seem like she'd damaged anything, but she walked very carefully just in case. The bionic hip still worked. Good news. Her leg still responded to mental commands. More good news.

Deciding she must not have done too much damage to it, she locked the front door behind her. Despite the fact water pooled in puddles at her feet, she went through her normal check of the house, leaving a trail of wet footprints behind her. Only when she knew she was alone and safe did she set her keys and phone down and start stripping out of the wet clothes.

Brad stood inside the mudroom off the kitchen and stripped off his shirt, then used it like a towel to swipe the sweat from his face. He plunked down on the bench and pulled off his muddy boots. In the dresser, he found a clean T-shirt with a University of Florida gator on it. Clearly, this belonged to Ken.

He'd hose his boots off tomorrow. In bare feet, he left the mudroom and walked into the kitchen, finding his dad finishing the last of the dishes. "Who was at dinner?" he asked, noticing the three plates in the dishwasher.

"Valerie." Phillip squeezed the water out of the dishcloth and wiped down the counter next to the sink. "We sent her home just as the storm started coming in. Didn't want her driving home in it. She texted your mom a bit ago and let her know she made it home safe."

Brad thought about the power outages and standing water on the road. "Glad she left. I think Jon and Ken are going to stay at that house tonight."

"Good. Do Jon some good to get some downtime with Ken." He shut the dishwasher and hit the button to turn it on. "He's seeking but doesn't know what he's looking for. Wish I knew what took his eyes off the truth in the first place." Phillip turned from the sink, drying his hands on a towel. "What about you? How are you, son?"

His father regularly did checks on his boys. He'd find himself alone with one of them and ask the question, "How are you, son?" It opened the door for them to express anything bad in their lives, anything good, anything fearful.

Brad highly respected his father. He made no bones about life, never made anything better or worse than it already was. But he was a fountain of wisdom, of tenderness, of discipline – whatever was needed at the time. Brad valued his father's opinion and sought it out his entire life.

Brad crossed his arms over his chest and leaned against the counter. "Honestly? More centered than I think I've ever felt. I've embraced my role and shed all the negative that was drowning me." He rubbed the stubble on his cheek with the palm of his hand. "I find myself getting so angry on Valerie's behalf. I did before, when it first happened, but having her here now...." He paused. "Couple weeks ago, we went swimming and I saw the scars on her back. I had to leave. I had to go to the edge of the property and just try to rip the wrought iron fence apart with my hands. Dad? I don't know what I'd do if Tyrone walked through that door right now."

Phillip raised an eyebrow. "You think you'd react violently? What if he's come to know Christ—like we've been praying for? What would you do then? Would you embrace him as your brother, or would you still want to hurt him?"

Brad felt his head flinch back as if Phillip had struck him. "Why would you ask me something like that?"

His father walked to him and put his hands on his

shoulders. "Because, son, that is how Christ says we're supposed to look at the world. We're supposed to see sinners as He did and love them as He did."

"Did you see what he did to her, dad? Weren't you at the hospital the next day? I see glimpses of it and it kills me inside, a little at a time."

Phillip stared at him with dark gray eyes. "I don't know everything he's done to her. That's true. But God knows. And I do know this. If Tyrone were on his knees right this second repenting and asking for forgiveness, he'd get it. We want to call ourselves Christians; we need to be willing to walk like Christ. Even as He hung suspended from a cross, beaten so badly He barely looked human, He asked *Adonai* to forgive those very ones who did that to Him."

Phillip lifted his hands then brought them down on Brad's shoulders hard. "Our lesson is there, son, and you are unsettled because your heart is torn between a very human desire for retribution that comes from the flesh and a soul desire to be like Christ. Let God deal with Tyrone. You let go of it and help Valerie redefine who she is."

He started out of the room but stopped and looked at Brad. "Your mom tells me Valerie claims not to believe anymore. We can pray for her, and witness to her, but I want you to guard your heart."

"Yes, sir." Emotion caught in his throat. He cleared it with a rough sound. "I know."

While she waited for Sami, Valerie rolled up her yoga mat and slipped the strap over her shoulder. As soon as her friend finished speaking to the instructor, she joined Valerie at the door.

"You subbing for her next week?" Valerie asked, referring to the conversation Sami had just had.

"I am. That's a little intimidating, if you want to know the truth." She pushed the door open with her hip. "I've never taught solo before."

"You'll do fine." They stepped out into the humid morning. Black skies made it look much earlier than it was. Valerie's hip objected to the movement of walking and caused a dull ache to throb down her leg. "I can't believe it's about to storm again."

"Especially after last night. Did you lose power?"

"It flickered, but just enough to make me wish I had a roommate. Or a dog." Valerie laughed, even though she hadn't slept all night. The ache in her hip and spine, and the storm that added sounds she couldn't identify, stripped her of any hope for sleep. "I think I'm actually going to take a personal day and go home and rest. The weather is hurting my hip."

She'd parked next to Sami, and they paused at their car doors. Valerie automatically scanned the back seat. "You sure you're okay?" Sami asked, her eyes sliding over Valerie's hip area as if she could see the artificial joint beneath her skin.

Despite the constant dull ache and the exhaustion creeping up the back of her neck, she nodded. "I'll get some rest, try to come in later this afternoon. I've already texted anyone who needs to know."

Sami opened her car door and raised a hand. "See you later. Enjoy the day. Hopefully, the storm will be gone by the time you get off work."

As Valerie drove home, she glanced at the stack of journals on the seat next to her, so very thankful she'd left them in the car instead of bringing them out into the rain last night. A part of her wanted to read them, but a part of her wanted to put them in a closet and close the door. She didn't feel ready to delve into the mind of the woman who gave birth to her. However, she'd promised Auntie Rose she'd read them, and she intended to keep her promise.

Eventually.

The ache in her hip became a shooting pain down her leg

and a burn in her lower back. Despite the warm temperature outside, she turned on the seat heater to high, hoping to soothe the muscles.

After last night's storm, Valerie wouldn't have thought that any more water could possibly fall from the sky. Despite her feelings on the matter, she pulled into her driveway just as the first raindrop splashed onto her windshield. Leaving her yoga mat and the journals in the car, she very carefully walked to the front door. Protected under the overhang of her roof, she unlocked the door just as the clouds above let loose and dropped buckets.

She locked the door behind her and did a quick check of the house. All clear. Ignoring some inner warning about bathing during a thunderstorm, she turned on the faucet of her bathtub to the hottest temperature she could tolerate and poured a cup of mineral salts into the water.

She stripped out of her workout clothes and opened the medicine cabinet. Her hand hovered over the Ibuprofen, but her eyes stared at the prescription pain medication. Did she need to take one? It might help her relax enough to sleep the pain off. She hadn't allowed herself that luxury in a long time. Months.

No. Over-the-counter medication would ease the ache enough so she could relax. She washed a few down with faucet water then waited for the tub to fill.

Finally, she slipped into the steaming hot bathtub, wincing a little at the temperature but knowing it would cool quickly. She eased herself into the water and lay back against her inflatable bath pillow. Taking a deep breath, she closed her eyes and slowly let her breath out, going through some mental pain management exercises her therapist had taught her.

By the time the water cooled, the tightening in her hip had eased. She gingerly got out of the tub and dried off, then walked to her room, noticing that she had a slightly less pronounced limp than when she got home. Her surgical scar itched, as it often did even after all these years, but she knew better than to even touch it. She threw on an oversized T-shirt and a comfortable pair of shorts then grabbed her soft blanket from the foot of her bed.

In no time, she lay curled on her couch, wrapped up in the blanket, a cup of cinnamon tea steaming on the table in front of her, and some cooking show playing at low volume on the television. Instead of watching the chef french some lamb chops, she watched the steam rise from her cup and found her eyelids growing heavier with every passing wisp of steam.

Brad hesitated before raising his hand and knocking on the door. The sun shone down onto the wet pavement, and the humid air hung heavy around him. He stepped back to make sure she could see him clearly, knowing she'd look through the fisheye peephole.

After about thirty seconds with no answer, he rang the doorbell. Through the stained glass on the side of the door, he saw movement. Seconds later, Valerie opened the door.

He could tell from her heavy eyelids and disheveled hair that he'd woken her up. That realization gave him a pang of regret. "Hey," he said gently, "sorry to disturb you. I was worried about you."

She opened the door wider and gestured for him to come in. When he walked into the living room, he saw the pillow and blanket on the couch and the cup of tea on the table. Valerie walked past him and crawled onto the couch, grabbing the blanket and wrapping it around her shoulders. She sat against the corner of the couch with her legs crisscrossed and the blanket covering her legs and waist. She hadn't spoken yet.

He sat on the other end of the couch. Some food program played on the television, but she had the sound so low he could barely hear it. "I texted a few times and, when you didn't answer, I just wanted to check to make sure you were okay."

With a raised eyebrow, she said, "You could have just called instead of sending me a text message. It might have woken me less abruptly than the ringing of my doorbell."

She reached forward and picked up her teacup. He noticed she grimaced when she took a sip. Without asking permission, he stood and took the cold cup from her then went into the kitchen. A box of cinnamon tea sat next to the electric kettle. Making sure it had water in it, he turned it on then opened cupboards until he found the teacups. Dumping the cold contents of her cup into the sink, he made them both a cup of tea, then carried the two steaming cups into the living room, setting hers on the table in front of her.

The cinnamon scent from the steam filled his nostrils. The aroma felt out of place on a warm spring day. It reminded him of fall, cooler temperatures, and football season.

"Thank you," Valerie mumbled, reaching for her cup.

Brad loosened his tie and relaxed against the opposite

arm of the couch. "You feeling better?"

"Yeah." She took a sip of tea and swallowed before she said, "I had dinner at your parents' last night. I left just before the storm hit, but it was already raining when I got home. I slipped getting out of the car and fell on my hip."

Concern made him sit forward. "Are you okay? Can I take you anywhere?"

Waving a dismissive hand in his direction, she shook her head. "I landed in the grass. I don't even think I bruised anything. I just twisted weird trying to protect my fall and hurt my back in the process." She set her cup on the table and pulled her blanket-covered legs up to her chest, wrapping her arms around them. "You have to understand how messed up my muscles are. I'll always have problems and I'll always be in some level of pain."

Intellectually, he knew that. It didn't stop him from wanting to fix it. "What do you do for the pain?"

She shrugged. "I ignore the prescription medication sitting in my medicine cabinet and instead do things like yoga and take baths with Epsom salts." Absently, she rubbed at the scar on her chin. "Most of the time, I pretend it's not there."

As if finally waking up, she reached for her phone. When she looked at the screen, she raised an eyebrow. "Six texts, Brad? Really? Do you treat all of your architects who take a personal day this way?"

"Only the ones I happen to care about," he murmured, then felt his cheeks heat.

"Care about, huh? Is that why you've ignored me for over a week?" She tossed her phone back onto the table and settled against the cushions with her tea. "I feel very cared for. Pampered, even."

Guilt had him bite back. "You know what? I suddenly remember how you tend to wake up in a bad mood. Sorry I bothered you."

He started to stand, but she said, "No, I'm sorry. You're right. The doorbell scared me. Waking up that way put me on edge."

His eyes narrowed. "Scared you? Why would the doorbell scare you?" He thought about how she triple-checked that she'd locked her door, how she checked the house when they got home from the restaurant. "Are you okay?"

He could see that her eyes welled with tears, but she blinked them back. "No, I'm not okay." She pressed her palm between her eyes. "I've not been okay for five years, Brad. I've lived with a form of PTSD that has me terrified whenever I'm alone. Wherever I am, whenever I am. I have worked with therapists and doctors and medication and diet and exercise and I finally just accept that I am afraid. Probably because a two-hundred-pound man threw me off a balcony after years of emotional and physical abuse, and I just wasn't strong enough to stop him."

A muscle ticked in his jaw and he realized he clenched his teeth. He purposefully relaxed his jaw. "So, what did all the doctors and therapists figure out? Is it the knowledge of what could happen, or the knowledge of helplessness about it?"

Unexpectedly, she smiled. "I appreciate the fact that you aren't coddling me right now." She inhaled the aroma of her steaming tea, then said, "The conclusion is a little of both. I know what can happen and I know how helpless I am."

"I see." His mind whirled with solutions and possibilities. "Do you have a counselor here in Atlanta?"

"Not yet. I planned to call my therapist in Savannah and see if she had a recommendation."

With a nod, he said, "Okay. Good." After clearing his throat, he asked, "Will you do something with me?"

She held eye contact while she took a sip of her tea. "What?"

He leaned forward and fiddled with the handle of his teacup but did not pick it up. "Come to a concealed carry class. My mom wanted to take a concealed carry class, and I told her I'd do it with her. It might be something good for you. We're going this Saturday morning at eight."

After several seconds, she finally asked, "You honestly think someone as paranoid as me should carry a gun?"

"I didn't say anything about you carrying a gun. I asked if you'd take the class with my mom."

Valerie pursed her lips and finally nodded. "Okay. I can do that."

Valerie sat next to Brad and Rosaline in the classroom in the back of the gun store and watched the safety video for the concealed carry class, wondering how she ended up here. A gun killed her parents. Law enforcement officers tended to shoot people who carried guns, especially people of her color. Did Brad not understand the taboo nature of such a thing?

Of course, he didn't. He had no reason to.

Even so, she did the worksheets, listened to the lectures,

watched the video, and soon found herself on the shooting range, hearing protection securely on her ears, goggles covering her eyes. She gripped Rosaline's .38 revolver the way Philip and Buddy had taught her and fired at the target of a silhouette of a man. Good shot, center mass. The next three shots grouped closely to the first. The fifth hit slightly to the right. It surprised her how well she did because she hadn't picked up a handgun in fifteen years.

She retrieved her target and kept her hearing protection on while watching Rosaline and Brad shoot. Brad instructed his mom then stood to the side and let her shoot at her target. When Rosaline finished, Brad wasted no time firing his shots.

Soon, she found herself signing the form that would give her the paper to prove she'd taken the class. "Take that to the courthouse, and they'll get it processed for you," the instructor said.

"Thanks," she said with a tight-lipped smile. She followed Brad and Rosaline out of the building. "That was an experience," she said.

"You did well," Brad remarked. "Are you going to submit your application?"

"Probably not."

"Oh, come with me," Rosaline said. "We'll do it together. Then I won't feel so weird."

"Why do you even want a permit?" Valerie asked.

"Because I don't have one." Rosaline winked and pulled the clip out of her hair, running her fingers through the frosted strands. "My women's group has a shooting club. I want to join. I think it would be fun."

That made sense. She smiled. "Okay. I'll go with you."

"Great! Let's go Monday at lunch."

"Sure." She looked over at Brad. "Assuming I can get off work. My boss is kind of a stickler."

"Hey," he grinned, "my boss just spoke. I don't argue with her."

He opened the door of his car for his mother while simultaneously opening the back door for her. She slipped into the seat and looked at the paperwork in her lap. Would she feel safer with a gun? Or would it make everything worse?

"Thanks for bringing me today," she said to him when he got into the driver's seat. He met her eyes in the review mirror and winked at her before starting the car.

"Glad you got something out of it." He backed out of the parking lot. "You're going to the game today with your uncle, right?"

"Yeah. He's picking me up in an hour."

"So, no time to stop for lunch, then."

"No." She looked at her watch. "I figured I'd grab something at the stadium." A stadium hot dog and some popcorn sounded so good right now. When had she last sat in Buddy's seats and enjoyed a hot dog while watching the Braves? Ten years ago? Eleven?

They'd had plans to go to opening night together, but they both had meetings at work and couldn't go. He ended up giving his tickets to someone with whom he worked. She'd promised him nothing would conflict with today's game.

Her mind wandered through growing up in those same seats and all the fun she and Buddy had watching the games together. Like so many other things, they were buried memories that she suddenly allowed to spring forth. How had she not thought about it for years? How did she not realize how much she'd missed it?

Before she realized the time had passed, Brad pulled into her driveway. She pulled her keys and her phone out of her purse and waited for Brad to open her door. As she slid out of the car, Rosaline said, "Monday, right?"

"Yes, ma'am. I'll be ready."

He shut her door and she looked up at him. "Thanks for suggesting this."

With a half-smile, he asked, "Was it as bad as it used to be when we were kids?"

Valerie remembered being afraid of shooting. She always went because she refused to let the Dixon brothers one-up her, but having an orphan's knowledge of what a bullet could do to a human body, she hated it.

Brad caught her crying behind Phillip's truck one time. At first, she denied it, but when he pressed, she finally admitted how much she hated when it was her turn to hold the gun.

She thought back through today. "Maybe sometimes, but others, no. I didn't enjoy the range, but I did learn some things about safety and legalities that I didn't already know. I really enjoyed spending the day with you and your mom. Thanks."

"I'll walk you to your door."

She looked around. "Brad, it's eleven in the morning. I'm sure I can get to my door. But I appreciate the chivalry."

As she walked past him, she squeezed his arm then waved at Rosaline.

Brad sat at the table and stared at his bowl of soup. His mother's voice startled him. "So, what do you think? Do you think she's going to be open to having a firearm in her house?"

Despite the impulse to shrug as a response, he simply met her eyes. "I don't have anything to do with it. I would want one. But I'm a different person than she is with different life experiences."

"You know she was thinking about her parents the entire class today, right?"

"Of course. She associates bullets with the killing of human parents. How could she not?"

"Yet you still took her."

"Yeah." He pushed his bowl away. "She told me about it when dad and Buddy took us all shooting one year. We were probably fourteen. She confessed how much she hated the annual treks out to the field for target practice and how every time the gun went off, she imagined her mother or father getting shot."

His mom stared at him for several seconds before nodding. "Is she in a place to be able to say no if she really doesn't want to do something, or is the passive abused woman just passively complying with your wishes to placate you?"

He took a deep breath through his nose. "Honestly, I don't think I bring out her passive side." He thought about how grumpy she'd been the day he showed up on her doorstep and how she had blown off his attempted chivalry when he dropped her at home. "My opinion? She doesn't want to feel like a victim anymore. She's desperate to just feel normal again. I think she went to the class because the idea intrigued her. Maybe she thought the class would help with that. I invited but I didn't push."

"No, you never push." She picked up her empty soup bowl and stopped by his chair to kiss him on the top of his head. "Thanks for taking me. Goodnight."

"'Night, Mama," he said. As she left the kitchen, Jon came in from the mudroom. "Hey."

"Hey yourself." He sat in the chair his mother had just vacated and grabbed a bowl from the stack next to the slow cooker. "How'd concealed carry go? Valerie didn't mention it."

"They both passed. They're going together to file for permits on Monday."

"Cool." He ladled potato soup into the bowl and grabbed a roll out of the breadbasket then slipped his baseball cap off his head.

"How was the game?"

"Braves won in the bottom of the ninth. Good game."

Brad looked at the mudroom door. "Dad didn't come home with you?"

"Nah. He and Buddy went back to the hospital to visit someone from church. Buddy drove. They were dropping Valerie off on the way." He shoveled three big bites of soup into his mouth before taking a bite of his roll.

"Who's in the hospital?"

Jon shrugged and swallowed. "Didn't recognize the name."

"Well, you haven't been recently. There are a lot of new people." He pulled his phone out of his pocket and shot his dad a quick text. The reply came almost immediately. "Elmer Jansen. Oh, he's the new janitor. Looks like he had a motorcycle accident and broke his leg. Yikes." He replied to the text and stood, lifting his arms over his head and stretching. "Want to do something tonight? Maybe we could get Ken over here for a card game or something."

Jon shook his head. "I'm going to go up to my room and get some work done. I have a couple projects coming up for bid." He shoveled more soup into his mouth and took another bite of roll. "Ken isn't free, anyway. He has a dinner meeting with some charity he's involved in." After washing down some soup with his glass of tea he added, "The house one."

"He must be about to do one of those houses-in-a-weekend things." He texted Ken, letting him know about Mr. Jansen. "'Night, brother."

"'Night."

He knew his dad would have told his mother about the accident, so he didn't bother her. Instead, he went up to his room and turned on his laptop. Jon wasn't the only one who had work that he couldn't ignore any longer.

Valerie stared at her reflection in the mirror, meeting her own eyes. She had zero desire to go to this church service. However, she and Buddy had such a great time yesterday at the game. He'd loved on her in a way that made her feel like no strife had ever existed between the two of them. If going to this service would please him in some way and served to make the man who had given up his youth to raise her feel happy, then she'd do it. Even if she didn't personally understand it and even if she personally thought the entire thing was a waste of time, Buddy deserved her respect.

She could see the determination on her face, but she could also see the frown. Why the frown? Shouldn't making

Buddy happy make her happy, too? It's not like she didn't know the church or the people in it. She'd grown up there just like her mother and Buddy had. Everyone she knew there had always treated her well, with love and kindness.

She supposed the hesitation came from entering a "house of God." She'd told Brad that she didn't believe in God anymore; however, she knew that didn't really encompass what she truly believed. Maybe some part of her believed in some kind of a god. Maybe not. She hadn't examined it for a long time. However, she certainly didn't believe in the God of her uncle, the One for whom her parents had abandoned her. If He existed, a big if, then He certainly didn't deserve any regard from her, did He?

But most of her didn't believe in any kind of supernatural being. Most of her believed in nothing. Nothing protected her in her relationship with Tyrone. Nothing healed her. Nothing helped her feel safe and secure inside the walls of her own home.

Walking into the church did not mean she had to give up her belief in nothing. Walking into the church meant she loved Buddy desperately and wanted to make him happy in a way she had the power to do. No one forced her or manipulated her. She would walk in with eyes wide open and try to keep her words polite.

Pep talk completed, she stepped back from her dressing room mirror and surveyed her outfit. She wore a light blue, sleeveless top with a black lace collar and a black and white striped skirt. Heeled sandals the color of her shirt and a thin black sweater complimented the outfit. She added black and light blue earrings that dangled, and pulled her hair up, letting the ringlet curls fall where they may.

The heels would hurt her hip if she stood too long in them, but she knew most of the time she would sit. Instead of wearing them out to the car, she carried them by their straps, intending to put them on in the parking lot, and wore flat black dress shoes out to the car.

In no time, she found herself driving toward the church. The last time she entered that building, she'd received her graduation gift from the congregation. How many people that she knew still went here?

She found a parking space and took the time to secure her heels, then grabbed her purse and walked toward the building. As she walked up the steps of the sanctuary, she heard someone call her name.

"Is that little Valerie Flynn all grown up?"

Turning her head, a grin spread across her face at the sight of Mabel Cunningham, her fourth grade Sunday school teacher. "Miss Mabel," she said, accepting the hug from the rather stout woman, "I am so happy to see you!"

"Girl, you look amazing. I can't believe how beautiful you are." They walked in together and somehow, Valerie felt very much at home. "Let's find that uncle of yours."

They stopped and talked to half a dozen people Valerie remembered from childhood. The telltale signs of age surprised her in a way. In her memories, this building had stopped in time and everyone remained exactly the same, which clearly did not reflect reality.

When she entered the sanctuary, she noticed they'd replaced the pews with chairs and the carpet beneath her feet was new. Modern electronics graced the sound system and screens adorned either side of the large stage. Mabel led her in that direction, down the aisle of chairs and scattered congregants to the stage, then out a door to the side of it. She found herself in the administration hallway. They passed the pastor's office, and next door, Mabel stopped at the door marked "Pastor's Study." She rapped on the door with three quick knocks of her knuckles then opened it.

Inside, she saw Buddy, Phillip, and a young black man she didn't recognize. When Buddy looked at her, his eyes widened and his grin lit up the room. "Well," he said on a breath, "look at you. Come in. Come in."

She looked at Mabel and thanked her, then went toward Buddy, hugging him then hugging Phillip. "I couldn't stay away today. Thank you for the invitation."

"It's a special day." He took her hand and led her to the younger man. "Danny, this is my niece, Valerie Flynn. Valerie, our pastor, Danny Brown."

The door opened again, and a blonde woman entered the room with a caramel-colored baby against her shoulder. She rhythmically patted its back and it snuggled against her neck. "Fifteen minutes, honey," she said to Danny.

"Great. thanks." He took the baby from her and she adjusted her shirt. "Madison, this is Valerie, Buddy's niece. Her parents are being honored today."

Madison's eyes widened and she turned to Valerie with a smile. "Oh, I wish I'd known you were going to be here. I would have made sure to include you."

Valerie held up a hand. "Please, no. I didn't know I was coming until this morning. I don't need to be included."

"Well, know that you are so very welcome here." She looked at her watch. "I need to get. Praise team is waiting. I'll see y'all later." She rushed out and Buddy put a hand on Valerie's waist.

"Let's get you settled before all the good seats are gone."

She waved at the men remaining in the room and let Buddy guide her back into the sanctuary. There, she saw Rosaline and all the Dixon brothers sitting in the third row, center aisle. He led her that way. "Rosie, look!" he said, grinning. "Val's here!"

Valerie hugged Rosaline and said hello to each of the brothers. It took a second for her to pick who was whom, because they all three wore shirts and ties. But she managed to get it right. "Hi, Ken. I heard you finished a house last week."

His eyes widened, as if surprised that she recognized him in a suit outside of work. "I did. It went on the market Monday morning."

"That's fantastic." She looked at Jon. "Jon, I'm surprised to see you."

He smiled crookedly. "I'd do almost anything for Buddy."

"Oh? What does he have on you? Must be pretty good."

Jon's grin showed some teeth. "I'll never tell. You look amazing, by the way. Beautiful as always."

"This old thing?" She teased, holding the skirt out. She felt a little nervous flutter in her stomach when she turned to Brad. "Hey, Brad. Thanks for inviting me."

He stared at her for a long time before he said, "Welcome home."

It felt natural when he ran a hand down her arm and took her hand long enough to lean forward and brush his lips over her cheek. She found herself closing her eyes and breathing in the smell of his aftershave. When he stepped away, she smiled up at him. "It sure felt like home when I came through the doors. Lots of changes, but so much the same. I even saw Miss Mabel."

Jon's eyes widened. "I loved Miss Mabel."

"Everyone loves Miss Mabel. I was so jealous you two had her." Ken gestured toward another part of the church. "I think she's the regional favorite."

Valerie settled into her chair next to Brad. She looked up as a screen lowered and covered the stage, then a series of photos filled that screen and the ones on either side of the stage. She recognized her parents, Buddy, Rosaline and Phillip Dixon, and the three other members of the team who had gone on that mission trip. Those three had returned. Her parents had not. Newspaper headlines came after the photos and the auditorium grew quiet.

"MISSIONARIES GUNNED DOWN IN DRIVE-BY"

"SUSPECTS IN CUSTODY IN FATAL SHOOTING"

"GANG VIOLENCE DOESN'T STOP FOR GOD"

"LOCAL CHURCH GRIEVES AS MISSION TURNS TO TRAGEDY"

Valerie expected to feel ambivalent about it. It's not like she could remember her mother's voice or her father's laughter. Her entire life consisted of Buddy and the Dixons. However, as the music played and the photos and headlines appeared, a well of grief inside her heart broke open as if it had lain dormant for twenty-seven years just waiting for release.

Brad's arm came around her shoulders as the tears poured from her eyes. She found as much comfort in his touch as she'd hoped, and she leaned into him.

The center screen rose, and, on the stage, she saw the musicians. In the front, holding a mic, she recognized

Madison Brown. Gone was the disheveled nursing mom she'd met twenty minutes earlier. In her place stood a well-groomed, beautiful woman in a trendy outfit, sparkling jewelry, and well-applied makeup. She started singing a slow song to match the somber tone set by the headlines and photos. Out of the shadows of the stage stepped four other singers, but she alone remained in the spotlight.

Valerie found herself pulled into the music. Madison Brown clearly had a gift for singing and entertaining and Valerie caught herself clapping, singing along, and losing herself. They sang songs she didn't recognize but enjoyed, and an old hymn she could have sung from memory.

As the congregation stopped to pray, Valerie did not bow her head but instead watched Danny come through the wings of the stage. He carried the baby, now dressed in a frilly pink dress with a sparkly bow somehow placed on her bald head. Madison scooped the baby out of his arms and gave him a gentle kiss on the lips before walking off the stage and taking a seat in the front row.

He straightened his suit, checked his mic, and picked his Bible up off one of the music stands. By the time the prayer ended, he stood in the center of the stage next to a glass podium.

"Today, we're honoring a team of missionaries who left Atlanta to minister to a very poor neighborhood in our own country. We worry and pray for missionaries in countries hostile to our God, but it never occurs to us that the danger could find us here at home. Twenty-seven years ago this week, while serving in a mobile hospital in Los Angeles, Dr. Cecil Flynn, and his wife and nurse, Alison, were gunned down in a drive-by shooting. Some teenagers affiliated with a gang had come to them seeking medical care. A rival gang chose that time to attack them while their guard was down. Cecil and Alison were inside the trailer with the teens, and they both sustained fatal wounds."

The screens flipped to a muted newsreel video shot live at the time. Behind the commentator, the scene was one of carnage and bloodshed.

"It's hard to reconcile that. Deuteronomy tells us that the greatest commandment is to love the Lord our God with all our hearts, minds, and strength. Jesus affirmed this and added that we are also to love Him with all our souls. From everything I've ever heard about this couple from everyone who loved them, if anyone embodied a love for God more than Cecil and Alison, I've never met them. Their tragic deaths seem so senseless and unfair.

"We ask questions. How do people who love God so much get gunned down in the street? How do they leave a toddler to be raised by a grieving brother? How does that happen?"

He paused and Valerie caught her breath. She'd asked those questions all her life. Was he about to bring her revelation?

"It's so hard for us to come to terms with death and tragedy. In our culture, especially, we treat death like it's some kind of rare thing that almost never happens. Oh, so-and-so died at the young age of ninety-one, or did you hear that so-and-so lost her baby? And everyone who hears the news looks shocked and appalled as if no one is supposed to ever die. You say somebody died? That's unheard of!

"The reality is, a hundred percent of us are going to die. Ten out of ten. Listen. Everyone who is born of woman dies.

Even our Savior died on the cross that day on Golgotha. He died, church. I'm not talking about what happened a few days later. Now, keep up. I am talking about his human body bleeding and dying on the cross. Church, consider that for a moment."

Pastor Brown set his Bible down and looked out into the congregation. In a low voice, he continued.

"When God created the world, He created perfection and harmony. It was Adam's job to tend the garden with the woman—I said the woman, that's right—the woman who had not yet been named Eve. At this point there's no Eve. She actually received that name Eve, which means life, after they had been kicked out of the garden. At this point, they are still in the garden. So, when the serpent tempted *the woman*, the Bible tells us Adam was 'there with her.' You hear that? There with her.

"A lot of people—mostly men, I'll admit it—a lot of folks want to pretend Adam was off somewhere working and doing what he should have been doing. But scripture is clear. Adam was right there next to the woman and he was not protecting her from the serpent. And when the woman gave in to temptation, Adam went into it with her and did not step up to protect her and protect the creation God had charged him to husband and steward. The result was the fall and the destruction of that once perfect world. The fall is our inheritance, and this fallen world now groans under the weight of sin to this very day."

Valerie had heard the story of creation since a very young age. She didn't really know where Pastor Brown was going with this.

"We already know this. God didn't create that sin. God

didn't force us into it. God didn't create that darkness. In the beginning, God said 'Let there be light' and there was light, church. This darkness was not God. This was sin. Sin is filthy. Sin is darkness. But, oh, church, sin is seductive.

"Sin brings about the type of coveting and hate that creates groups of young people who war with other groups of young people. Throw in drugs. Toss in fornication and other vices. Rationalize it all with a secular worldview that makes each one his or her own god. Layer on some poverty, deep poverty that spans generations. The kind of generational poverty that winks at theft and deceit and a little bit of violence here and there 'cause you gotta do what you gotta do to survive when you're that poor. Right? Add racial tension. Add some grandstanding politician claiming to make this better when all they really want to do is alchemy. They just want to turn blood into gold; turn a profit off the misfortune of others. What does all that give you when you mix it all together?"

Pastor Brown bowed his head for a heartbeat then looked up and proclaimed, "You get a hot mix of explosives stored in a room full of sparks. Someone lit a spark that day twenty-seven years ago, and four people died just to end the lives of two with as much fanfare as possible. It leaves us all shaking our heads, sad and confused.

"But that was not God, church. God is not the author of confusion. That was darkness and sin. The Bible tells us that God is light and in Him is no darkness at all. We are the followers of God, and He created this world. We Christ followers, we here in this church today, we are the ones who run counter to this world of sin and darkness. We aren't the norm. We're swimming against that dark tide.

"Satan is a roaming lion seeking whom he can devour, and there are masses and masses whom he has consumed since the very day the woman ate of the fruit and Adam stood there with her just watching it happen.

"We can try to stop the darkness, but Christ Himself tells us that there will always be war and rumors of war. He said, 'in this world you will have trouble. But, take heart, I have overcome the world.'

"We are going to have trouble. It's unavoidable. But it's what we do with it, how we react, how we process it that determines if the darkness is going to suck us in and devour us, or if we're going to continue to be followers of the light."

Valerie found herself wrapped up in every word he said. She held her breath, waiting to see what would come next. Her heart pounded as if she'd run a mile, and she felt sweat on her temples. Around her, people murmured in agreement with the things he said. Occasionally, someone clapped one or two loud claps, or shouted, "Amen!", or "Uh, huh!" It took all her self-control to sit still and not lean forward, trying to get as close to his words as possible.

Danny continued. "The Bible is wrought with strife and death, pain and despair. Humans on this fallen earth are not immune to the darkness. Followers of God, Christians, still suffer, still grieve, still hurt. And we still die in ways that are violent, in ways that seem unfair, in ways that leave the living grieving and wounded and deeply hurt. It is part of the human experience.

"But church, none of it is for naught. Romans tells us that all things work together for good for those who love God and are called according to His purpose. All things. Not just good things. He can take all your experiences and turn them to good if you embrace the love He has for you. If you let Him love you the way only He can."

Valerie's forehead tightened in a frown. She did not seek this answer! Bad things happened and nothing could explain them because some man who supposedly lived thousands of years ago didn't protect his wife from a talking snake? That didn't resonate with her.

Even as she thought the words, she felt an ache in her heart. She clenched her fists, refusing to give in to the well of emotion that surfaced. She told herself that she only reacted to the day, the memories, the pictures, and it had nothing to do with the preacher Danny's words.

He concluded his sermon. "Today, we're dedicating a building to these two who loved God with all their hearts and served Him with everything they had. Their deaths left our church hollow for a long time, orphaned a little girl who was just a few years older than my infant daughter, and launched a bachelor brother into unplanned parenthood.

"Dr. Flynn went on a mission to heal and the very sinners he wanted to help cut him down. But he knew the Great Physician, church. Nurse Flynn went on a mission to comfort and nurture and nurse those who were in pain. She left this world clutching her husband's fingers. But she left this world and went on to glory, church. It is well with their souls. How's your soul doing today? Is it well? Is it hurting? Is it broken? I know a mighty healer who can make you whole. He made the lame to walk again. He made the blind to see. He loosened the tongues of the mute. He cleansed the disease from the lepers. He can heal you. He can make it well with your soul. You just have to let Him."

Music started somewhere behind him. In the shadows,

Valerie could see Madison standing still, microphone in hand, head bowed, no baby in sight. When she started singing, she sang softly. "*When peace like a river, attendeth my way....*"

People around Valerie sang along with her, softly like her, letting her set the tone. Danny spoke above the music, finishing up his sermon, walking up and down the stage as he addressed different sections of the congregation. That lasted about ten minutes longer, as people sang, went forward to pray, and Danny occasionally spoke.

Finally, the service ended. Valerie didn't realize how tense she'd gotten until her neck muscles started to relax. Danny announced lunch in the new building. She picked up her purse, anticipating following the Dixons to where she needed to go. Buddy appeared at her arm. "We have a table set up as a head table at the lunch," he explained.

Inside, she recoiled at the thought. But, outside, she smiled and said, "Great. Lead the way."

Soon she had a plate of potluck sampling and she sat between Madison and Buddy. Danny joined them late, carrying baby Miriam. "Lila said she ate all of the banana you left her in the nursery."

"Good," Madison said, smiling as she took her, "maybe she'll let me eat in peace."

Valerie smiled at the little chubby face with the dark chocolate eyes. "How old is she?"

"Six months tomorrow. Hard to believe."

Miriam reached for Valerie, lurching toward her and almost launching herself out of her mother's arms. Madison laughed and said, "She loves darker skin. I swear if anyone darker than me is around, she won't even look at me. My mother-in-law has spoiled her."

Valerie took her, but didn't quite know how to hold her. She wiggled around and clutched at Valerie's collar. After a few clumsy moments, Valerie felt confident as the baby settled against her shoulder and fingered the lace collar of her shirt. "She's so sweet." She put her nose against the bald little head and breathed in the smell of baby. "How do you get anything done with her around to distract you?"

"Easy. I just don't get it done." Madison laughed. "Actually, that was only true for a couple months. We've got a rhythm now, don't we Miriam?"

Brad approached the table carrying a plastic cup of tea. "You're a natural," he said with an enigmatic smile.

Valerie felt her heart rate speed up as she stared at the light in his gray eyes. "I've never held a baby before."

"See? Natural." He looked at his watch. "Ken and Jon wanted to go fishing today on Lake Oconee. Care to join us?"

Despite her plans otherwise, she was tempted. "I wish I could. Sincerely. But I've not been home much this weekend and I have a full week. I need to go home and work some this afternoon."

He nodded and looked at Buddy. "How are you? That was rather an emotional service."

Buddy cleared his throat and Valerie glanced over at him, surprised to see the shimmer of tears in his eyes. How had she not asked him? He must have been wrecked by that sermon and the music and the pictures! Suddenly, she felt very sorry and very selfish for going into her own head the way she had. "I thought it was beautiful. I know Cecil would have been pleased. Alison would have, too."

Valerie reached for his hand. "I'm glad they would have

been pleased. And I'm especially glad you liked the service." She turned and handed the baby back to Madison, then turned her body to face her uncle. "You are so important to me. I don't think I express it enough."

"I don't doubt it, child." He patted her hand. "You being here was just the icing on the cake. Thank you."

She stood, hoping to walk out with Brad. "I'm going to go." She bent and kissed Buddy's cheek. "Have a good afternoon."

After telling Danny and Madison goodbye, she tossed her paper plate in the garbage, then grabbed her purse and walked out with Brad and his brothers. The ache in her heart continued and she knew she needed to get alone and give in to a good, long cry. Ken and Jon separated from them in the parking lot, but Brad continued to walk next to her until she reached her car.

"You okay?" He asked, his eyes searching her face.

"It was very emotional, as it was meant to be. I found myself caught up in it." She cleared her throat and looked up at him. She fought the temptation to step forward and put her head on his chest. "I'll see you tomorrow."

Chapter 17

B **rad** changed clothes next to the door of Ken's truck. Wearing a pair of swim trunks and a tank top, he enjoyed the feel of the sunshine on his bare skin. He slipped his feet into a pair of work boots, grabbed the tackle box and pole from the bed of the truck, and walked to the dock. Jon and Ken already had bait in the water. Jon sat back in his chair, a baseball cap pulled over his eyes. To the outside world, he looked completely relaxed and almost asleep; however, Brad knew that the second Jon's pole so much as twitched, he would have it in his hand.

"Valerie okay?" Ken asked as he held the bucket with the bait in it out to him.

Brad chose a large minnow and scooped it into his hand,

then secured it on the hook. "She was on the verge of breaking down. But I could tell she wanted to be alone."

"Powerful sermon," Ken said, looking at Jon. Jon shifted his hat and glared at his brother.

"It was a great sermon. I'm sure it filled Buddy with all sorts of comfort. He's a good man. He deserves it." He pulled his hat down over his eyes again and feigned sleep.

Once Brad cast his line into the water, he pulled up a chair and opened a bottle of water. It felt so good to sit outside. "We need to plan a day out here," he said. "Invite some friends. Grill some steaks."

"How about Memorial Day?" Ken asked. "Maybe make it a weekend? We could put together some campsites."

"That's a good idea."

"Mom can help with invites."

Brad looked around. "I wonder if we can get a party tent or something to put up."

"And dad's big grill. The one in the boathouse is too small for a crowd."

"Make sure Val's invited," Jon said, smiling though he did not move his hat. "Brad wouldn't have any fun without her. He'd be all, you know, mopey."

"You're so pretty, Jon," Brad observed. "I don't know how you stand it."

"You've waited your entire life for her to come back, and now that she's here, you're nowhere near her. You're sitting here with us killing bait on a Sunday afternoon." He lifted the brim of his hat again. "Who's the pretty one?"

Brad clenched his teeth instead of replying. He had invited Valerie. She needed to work. Why would he infringe on that? Besides, he reminded himself, he couldn't acknowledge nor give in to any deeper feelings until she found her way back to God. Unevenly yoked was bad. He almost said it out loud to reinforce it.

Instead, he said, "Yeah, I'm fishing with you and when it comes to me and Valerie, there's plenty of fish in the sea. We're different people from who we were fifteen years ago."

"You saying you're not pursuing Valerie anymore?" Jon kept the question casual.

"That about sums it up."

Ken chuckled. "Yeah. Keep telling yourself that. You can't see that awestruck look on your face every single time you look at her."

Brad opened his mouth to make a sharp retort, but Jon cut him off. "Hang on. Hang on a second. Seriously. You're seriously not pursuing Valerie anymore?"

"That's what I said," Brad answered again.

Jon leaned forward a little bit. "So, I take it you don't mind if I give it a shot since you're finally out of the way."

Even though he knew Jon was intentionally provoking him, Brad couldn't dampen the instant feeling of anger that flushed his cheeks and tensed every muscle in his body. Faster than Brad could form a retort, Jon leaped to his feet and had his fishing pole in his hands. Minutes later, he pulled up a medium-sized bass.

"Whoooeee!" Jon whooped. "Look at that. You're right, Brad. Plenty of fish. Plenty of fish."

"Jon." Brad relaxed his shoulders and rotated his head on his neck to release the tension in his neck and jaw. He looked Jon in the eye. "Jon, I'm just going to say this for the record. If you ever actually do mess around with Valerie, I can't see it's going to end well for any of us."

"Oh, yeah," Ken observed. "You are clearly done with Valerie, bro. It's obvious. You have *finally* moved on."

Brad let Ken's comment go as Jon chuckled while he wrestled the hook out of the mouth of the fish. Instead, he fiddled with his own line, pulled it in and recast it, then settled back in his chair, ignoring his brothers.

Sitting at her table with a steaming cup of coffee next to her laptop, Valerie logged into the VPN and then into her workstation at Dixon Contracting. As soon as she had a calendar pulled up, she started logging the week's meetings into her organizer. She had her phone synced with the online system, but she could think better when she looked at it on the screen.

Knowing what meetings the week held for her gave her a better handle on what projects needed her attention in what order. Systematically working through the list, she organized her week, praying that nothing blew up and interfered with her schedule.

When she finished, she contemplated starting work, but her eyes kept going to the stack of journals sitting on the other end of the table. She glanced at the clock on her laptop. It was only four. She could read for a little while then get some work done.

Taking her coffee and the first journal in the stack, she went into her living room and curled onto the couch, resting her back against the arm. She took a sip of coffee, savoring the flavor, then set it on the end table next to her and opened the journal.

A folded piece of paper fell out of the first one. She opened it, finding a flier from the church about which Rosaline had told her. "RECOVERY FROM DOMESTIC ABUSE." She skimmed the flier and read about the support group meeting Thursday nights, a safe place to share and connect with other survivors.

She had sat in on a support group her therapist in Savannah had recommended but didn't enjoy listening to the stories the women told. She had only attended a few times.

Setting the flier aside, she turned the page in the journal and translated the date on the first page. Her mother had written this when she was 17 and still in high school.

> My counselor suggested I try prayer journaling. I feel silly doing it, because it's not like God isn't going to remember my prayers. But, maybe it's not for God. Maybe there's another reason.

Valerie smiled. That sounded like something she'd write. She skimmed a couple pages and found an entry covered in waterdrop stains. Tears? Maybe.

> I'm so tired of being scared all the time. No matter how much I pray, the fear remains. How do I do this? How do I walk into that school and have everyone laugh at me, knowing what happened, knowing what he did to me? Even though the attack happened at school, I'm scared in my own house. Why? Dr. Turner assured me it was normal, but I don't feel normal. I feel

used. Like something someone would throw away. Garbage. No longer with purpose.

What? Valerie went back through the pages she'd read, but she couldn't find another reference. Her heart rate picked up speed and a little sweat beaded at her temples.

It took another two weeks of just random high school girl life before she read anything else significant.

Cecil Flynn got suspended today while defending me. Some of the football players said something to me when I walked past them, and Cecil completely lost it! Jordan Kietch had blood pouring down his face from where Cecil slammed his head into the locker.

His dad was mad when he came to pick him up. I heard him telling him it better not mess up his college applications.

Valerie found herself smiling. *Go, Dad*, she thought, as she turned the page. A couple weeks later, she found the entry she subconsciously sought.

Cecil asked me to prom! He knows what happened to me, but he doesn't care. He told me that anyone who blamed me for the attack wasn't worth listening to. He even told me he'd go with me to court when it came time for me to testify. I don't know if I want him there, though. The DA said they're going to ask for details, and I don't want him to hear them.

Prom! Pulling myself out of the mud last fall, walking home missing my shoe,

I remember thinking how nothing would ever be good again, or normal again. And here I am, off to look for a dress with mama. I know which one I want–the off-the-shoulder shiny green one with ruffles. I can already see Cecil in the tux with a matching bow tie! Sigh!

She reached the end of the first book and realized her coffee had gone cold. With a grin covering her face, she walked into the kitchen and dumped the cold coffee into the sink. As she refilled the cup, she thought about the fact her mother showed signs of the same kind of fear that overwhelmed her on a regular basis. Somehow, she felt less alone now.

New journal in hand, she settled back into her space and eagerly turned the page.

Cecil took me to his church today. Afterward we went to lunch with his family to celebrate his brother Buddy's birthday. At the party, I met Rosaline. I knew her from when I was a sophomore and she was a senior. She's married to Buddy's best friend, Phillip. Cecil really just bloomed around his family. At school, he's so quiet. With me, he's so attentive and caring. But there, he relaxed, had fun, joked with Buddy and Phillip. It was like he was finally able to be himself. Am I holding him back from something? Maybe he needs to be with someone other than me. Maybe I don't let him be himself. Oh, God, how am I supposed to know what's right and what's good?

She read through graduation, a brief breakup that actually caused her to cry even though she knew they got back together, and the beginning of her mom's freshman year at college.

I don't know how I thought I could do this. I'm so afraid to come home at night. My roommate is never there. There are so many sounds in the dorms that I cannot relax and go to sleep. I swear as soon as I fall asleep, I hear someone trying to open the door. What made me think I could do this?

Cecil is across the campus. He walks me home every day, but then he has to go home in the dark. It's the worst place ever. I hate it here. The classes are stupid and don't have anything to do with nursing. Why am I here? God, I know I'm in Your will, but it sure would be nice to be able to sleep. Just putting that out there.

At the end of the journal, she read the last entry.

Cecil wants to get married tomorrow. We'll just go do it and explain to everyone later that we didn't want to wait anymore. He's tired of me being miserable. We can live together, and I can feel safe again. We will go to school together, and I'll get a job as soon as I graduate so he can finish medical school. We've done nothing this week but talk about the details. I'm so excited. Mama is going to be mad, but she'll be happy, too, because she loves him. So do I.

As she read through two journals that chronicled their time in college and her father's time in medical school, the death of Cecil's father, the death of Alison's mother, she had to stop and turn on the lamp next to her. Somehow, the sun had gone down. She grabbed another journal.

We got the due date today. Baby Flynn will come two weeks after graduation. Oh, Lord, please let it wait and not be early! Cecil needs to focus as he approaches finals, and I really want to be at his graduation. We've worked so hard. Doctor Hart said I can work up until the moment I give birth if I want to. I need to, that's for sure.

I know this was a year earlier than planned, but God, thank you for this incredible blessing. I already love this baby so much and I don't even know what it is!

Rosaline has it confirmed. The doctor first told her twins, but she's actually having triplets! She's been so sick, and I've been too overwhelmed with everything to be a good friend. God, please help me release some of my stress and worry so I can help her. She's so scared, and I'm so excited and I feel a little guilty.

It took Valerie a moment to realize that her mother had

written about her! These words were written thirty years ago. Emotion clutched her chest and she felt a slight tremble in her hands as she finished that journal and picked up the last one.

Halfway through the book, she came to the end. No more. She re-read the last entry.

> God, we are really apprehensive about leaving Val with Buddy. I know he loves her. Actually, he adores her. But a week is a long time to be away from her. I wanted to take her, but because we'll be working such long days, Cecil put his foot down. Maybe I should stay home? No, even as I write the words, I can feel your displeasure at that. Okay, God, I'm heeding the call. One week in South Central Los Angeles. Please watch over our baby girl. Let Buddy allow Rosaline to help him. Grow the relationship between Buddy and Valerie so that they're blessings to each other. If for some reason we don't come back, let my community come together and help Buddy and Valerie. We love you so much, God, and we place it all in your hands.
>
> Okay. Done. Time to pack Valerie to go to Buddy's. Maybe this will inspire him to find a wife of his own and have children.

And that was the end of it.

How could that be all? She'd had her mother for an entire afternoon, and now she was gone again. Somehow, she could hear her voice. Somehow, she could smell her lavender lotion—the same lotion Buddy kept for her in her childhood. He would dab a little onto her hands every once in a while so she could remember the way her mom smelled.

She very carefully set the journal on the coffee table, as if setting down a precious breakable item. She grabbed a couch pillow and hugged it to her chest tightly as tears streamed from her eyes. Her parents had been amazing, wonderful people who loved each other, loved their families, and loved her. They loved her. They didn't choose God over her. They didn't want to leave her.

Her entire life, she'd carried resentment for her parents deep inside her heart, resentment that led her far away from everything she'd been taught to believe was good and right. It pushed her into an adulterous affair, a separation of herself from everyone she knew and loved, and eventually into danger.

Somehow, the knowledge of the love her parents had for her, of the hesitation to leave her even to the last minute, softened a hardness in her heart that she didn't even realize was there until it was gone.

Somehow, in the last four hours, immersing herself in the prayers of her mother, she'd let all of it go, and it came out of her in big gasping sobs.

Everything she learned, everything Buddy and Rosaline and Phillip taught her from her earliest memory came rushing forward. Love, joy, peace – those were the things she never could grasp in adulthood. Those were the things that waited for her right here.

She knew the truth. It wasn't a lack of knowledge. It was an intentional separation. Now, as she fell to her knees and sobs ripped themselves out of her as if from the depths of her soul, she clung to the truth, desperately seeking the hand of Christ to reach in and pull her out of the mire she'd built around her.

"Please forgive me," she cried out into the empty room.

This week had dragged on and on. So much so that at 4:58 on Friday afternoon, Valerie decided to call it done. She logged out of the computer system and pulled her laptop out of the docking station. She slipped it into her bag, made sure she had her tablet, and pulled her purse out of her desk drawer. She couldn't remember the last time she'd left work with such enthusiasm.

As she left her office, she turned off the light and let the door click shut behind her.

"Hey, Val," Ian Jones greeted, pausing as he walked down the hall.

"Hi, Ian. How's Calla?"

"So busy. Their reservations have been full since

opening. I can't tell you what a relief it is to see it succeed. She's worked so hard."

"She has. It's exciting to see it happening."

"Will we see you at the lake on Monday?"

She had an immediate impulse to say no. A big party did not constitute a good time to her, but she knew she'd come to the Dixon brothers' Memorial Day party because they were family. Mainly, if she were honest with herself, because Brad would be there.

"I plan to come. Is Calla coming, too? Will you be able to tear her away?" She asked it with a smile, making sure he knew she meant only to tease.

He laughed and shrugged. "She said yes. We'll see." He looked at his watch. "Got to run. My grandmother is expecting me for dinner tonight. Have a good weekend."

On her way to the elevator, four more people stopped her, asking if they'd see her at the lake. It sounded like the entire office planned to attend. The more she thought about it, the more fun it sounded. It might be nice just having some downtime with the people she worked hard with every day.

Instead of going down, she went on up to the executive floor and made her way to Brad's office. As she got closer, her pulse started to increase, and she felt like she needed to catch her breath. She hadn't seen him for any reason for a month. When she first started here, he'd just show up at meetings whether she saw his name on the invites or not. Ever since the dedication at the church, nothing.

Crickets.

Not even crickets. More like a deafening silence.

What would she say if she saw him? Probably just hi. Probably let him lead the conversation. And he'd probably act very cool and dismissive and walk away as soon as he could.

But, today, she wouldn't see him. A part of her hoped he'd come out of his office just in time, but she had an ulterior motive. She pushed the door open and stepped into Sami's office.

She wore a miniature Uncle Sam hat perched on top of bright red curls and a blue jumper covered in white stars. A blue star adhered to the corner of one of her eyes, and silver glitter eyeshadow made her eyes glow. Just as Valerie came in, Sami hung up the phone.

"Perfect timing!" She grinned and clicked two buttons on her computer. The screen shut off as she stood up. "I am so ready for this weekend!"

"Me, too. It's been such a long week." She couldn't help but glance at Brad's door then back at Sami. "Are you going to the party on Monday?"

"Dixon brothers' party? Probably. I originally wasn't because my church has a picnic planned. But Calla wanted to go to the lake, so I'll probably come, too. She's my sidekick at church things."

Valerie paused and looked at her. "Wait. Did I hear you right? You go to church?"

Sami raised an eyebrow and crossed her arms. "Yeeeees?" She dragged it out slowly, made it sound like a question. Then she added, "Why?"

"I just...." Valerie pursed her lips and wondered what else to say. She cleared her throat. "I've been reading my mother's journals for the last couple of weeks."

"Your mother the missionary," Sami clarified superfluously.

Valerie nodded. "I've been wondering what to do with some thoughts and feelings I have."

Sami opened the bottom drawer of her desk and pulled out a blue straw bag. She walked around the desk and stopped in front of Valerie. "I'm happy to talk to you about it, if that's what you want. And if you don't want to talk about it, I'm happy about that, too. Let me know."

"Thanks." Did she want to talk to Sami about it? Would that affect their friendship? "I grew up in church, with the Dixons. But when I left home, it seemed less real to me. Because my parents were killed on a missionary trip, it became easy to make God fake and their decisions selfish. But ever since I read my mom's journals, everything I once believed in so much started to come back to me, and I don't know if it's the influence of my environment or if it's a true conviction from a living God."

"I can see why that would be confusing," Sami nodded, her eyes very serious under their sparkly eyeshadow. "I grew up with no church. My mom was intentionally a single parent. She was a career woman who looked at her biological clock one day and realized she was almost too late to have kids, then went out and got pregnant. I was in a church daycare until I was 5, then a Catholic school until graduation. The only basis for religion I had was from that. It took a group in college to really open the door wide for Christ for me. I believe it wholeheartedly and have no doubts. And I'll tell you something else. I believe God is talking to you through your mom's journals."

Valerie raised an eyebrow. "You say that. You think I'd actually be able to hear a voice?"

Sami's lips pressed together, and Valerie watched her

face, saw thoughts come and go as she considered what to say. Finally, she put a hand on her shoulder and squeezed. "My friend, I believe if you trust your mom's heart and words and listen—and just let Him in, you'll hear his voice. No doubt. I think you'll even be surprised at what you hear." She straightened and gestured toward her door. "Ready to start this long weekend?"

Brad lifted the string of lights with both hands as he climbed the ladder, using his shins against each rung to help balance himself. The temporary wooden structure would have canvas stretched over the roof once they got the lights strung. While he fastened lights to the frame, he heard the sound of a truck idling. He glanced over and saw the crew unload the large portable restroom facility complete with working sinks and flushing toilets. Ken hooked up the water tank while Jon helped unload another truck full of tables and chairs. He strung lights as far as he could reach, then gingerly stepped down the ladder, shifted it over several feet, and climbed again. From his vantage point, he saw his mom go to the back of his father's truck and pull out a plastic bin of tablecloths. She carried it into the fishing shack and came back out again for another box.

Growing up, his parents regularly threw Memorial Day parties. His mom liked it because that last Monday in May the summer heat typically warmed the air compared to the Fourth of July heat that beat down like a heaven full of hot hammers. But, for the last seven or eight years, they just hadn't. His dad would mention it about a month out, and his mom would put it off. Or she'd mention it and they just wouldn't start working on it. He was glad Ken had initiated the idea this year.

As he climbed down the ladder, he checked his watch. Nearly four, and he wanted to get back home and take care of some emails before the weekend officially started. He plugged in the lights and shielded his eyes with his hands as he looked up into the bright sky and confirmed all the strings of lights lit up, then unplugged them and walked over to his dad's car. Two more plastic containers remained. He stacked them together and carried them both into the shack. His mom had set up a temporary staging room to prepare the tables.

"Where to?" he asked.

She set a bin next to a worktable and said, "Those are plates and cups. Set them back over there by the sink."

After he set them down, he said, "I'm going to go get some work done at the house. Call my cell if you need me to bring anything back with me."

"Thanks, hon, but there's still plenty of time to figure out what's missing. I'll take care of it tomorrow before I come out here to make centerpieces."

He bent to kiss her cheek. "You realize that people would have been pleased with hot dogs wrapped in tin foil?"

She laughed but shook her head. "Not how I do things. You know that. People are expecting Rosaline Dixon, even though you boys are technically the ones throwing the party."

"Well, we appreciate you making us so look so good, even if it's just to keep you from looking bad." He said it with a smile, and she laughed, clearly knowing he teased her.

"See you at home."

The drive home took twice as long as it should have. Most of the time, he left the lake during the evening on a weekend. Now it was five o'clock on a Friday, on a holiday weekend. Atlanta served as the hub for several interstate highways, and travelers inevitably had to go through Atlanta to get almost anywhere else on the east coast. If he'd thought about it, he would have spent another hour or two at the lake then started home. He would have gotten there at about the same time without the extra hour or so on the road.

He let himself into the quiet house and went straight for the kitchen. In the fridge, he found leftover meatloaf, and he used that to make himself a sandwich. Armed with a plate holding his sandwich, potato chips, and a pickle spear, he went upstairs to his room. He felt energized, even happy, after working with his family on something they all loved to do. He wanted to pour some of that good energy into his work.

Just as he booted up his laptop, the sounds of the doorbell filled the house. From his room, he looked down and saw Valerie's car in the driveway. His pulse raced as he rushed downstairs, crossed the foyer, and threw open the door, finding her walking back down the steps.

"Hey," he said as she turned. "Sorry. I was upstairs. Big house."

The startled look left her face and she smiled. "Hi. Sorry to bother you."

"No reason for sorry. No reason to even ring the doorbell, for that matter." He held the door wider. "Come on in."

As she walked by him, she left in her wake the smell of her light strawberry scent. He closed his eyes and gently inhaled, letting the aroma fill and tease his senses. He shut the door behind her and followed her into the foyer. "Mom and dad are with the guys at the lake."

At the table in the center of the room, she paused. "Oh. Okay. I'd hoped to talk to your mom."

"I know I'm not as pretty as she is, but I'm here if you need an ear."

With a raised eyebrow, she quickly said, "I've seen so little of you that I almost forget you're here."

He knew his removal from her life probably confused her a little bit, but it kept him sane. The more time he spent in her presence, the harder he found it to deny his attraction for her. "As you know, it's been a super busy time at work," he said, using a very poor excuse. "I get pulled in a lot of different directions in the spring and summer. I barely find a free minute in any given day." He gestured toward the back of the room. "Come outside. We'll sit in the gazebo."

"Are you going to rescue me?" she asked, leading the way. It made him think about the times she'd played a helpless princess in the tower, trapped in the gazebo as one of the brothers battled the other two with plastic swords to rescue her.

"I wonder if we could talk Ken and Jon into playing again," he said. "Though I think you've probably proven that you can get yourself out of the tower."

She looked over her shoulder at him, her lips in a thin line. "Sure, by being thrown out of it." His face fell, and clearly she saw it because she immediately said, "I'm sorry. That wasn't nice."

Clearing his throat, he brushed by her and led the way into the dining room and through to the kitchen. At the back door, he stopped and waited for her to catch up before opening the door and stepping aside to let her by. "You need to quit apologizing to me."

"I'm so—" She stopped and lowered her eyes, then turned and walked straight to the gazebo with her shoulders back. He followed more leisurely. When he got to the gazebo, he found her standing with her back against the railing, her arms folded in front of her almost in a defensive manner.

"Is that what you learned to do? To constantly apologize?"

"I beg your pardon?"

"When Tyrone was using you to prove to himself that he was a man, did you constantly apologize?"

"Actually, it's classic behavior for—"

Feeling angry at himself and enraged at Tyrone, he held up a hand to cut her off. "Forget it. That was rude. Please forgive me. Sincerely."

He watched the hesitation on her face before she relaxed and nodded. "I accept your apology and will try to refrain from saying 'I'm sorry' from now on." She sat on the bench and looked up at him. "How are you? I've missed seeing you regularly since our 'date date, like a romantic date' night."

Intentionally forcing himself to relax, he sat next to her and turned his body in her direction. "I've been great. How are you since the dedication at the church? It seemed to have an emotional effect on you."

She took a deep breath through her nose. "You know, I've been so angry for so long that I just didn't know how to let it go. Your mom gave me my mom's journals to read and they really opened my eyes to a lot of things. Now I find that I'm seeking God, wanting to rediscover a love that I had once but not sure how to go about doing it."

The flood of joy in his heart overwhelmed him. He reached for her hand and watched her start to recoil at the sudden movement, then intentionally place her hand in his. "I think once you acknowledge to God that you're seeking, He'll find a way to let you hear Him." Her fingers felt cool in his hand and he covered them with his other hand, wanting to give her some warmth. "How can I help you?"

Unexpectedly, her eyes filled with tears. "I was hoping Auntie Rose could help me. I remember her always being ready with words of wisdom when we needed it, and my mom's journals were filled with her and her insights."

Brad looked at his watch and at the sky. "I could call her, ask her to come home."

"No. It's okay." She pulled her hand out of his and pushed her fingers against her eyes as if to try to stem a coming flood. "It's waited this long." Releasing a long breath, she stretched her legs in front of her and crossed them at the ankles. "It's been a long couple of weeks."

In the silence that followed, Brad searched for the right thing to say or do. He came up with, "Do you want to go for a swim?"

"Not particularly." Leaning her head back against the railing, she closed her eyes. "Remember that big hammock that all four of us tried to get into and ended up wrapped up in and your mom had to cut us out?"

They'd been about six. He remembered his mom didn't get mad because they got stuck. She got mad because she'd specifically told them they couldn't get into the hammock. He chuckled. "So many memories, so many punishments."

"We were a bit of a handful. I can't imagine how she did it."

His answer came out without even thinking about it. "With love. She loved us. Still does."

"Love conquers all," she murmured.

Love conquers all. Maybe it would conquer her heart and lead her back to God. "And God is love," he remarked, quoting first John.

Valerie straightened her spine and she suddenly had to confirm her suspicion. "Brad, is the reason you left my house the night of the restaurant opening because I told you I don't believe in God anymore?"

Her directness surprised him, and he answered honestly. "Yes. I don't have the freedom to pursue a relationship with a woman who doesn't have the same heart for God that I do. The Bible warns against it, and common sense tells me it would weaken my faith rather than increase hers."

She opened her eyes and stared at him, her eyes serious, hard, searching. "My seeking has nothing to do with you. Nothing at all."

He raised an eyebrow. "I didn't assume it did. I'm sure it has everything to do with being back home and getting thrown back into the mix of faithful people. You can't hide anymore."

"You think I've been hiding?"

Standing, he paced across the gazebo and looked up, spying the very edge of the box they had put up there almost fifteen years ago. He only noticed it because he knew it was there. "I think you were hurt and took it out on everyone. Acting out of that pain put you in a situation that ended up physically harmful, and that fed your hurt. The fact, though, is that you're safe here, Valerie. You're physically safe, you're emotionally safe, and you're spiritually safe. No one is going to hurt you here."

She sat quietly for several moments, then said, "I never imagined I'd be hurt anywhere. I was wrong, though, wasn't I? I became a victim. I turned into a victim. Do you know what that does to someone?"

"I only know what I've seen in you." He crossed to her again and sat back down. "I don't think you know how much it affects me to see the changes in you that are a result of your relationship with Tyrone. It makes me want to go let him feel my wrath. Kind of less than charitable, but there it is. I've talked to my dad about it and he's given me some good solid wisdom that I need to be willing to listen to."

"If I remember my Bible correctly, I don't think wrath is left out of it." She chuckled and sat up. "I very, very much want to uncover my way back to God. Can you help me?"

Brad cleared his throat as emotion tried to close it off. He held a hand out, palm up, and said, "Will you pray with me?"

Valerie sat next to Brad and listened to Danny Brown as he talked about Jesus feeding the multitudes. "We say He fed 5,000 like that's this massive number and should be amazing to us. But, church, we refer to it wrong and have forever. Jesus didn't only feed 5,000 that day. Read the words again. He fed 5,000 men plus women and children." He paused for several breaths, then said, "We're talking ten, fifteen thousand, church. Think about it. He did it without effort. He did it in front of tens of thousands of hungry people. What can He do for you? What part of you needs to be fed? Don't fool yourself into thinking He can't because He did. And He will. He will because He loves you and He wants you fed."

She let his words sink in through the rest of the service and through the lunch with the Dixons that followed. Buddy sat next to her at a table next to the pool and listened to her work through what she felt like inside after listening to the sermon.

"Tyrone broke me," she admitted. "I'm afraid a lot, which isn't reasonable because he's not here. He's in prison, and no one else will ever hurt me. But I am. I was reading my mom's journals that Auntie Rose gave me, and she went through something that made her afraid, too. Can you tell me about it?"

Buddy swallowed hard and tears filled his eyes. "She was attacked and sexually assaulted by a football player after a game in high school. The police didn't believe her. The school didn't believe her. There wasn't enough evidence for a guilty verdict. White boy from an affluent family, black girl from a middle-class family. And, he tormented her as often as he could."

Tears fell from Valerie's eyes. "How horrible."

"One of the reasons she loved your dad so much was because he never once made her feel like less of a person because that happened to her." He leaned forward. "She was afraid at night. She'd push her chair in front of her bedroom door. One time she admitted that it didn't make sense because he never broke into her room and attacked her there. I think what happened to her is what happened to you. You understand that something terrible *could* happen, and there's not a lot you can do to stop it because someone might be bigger and stronger than you. That would damage a psyche."

He sat back and picked up his glass of tea. A ring of

condensation remained on the table. "Once she and your dad were married, the fear gradually faded. One day, she realized she hadn't had a panic attack in weeks. At one point, it was all just a bad memory."

Valerie would love to experience a day without a panic attack. Did she have any hope for that? Or did Tyrone break her too permanently and completely? She thought about it as conversation happened around her, searching herself inside, examining her mind and heart. Auntie Rose's voice pulled her out of her own head.

"Buddy, the boys are going to the lake to finish prepping for tomorrow if you want to help," Rosaline said as she stood and gathered lunch plates. "I'm going to start cooking."

"I'll stay and help you cook, Mama," Brad said. "We have a really great handle on the lake for tomorrow."

Phillip drained his glass and stood. "Did you take the fishing poles and tackle out there?"

"Yes, sir. Put some worms in the mini fridge, too. Ready for the kids."

"Perfect." He pulled his keys out of his pocket and gave Rosaline a gentle kiss. "See you tonight."

Everyone but Brad, Valerie, and Rosaline left. Valerie carried lunch dishes into the kitchen and loaded the dishwasher while Brad started peeling and chopping onions. Once she cleaned the counters and put soap in the dishwasher, she turned to Rosaline. "What can I do?"

"Deviled eggs. They're in the fridge," she said, raising her voice over the sound of the food processor she currently used to shred cabbage .

Valerie opened the refrigerator door and saw the large bowl of eggs. "These are already boiled?"

"Yes."

Rosaline used a remote control to put music on, and the three of them worked without speing for several minutes, listening to the music. Valerie steadily peeled and rinsed eggs. She counted about three dozen. Once she had them peeled, she cut them in half and scooped out the yolks.

Soon she filled containers with eggs filled with a relish and mayonnaise filling and sealed the containers, then stacked them and put them in the fridge. For ease of transport, they would put the filling into the egg white shells at the lake tomorrow.

"What next?"

Rosaline put cabbage and carrots in a huge stainless steel bowl and used both hands to stir the coleslaw dressing into them. "Jon made a sauce last night and I put some beef short ribs in the fridge to thaw. Go ahead and get them marinating in the sauce."

While Valerie transferred ribs from one container to another, she thought about what Buddy told her. Of course, she'd inferred what happened to her mom from reading her journal, but she hadn't thought about how she didn't write about the fear a whole lot after her father came into the picture. It interested her how the relationship would have made the fear fade away.

"How many people are you expecting tomorrow?"

"Maybe a hundred. Not positive. We have the ribs, hamburgers, and hot dogs, and I have friends bringing more salads. However many come, we're going to have too much food."

Valerie laughed. "We always did."

Brad bagged the onions he'd sliced for hamburgers and

gave Rosaline three separate bowls of chopped onions. "Next?"

"Wash and prep the lettuce for hamburgers, then slice tomatoes and prepare them for transport."

After Valerie finished putting the ribs in the marinade, she helped Brad slice tomatoes. Soon, they finished all the food prep and Rosaline released them from the kitchen. "Go enjoy the afternoon. We've done all I want to do."

Brad looked at Valerie. "I really have some work I need to get done, but I can probably spare another hour. Do you want to swim?"

She'd planned on working that afternoon, too, but the thought of spending an hour in the sunshine appealed to her on a massive scale. "I packed my suit in case I had a chance. Let me go get it from my car and I'll meet you out there." Standing in the kitchen for so long made her hip ache, and swimming would loosen her muscles without any impact. She grabbed her bag out of her car and used the guest bathroom to change out of the dress she'd worn to church. Barefoot, she grabbed a towel from the closet by the back door and walked out to the pool. They had retracted the glass walls and roof weeks ago when the weather had warmed. She found Brad already out there, kicking off a pair of flip-flops.

"Is the water warm?"

"I turned the heater off a couple weeks ago. So, it's as warm as the weather's been." He walked over to the deep end and winked at her. "Afraid to just jump in and give it a test?"

He executed a perfect dive and smoothly entered the water, emerging several yards closer to her. He shook his head to get the water out of his eyes and looked up at her. "It's nice. Come on in."

She didn't fully believe him, but didn't want him to call her a chicken, either. So, she walked over to the same spot he'd dived from and jumped into the water. She fully anticipated the shock of cold and felt pleasantly surprised as tepid water enveloped her.

Instead of swimming to Brad, she paddled, kicking her legs out against the force of the water, letting the resistance work her muscles. Brad swam up to her and faced her. "Would the hot tub feel better?"

"No. This feels good. I'm glad you suggested it." She lay her head back and closed her eyes, letting the hot sun soak into her skin. "Tomorrow is going to be fun. It's been too long since I was at a Dixon party."

"It has been. What was the last? Graduation?"

"Yeah. High school. I didn't come for your college graduation." She lifted her head and smiled. "We had it here, remember? The big pool party."

"I remember." His eyes grew serious. "I remember asking you to reconsider college and go to Auburn with us."

"It was too late then." She kicked backward and stretched out her body, floating on top of the water. She had to close her eyes against the glare of the sun. "This feels incredible." Slowly, she stroked her arms and gently kicked her legs just enough to barely move but stay afloat. When she reached the edge of the pool, she lazily turned around and went in the opposite direction. After three laps, she pulled herself out of the water and picked up her towel, wrapping it around her shoulders. She sat in a chair under an umbrella and watched Brad swim laps. Eventually, he got out and sat next to her.

"You know what?"

"What?" he asked.

"I haven't been fishing since the last time I went fishing with you and, hmm, was it Ken?"

"I don't remember." He gestured with his hand in the general direction of east. "I stocked up on bait and poles for tomorrow. You should be able to fish."

Brad fully relaxed while fishing. At least, that's what used to happen. She assumed he still did. With a smile, she said, "I'll like that. But I'd like to go fishing with you again. Not at a party. Not with your brothers. Just you and me. Do you want to do that?"

With amusement in his eyes, he asked, "Like a date?"

Chuckling, she said, "Yes, Brad, like a date-date. A romantic fishing date, even."

"I'd like that very much. Let me look at my schedule and I'll tell you when I'm free to go." He picked his watch up off the table and looked at it. "In the meantime, I need to get to work. I took Friday and yesterday off. I have a lot of catching up to do."

"I need to go, too. Thanks for spending this hour with me." She stood and wrapped the towel around her waist. "I'll see you tomorrow. Let your mom know if she needs anything, to call."

Brad clicked "send" on the email, then sat back and rubbed his eyes. He didn't resent working until eleven Sunday night, but he was happy that he didn't have to work tomorrow. He would have a chance to relax, knowing he'd caught up, and just enjoy his guests. Of course, most of his guests worked for him or with him, so work would come up. Just, hopefully, not too much.

He picked up his dinner plate and cup and took them downstairs. After washing them and stacking them in the dish drainer, he turned off lights and walked through the downstairs rooms, making sure all was well in the Dixon household.

When he went into his dad's study, he was surprised to find Jon on the leather couch, legs crossed on the table in front of him, arms crossed over his chest. He had his eyes closed. Brad bent and touched his shoulder. "Hey, bro," he said.

Jon immediately jerked awake and grabbed Brad's hand. For a brief moment, he looked scared, confused, and startled. Then he relaxed and smiled. "Hey."

Brad could smell an overpowering odor of beer. "What are you doing in here?"

"Oh, uh, I didn't feel like going up the stairs." He pushed himself to his feet and slightly wobbled. "I'm cool, though. Just had to close my eyes for a second."

"Let me help."

Jon pushed away and held his hands up. "I said I'm cool, Bradford. Back off, br—bro." He muffled a belch, then walked out of the room in a relatively straight line. Brad sighed before sitting on the couch and rubbing his face. What made Jon hurt so much? What had him doing this to himself?

And how could he help him?

He'd always been the one to want to fix everything for

everyone. But if he didn't know what hurt Jon, he couldn't do anything about it. Assuming he could do something about it.

He felt like he knew nothing about his brother anymore. He took every job he could away from Atlanta and spent months away from home. Clearly, he felt the need to escape. This last trip to Egypt, though, something had changed him. He'd come back darker, defiant, unbending. And now drinking to excess.

Feeling a bit helpless, Brad stood and walked out of the room, stopping at the front door to make sure Jon had locked it. And, if he was honest with himself, to make sure Jon hadn't driven home. Not seeing the truck in the driveway gave him a bit of relief.

Back upstairs, he tapped on Ken's door and opened it. Ken rarely stayed here anymore. In between houses, he'd use his old room until the newest house had running water and a good roof. He found Ken sitting at his desk, a drafting program open on his laptop. He looked up as Brad opened the door. "Hey."

"Little late, bro. Everything okay?"

Brad rubbed the back of his neck. "I just found Jon passed out in dad's study."

"Yeah. I heard him come in about two hours ago."

"Something's eating at him. Do you know what's going on?"

Ken shook his head. "No, I do not. I don't pry like you, though."

"Pry?" Brad laughed. "Is that what it's called?"

"That's what it becomes at some point." He shut the laptop and pushed away from his desk. "Do we need to arrange an intervention, or do you think we need to just love him?"

"I feel like I'm hearing sarcasm."

"You always had a good ear. Trust your feelings. I swear, sometimes you remind me of the annoying little sister I never had and never wanted." Ken walked closer and slipped his hands into his jeans pockets. "Jon's just as intelligent as you are, probably more so, and was raised in exactly the same environment. Leave him be. He'll work out whatever's on his heart. He just came home from Egypt. There's no telling the experiences he had there. He has to process whatever this is."

"And if he gets hurt in the process of me leaving him be?"

Ken chuckled. "Then you have my permission to wag your finger in my face and tell me you told me so before you tattle-tale to Mom and Dad." He leaned his shoulder against the wall. "Like any prying little sister."

Properly chastised, Brad backed out of the room. "Good talk," he said, trying not to laugh at himself while still feeling a touch of concern for his brother. "See you in the morning."

He paused at Jon's door before going to his room. He wanted to talk to him, but he would wait until tomorrow.

Back in his room, he got ready for bed. As he brushed his teeth, he looked at the list of dates he'd made once he had access to his calendar. Impulsively, he picked up his phone and typed out a text.

HEY. THESE ARE THE DATES I'M FREE FOR FISHING. LET ME KNOW WHICH WORKS FOR YOU.

Turning out his bathroom light, he smiled and thought about Valerie asking him on a fishing date. He couldn't imagine a less romantic environment, but he loved that she wanted to go with him. He'd pack a picnic. Maybe offer to cook her their catch.

Just as he settled into bed, he heard his phone chirp with her reply. She'd picked Wednesday afternoon. Just a few days away. He'd see her tomorrow, too.

As he drifted off to sleep, he realized he still smiled.

Valerie watched one of the teenagers jump onto the rope swing and swing out above the water and let go, landing with a loud splash. His friends cheered him on.

She laughed and looked at Jon, who stared at the group with squinted eyes. "Did you put that up?"

"I did. I'm just watching it and making sure it's gonna hold." His face relaxed as another teen took the challenge and splashed into the water. "Looks good. Cool." He shifted the baseball cap on his head. "Remember the one dad built us? I didn't listen to the way he told us to do it and ended up with rope burns on my hands. I didn't realize how badly I'd hurt myself until I got into the shower that night and the shampoo touched my palms."

"I do remember!" She pointed at the rope. "I notice you added a wooden plank for their feet. No rope burns today?"

"Shoot, I didn't put that on there for them. I did it for me. I'm almost thirty. Why would I want to hold my body weight up with my arms if I have the tools and skill to make a platform?" He laughed and raced over to the water's edge, pulling his shirt over his head. He grabbed the rope and jumped up on the wooden piece. He hooted and hollered as he swung over the water and jumped in. Valerie laughed and clapped him on.

"Why didn't we think of the wooden step when we were young?" Brad asked as he walked up to her.

"It is a clever idea. I'll give him that." She smiled up at him. He wore a pair of red swim shorts and a black T-shirt with horizontal white stripes. He clearly hadn't shaved all weekend, and the stubble of beard on his face made her want to rub her hands on his cheeks. "Want to give it a go?"

She looked down at her outfit of a white tank top and denim shorts. She hadn't even thought of packing a swimsuit. "Not particularly." They watched as Jon swam to shore and shook his head to clear the water out of his hair. He picked his hat and shirt back up then jogged up to them. "The water's a wee bit cold," he said, rubbing his arms. "Why didn't I think of that?"

"The difference in May and July." Brad laughed. "Dad said to tell you the ribs are ready to come off."

"Yum." He slipped his shirt over his head. "Been slow cooking them all morning."

Valerie scanned the crowd and the decorations. More than a dozen tables covered in red, white, and blue tablecloths filled the yard. Vases filled with red and white flowers graced with small American flags sat in the center of each table. Under the large white tent decorated with American flag streamers sat tables filled with food. Someone had set up a volleyball net and a small group of teenage girls batted a ball back and forth. Kids flooded the dock with their fishing poles. "You guys did an amazing job. I love how you all came together and did this."

"We work well together." He pointed to his parents who sat in camp chairs talking to a group of friends. "And my mom trained us all well."

She thought about her life in Savannah and what it was like outside the Dixon circle. "You have no idea how blessed you are, do you? Your family is special." Her stomach growled. "I'm ready for some of those ribs."

She felt Brad put a light hand on the small of her back as they walked from the lake edge to the tent that held the tables of foods. At the doorway of the tent, Brad had installed fans to help keep the flies at bay. As they walked in, she enjoyed the cool breeze they created. Immediately, she smelled the spicy tang of freshly grilled meat. She grabbed a plate and worked her way down the line of tables, adding a little bit of potato salad, fruit salad, and coleslaw to her plate, then a beef short rib.

Brad helped himself to a hamburger and a hot dog and dressed them both at the table that contained all the condiments and toppings. He grabbed a bag of potato chips, and they departed the tent through the blowing fans.

Brad frowned at the doorway. "I know there's probably a better way to do it, but it was what I thought of Saturday afternoon."

"I think it works fine." She popped a piece of watermelon in her mouth. "I didn't see any flies in there, and you and I both know the food would be covered if it was out here."

"True." They found two seats at a table next to Calla and Ian.

"Hey! Where's Sami?"

"Swinging from a rope," Ian said, nodding with his chin. Valerie looked where he gestured and saw Sami standing on the rope swing, laughing while Jon yelled at her to let go and fall into the water.

She and Brad started laughing. "She's going to end up making Jon come save her," Brad said. "It's not safe to jump when it's close to shore."

"She'll be fine," Calla said, pushing her glasses up the bridge of her nose. "I'm trying to talk Ian into going with me, but he won't."

"Well, to be fair, I'm not twelve," he joked. "Plus, I'm not wearing a suit."

"Those sound like good excuses to me." Brad laughed. "I'll let Jon go and pretend he's me."

"Did you guys do that a lot growing up?" Calla asked.

"Only always," Valerie said. "They couldn't fool me, and they couldn't fool their mom, so they didn't get away with it too much. But they tried. Especially in school."

"Ken tried to get me to take a test for him one time in seventh grade, but the teacher told us he'd have Valerie confirm identity so it didn't work."

Calla looked at Valerie. "How can you tell them apart? I tried the whole time I worked there, and never could tell except by how they were dressed."

Valerie studied Brad's face. "I see lots of subtle differences," she said, somehow unable to tear her eyes from his gaze. Her heartrate skittered and she licked her lips. "It's in the shape of their eyes and mouths."

"You're kidding, right?" Ian asked.

"Nope." She finally looked away and felt like she'd broken a spell. She smiled at Ian. "But we were born within weeks of each other and I've grown up with them. Auntie Rose would tell you the same thing."

"Mm-hmm," Calla said with a raised eyebrow. "I'm sure it's like a sister thing."

"Hardly sister," Brad remarked.

"Mm-hmm," Calla said again, half smiling. "Thought so."

"Calla," Ian said under his breath.

Valerie felt a little embarrassed but didn't know exactly why. Brad said, "It's okay, Ian. We came to Calla's opening as a couple on a date. I'm not hiding anything."

A soaking wet Sami wearing a pair of blue shorts and a red tank top rushed toward them laughing, carrying her sandals. "Y'all have got to do that," she said, pulling out a chair next to Calla and landing in it with a wet sound. "The water's great."

"Yeah, no," Valerie said, shuddering. "All I can think about when I look at that rope is how many water moccasin nests must be among the roots of that tree."

Sami's laughter immediately stopped. "Really? Did you seriously just say that?"

Valerie laughed and covered her mouth with her hand. "I'm sorry! I didn't even think before I said it. I just am afraid of freshwater. I had a friend get bitten in high school."

"Well that will keep me off the rope the rest of the day." She leaned back in her chair and crossed her arms over her chest, letting her lower lip come out in a pout. "Water moccasins," she huffed.

"You fish freshwater," Brad said.

She thought about their upcoming fishing date. "Sure. I don't have to go into the water to fish. Besides, you'll be with me." She winked at him. "I know something about you, Brad. You'll protect me from the snakes."

Giving a barely perceptible nod, he looked at Sami. "You know all the splashing and laughing and giant human beings in and around that tree all morning would have scared away any snake in the vicinity, right?"

"And the 'gators," Ian added, dimples appearing in his cheeks as he grinned.

"'Gators. right." Sami slapped her hands on the table and stood. "Sounds like it's time to get lunch." She left a puddle of water on the plastic seat of the chair and headed off to the food tent.

"We took all her fun away," Valerie said on a laugh.

"Hardly. She's probably devising a way to turn all that information into a dare for the teenage boys. Scare them and make them jump anyway." Calla took a sip of her water. "But I get your point. Once you think about it, it's hard to relax and have fun."

"I'm good in public swimming areas. They get used all the time so they tend to not be inhabited with dangerous fauna. It's mostly untouched places like this I don't trust." Valerie bit into a short rib and enjoyed the mingle of spices and tang from the sauce on her tongue. The meat melted in her mouth. She set the rib on her plate and licked her fingers.

"Those ribs are amazing," she said to Brad.

"Jon's sauce. Can't be beat. He needs to bottle that stuff. He starts with raisins and goes from there." He picked up his hot dog. "I had one earlier or I would have gotten another. Want to make sure there's enough for everyone."

Calla dug her phone out of her pocket and checked an incoming text. Ian watched her as she typed. "Day off, love, remember?"

"He's just asking for the security code for the safe. And he apologized three times in the text asking for it."

"Why doesn't he know the security code?"

"Well, I told it to him, but he's never actually opened it."

Ian leaned toward Calla and gently covered her fingers, preventing her from typing any more into her phone or sending the text. "First of all, don't text him the code. Call him and recite it, and make sure you aren't on speaker. Second, you and I are going to have a conversation about delegation. I want you to enjoy this, not get burned out in the first year."

Calla dialed the phone and strolled a short distance away. Ian looked at Brad. "Ken said you're going to Florida for the mission trip this year?"

"Yeah. Jon and I are giving him a break from flying this year. After the last hurricane, there's more than enough work to keep us busy for the week."

"Is it just a brother thing, or could someone else join?"

Brad's eyebrows drew together. "It's kind of a brother thing. And we want some downtime with Jon this year."

Ian nodded. "Understood, friend. Let me know if you need anything."

"We're good. Ken drew up a list and coordinated with

our office in Panama City. Probably be the smoothest mission trip ever."

"You head out September first?"

"Yeah. Be gone until the ninth."

Valerie finished her rib just as Sami sat down, her plate loaded with a hamburger and three different salads. "I never can decide at things like this, so I end up eating way too much."

"That's good," Valerie said, "because there's a lot of food."

Sami looked around. "Good crowd, though."

Brad stood with his empty plate. "I'm going to get more water. Can I bring you anything?"

Valerie shook her head. "I'm good. Thanks."

As he walked away, Calla walked back over and caught her watching Brad's departing profile. "Looking good I take it?"

She watched Brad stop and talk to someone on his way to the cooler full of water. She liked the way he moved, with confidence and grace. "Yeah, I think so."

"Good. He needs you." Sami shoved potato salad in her mouth and pointed at Valerie with her fork. "You're perfect for him."

Ian got to his feet. "Sounds like girl talk, so I'll just excuse myself. I need to go talk to the elder Mr. Dixon." He put a hand on Calla's shoulder and gave her a look of pure love. "Need anything?"

She smiled up at him and shook her head. He bent and gave her a brief but gentle kiss, then walked away. Calla grinned at his departing back then looked at Valerie. "He's kind of perfect for you, too," she said, and Sami murmured her agreement around a mouth full of food.

Brad sat in a lounge chair on the back porch and closed his eyes. His body felt fatigued, but he had a content mind and a happy heart. It was nearly midnight when everyone got home after the party at the lake. He planned to send some laborers out to the site tomorrow to load up the chairs and tables and finish the cleanup.

The door behind him opened and he didn't even open his eyes as he listened to his dad sit in the chair next to him. "Y'all did an amazing job with the party," he said.

"Thanks. Ken did a lot of work ahead of time, building the structures. Mom worked hard."

"You and Jon did, too. Your mom loves to throw parties. Thanks for giving her that. It's been a couple years."

"I think she's been holding out for weddings and baby showers that haven't happened yet," Brad said with a grin.

"And grandchildren birthday parties. You three are killing her with all this bachelorhood," Phillip confirmed.

"Can't rush God's timing."

"True." He sighed and Brad finally looked at him. His father had always been a very strong, imposing figure. Lately, Brad had started to notice how age had begun creeping up on his dad. His hair had grayed and thinned, his middle thickened and sagged. The lines on his face deepened and he had to wear glasses all the time now. Brad didn't enjoy thinking about his dad's aging.

"So," Phillip said, "tell me what's going on with Valerie. The last time we talked about her, you appeared burdened with angst."

"Dad, I'm twenty-nine. I was hardly angsty."

"Yeah. Sure." He laughed and waved a hand at him. "We'll go with your side of it. Tell me anyway."

What could he say that his dad didn't already know? "She read her mom's journals. She came over to talk to mama about it, but I was the only one here. We ended up talking, then praying together. You saw her at church yesterday."

"I did. I didn't want to press her, though, and she hasn't said a lot to Buddy."

"She read the journals weeks ago. I think they've been on her mind since the dedication."

"You say you prayed together. Then what?"

"I don't know. We're going fishing Wednesday after work. We'll be alone, and that's pretty rare. I'm looking forward to it." He really looked forward to it, but also felt a little nervous for some reason. It didn't make sense to him. He'd known her his whole life. What reason could he possibly have to be nervous about spending a couple hours alone with her? "I'm going to pack some of the leftovers for a picnic."

"She's already talked to your mom about making a picnic for you."

Brad raised an eyebrow. Somehow, that thought made him really happy. "Really? Sounds like you might already know the answers to these questions of yours."

"I know what current activities are going on under my own roof. What I don't know is your current state of being and if there's anything I can do for you."

His current state of being? How did he word that? "Well, hmm." He cleared his throat. "Dad, I've been in love with

Valerie since I could form the rational thought. Every important memory from my childhood and adolescence involves her. She broke my heart a couple different times in a couple different ways, but I still love her. My deal with myself was that I would not be unevenly yoked. As hard as it was, I meant it. Having her come to me, to pray with her, to talk to her about her spiritual yearning and seeking means as much to me as if she threw herself into my arms and declared undying love for me."

He paused and smiled. "Well, maybe not as much, but you know what I mean."

"I know exactly what you mean." He shifted in the lounge chair and turned his body to face Brad. "And Tyrone?"

Brad's heart lurched in his chest. "Yeah. I need to forgive Tyrone."

Phillip put a hand on his knee. "You need to. Not for Valerie. Not even for Tyrone. You need to let it go for your own heart and soul."

"I know." He let out a breath and looked at the sky. "I know that more than you know."

"You've never kept your feelings for Valerie secret. Your mama and I worried about your heart when she left, when she moved in with Tyrone, when she was hurt so badly. We pray for you, and we pray for your future wife, whomever that may be. God already knows. We love you and we love your eventual wife. If you ever need anything, someone to talk to, someone to pray with, I am here and so is your mom." He pushed himself to his feet and started back inside, pausing with his hand on Brad's shoulder. "Buddy will be less encouraging. Be prepared for that."

Phillip knew Buddy had issues with Brad's lack of skin pigmentation. He wanted Valerie's husband to come from what he called her "own people." He had pulled her away from their home and put her into a different school on that very basis. Brad didn't understand it, and Phillip didn't understand it. Despite their lack of understanding and their disagreement with the notion on its face, they respected Buddy as Valerie's blood kin. "I'll pray about that."

"Good. That is the right answer." He put his hand on the door but stopped again. "Quit worrying so much about Jon. He'll make it through. Don't try to father him. That's my job. He needs a brother who loves him, not another parent."

Phillip waited while Brad let that sink in. Finally, he said, "Yes, sir."

After another twenty minutes, Brad went inside and locked the door behind him. As he poured his glass out into the sink, Ken walked into the room. "I have a team of eight going out to the lake tomorrow. They'll have it taken care of in a matter of hours."

"Great. That works." Brad rolled his head on his neck. "I was not looking forward to doing it." He laughed.

"Me, either." He pulled his keys out of his pocket and hung them up on the hooks by the back door. "I'm ready to move into the apartments whenever you are. Got an offer on the house today."

"Send me the plans so I can look over them."

"Already in your email. I was going to ask Valerie to give me some insight into the color samples."

"Yeah, good idea."

"There's an office that has its own bathroom. We can install a shower then use that as living quarters."

"Sounds good. How much money do I owe you?"

"I'll finish up the estimate after getting with Valerie and let you know what your half is."

"Maybe Jon wants in on a third of it."

"I checked. He was about half interested. I'll check again and make sure before we divvy up costs."

"Looking forward to it. As sore as I am after prepping for the party, I clearly need to get back to some manual labor on a regular basis." As he left the room, he called over his shoulder, "Goodnight."

He double-checked the doors then went upstairs. On his way to his room, he paused at Jon's room, seeing the glow of his light from under the door. He rapped two knocks with his knuckles and opened the door. Jon lay against pillows in his bed watching a replay of a Braves game on his television. "Hey," Brad said.

"Hey, yourself." Jon pointed the remote at the tv and paused the game.

"The rope swing was a huge hit. Great idea."

Jon smiled. "It was fun. The older kids liked it. Made them put their phones down for five seconds."

"Brilliant." Brad chuckled. "Sami even had fun on it."

"Yeah, until Val scared her off." He ran his fingers through his hair. "You should have heard her goading some teenagers about snakes and alligators. Suddenly, it became a challenge and the more that went on, the more everyone had to keep going. Hysterical."

"Goodnight, bro."

"'Night."

Feeling like maybe he had reset their relationship before it had gotten too far out of bounds, he went to his room to get ready for bed. As he brushed his teeth, he thought about Valerie, his dad, work, Valerie. Turning off the bathroom light, he took a deep breath and closed his eyes, willing his mind to settle down and take a break from the thinking and worrying.

Chapter 21

Valerie sat in the camp chair and watched the tip of her fishing pole. Brad caught a bass earlier and it swam around in the bucket waiting for a partner. "I never catch anything," she mused. "I remember once I kept moving around because all you boys were catching fish right and left and I couldn't even get a nibble."

Brad didn't have anything in the water. She had a feeling he did that so she could catch something. "You caught that stingray in Florida that time."

"Yeah, fishing for flounder."

Brad grinned. "Still. I never caught a stingray in my life."

Valerie shifted the baseball cap on her head and grinned at him. "You might as well hold the pole so we can catch dinner before the sun goes down."

He smiled a gentle, lazy smile that made her stomach do funny things. "I'm in no hurry." He kicked his feet out in front of him and crossed his legs at his ankles. "How was work today?"

"Nonstop. I grabbed a sandwich from the deli and ate it in the elevator going from one meeting to another." She retrieved the bottle of water from the cup holder in the arm of the camp chair. Condensation made the label fall off. She ran her finger over the remnants of glue. "I'm doing design work at home because the days are full of meetings."

"Was it like that for you in Savannah?"

She thought back to her little shared office and the influx of work. "In cycles. I'm assuming this is similar with greater volume and more staff."

"Sure. Lots of jobs are beginning. That's a busy time for you guys in design and engineering. The project managers are winding down jobs, coming home, getting ready to get back out there. Everyone's time seems to be busy at different cycles."

He rubbed his eyes with his fingers, and she realized how tired he looked. "Except for you," she observed. "You are in the thick of all the cycles."

"Except me." He sighed. "Poor little me who worked until nearly midnight the Sunday before Memorial Day so I could enjoy the picnic." He raised his water bottle in a toast toward her. "All because I drew the short straw."

"Wait, what?" Fishing pole forgotten, she leaned forward and put her elbows on her knees. "Did you guys actually still draw straws like when you were kids? You drew straws for your current positions?"

He laughed. "Did you not know that?"

"No, I just assumed you were picked because you were more gifted in leadership than your brothers. You've always been more organized, neater."

He shook his head. "Dad wanted it to be placed in God's hands, not his. He didn't feel like he could make a fair decision. So, we drew straws. Later, he told me he knew it would be me. But, who knows, he might have said that to any of us."

She studied his face, the seriousness in his gray eyes, the order he'd created around him even in a fishing spot on the river. "No, I think he knew it would be you. It did not surprise me when you were named president. I think anyone who knows you, who knows all three of you, expected it to be you."

"Everyone but me." He stood and walked over to the cooler, digging in it until he pulled out an apple. "I couldn't believe it was me. It's only been recently that I've relaxed and accepted it." He settled back in his chair and took a bite of the apple, crunching into the crisp flesh. "You know, when dad and Mr. Mason first started Mason-Dixon contracting, they only wanted to build affordable houses."

Valerie snorted. "You and I both know there's builders making a killing from south of the All American to north of Lawrenceburg building little mini-mansions on the cheap and selling them for millions. That's anything but affordable."

Brad nodded. "That supply will keep coming down the pike as long as there is a demand, too. No end in sight."

"Very different from the vision Mason-Dixon had, I imagine."

Brad pursed his lips. "Mason-Dixon grew too fast. The demand outpaced their vision. Eventually, they split and both created huge names for themselves. They built so much of this city. Dad never planned on having thousands of employees over several states. He just wanted to build affordable houses. But he embraced it and he did it well. If I sit and think about it, I get overwhelmed with the responsibility. I don't want to ruin his legacy."

She stayed silent for several minutes before she said, "I seriously doubt you'll do anything to ruin his legacy. But, as he officially retires and you fully take the reins without his presence, if you make changes or do things differently in various areas, that's completely acceptable. Because you're taking his legacy and turning it into your own."

"Assuming I have children to whom I can pass it down."

She picked up her pole and slowly reeled in the bait. "You don't want children?"

"Of course, I do. Lots and lots of them." He took another bite of apple. "But first comes love, then comes marriage."

Valerie laughed. "Then comes baby in the baby carriage."

"Bingo." He finished the apple and tossed the core into the water. "Lots of folks get that out of order these days. I found it works much better when you do things in order. I'll leave the timing for all of that to God, like always."

They sat in silence for several minutes. Valerie couldn't help but think about the things she'd done out of order in her life. She tried to push the thoughts away and not let any darkness into the sunny day. Finally, Brad asked, "Are you happy you came home?"

Standing as she checked her bait, she looked down at

him. "I could have gone anywhere. Your dad would have put me in any Dixon Contracting office or written me a referral. This was where I wanted to come."

After she cast the bait, she tightened the reel and sat back down. "I already know all those facts," Brad said, "but I asked if you were happy you came home."

She lifted the chair by the handles and turned so she could face him instead of the water. "I have learned so many things about myself, about my parents, about you. None of that would have happened if I hadn't come home. I'm glad I came. But, frankly Brad, I haven't been happy in years. I don't know if I know how to be anymore."

He sat forward and took her hands in his. "You don't have happy moments?"

Contemplating what he said, she pursed her lips and tried to form her answer correctly. His hands were warm, strong. She loved the feel of his skin against hers. "I have moments where I feel happiness. But reality always pushes in, physical pain, regrets, all of it comes back. I don't know what that means about me or my psyche. I'm not saying I dwell in misery, but I am definitely not existing in a state of happiness."

"What would make you happy?" She could tell by the fierce look in his eyes that he was not teasing her, that the question was serious. She had a feeling that if she had an answer, he'd move heaven and earth to make it so.

"I think," she said, breathing out, "that I have to find a way to come to terms with decisions I made in my past, to forgive the younger me. I think I live in a constant state of regret and when I can let that go, then I'll find happiness." She smiled. "I was happy when you said you'd take me fishing this week. I was happy to look forward to this evening all day. I know I'll be happy as I cook up that fish you caught. I'm able to experience moments of happiness."

"Valerie, if you need anything, or if there is ever anything at all I can do to make you happy, let me know. Whatever it is. I promise I'll make it happen."

"I believe that," she said in almost a whisper. "Thank you."

Out of the corner of her eye, she saw the fishing pole bend in half and the seriousness of the moment disappeared as she jumped up and caught it. Laughing, she set the hook and slowly reeled in her fish. It fought, she fought, Brad gave advice, and she worked it until she got it all the way onto shore.

Brad reached down and picked it up and used a pair of pliers to pull the hook out of its mouth. It landed in the bucket with a splash and both fish started swimming in circles.

"I think it's as big as yours," Valerie said, admiring her catch.

"At least." He rubbed her shoulders. "Good catch. Do you want to keep them both?"

She pursed her lips and contemplated the question. "It's a lot of fish for the two of us, isn't it?"

"I think one is plenty."

"Okay. Toss yours back."

"Well, of course," he said, reaching into the bucket with both hands to scoop out the fish that had spent a good part of the afternoon contained. "I wouldn't think of tossing yours back."

After he slipped his fish back into the water, he talked

her through killing and cleaning her catch. “It’s way easier to do it out here,” he explained, “than in your kitchen sink. Just toss the waste back into the river. Circle of life.”

Valerie used his fillet knife to clean and gut her fish, then rinsed it out in the water in the bucket. She knew she’d rinse it again at her house. Brad had brought a plastic bag to transport any catch in and after putting her fillets of fish in it, she sealed it and put it in the cooler with the leftover snack she’d packed.

“Now to dinner!” she exclaimed as they packed up the fishing poles and tackle.

Brad tossed everything into the back of his truck and held the door open for her. She felt ridiculously proud of her catch and couldn’t wait to cook it. As he drove to her house, she turned slightly in the seat and faced him. “Thanks for taking me fishing.”

“Best romantic date ever,” he said, looking over at her and winking. “Seriously. It’s a mixture of two of my favorite things; you and fishing.”

Her breath caught at his words but she kept her comeback light. “Right up there with fishing, huh? That’s a lot of pressure.”

“You don’t even have to try.” In no time, he had pulled into her driveway. He carried the cooler in and she went straight to the kitchen. “I already have coleslaw. Your mom sent it home with me on Monday. And I made a hush puppy batter this morning. All we have to do is cook some potatoes and these fillets.”

After setting the cooler on the ground, Brad walked to the sink and washed his hands. “Just tell me what to do.”

While she seasoned the fish and put the fillets under the

flame of the broiler, Brad sliced potatoes and added them to the oil she'd heated up in a frying pan. In another pan of oil, she added scoops of the cornmeal and green onion hush puppy mixture. When the little balls of bread rose to the surface and turned brown on the bottom, she turned them over and let them cook another two minutes, then pulled them out of the oil and let them drain on a paper towel covered plate.

With the first batch of hush puppies draining, she opened the broiler drawer and checked the fish. Using a spatula, she turned them and closed the drawer.

Thirty minutes after getting home, the two of them sat at her table. Brad held out his hand and she placed hers in it and bowed her head while he prayed.

"God, you are a God of wonders, a God of healing, and a God of love. We thank You for everything that You are and everything that You will be. Please bless this food to the nourishment of our bodies and our bodies to Your service."

His prayer resonated with her heart. God was a God of healing. Not just of bodies, but of minds and spirits. Seeking healing through Him, forgiveness for herself and her mistakes, might break through this fog of merely surviving and help her find a way to bring joy and happiness back into her life.

She liked the feel of her hand in his and hesitated a second longer than necessary before letting go. Nervous, she put her napkin in her lap and picked up her fork. "You fry a mean potato, Mr. Dixon," she said around a mouth full of food.

"My mama raised me right."

She laughed and immediately relaxed. They chatted as

they ate. About work, about his brothers, about Buddy. "He isn't sure where he fits in my life anymore," she said, thinking about the man who gave up everything for her.

"You intentionally shut him out. To protect him from your life, I'm sure. And while everyone understands that intellectually, you probably have to be intentional about bringing him back in now." He pushed his empty plate aside and leaned forward on his arms. "I've done that to Jon without realizing it. He's going through something. He's dark. He's drinking too much and angry too often. I found myself parenting him instead of supporting him and it affected our relationship. It took my dad saying something to me to make me realize it."

She looked at him, at the worry clouding his eyes, at the lines of strain around his face. "I imagine it's hard to go from boss to equal depending on the environment."

"Even you had a hard time with me being the boss," he remarked.

She ran her tongue over her teeth. "I think I might be over that now."

"Yeah?" He reached out and took her hand. The move startled her, and she tensed up before she realized it. "Good."

Intentionally relaxing, she pulled her hand away and stood, gathering his plate and hers. She took them to the kitchen and put them in the sink. When she turned around, she found him standing in the kitchen door.

"I'm going to leave now," he said, his voice deep. "I'll see you tomorrow."

She clasped her hands in front of her and nervously wrung her fingers. "Oh, okay." He turned and she followed him to the door. Before he opened it, he stopped and faced her. She was right on his heels and almost ran into him. He grabbed her shoulders to steady her and looked down at her.

"Thank you for catching and cooking dinner. I had an amazing time."

Heart pounding, mouth dry, she smiled a tight smile and stared into his eyes. "Me, too," she said. "Thanks for, uh, taking me up on it."

When his hand cupped her cheek, she stopped breathing. Was he going to kiss her? Was Brad Dixon about to kiss her?

When he released her and opened the door, she felt a sudden sense of disappointment. In a nervous gesture, she licked her lips and watched him get into his truck. She raised a hand goodbye as he backed out of the driveway.

Only when she shut and locked the door did she realize she had come home with him and never checked the house.

Amazed, heart pounding, she grabbed her keys and cell phone and did a cursory check, but for once she didn't feel surprised to find everything in order and nothing at all out of place.

Brad pulled into the parking lot of the apartment building they would renovate. He had the keys in his pocket, so he grabbed his tablet and let himself into the office that he and Ken would call home for the next several months. He didn't want to go home and think about how Valerie had tensed up when he touched her. He would rather just work, put it out of his mind.

The office had a main waiting area, two offices, and a bathroom. They would convert the waiting room into a living space and kitchenette. They had the couch, chairs, refrigerator, and appliances in storage from the last renovation job. Using his fingertip, he drew on his tablet and created rough plans for the space. The bathroom looked like a shower could fit in it if they got rid of the sink. They could use the kitchen sink. Each of the offices would serve as a bedroom. They had plenty of room for single beds and dressers, and each could have a sink and mirror installed.

He made notes, he wrote plans, he sent Ken three texts and adjusted plans based on the replies he received. He sent an email to one of the crew chiefs to have four laborers scheduled for tomorrow to move the furniture and appliances out of storage and bring them here.

Hours later, he found himself in Jon's room, nursing a beer long gone warm.

"Do you think she's afraid of you?" his brother asked.

Did he? He analyzed the question. "I think she's aware of what a man can do to a woman, and she has to force herself not to expect it from me. But I don't think it's actual fear." He set the half-empty beer down and stood, shoving his hands into the pockets of his shorts. "I wish I had stayed and asked her. Why did I leave?"

Jon put his empty beer bottle back into the cardboard carrier it came in. "You left because you don't want her afraid of you and you couldn't stand the thought. It's understandable. But, dude, you're going to have to confront it or else you'll never ever get anywhere with her."

Brad paced to the window and looked at his reflection in the light. How could he possibly address it? "I have this rage inside of me that wants to pull a Superman and fly around the world backwards, reset time. It's like this energy that consumes me."

Jon sighed. "Rage, huh. Yeah. I understand." He stood and crossed the room so he stood in front of him. He leaned his back against the window frame and crossed his arms in front of his chest. "You can't, though. So how are you going to settle this rage? What's the source? Tyrone, who hurt her? Valerie, who bucked everything we were raised to believe and moved in with a married man? Buddy who took her away from you when she was 15? You haveto find it, backtrack until you get to where it starts, then you have to deal with it there. Until then, your soul is going to be unsettled, and you won't be good for her."

Brad studied his brother. They looked alike. Most people couldn't tell them apart. To him, though, they had so many differences, he wondered how they even came from the same parents. "Where did such wisdom come to someone so young and attractive?"

Jon's lips formed a thin line. "I can't talk about it." He walked up and slapped Brad on his shoulder. "I love you, man. I want to see you content and happy. If I can help, let me know."

"Likewise, brother."

Valerie sat at her desk, working the design program and observing the results on the two screens above her desk. She calibrated the program so she could see the colors the way she needed to see them, and worked through tile, wallpaper, paint, and fixture options to try to best reflect the needs and desires of the shopping mall project.

She'd received bids from local artists who wanted to do sculptures for the three central areas. In each of them, she added the lower bidders' work samples so the owner could envision how they worked with the surrounding ambiance.

When a knock sounded at her door, she said, "Come on in," without even knowing who bid entrance. It surprised her to see Jon come into the room. "Hey, Jon," she said, barely glancing at him.

"All right. Tell me. How do you know it's me so quickly?" He slipped into a chair in front of her desk and hooked his ankle on his knee.

"Umm," she said, saving her work and turning to face him. "Sorry. What?"

"How do you know it's me so quickly?"

"Because Ken would be in jeans."

He lifted the collar of his suit coat. "And yet, I'm dressed like Brad."

Her eyebrows came together. "Hardly."

With a finger pointing at her, he laughed. "You know, lately, you group Ken and me together and make Brad his own separate entity."

Thinking of Brad, she felt her pulse quicken and put her chin in her hands. "Brad is a separate entity," she said in a dreamy voice with half a smile. "Why is that such a big deal?"

"Because, my friend, when we were in college, Ken convinced him to ask this woman on a date. She was this beautiful redhead whose name I cannot remember for the life of me. Anyway, we were at this party, and she cozied up to me. I told her I was Jon, not Brad. She asked me why that mattered." His cheeks turned red and he cleared his throat. "Brad overheard her. I honestly don't know if he's ever dated again. If he has, he's never talked about it."

That surprised her. "You're kidding, right? We're 29."

"Right. And he's always had his sights set on one particular woman. Don't think he's ever actually been interested in anyone else. That fiery redhead's attitude in college certainly drove that home."

Flabbergasted, Valerie shook her head. "I honestly can't fathom that."

"Well, there it is."

He settled more comfortably in his chair but made no apparent move to say anything else. This prompted her to ask, "Is there a particular reason you came in here?"

With his gray eyes lighting up in a smile, he said, "Honestly? No. Not really. I just had a suit on, and I wanted to see if you'd think I was my brother."

Angry, she narrowed her eyes. "Well, in that case, you've had your fun. Now, leave me alone. I have so much work to do before a meeting in," she glanced at the clock on her desk, "twenty-two minutes."

With a laugh, he stood and walked out of her office. She scowled at the door before she turned back to her computer and went back to work.

It took her a couple minutes to fully get herself mentally back into the task at hand. She could only think of a redhead cozying up to Brad in the way Jon described. "Enough," she said to herself, "it's not like you weren't cozying up to someone you shouldn't be with."

The pep talk helped her get her mind back on her job and she rushed through the plans until the alarm she'd set on her phone signaled that she had enough time to save the presentation to the office system and get to the conference room.

Due to the owner's attendance in the meeting, it took place on the executive floor. She made sure everything saved properly, then grabbed her tablet to control the presentation and rushed to the elevators. When the doors opened, she felt a jolt of surprise to see Brad standing in the car. His eyes widened when he saw her.

"Hey," he said warmly.

"Hey, yourself." She could feel her smile literally stretching her cheek muscles. She quickly pushed the shut door button, hoping no one else would get into the elevator with them. "How are you?"

She intentionally stepped closer to him. The smell of his aftershave filled the whole car. Reaching out, she put a hand on his forearm. He let go of the car railing and turned his palm so he could grip her forearm like she gripped his. She wished he'd pull her closer, but he did not.

"I'm great," he said softly, rubbing a thumb on her wrist. "You look really nice today. And you smell good."

In reflex, she glanced down at her bright green pantsuit that she'd paired with a white top and a jade-green necklace. "Thanks." She shifted her feet and looked at her white heels. "After Memorial Day. Your mom would approve of the white shoes."

His smile softened his entire face. "Yes, she would."

When the elevator dinged, he let go of her and straightened. "Is it too much to hope that you're headed up to see me?" The doors silently slid open and they stepped out of the car. She saw the owner in the conference room, waiting on her with the head architect and structural engineer.

"Alas, I'm not. I'm headed into conference room one. But I can come see you after. Let you know how the meeting went."

He smiled down at her and said, "That would be great. I'm going to need you to take your time and cover every detail of this meeting with me privately. Okay?" Instead of walking toward his office, he opened the conference room door for her and followed her inside. "Mr. Jordan, great to see you!"

They shook hands and Brad sat at the end of the table. "Uh," Valerie said, "I think you're going to approve of the designs I implemented into Owen's plans. Let's get started."

Brad let Valerie precede him into his office area. He noticed Sami's empty desk and realized that lunchtime had snuck up on them. He reached around her and opened his inner office door for her. As he followed her in, he shut the door behind him.

"I think he's going to approve the artist that I liked," she said, setting her tablet on the low coffee table in front of his couch. "I hope I didn't try too hard to sway him in the meeting."

He opened the mini fridge and grabbed them each a bottle of water. "It's your job to sway him to a good design. You're the one with the talent and training."

He gestured to the couch and she sat, leaning back against the cushion. He sat in the chair adjacent to her. "When I majored in architecture, I honestly thought I'd be designing buildings. I never had a concept of doing design."

"What changed?"

She pursed her lips and looked over his shoulder as if seeing a memory. "I took an interior design class in college as an elective, but it still counted toward my major. It was an amazing class, and the teacher clearly had a love for art.

It spurred the desire in me, and I started shifting my courses of study into design and colors versus engineering and structure." She looked at him again, her brown eyes the color of caramel. "I'm still an architect, of course. I could still design that building. I'd just rather color it."

Her laughter filled his office. Filled his heart. He could not help but smile in response. "At least we know it would be a pretty building."

"Exactly."

She looked at her watch. "Thanks for the water. I haveto go eat at my desk and get some more work done. Yesterday's fishing expedition took a couple of hours away from my schedule."

He raised an eyebrow. "Should I apologize?"

"Absolutely not. It was wonderful. But it is what it is." As she stood, she took three long gulps of the water. "See you later?"

He stood with her, reached for her hand before he could talk himself out of it. The startled look came into her eyes again, but this time, he paid attention and saw her fight it back, felt her muscles relax. "I'll never, ever hurt you, Val. Not ever."

Immediately, tears came to her eyes and he felt the pulse on her wrist skitter. "Do you think I don't know that?" she whispered.

He stepped closer and put a hand on her cheek. "I just needed you to hear me say it."

As she nodded, a tear fell out of her eye and burned a path over his hand. "I trust you, Brad. It has nothing to do with you."

He searched her eyes, seeing nothing but the Valerie he

knew. Finally, he nodded and let her go, stepping back and putting his hands into his pockets. "Have dinner with me tonight."

She picked up her tablet and turned to look at him. "I am not free tonight. I have plans with Sami and Calla. But I'm free tomorrow."

The initial disappointment he felt at her immediate no dissipated almost as quickly as it appeared. He picked his phone up off his desk and accessed his calendar. "Saturday?"

With a laugh, she walked to the door. "Saturday. Glad we could work that out. Pick me up at six?"

Seeing a meeting with Ken at the apartments for four, he said, "Thirty."

"Six-thirty. I'll be ready and waiting."

She walked out of the office without a backward glance.

Wishing she knew where Brad planned to take her for dinner, Valerie studied her closet and finally decided on a silver sleeveless dress. She paired it with silver heeled sandals, a blue and silver scarf around the waist like a belt, and a blue necklace and earrings. Part of her worried he planned to take her to a casual restaurant, but she thought he'd probably tell her if he'd made plans in that direction.

When he rang her doorbell, she already had her purse in hand. Relief at seeing him in a suit made her grin. "You look nice," she observed, stopping to lock the door behind her.

"I would say the same about you, but it would be an understatement. You look stunning."

She followed him to his truck and stepped back as he opened the door for her. Pleased, she continued to smile as he got into the truck and started driving. "I worried I'd overdressed. I almost talked myself out of it."

"Oh, man. I'm really glad you didn't talk yourself out of it. That could have been, um, awkward." He glanced her direction. "That color looks really good on you. Hard to keep my eyes on the road."

Heat flushed her face and raced down her neck. "I just don't even know what to say," she said softly.

"I'm not saying it to earn a response. Just stating a fact."

He drove them into the downtown area, pulling up to a valet outside the golden awning of the Atlanta Downtown Viscolli Grand Hotel. Valerie looked up and saw the rooftop restaurant. "I've read about this. How did you score reservations? Are you friends with the manager? Is this a Calla hookup?"

"No. The owner."

"The owner? Of this place?"

As he opened her door, he said, "About a hundred years ago, I helped build it. It took a call to the owner and the table was ours."

She laughed as they walked into the hotel lobby. Green Italian marble floors, black leather furniture, gleaming brass accents, and rich oriental rugs all screamed old-school elegance and sophistication. They walked straight to the elevators and a forest green uniformed attendant pressed the call button for them and held his keycard over a magnetic reader until it lit up green. "Twentieth floor, Mr. Dixon."

When the doors shut, she looked at him with mirth. "Mr.

Dixon, eh? How did he know your name?"

"I imagine he was told I'd be coming. We worked closely with the staff renovating the hotel and building the restaurant. It wouldn't take much for them to know to look for me or recognize me when they saw me. That, and I think they have some clandestine system here with the valet and the concierge and whatnot."

The elevator went straight to the top without stopping, probably as a result of the attendant swiping his card on the ground floor. They stepped into a foyer area outside the main doors of the restaurant. As they approached the reception desk, the blond man in a tuxedo looked up and smiled. "Mr. Dixon. Welcome back to the Viscolli. It's our pleasure to serve you this evening. Your table is ready. Right this way, please."

They walked through the crowded dining room to a table for two next to the window. The *Maître D'* held the chair out for Valerie and handed her a menu. After informing them of their waiter's name, he left to return to his post.

Valerie skimmed the menu, stealing glances at Brad who had set his down to watch her. Finally, she put her menu to the side and propped her chin in her hands. "I cannot even think about what I want to eat, imagining how good everything is going to be."

"Good point. Let's simplify." He sat back in his chair. "Chicken or beef?"

"Hmmm. Beef."

"Okay. Beef or fish?"

"Oh, beef. Definitely."

He glanced briefly at the menu. "I'd recommend the

fillet. It's aged prime and so tender it will melt in your mouth. And the chef does some amazing things with sides. There's this root vegetable tartan thing that looks like a work of art."

She smiled coyly as she leaned back and crossed her arms over her chest. Trying to sound like a Dickensian waif, she said, "Please, sir, I'll leave the ordering to you. You clearly know the landscape. Do you bring all your special lady friends here to impress them?"

Brad frowned. "I've only ever had business dinners here." His expression suddenly lightened. "You're the first 'special lady' I've ever brought here."

"Really?" Valerie's tone of voice sounded more skeptical than perhaps she intended.

Brad set the menu down and captured her eyes. "You're the only special lady I've ever wanted to impress, Valerie."

Those words caused a flush to move from her chest, over her neck, and across her face. It took willpower not to fan herself.

They chatted comfortably in between service of bread, salads, dinner, and dessert. She let Brad handle ordering everything and enjoyed every bite. Even the coffee they had with dessert tasted rich and savory and gourmet to her tongue.

"I'm moving out tomorrow after church," he announced after swallowing the last bite of a plum torte.

"Into the apartment building?"

"Yeah. Plumber hooked up the shower yesterday. I've had a crew clearing out and moving furniture in all week."

"Do you need help moving?"

"No, but I'd love your company. We can get lunch after

church and then head out. Everything's already packed."

The waiter approached. "Mr. Dixon, Mrs. Westcott would like you and your guest to enjoy a complimentary dinner tonight. If there is any way we can be of service, please feel at home and enjoy our hospitality. All the amenities of the Viscolli Grand are at your disposal. Please enjoy."

His eyes widened slightly before he laughed. "Well, that is very generous of her. Please convey my thanks."

The waiter didn't reply, he just made a little bow and retreated.

Valerie leaned forward. "And exactly who is Mrs. Westcott? A special lady friend you neglected to mention, perhaps?"

The question took Brad by surprise and a little bark of laughter escaped before he explained, "Not quite. Madeline Viscolli Westcott. Owner of the hotel. She was learning the ropes when we broke ground, and this was her first major project. I gave her some advice that saved her a boatload of money."

"A boatload of money that would have been yours," Valerie remarked.

He shrugged. "Irrelevant. It was the right thing to do."

Her heart swelled with emotion that she didn't know how to identify. Brad Dixon was a good man. He didn't just pretend to be a good man to impress people around him. Like his father, his goodness went into his soul and radiated out.

Without thinking about it or hesitating, she reached out and covered one of his hands with both hers. "You're a good man, Bradford Dixon," she said softly. "It makes me very proud to be with you tonight."

He turned his hand so their palms touched. He lifted their joined hands and pressed a kiss to the back of hers. Without remarking on her comment, he stood, retrieved his wallet, and set a large bill on the table. "Ready?"

He helped her to her feet and kept a hold of her hand as they walked through the restaurant, lacing his fingers with hers. They shared the elevator down with another couple, and she stepped closer to him until the side of her body pressed against his, their hands clasped and resting on the small of her back. Even in heels, her head barely came to his shoulder. She imagined how easily she could just lean into him and rest her head against his arm.

They drove back to her house in comfortable silence. Valerie's mind wandered until she asked, "Where is the apartment?"

"About two miles from your house." He gave her quick directions.

"I'll go home after church and change first," she said. He pulled into her driveway and put the truck into park. "Would you like to come in?"

She turned to face him and could see the intensity in his eyes as he looked at her. "Yes, but I won't," he said, his voice deep. "I'll walk you to the door, though. If you'll condescend to let me, that is. I know you're a big girl now and all."

Valerie took the teasing on the chin and waited while he opened her door. He kept a hand on the small of her back as he walked her up her drive. She pulled her keys and cell phone out of her purse and turned to look at him. "Thank you for an amazing meal and a wonderful night."

"We should be thanking Mrs. Westcott, apparently." He

smiled and leaned his shoulder against the brick wall. "I'll have to call her in the morning."

Unlocking the door, she stepped inside and turned to face him. Inside the threshold, and in her heels, she could almost look him in the eye. "Goodnight, Bradford Dixon," she said.

"Goodnight, Valerie Flynn." He straightened and slipped his hands into his pockets. "Go ahead and lock up. I'll wait."

Her breath hitched in her throat, partially in embarrassment that he would have guessed her compulsions, partially in relief because they'd come home in the dark and it made it worse. "Thank you."

She didn't elaborate and he apparently didn't need her to, because he only nodded and kept standing there. She knew he'd see the lights go on in each room, but she worked through her shame about it and did the thorough house sweep. About a minute later, she heard his truck engine start and watched the lights flash against her hall wall as he backed out of the driveway.

Valerie got out of her car in the parking lot of the apartment building. She recognized Brad's truck backed up to the building marked "office," and saw a brand-new truck parked next to it that she assumed belonged to Ken.

She looked up at the sky. The sunny spring weather had started to surrender to the heat of summer, and the heat of summer brought afternoon thunderstorms to northern Georgia. The clouds looked like a dark bruise against the summer sky, and a cool breeze stirred the muggy air.

She went through the open door and into what used to serve as the office of the apartment complex. It took a moment for her eyes to adjust. A brown leather couch, a recliner, and a square coffee table sat on the orange shag carpet. Where the carpet ended, orange ceramic tile began. Her interior designer self comically recoiled at the décor.

Jon stood on a stepladder and lifted one end of a large flat-screen television onto a brace on the wall while someone she did not know lifted the other end. He glanced her way and lifted his chin in a greeting but did not speak. Instead, he offered instruction to the person helping.

She could smell freshly cut wood, stale carpet, and a mildly unpleasant odor of mildew. She wandered through the room. A cooktop leaned against the back wall next to a kitchen sink and a rolling cart that held a microwave.

A hallway with a bare plywood floor branched off to her right. As she walked down the hall, she saw a bathroom on the right. Next to the bare shower, she saw a box of towels. A few feet ahead, she saw a doorway to her right and glanced in. A metal bed frame held a bare mattress and box springs. A sink and mirror sat in the corner next to a dresser. Two suitcases and two big moving boxes sat on the floor next to the bed.

Following the sound of voices, she went to the last room on the right. There she found Ken and Brad. Brad stood on a stepladder and fastened vertical blinds into the window frame. Ken had an open box next to the dresser and transferred clothes from the box to a drawer.

"Hey," she said, lifting a hand.

Brad glanced her way. "Hey," he said, then ducked his head and looked closely at the blinds. With a metallic click, the blinds snapped into their housing and he stepped off the ladder. "Thanks for coming."

"Happy to help. Where do you need me?"

"I have to run back to the house and grab Ken's drafting table and some tools. Do you want to help with that, or unpack here and I'll take him?"

"Wherever I can be most helpful," she said.

Ken shut the dresser drawer and pointed at the half-empty box. "Why don't you unpack? That way, Brad and I can probably be more efficient. We aren't keeping the boxes. Jon can haul them out to the recycle if you get done."

She smiled. "Sounds good."

Brad stopped next to her and bent, brushing his lips against her cheek. "Thanks for helping."

Her cheek tingled where his lips had touched. She smiled a nervous smile. "Sure."

Ken slapped Brad's shoulder. "We'll take my truck. Got to break it in."

"You're just enjoying all the gadgets."

"What gadgets?" Ken asked, mocking shocked indignation.

"'What gadgets?'" Brad repeated, assuming a mocking tone of his own. "The cab looks like mission control at NASA."

When they left, she checked the dresser, inspected the closet, and made logical assumptions about where clothes belonged. In no time, she'd emptied two boxes and a suitcase. Worn steel-toed work boots, sneakers, and one scarred pair of leather dress shoes in need of a good polish made her guess she'd just unpacked Ken.

In another box, she found toiletries in plastic bags and bedding. She set shaving accoutrement at the sink and carried shower accessories to the bathroom, then made the bed. Everything in that room unpacked, she carried the boxes to the front room and found Jon on the floor next to a speaker wiring something in the back. The man who had helped hang the television had left.

"Hey," she said, "should I break these boxes down?"

He took a screwdriver out of his mouth long enough to say, "I would save me the trouble." He gestured toward a tool bag. "Boxcutter's in there somewhere. It's blue. You done unpacking?"

"Not yet."

"Do them all at once, or I can when you're done."

Seeing the logic in that, instead of flattening the boxes, Valerie stacked them next to the couch and went into the other bedroom and started putting clothes away there, too. Here she found garment bags of suits hanging in the closet, nice leather shoes in varying shades of brown and black lining the two-tiered shoe shelf in the bottom of the closet, and dry cleaner bags of starched dress shirts.

She unpacked the suitcases, using the same organization as she had in Ken's room. She placed the walnut jewelry box of cuff links and tie tacks atop the dresser. As with Ken's, she put shaving elements at the sink and the other toiletries in the bathroom. Just as she nested the suitcases together and zipped them closed, she looked up and saw Brad in the doorway.

She straightened and wiped the sweat off her forehead. "I hope you guys are installing air conditioning."

"First thing. I have units coming for each room. I had to figure out which storage facility I'd put them in from the last job."

She carried the empty boxes out of the room, following him. Brad grabbed the boxes out of the kitchenette and tossed them toward the other boxes in the central space where Jon had already broken down a bunch of them. Jon said, "Hey. The recycle bin isn't here. It was nearly full, so they took it already. They're dropping a new one tomorrow morning. We can store this cardboard next door until then to get it out from underfoot."

Brad collected most of the torn down cardboard and carried it out like a giant sandwich. Valerie collected the remainder and followed him out. They left the office and stepped outside.

The wind had picked up and the cool breeze felt nice. Brad stopped at the unit next door to the office and pulled a key out of his pocket to unlock it. Without going in, he tossed the boxes in his hands inside then took hers and tossed them in also. Then he shut the door and locked it. "There," he said with a smile. "All put away."

She watched Ken and Jon carry tools into another unit. Brad gestured in that direction. "We need to get the truck unloaded before this rain hits."

"Is everything going in that unit?"

"Yes." He stopped at the cab and reached inside, grabbing a pair of tan leather work gloves which he held out to her. "Put these on."

The extra-large gloves swallowed her hands but protected her from the dirt and grime on some of the tools. They carried saws, drills, tables, sawhorses, and boxes of tools from the truck to the unit. As Ken shut the tailgate, the first drops of rain fell, and they all rushed back into the office converted into an apartment.

"Thanks, guys, for helping." Ken went to the sink in the kitchen and washed his hands. "Brad and I would still be unpacking the first load."

"I hooked the television up to the router," Jon said. "Your WIFI password is on a sticky note on the router."

"Perfect." Brad shook Jon's hand. "You available to come to a meeting Wednesday morning?"

Jon's eyes narrowed. "What's up? Your voice sounds weird."

Brad sighed. "Got to do what I got to do. We have to let Mitch Conway go."

Jon whistled under his breath and took his baseball cap off. "That's not going to go well."

"No. Nothing about it will go well. I could use the backup."

"You want me to be you?"

Valerie didn't understand what they were talking about, but the excited look on Jon's face made her start to laugh. Because of the serious expression on Brad's face, she covered her mouth and coughed instead. Brad said, "No. It's my thing. I just need a wingman."

Jon pulled his phone out of the cargo pocket of his shorts and swiped up. "What time? Let me check my schedule."

They hashed out details then Brad looked at Valerie. "We're done with the moving in."

She looked at her watch. She had enough daylight left to go to the grocery store so she could spend the evening meal prepping. "Okay. I need to go to the grocery store."

"I do, too. I'll follow you."

Knowing she'd have company in the store lifted her spirits. "Okay." She told him which store in case they got separated and told Jon and Ken goodbye.

"I'll text you a list for me," Ken said as he dried his hands.

"We need coffee, but we forgot to grab the coffee maker from the house."

Jon pulled his keys from his pocket. "I'll bring it to work tomorrow. Save you the trip."

"Thanks."

Valerie dashed through the rain to her car. When she shut the door, she pulled some tissue out of her purse and used it to dab at the raindrops on her face. Since Brad knew her destination, she didn't worry about waiting for him. Instead, she drove the mile and a half to the large shopping center nearest her house. The rain hadn't even pretended to let up when she pulled into a parking space, so she got her umbrella out of the back seat and used it for cover as she dashed into the store. After getting a cart, she waited by the door until she saw Brad coming in. She shivered a bit as the air conditioning met her wet arms and legs.

"I probably should have met you at your truck with my umbrella," she said, slipping it into a plastic bag.

"After working in the non-air conditioning all afternoon, the rain feels great."

He started to grab a cart then said, "Why don't we share, and we'll split it at the register?"

"You want to share grocery carts, Brad? Is this like a grocery store date?"

He grinned. "A romantic grocery store date-date."

They began to work through the store. She explained how she'd spend the evening preparing meals that she'd freeze or refrigerate. "It saves eating out all the time. Healthier, cheaper."

"Great idea."

"I did it in high school. Your mom actually helped me

menu plan with it and set up the system."

He frowned. "I don't think she did that for us."

"Of course not. She didn't work."

"She had triplet boys. I think she'd object to the notion that she didn't work."

With a laugh, Valerie said, "She didn't leave the home so she could spend time in the kitchen every day. You know what I mean."

"I do. And I'm very grateful that mom worked as a homemaker. I know dad is, too." He winked at her and they finished their shopping in the produce aisle. She contemplated some fresh summer squash while Brad filled a bag with green apples.

"Valerie?"

Hearing her name, she glanced up and spotted an intern from work. "Oh, hi, Donna."

Brad set the apples in the cart and touched Valerie on the back of her arm. She glanced at him. "Have you met Donna? She's an intern in the engineering department."

"I have not had the pleasure."

Donna's face turned red and she stuttered, "Hi, Mr. Dixon."

"Nice to meet you, Donna." He looked at Valerie. "Done?"

"Let me just grab some zucchini." She lifted her hand. "See you tomorrow, Donna."

"Sure thing, Valerie."

She slipped four zucchinis into a produce bag and caught Donna staring at her from the other side of the produce department. She looked up at Brad. "I have a feeling we're going to be the source of some rumors."

He narrowed his eyes at her. "How so?"

"Well," she said on a breath, "Donna is in NAWIC with us, and I've noticed she is prone to gossip."

He winked down at her. "Shall I kiss you? Make the gossip really juicy?"

Valerie gasped and laughed. "I will not have our first kiss be in the produce department of a grocery store."

He slipped an arm around her waist and grinned. "Oh? Is that so? But this is a romantic grocery store date-date."

Still laughing, she slapped a hand onto his chest. "Absolutely sure."

With a mock sigh, he let her go. "Fine. Apparently, you get to dictate where our first kiss will be. I guess I should cling to the idea that there will at least be a first kiss and let that tide me over."

"Such drama." She gripped the handle of the cart. "All set?"

"Yep."

"I'll make it up to you by making you some zucchini bread."

He casually put his hand on her lower back as they walked to the checkout. "See, here you are speaking my language. It's no wonder you so consume my thoughts."

Valerie tossed her empty yogurt container in the break room trash and went into the bathroom adjacent to the break room. She heard a couple of women come into the room a few minutes later. She exited the stall just as they went in.

"I'm telling you, Diane, I saw them together myself. Plus, someone else saw them together at that Memorial Day picnic we weren't invited to."

Valerie froze in the middle of washing her hands. She knew, without a doubt, that this unknown woman spoke of her and Brad. Unable to ignore the impulse, she stayed by the sink instead of leaving.

"Who is she? I'm not putting a face with the name."

"The new black architect chick. Don't you remember? Something happened to her when she worked for the Dixons in Savannah. There's been a lot of hush-hush conversation about it."

"Oh, I think I know who you're talking about." The toilet flushed and she could barely hear the sound of the metal lock sliding over the rushing water. "Her? Seriously? What makes her Dixon material?"

"Sounds uppity for sure. Social climber."

The stall opened and the file clerk receptionist, Diane, came out adjusting her belt. Valerie stood with her back to the sink, arms crossed over her chest and legs crossed at the ankles, giving the air of nonchalance. Diane had the courtesy to freeze and turn red. However, she did not say another word. Valerie raised an eyebrow and waited while Donna continued the conversation.

"Must be something. No one's ever been able to get a Dixon to look twice. I'm not sure which one she was with, but it was one of the brothers for sure. Probably Jon. Rumor has it he's a little wild."

She came out of the stall and froze when she saw Valerie. For several seconds, they just stared at each other. Finally, Valerie pushed away from the sink and said, "I was actually socially climbing up Brad." When their eyes widened, she nodded and said, "Ladies."

Valerie left the bathroom keeping her footsteps purposeful and slow. She calmly headed straight to the elevator, praying she could maintain the cool composure as long as she needed to. When she pushed the button for the executive floor, she wondered if she needed to see Brad or Sami. Honestly, anyone who didn't hate her would do.

By the time she made it into Sami's office, the panic attack had started. Her heart pounded and the edges of her vision had blackened so she could barely see in front of her. Every breath felt like it contained zero oxygen, and her stomach rolled with nausea. Sami wasn't at her desk, so she burst into Brad's office.

Phillip sat in the chair in front of Brad's desk, and they both looked up sharply when she burst in. Before she could speak, Brad had crossed the room and had her in his arms. "What happened?" he demanded.

The words could barely come out. Every word burned her throat and she thought she might throw up or pass out, neither of which appealed to her. Somehow, she told him. When she got to the words "black architect chick," Phillip demanded names.

"I only know first names. Donna, an intern in engineering, and Diane from the file room."

Brad helped her to the couch. Before sitting next to her, he got a bottle of water out of the mini fridge and opened it for her. The cold water shocked her dry mouth.

She knew Phillip had picked up the desk phone to call someone, but she didn't know who and couldn't make out what he said through the roaring in her ears. She looked up at Brad. "I don't know if I can work in a place where I'm such a source of gossip again. I barely survived the last time. It was only because it was Dixon that I even stayed."

He cupped her cheek with his warm hand and wiped at a tear with his thumb. "I can't stand the thought of someone hurting you this way, but the idea that you would stop whatever is happening between us because of catty women gossiping doesn't resonate well with me, either." His touch was gentle, his words soft, but his eyes stormed with emotion. Fury, concern, care. "It should bother you that they think so low of you."

Phillip walked toward them. "I have HR coming to my office. You want in?"

"No. Do whatever you can." He didn't break eye contact with Valerie while he spoke.

"What are you going to do?" Valerie demanded, pushing away from Brad and standing.

"That's what I'm going to find out." He put a hand on the door handle.

Brad speculated, "Chances are good that there's absolutely nothing we can do outside of a first written warning and some mandatory retraining on our company policies. But they'll know they overstepped, regardless."

Phillip said, "Doesn't apply to the intern. There are dozens of interns waiting in the wings. She can go back to school with a letter to the dean for all I care."

"Uncle Phillip," Valerie said on a sigh, but Brad held up a hand.

"Let him protect you." He put both hands on her shoulders. "Be thankful I'm not going with him. If I did, I might have to take some retraining under the supervision of

HR."

She leaned forward and put her forehead on his chest. His arms came around her and she felt so very safe. She closed her eyes and took a deep breath through her nose, feeling better, less panicky, more in control. Finally, she gripped the collar of his suit jacket and lifted her head. He looked down at her, his eyes less stormy, calmer too. Without a word, he cupped her cheeks with both hands and lowered his mouth. When he hesitated, she tightened her grip and pulled him to her as she raised up on her toes to meet his mouth.

For weeks she had wondered what kissing Brad would feel like, but nothing she imagined even came close. The second their lips met the remaining traces of the panic attack slipped away.

His lips felt warm, soft, and as she took a deep breath through her nose, the smell of his aftershave filled her senses. She placed a hand on his cheek, feeling the smooth skin under her palm, and he pulled her even closer, deepening the kiss as she wrapped an arm around his neck and stood on her toes. She felt like she could just stay like this forever, letting Brad consume her every thought, her head spinning, her heart pounding, her toes curling. She felt his hand on the back of her head, gripping her hair and holding her steady as he kissed her and kissed her.

She didn't know who ended the kiss. It just gradually became gentler, until he lifted his mouth and brushed it over her cheeks, her eyes, her forehead, then wrapped his arms around her again. How long they stood there, she didn't know. But she listened against his thick chest as his heartbeat slowed from fast and furious to steady and strong.

Finally, she stepped back and broke the contact with him. She ran her hands down the sides of her dress and looked at him. He slipped his hands into his pockets and stared at her without speaking.

"Well," she said on a breath, "I think that's way better than it would have been in the grocery store."

He chuckled softly and smiled. "You're probably wrong. I think it would have been amazing anywhere."

"I guess we'll never know." She crossed the office and put a hand on the door handle. "Thanks for bringing me back from the panic vortex."

"Well, as long as I'm useful."

Laughing, light, walking on air, she floated from his office and went back to work.

Brad took a deep breath and steeled himself to go into the meeting. They had already had one HR issue today. He did not look forward to the coming confrontation. Jon looked at him with a raised eyebrow. "Ready?"

"As ever, I guess," he said under his breath, and opened the conference room door.

Mitch Conway sat at the head of the conference table. A video of backhoes digging up dirt played on the screen behind him. Six men sat around the table, copies of a scheduling report in front of them.

When Brad and Jon entered, everyone looked up, surprised. Mitch scowled and said, "Can I help you, gentlemen?"

Brad stood at the end of the table, facing Mitch. Jon sat down to his right. "I have been going over the schedule and the jobsite meeting minutes, Mitch, and I'm afraid that I can't see how you're so far behind."

He'd preloaded the computer and overrode the presentation Mitch had begun with his own. A chart appeared showing the original schedule and the current progress. "I see no weather concerns, no equipment concerns, and no true site issues. What I see is a water treatment facility outside of Lexington, Kentucky, that required the initial plumbing work for the building to be started by April first, and we're still looking at pictures of site work equipment. I'd like you to explain."

Mitch stood and faced Brad across the table. He'd worked for Dixon Contracting for seventeen years and had challenged Brad from the moment he started taking over for his father. Someone overheard him saying that the "boys" hadn't earned his respect yet. Brad had let it go until now, because historically, Mitch knew his job as a project manager and did it well. But with this Kentucky job, something obviously had happened.

A source on the site informed Brad that Mitch would show up on the site maybe three days a week, Tuesday through Thursday, and never made an appearance on a Friday or a Monday. It turned out he had been spending four-day weekends in casinos in Indiana just across the Kentucky River. Initial inquiries with the jobsite computers and a dig into Mitch's finances revealed some serious financial stress coupled with what Brad discovered were some heavy gambling debts.

Brad suspected that Mitch had cut a shady deal with the site work contractor, which allowed the contractor to overbill Dixon Contracting for extra time and resources needed on a site that didn't require extra time or resources. It caused Brad to order a full audit on all Mitch's jobs going back ten years, and he started to see a trend.

"Your daddy is the one who assigned me to this job. I suggest that if you have a problem with my management of it, then you take it up with him." He sat back down as if he'd said all Brad needed to hear.

"I'm afraid it doesn't work like that," Brad said, still standing. "I asked you a very specific question, and I won't repeat it. But you have about three seconds to give me an answer before this conversation goes where you don't want it to go."

Mitch did not stand again and sat passively still for the three seconds. Brad finally nodded. "I'm putting Edward Branson in charge of this project. Mitch, you can gather your things and meet me in security."

He surged to his feet and rushed toward Brad. "I will not take direction from some spoiled, pompous, little rich kid who thinks he has power over me just because he wears a tie!" he yelled.

When he reached Brad, he tried to grab him by the jacket front, but Brad sidestepped and performed a Tae Kwon Do move that had Mitch landing on the ground with his feet swiped out from under him. He kept a hold on the man's wrist with both hands and used it to keep him subdued.

Brad carefully placed a foot on Mitch's chest and looked up, spotting the security team he'd called to be on standby outside the glass wall of the conference room. He nodded them forward. It was then he spotted Valerie standing with a couple other people who had gathered when the commotion started.

As soon as the security team had secured Mitch and escorted him down to the security office where they would wait for the police, Brad and Jon moved to the head of the table. "If anyone else has a problem with my authority over this company, I invite you to voice your concerns now." He paused for a minute. "Nothing? Now is the time to say something."

Straightening his jacket and the cuffs of his shirt, he sat at the head of the table. He ignored the slight tremble in his fingers knowing that adrenaline caused it. No one moved nor spoke. After a brief pause, Brad nodded and said, "I'm putting Edward Branson in charge of this project. He's spent the week reviewing what's going on and is ready to answer any questions any of you may have. We will be replacing the site work contractor and we will be fast-tracking from this point forward. Ed will let me know if we have to crash the project to meet our deadlines, but make no mistake gentlemen, we are going to meet our deadlines from this moment on."

He looked up as the conference room door opened and Ed Branson ambled inside. "Ed, I believe you know everyone."

Valerie sat in her desk chair and stared at the screen in front of her. She didn't see the layout of a hospital atrium. Instead, she saw how effortlessly and easily Brad had restrained an angry man. She knew he'd studied martial arts his entire childhood and adolescence. She had no idea he would ever have a reason to put that study into use in the real world.

The idea that he had done it without flinching, without hesitating, without breaking a sweat. She had witnessed it. After security removed Mitch, Brad just went on with business as usual just as cool as a cucumber. No regrets? No remorse? What did that mean?

A sharp rapping sound startled her and broke her out of her thoughts. "Come in," she called, picking up a pen to make it look like she hadn't actually sat here for the last twenty minutes staring into space.

When Brad walked into the office, her heart leaped almost painfully in her chest. Sweat broke out on her forehead and she stammered as she stood up. "B-brad," she said, then took a sip from her water and started over. "Hi, Brad."

He walked to her desk and slipped his hands into his pockets. "Valerie," he said softly, "tell me what's going on in your mind. What are you thinking about right this second?"

"I'm just working on the hospital in—"

"I didn't ask what you're working on." His voice had taken a hard edge to it. He took a step closer and his pants leg brushed against the edge of the desk. "I asked what is going on in your mind. Please answer the question I asked you."

Fear clouded her vision. She recognized the flight response and closed her eyes, putting a hand on her forehead. "I saw you...." Lowering her hand and opening her eyes, she said again, "I saw you and you didn't even hesitate.

And he hit the ground like he weighed nothing. How could you do that so easily?"

"The truth is, Valerie, that I knew he would attack me. I'd seen him do it to another man once on a job site when I was a teenager. I saw him lose his temper another time and beat a board into the ground until it broke in half. His wife left him a long time ago and they aren't on speaking terms. I suspect I know why."

She processed that information. "Still, you—"

"Planned for it," he said every syllable very crisply. "I practiced with Jon this morning before work. I utilized my training, pulled my black belt memory forward, and practiced a couple scenarios that ended up without anyone seriously hurt." He tapped the top of her desk as if making a point. "You realize security was all around that conference room. That was also at my direction. I'd planned for all of it."

Everything came together clearly for her. "Oh," she said, feeling foolish, relaxing so rapidly that her neck muscles ached. "Oh."

"Yeah. Oh." He turned to leave and turned back around. "You know what? I have never hurt another human being in my life with any intention. This morning was self-defense, and I restrained him without hurting him. You saw me do it, but I could tell by the look in your eyes that you assigned all sorts of uncharitable motives to my actions and my intent."

He turned again and walked toward the door. "Brad!" He turned around and saw her rushing toward him. "I'm sorry."

"You're sorry?" He closed his eyes and she saw the anger cross his face. When he opened them again, he glared at her. "How many more times in your life are you going to apologize to me?" He put his hand on the doorknob. "I don't want sorry, Valerie. I want you to know deep in your soul that you do not have to be afraid of me. I want you never to assume I'm about to beat you up or hurt you in any way. Because, the truth is, I'd kill anyone who tried. I want you to realize that I have loved you from the moment I had the maturity to process those emotions, and that if you had only understood that at the time, none of this would have had to happen. And it kills me that it did. It kills me inside. But I am not Tyrone, and I would never, ever, hurt you physically, or emotionally, or spiritually."

He opened the door to leave but hesitated and shut it again. "When you believe that, you can come find me. Until then, I cannot deal with you looking at me in fear. I won't."

When he left, she leaned her shoulder against the closed door and covered her eyes with her hand, trying desperately to hold back the flood of tears. How could she stop reacting? Where would that come from?

He had said he loved her and if she had realized it, none of it would have happened? It seemed unfair to put that on her. Why hadn't he stepped up and told her how he felt at the time? How could he mean what he said? Did he really feel that way?

Of course, he didn't. He just dramatically assigned current adult emotions to a childhood memory of fondness brought on by proximity. If he'd loved her like that, she would have known. She so desperately had wanted him to. And then what? What would that mean?

She wiped the tears from her eyes and straightened. It meant nothing. The past happened and she couldn't go back and fix it, and neither could he. How dare he say something like that?

She stormed back to her desk and plopped down into the chair. She would not go find him. He could just keep his blame and accusations to himself and come to her when he was ready to apologize.

Brad swung the sledgehammer and felt the drywall give under the force of the blow. He pulled back and swung, again and again, making a giant hole in the wall. After about ten solid minutes of swinging, he set the hammer down and took off his safety glasses, wiping at the sweat on his face with his shoulder.

The apartment door opened, and his father came in. "Safe entry?" he joked.

"Sure. Stopping for a minute."

"Glad to see you found a useful outlet for your moping." Phillip walked over to the room plan hanging on the wall. He studied it and then turned and studied the room.

"Is that what I'm doing?" He tossed the glasses onto the floor next to the hammer and took off his work gloves. "Moping?"

"Seems like. I heard what happened with Mitch today."

"Well, of course you did. People still consider you in charge." He sounded like a bratty teenager and reigned in that attitude.

"Well," Philip said with a deep breath, "I was in charge for a long, long time. As long as I am present, it's going to be something people think. As this next year, my last year, comes up, I will be spending less time there and the transfer of power will be complete and permanent." He leaned back against the kitchen bar and crossed his feet at his ankles. "But I don't mind that you said that. You, of course, are just venting in your way. So, what happened with Mitch?"

Brad told him the story. "Jon and I had sparred in the morning to prepare for that eventuality."

"This isn't your fault, you know." Phillip sighed. "I should have done something about him a long time ago."

"It's easy not to act when you don't have anything concrete. You have a lot of employees, dad. You can only do what you can do and know what you know."

"You knew, though." He sat forward and propped his elbows on his knees. "You knew enough to know. Maybe...."

"Maybe we need to let people be people and not judge based on suspicions. I was prepared. I would have preferred to be wrong."

Philip inclined his head in an agreement. "Then we'll leave it at that." He gestured toward the hole. "And the venting? The moping? I assume it has something to do with a beautiful architect who was slandered in our little workplace today and who has occupied so many of your thoughts over the years?"

"Maybe she won't occupy them so much anymore." He walked to the bar and grabbed his bottle of water. "I should have followed my instincts before. There was a time for us, but too many things have changed."

Philip sighed. "I would reckon, son, that she has no idea what you went through. I would imagine that to her, you said goodbye at graduation and then life went on for you without a second thought of her."

"Why in the world would she think that, dad?"

"Because you never once, not even one time, told her

how you felt, did you?"

Brad opened his mouth then closed it again. Had he? Surely.... He sighed. "No. I just pined and wished."

"Silently."

"Silently." He drained the bottle and crushed it. "I should have said something."

"Even if it was to give her something to think about. She could have easily rejected you, of course, but at least you would have tried. Now you're angry with her for leaving you. For putting herself in harm's way. That has to stop, son. She's not at fault here. She was a victim of smooth-talking seduction by a predator, plain and simple."

His dad left not long after. Brad put the gloves back on, slipped the glasses onto his face, and picked up the sledgehammer. As he swung and broke drywall, he thought about it. He *had* harbored some anger toward her, some blame. Rather unhealthy thinking.

"God," he said between blows, "help me cleanse my mind of such contorted thoughts. I need clear thinking and logic, not emotion and blame." After a few more blows to the wall, he added, "And I need to forgive Tyrone. Like for real."

He swung, prayed, swung, prayed, and eventually, exhausted, fell into his new bed in his new room, his shoulders and arms aching from the exertion, his mind exhausted from the prayers. He closed his eyes and felt the world spinning seconds before he fell asleep.

Valerie sat across from Calla in the empty restaurant. She copied her friend's movements and folded the napkin in front of her to her specifications then put it in the stack next to her. Through the kitchen door, she could hear voices, occasional banging, and rattling. The sharp smell of garlic combined with a sweet caramel smell that confused her brain.

"Did he really just flatten the man?" Calla stopped folding and looked at Valerie. She nudged her glasses back up her face.

"It was fascinating. I've seen him do it before, of course, practicing with his brothers when we were younger. But you never think that kind of thing would happen in the real world. It was really...."

Calla grinned. "Exhilarating?"

With a chuckle, Valerie picked up another napkin. "I'm sure it should have been to any normal red-blooded woman. However, I reacted badly."

For a few moments, Calla didn't speak. Finally, she said, "So you removed that other guy from the picture and in your mind substituted yourself. Suddenly, you saw how easily Mr. Di—I mean, Brad—could hurt you."

She had simplified it, of course, but that was basically it. "Right." She sighed and slapped a newly folded napkin onto the pile. "And he knew it."

Calla leaned forward and put a hand on her forearm. "Do you honestly think he ever would? I mean, really? Do you even think he has it in him?"

Valerie opened her mouth to deny it immediately, then shut it again. What did she think? "I think that I learned how powerless I actually am. It's not that I think he would or that he wants to. It's how powerless I am to stop him if he does."

Calla sat back and stared at her. Finally, she said, "I don't have your experience. It's not up to me to say what you should or shouldn't think or feel. But I will tell you that assigning someone else's evil to another person isn't going to help you. There will come a time when you believe that, or else you're going to just be scared and paranoid the rest of your life."

Thoughts crashed against each other in her mind. She couldn't focus on one thing to think about. She quit trying to act busy with her hands and sat back in her chair, crossing her arms over her chest defensively. "I don't want to think that way," she said quietly. Hot tears pricked her eyes. "I want to be able to relax and enjoy life. I don't seek out the thoughts."

Calla immediately stood and rushed to her side of the table. "Oh, honey, I didn't mean it that way." She sat in the chair next to her and angled her body toward her, putting an arm over the back of her chair. "I wasn't criticizing. But, in all these years of therapy you've had, you've never turned to God with it. Maybe if you relax, open up to Him, you'll find peace that will settle into your soul. That's when you will be able to love and be loved without fear."

She had never tried any counseling that would bring her closer to God. Did it work that way? Did a personal connection exist that would help heal her? She thought about her mother's journals, about her certainty through everything in life that God talked to her and that He cared about what happened to her. Could she find that, too? How did one go about doing that?

"Maybe you're right. It seems like I remember something Auntie Rose gave me, some sort of support group through the church. I'll look that up and see. Maybe they can help me know how to pray and what to pray for."

"I think that's perfect." Calla put a hand on her shoulder. "In the meantime, I'm here if you need me. So is Sami."

Valerie smiled. "Thank you."

Following the classroom signs, Valerie made her way down the church hallway until she came to the right classroom. Nerves danced in her stomach, and she put her hand flat against them as if to quiet them. Letting out a deep breath, she opened the door and stepped inside.

Valerie didn't know what she expected. Her last experience with a support group for survivors of domestic abuse had taken place in a YMCA community room. Everyone sat in a circle in metal chairs and uncomfortably stared at each other, while a couple people took turns talking about how bad they'd had it. At the time, she felt like it was a giant pity party and a huge waste of her time.

When she walked into this classroom, though, she stopped short, thinking she'd come to the wrong room. Madison Brown and a white woman with curly dark hair stood at a snack table, taking plastic wrap and lids off brownies, veggie trays, and a cheese ball. In another part of the room, two Hispanic looking women talked and laughed, their faces happy and relaxed.

When she walked into the room, Madison left her station and approached her. "Valerie Flynn," she said warmly, "I had hoped you'd find out about us and join us."

Of all the things she imagined Madison would say, that did not approach anywhere near the top. "You did?"

Instead of shaking her hand, Madison hugged her then stepped back and turned, keeping an arm around her shoulder. She walked them over to the snacks. "Yes. When you went through what you went through, this whole church was praying for you. The day it all happened, we had a prayer vigil here for you until you came out of surgery."

They stopped at the table with the food and Madison released her, stepping away and turning to face her. "Of course, we don't know everything that happened. No one does, and Buddy keeps mostly to himself. But I know some of it. I've seen you attending regularly the last few weeks and wanted to invite you but didn't know how to approach you properly."

"Wow. I, uh, I'm a little overwhelmed by that." The thought that the entire church had done that first embarrassed her then provided her with an unexpected sense of security and belonging.

"I imagine you are." She gestured at the woman who currently unwrapped a stack of small dessert plates. "Crystal, this is Valerie. Crystal is my right-hand with this group. I could not do it without her."

Crystal put the plates down and put out her hand. "Valerie, welcome." Her eyebrows drew together. "Flynn. Are you related to Buddy?"

"Yes. I'm his niece." She looked toward the door as an older black woman came in. "It's nice to meet you, too," she said, turning her attention back to Crystal.

Madison gestured to the group across the room. "We'll all have a chance to get to know each other later. I just want you to feel comfortable here. We have an agreement that nothing that is said here is ever repeated, even to our significant others. It is a safe room." She looked at her watch. "We'll give it another few minutes. We're missing about three regulars."

Twenty minutes later, Valerie sat in a comfortable wingback chair, a steaming cup of tea in her hand, a plate of strawberries and grapes on the little table next to her. She felt less anxious, more relaxed, and, strangely, safe. Madison had opened them up with prayer, everyone went around the room and introduced themselves, and then Madison started talking.

Valerie listened to every word with rapt attention as

Madison talked about the abusive boyfriend in college who had broken her jaw while sexually assaulting her. She talked about going back to him even as she struggled to nourish herself with a jaw wired shut, crying for him to forgive her, putting herself in jeopardy without ever considering leaving.

So many things she said, so many trigger words, resonated with Valerie. Tears fell down her face as Madison related the experience of killing an unborn child to make him happy then waking up one morning as if from a dream and realizing she had nothing right or good or acceptable about her current circumstances.

"It's easy to sit back on the outside and see what was wrong. I didn't even know the depths of hell I'd entered until I took myself out of it and went home to my parents." Madison looked each woman in the eye. "I went to doctors and therapists and groups and nothing fixed me. Not until I let go and forgave myself, forgave him, and let God have His way in my heart. That's why we're here tonight, sisters, so that we can help each other, pray for each other, and bring each one of us to a place where God fills even those dark places inside of us that are closed off to Him because we're ashamed, or scared, or afraid to let go of that darkness."

She tapped a finger on her chest in the spot over her heart. "I not only had to face God about my circumstances, but the choice I made to end the life of an innocent child He had started to knit in my womb. And you know what?" A tear slid down her cheek. "He forgave me, He loves me, and He wiped that slate clean. Now I have my beautiful Miriam, and every time I look in her face, I feel His love of me as my Father, and I know that the depth of forgiveness I sought actually exists."

Silence settled over the room for a few moments, then one of the women sitting next to Valerie spoke. "I don't know how to get beyond the end. I got out. I got help. But my mind won't let me go. I think about the years lost and the relationships I let fade all in the name of trying to make a man who hated himself and hated me love me." A sob ripped from her chest. "How do I make that go away?"

Oh, how much she knew what this woman felt and thought and feared! Valerie could not stop the tears from falling from her eyes. Madison walked over to the woman and knelt next to her chair. "You can't do anything except forgive yourself, forgive him, and turn to God. There are no wasted years. There are no wasted relationships. God's word tells us that He'll take even the bad things and make them good. His love is infallible. When you are able to trust Him enough to accept that love, then you will start to feel His work inside of you."

She stood and walked over to a whiteboard. "I'm going to go over some verses with you that will help all of us see what I'm talking about."

Valerie reached into her purse and pulled out her Bible. She'd had a feeling she would need it tonight. Using her napkin, she dried her face and her eyes and opened the Bible to the book of Romans, prepared to hear every word Madison spoke.

An hour later, she stood and tossed her empty plate and cup into the trash can. She felt energized but at the same time sad to see the meeting end. She walked up to Madison. "Thank you for sharing your story," she said.

"I try to about once a year. I encourage everyone to

share, but not all of us are as comfortable baring the depths of our souls to a group of women they may or may not know." She laughed, obviously teasing. "Just know that if you ever need a friend, someone who understands, I'm here."

"I appreciate that." She slipped her purse over her shoulder. "I am trying to find a way to trust in a relationship. I think you gave me some good tools and a starting point."

Madison put a hand on her shoulder. "And a group that I hope you will return to."

She nodded. "It is definitely on my schedule. I'll see you Sunday."

Valerie stood on the gazebo platform and watched a fat bumblebee crawl through a magnolia bloom. The sound of footsteps on the path made her tense, and she turned. When she saw Brad, a nervous butterfly started dancing in her stomach replacing her fearful tension.

"Permission to come aboard?" he asked gently.

Despite her feelings about him right now, she said, "Aye," which was far from what she wanted to say. However, since he asked her to meet him, she thought she ought to let him, "come aboard."

"Thanks for coming over."

He wore a pair of khaki shorts and a black golf-style T-shirt with the red Dixon Brothers Contracting logo over the pocket. She hadn't seen him in several days. His drawn face looked tired, with dark circles under his eyes. Out of character, his hair looked shaggy and he needed a shave.

"I wanted to hear what you had to say," she said coolly. She gingerly lowered herself to the bench. Her hip ached today, which made her think some summer storm system bore down on them.

"My dad came and talked to me the other night and made me realize something."

"Oh?" She bit her tongue on words like, "That you've been a jerk? That you've blamed me for what happened." Saying something like that would not make this planned meeting end any sooner.

"Yeah." He walked over to the bench next to her and stood on it. Looking up, she watched as he lifted his arms and jumped, grabbing the beam above him. With apparent ease, he pulled himself up and grabbed something from on top of it. He swung down with a loud thud, then hopped off the bench. When he handed her the box, she gasped.

"Our dreams and desires box," she whispered, examining the metal tin, noting the rust on the edges where the lid met the box. She looked up at him, and he sat next to her but did not touch her. "We're supposed to wait until we're thirty to open this."

"I think we've waited long enough," he said. "Go ahead."

She pried open the lid and rust dusted her lap and coated her hands. Reaching in, she pulled out her envelope, trying to remember what she'd written. The seal easily came loose on the envelope.

She cleared her throat and read out loud.

"I would like to come back and live at the castle. I want to stay and hate that Buddy is moving us away. So, I'm going to go to college, become an architect, and move back into our cottage. By thirty, if I'm not married to Brad, I hope I'm married to a man who loves me and who doesn't mind that my best friends are three identical men, because they'll always be a part of my life."

Her breath hitched and tears came to her eyes. "How had I forgotten this so thoroughly?"

"If you're not married to Brad?" He cleared his throat. "I never knew you felt that way, Val."

Regret warred with embarrassment. "I never dreamed you'd feel the same way. I thought you thought of me as a sister."

He leaned close and reached around her to pull out his envelope. He handed it to her. "Please read mine."

As with hers, the gum on the envelope had long given up its stickiness. She pulled out the single notebook paper and a photo. She looked at the photo first—a picture of Brad and her sitting together at Thanksgiving dinner. When Rosaline had prompted them for the picture, Brad had put his arm around her chair and leaned close to her.

Valerie's hands began to tremble as she unfolded the paper. She cleared her throat and read Brad's neat handwriting.

"My hopes and dreams: to marry Valerie Flynn and love her every minute of my life while we live in the cottage on the estate so our children can grow up surrounded by our family. I dream of a day when skin color means nothing, especially because that's why Buddy is moving her away from us. One day, diversity won't be a word that is used build barriers and rip people apart. I love Valerie, and one day she'll see it and love me, too."

With careful movements, she folded the paper and slipped it back into the envelope. Brad sat down next to her.

"Dad reminded me that despite my longing, my deepest desires, my biggest hopes, I never once told you. I sat back and just hoped you'd notice." He paused and she looked at him. The storm in his eyes made her breath hitch.

"You were the only woman I ever loved. I loved you so much, but I wasn't very mature about it. I thought that you would just see it and feel it like I did. So, I kept quiet and expected you to just come to your senses someday."

He shook his head. "That was stupid. And I'm sorry. And I'm sorry that you left for college without a word from me. That's my fault, too. At the time I thought if it was meant to be, you'd just come to me. Rather passive of me."

Her mind swirled. How did she process this? "What would have happened if one of us had just said something?" She clutched both letters, intending to examine them when her mind stopped whirling. "I have to go."

When she stood, he reached out and took her hand. "Wait, please."

She jerked her hand away reflexively and watched as a look of resignation crossed his face. "Brad, here's the problem. I am going to react. I'm going to flinch and jump and startle. I'm going to obsessively check my environment and double-check my house and make sure all my doors are locked. I am way better than I was three or four years ago. I'll be better three or four years from now. But like my limp, I cannot help how I react to movements and actions, especially of men. You don't like it. You think I'm reacting to *you*, but I'm not."

He stood and reached for her hand again. "I think I'm starting to understand that. I apologize for taking it personally. I think part of it was worrying about what it was doing to you."

"It doesn't do anything to me. It's just reflex."

He stepped closer and ran his hands up her arms. "Then I'll learn not to worry about you over it, if you'll give me another chance to not be a presumptive jerk."

Feeling the chaos in her heart start to settle and right itself, she leaned forward and put her forehead on his chest. "Deal," she whispered as his arms came around her.

Brad stepped off the elevator and immediately saw Ian coming out of the conference room. "Hey," Brad greeted, shaking his hand. "Thought you were gone for your summer mission trip."

"Six a.m. tomorrow," Ian said, slipping his phone into his pants pocket and gesturing with the thin tube of building plans. "I should have left an hour ago, but we had something come up with the HVAC at a job. Had to stay and finish that."

"You know, there are other engineers here." Brad laughed and slapped a hand onto his shoulder. "You have a good trip. Give Calla our best."

"You bet." They walked in different directions. Brad

stopped and talked to two more people before he made it to Valerie's office.

He tapped on her door then opened it at her bidding. He found her sitting on the floor, surrounded by fabric color samples. She had a pencil between her teeth and a pad of paper in her lap. When she saw him, she smiled around the pencil.

"Miss Flynn, I was coming to see if you want to have lunch with me."

"Mr. Dixon." She slipped the pencil behind her ear and gestured at the floor. "I need a few more minutes. I'm almost at a stopping point."

He crouched next to her and fingered a swatch of cloth the color of dark mustard. "What are you doing down here on the floor?"

"In Savannah, our workspaces were so small, so to work with a bunch of samples or something, I'd go into the break room and take over the floor. I just got used to it as a way to help me really think. Something about being down here helps me isolate my thinking and draws out my creativity." She reached forward and picked up a bluish cloth and a tannish cloth. After reading the labels, she made notations in the notebook and set them to the side. She did the same thing about three more times, then smiled up at him. "All done."

She gathered all the samples into different piles and put some of them into a file envelope, then she shifted to stand. It pained him to watch her shift her body to stand up. He could tell the movement hurt her hip and back. Nothing about the movement looked fluid; nothing looked natural or graceful. Once she got to her feet, she limped to her desk and put the notebook and pencil down before she used the desk as a brace to stretch.

"Sorry. Sitting on that floor makes everything tighten up."

It bothered him, but it didn't appear to bother her, so he tried not to make a big deal of it. "Would it be better to use a conference table?"

"You'd think but it doesn't feel the same. Must just be because of the way I trained my mind. Or, I like being down in the midst it all and that's how I have to do it." When she stepped away from the desk, she moved with more ease and less obvious pain. She pulled her purse out of a desk drawer and grabbed her ID out of the computer's key-card reader. "Okay," she smiled, "ready."

He had his hand on the doorknob when she stopped and smiled up at him. "This is the third time this week we've had lunch. At this point, when we walk out that door, people are going to start talking. Are you ready for that?"

"Are you?" His smile and his glance made Valerie catch her breath. He could barely wait to have the world acknowledge them as a couple.

Her laughter filled the room. "If I weren't, I would have said no to lunch. I just don't know if you, as a Dixon whose life has been spent slightly separated from the pack, can fathom the amount of gossip that goes on in an office environment. What happened a few weeks ago in the women's bathroom was just the tip of a proverbial iceberg."

Brad thought he was ready for any interoffice gossip. Her words made him question that notion. Maybe he needed to back off and let her lead a public romance.

He ran his tongue over his teeth and smiled a little

closed-lipped smile. "Well, Valerie, while I appreciate the schooling, I can assure you that I know all I need to know about office gossip. And, the best way to kind of get ahead of that is to come to your office three days in a row and take you to lunch. I might even convince you to let me hold your hand walking back into the building. That should really bring it all home, don't you think?"

She looked up at him, processed everything he said, then threw her head back and laughed. "You are what your mama would call incorrigible."

"I am that." He held the door open and let her precede him out into the office area. "I actually have to restrain myself quite often."

Three steps into the cubicle area, Valerie stopped walking. He almost stepped into her. She pivoted and grinned up at him before quickly rising to her toes and giving him a quick kiss on the mouth. He was so surprised that he could only grab a shoulder in response. "I, too, can be incorrigible. How do you think I learned the word?"

She winked and turned back to keep walking to the elevator. His lips tingled and hungered for a longer, deeper kiss. His heartbeat roared in his ears. Brad paused for half a second before resuming his course. He fought against the desire to look behind him and see if anyone watched or whispered at their backs.

Once in the elevator, she leaned against the wall and smiled up at him. "So much for sealing it," he said.

"Better to just rip that bandage off." She laughed. "Where do you want to eat?"

Valerie leaned back against Brad's chest and laughed at the joke Ken just told. They sat in the middle of the floor of the apartment Ken and Brad currently had ripped apart for renovation. For the last three weeks, she'd brought them dinner two or three nights a week and shared it with them. Tonight, they had just finished polishing off barbecued chicken and potato salad.

"Thanks, Val," Ken said, stacking his plate into the empty picnic basket. "You're spoiling us. I'm used to Brad or Jon bringing takeout in the middle of the night. About once a week, mama takes pity on us."

"I'm happy to do it, especially because it means I can work time into seeing Brad. Apparently," she added dramatically, "he's committed to you and can't leave all the work to you, blah blah blah."

She felt Brad's chuckle before she heard it. "That's pretty much what I said."

Her phone chirped with an incoming text. She leaned forward and pulled it out of the pocket in the basket. "That's Buddy," she said. "I need to call him back."

"Of course." Standing from sitting on the floor always proved to be a chore. Brad deftly got to his feet and held a hand out to her, pulling her up. She winced and limped away, stopping to stretch her leg muscles as she dialed the phone.

"Hey, Buddy. What's up?"

"I came by, but you're not there. Are you somewhere I can meet you?"

With a frown, she said, "Sure. Do you know where Brad and Ken are renovating an apartment building?"

"Yeah. Sure. I figured that's where you were. I'll be there

in about five."

"I'll be waiting." She hung up the phone and stared at it for a moment.

At her elbow, Brad said, "Everything okay?"

He ran a hand over her back, and she had a feeling he'd be able to feel the tension in the muscles there. "No idea. He's on his way over here."

Needing something to do while she waited, she packed the basket then turned to Brad. "I know you guys have plans of what to finish before bed tonight. I'll get out of your way."

She slipped the strap of the picnic basket over her shoulder and started to walk away, but Brad grabbed her arm. "Hey," he said softly, pulling her closer, "you aren't in the way and you're more important than any self-imposed deadline we set." He cupped her cheeks with both hands and looked down at her. "If you need me, I'm here."

Her smile didn't feel natural or real. "I know. Thanks."

He gave her a gentle kiss and she wondered if she would ever get used to how right, how perfect it felt to feel his lips against hers. Her swirling thoughts vanished into a vortex of nothingness and the only thing that existed was the feel and taste and smell of him. Each time they kissed, she soared above her daily mundane existence and escaped into this feeling of complete adoration.

Their lips parted and suddenly she could breathe again, open her eyes and see again, feel the ground beneath her feet again. She sighed and grinned.

Three weeks had passed. Three weeks of stolen moments and interludes, taken as breaks in busy lives.

"Well," Buddy said from the open doorway, making the word sound like it had two syllables.

Valerie jerked away, feeling uncomfortable and a little guilty. Buddy knew about Brad. He'd seen them holding hands in church, swimming together at the Dixon estate, arms around each other while watching a family movie. She didn't know why she felt nervous. She turned toward him and smiled. "Hi."

"Valerie. I need to speak to you in private."

Without another word, he turned and walked out of the apartment. Valerie looked up at Brad and saw his worried frown. "I'll be back in a few minutes," she said, handing him the picnic basket then rushing out after Buddy.

As soon as she got outside, he held up an envelope. "This came for you today."

"To me?" With a frown, she reached for it. "Why would it come to your house?"

"I'm your emergency contact and the Georgia prison system does not have your current information."

Her stomach fell out from under her and suddenly her entire world, her entire focus became that envelope. What? Why?

With shaking hands, she took it from him and opened it. She recognized Tyrone's scrawl before she even had the letter open. A sob came out of her soul. She didn't even realize she'd made a sound until she heard it.

"Is this the place to be reading that?" Buddy asked. He put a hand on her arm, but she jerked away.

"This is fine." How she managed to voice the words around the parched mouth and tight lips amazed her. She opened the single page and had to re-read the beginning twice.

Dear Val,

I realize you don't want to hear from me. But I felt that writing you would go a long way toward your healing... and mine.

You may or may not have heard that I come up for parole in two weeks. I want you to know that I have no intention of seeking parole.

In the five years since I have been in prison, I have developed a close relationship with our chaplain. About six months ago, I came to know Christ as my personal Lord and Savior.

I know this seems strange. I was such an evil man before. But, since then, I've worked hard to make changes in my life, in my heart, in my mind. Writing you and telling you was of the utmost importance to me.

I know you won't feel safe until I am able to prove the changes inside of me. I know there is no recompense for what I did to you, but I pray that by finishing my complete sentence, you can have a little extra time of peace.

That is why I will not go before the parole board.

I pray that you can forgive me someday. There is nothing I can do or say to make up for what I have done but I beg you to forgive me.

Yours in Christ,
Tyrone

Valerie felt tears streaming down her face as she wadded the paper up in one hand and jammed it into her pocket.

"Valerie?" Buddy asked, his face drawn with worry.

"No." She shook her head. "No, no, no. No way. No."

Escape. Just run.

Whirling, she ran to her car, pulling her keys out of her pocket. She glanced over at the apartments as she drove out of the parking lot and saw Brad standing with Buddy, looking after her with a look of confusion on his face.

Brad waited in the living room while Valerie went into the kitchen to make tea. Normally, he would have followed her into the room and watched her work, but he sensed she needed some space. His unannounced arrival three minutes before had thrown her off somehow.

Buddy had convinced him to come after her. He didn't go into any detail except to say she'd received a letter that upset her. He gave her twenty minutes, and when she didn't come back to the apartments, he decided to go to her house. He used the excuse of returning her picnic basket to her.

Next to her keys, he saw the crumpled envelope and could make out the "Department of Corrections" on the return address. His stomach hurt at thoughts of what the letter might contain. Threats? Insults? Accusations?

Valerie finally came back into the room, carrying two steaming mugs. Her puffy, red-rimmed eyes told him she'd been crying. Even so, she didn't appear extra jumpy or on edge. Instead, he could detect a slow simmer of fury. Despite that, she calmly handed him his mug.

"Thanks." He took a cautious sip and tasted peppermint. "What happened?"

"No small talk with you. Just cut to the chase," she said, moving to the chair. She set her untouched cup of tea on the coffee table and sat on the edge of the chair cushion. "I got a letter."

"That's what Buddy said." He sat on the couch close enough to her that he could reach out and touch her if she needed him to. "From?"

"From Tyrone." She said his name in a whisper, then cleared her throat. "They sent the letter to Buddy's address because mine is not accessible."

"Right." They sat in silence for several minutes until Brad said, "What did the letter say?"

She leaned back into the chair and covered her eyes with the palms of her hands. "I don't even know how to start."

He reached out and put a hand on her knee. "How can I help?"

"You can explain to me how fair it is that I have to share eternity with Tyrone Baker."

Maybe he'd expected her to say something shocking, but not that. "I beg your pardon?"

She surged to her feet and crossed the room, snatching the letter up and coming back, tossing it into his lap. "Read it yourself."

With surprisingly steady hands, he pulled the single piece of paper from the envelope. It took seconds to read it, much longer to digest what it said. Then he had to process what she said about it. "Wait. You're upset because he's become a Christian? Do you think this is sincere?"

"Oh, I absolutely believe it. I have no reason to doubt it." She paced to the dining room table and back again. "It's infuriating to think that with everything he did to me, he can just," she held up her fingers and snapped them, "be redeemed."

Maybe he understood. "Valerie—"

"It's. Not. Fair." She enunciated every word.

"Maybe not to your human mind and heart. But God is a just God, and He makes it clear that—"

"Is that what you think I need to hear? More platitudes from Sunday school?" She interrupted him with a growl.

Standing, he crossed to her and made her stop her pacing by standing in her path. He put his hands on her shoulders and gently massaged the tense muscles. "Here's some truth. When I saw the scars on your back and shoulders that first time we went swimming, I was overcome with a desire to kill Tyrone. It was an overwhelming reaction and if he'd been anywhere near me, I probably wouldn't have been in control of my actions. I had to excuse myself."

Valerie's eyebrows drew together in a frown. "I asked you what had happened. You never said."

"I wasn't ready to discuss the things that happened to me because of what happened to you. That wasn't your burden to bear. I talked about it with my dad a few times and seriously prayed about it. I had to come to a place where

I could forgive him." He ran his hands from his shoulders to her upper arms and back up to her shoulders. She tensed up but he kept rubbing. "You know, the apostle Paul was a pretty hardcore anti-Christian man. He persecuted Christians and was even present and complicit in the stoning death of the disciple Stephen."

She looked up at him with tears burning in her eyes. He could feel the tension in her body radiating through his hands. He continued. "When Paul had the encounter with Christ on the road to Damascus, he tried to join the Christians and they didn't trust him. They thought he was just pretending so he could infiltrate their ranks."

"So?"

"So, Valerie, there is nothing new under the sun. You are not the only person to feel this way about a once personal enemy coming into the fold of Christ. From our perspective, it doesn't seem fair that someone who perpetrated a heinous crime against us would be allowed the same grace as what is available to us. But what we don't see, with our limited perspective, is that we are as undeserving of God's grace as anyone else. Christ died for Tyrone's sins as much as He died for yours."

She shrugged his hands off and stepped away from him. "He ruined my life."

Brad nodded. "I get why you would say that. But I don't think you're ruined forever and ever. I think if you can forgive him, you'll start to move on."

She whirled around and lifted her chin in a regal manner. "Forgive him?" She spat out. "Forgive him? How dare you—"

"I don't dare. I'm simply repeating what Christ said.

'Forgive one another, as I have forgiven you.' It's up to you to forgive Tyrone for what he did to you. It's not up to you to cling to the past and use it to justify letting memories and thoughts of him continue to dig a pit in your heart."

The tears fell down her face. The anger left her expression and a mask of hurt settled over her features. "Why are you taking his side?"

"Valerie, baby, I am only on your side. You are the most important person on the earth to me and I want so desperately to help you, to see you healed. But I'm not going to nurture your negative thoughts. I'm only ever going to tell you the truth."

"The truth, huh?" Throwing herself back into her chair, she pulled her legs up to her chest and wrapped her arms around them. "Here's some truth for you. Tyrone Baker deserves death. He does not deserve eternal life."

Brad slipped his hands into his pockets and closed his eyes, praying silently that God would give him some brilliant divine guidance into how to handle this conversation in a way that neither destroyed Valerie's faith nor their brand-new relationship.

"Do you remember the story of Jonah?" He asked quietly.

"I was raised in the same church as you."

"Do you know what kind of city Nineveh was?"

She raised her head and glared at him, finally speaking in a very sarcastic tone. "Evil?"

He nodded. "Very much so." He sat down again. "Evil as in there are historical passages that talk about the military rulers cutting off the heads of hundreds of people and stacking them into a pyramid. Forced incest. Demon worship. The works."

She waited a few heartbeats before replying. "And?"

"And God sent Jonah there to pass judgment on the city as a whole, a city of about 120,000 people, to give them a deadline for repentance. If they did not repent and turn from their evil ways, God would destroy their city as He had destroyed Sodom and Gomorrah. If they did repent, He would not destroy them."

"I told you I know the story, Brad."

"Yes, I know you do. Do you remember how it ended?"

The tears had dried on her face. "I can barely wait for you to enlighten me."

"Jonah was angry. He didn't think they deserved God's mercy. He didn't think they would accept His grace. But they did, and Jonah sat and pouted over the fact that he couldn't watch a city of 120,000 men, women, and children be destroyed. God made it clear to Jonah that he did not have the right to be angry over God's decisions."

After several moments, she said, "Are you saying to me that I don't have the right to be angry?"

"I'm saying that you had a right to be angry, hurt, scared. But now that he has repented and become a follower of Christ, you don't have the right to be angry at God for offering him the same grace you received, because you didn't deserve it any more than he did, any more than I did."

A muscle ticked in her jaw and she glared at him. Finally, she said, "I'd like you to leave now."

"I know." He stood and looked down at her. "But hear this. I love you. I have always loved you. I am only speaking to you in love and compassion, and I pray that my words have done nothing to cause you any more pain."

He left, wishing she hadn't asked him to, thankful it took her so long to ask so he could say everything that had been placed on his heart. Now he could just pray for her. Pray for her heart. Pray for her soul. And pray for the two of them.

Valerie walked into the room in the church where the support group met and found Madison alone. She had asked to meet Madison thirty minutes before the support group meeting, hoping no one else would arrive that early.

Madison approached her as she entered the room. "I'm so happy you reached out to me," she said, gesturing toward two chairs that sat facing each other.

Valerie sat down and crossed her arms over her chest. She desperately wanted to have someone on her side right now. After Brad's... what did she call it? Betrayal? That's what it felt like. After Brad's betrayal last night, she could hardly think or focus. She'd called in sick and spent the morning reading her Bible, finding the places Brad specifically brought up, seeking something other than the black and white words.

They sat and without preamble, Valerie told Madison about the letter from Tyrone and about her conversation with Brad. Madison's smile slowly faded, and she leaned forward, her hands out, palms up. Valerie uncrossed her arms and lay her hands in Madison's.

When she finished speaking, the silence stretched for perhaps the space of three calming breaths. Then her new friend spoke. "Valerie, do you know anything more about my story than what I shared your first night here?"

"Nothing specific, really. All I know is what you've shared here."

"I didn't think so." Madison closed her eyes and Valerie saw them flutter behind her shut eyelids, as if searching for exactly the right words. Finally, she opened her eyes again, took a deep breath, and quietly said, "I know it's hard for you to grasp the idea of forgiveness, but please believe me when I tell you that I understand exactly where you are right now and I also know where you can be."

Valerie frowned. "I don't know what that means."

Madison squeezed her hands, as if conveying unspoken support. "I was nineteen, my boyfriend was a really bad guy. He raped me when we first started dating. It was a violent rape. Not only did he choke me nearly to death, but he also broke my jaw by punching me with his closed fist." Madison ran a slow finger along the length of her left jawline, as if the faint scars there were still fresh.

"I told myself it was because he was drunk, and it wasn't anything else. So, when he said we had to move in together, I didn't argue. After I moved in with him, I thought he would change. He did, in a way. He drank a lot more. He smoked pot a lot more. He also ridiculed me, humiliated me, used words to break me down, and occasionally he would manhandle me and toss me around. Nothing too bad, just really rough, you know?" Madison stopped talking and searched Valerie's face, as if checking to ensure she could continue.

With a nod, she said, "About a year later, feeling spunky and brave, I told him off and he closed-fist punched me again. That's when I left."

Valerie felt her throat start to close and remembered the

feel of a fist hitting her cheek, of the pain so intense that at first nothing else existed.

"This was about two months after I'd found out I was pregnant. It was about two months after the day he drove me to an abortion clinic and told me he couldn't be with me if I had the baby. So, I didn't argue. I went inside and I murdered my unborn child."

Valerie nodded. "That's what you said before," she whispered.

"What I didn't say was that I got a knock on my door years later, about six months after I graduated college, in fact. I opened my door and thought my world was going to fall out from under me when I saw him standing there on my stoop wearing a suit and tie with a very sincere and repentant look on his face."

The gasp escaped Valerie's mouth as if she had opened the door and Tyrone stood there. "What did he want?"

Madison smiled. "He wanted to beg my forgiveness. He wanted to tell me about how he'd found Jesus. He wanted me to know that he was going to seminary. He told me the memory of how he had treated me back then—and his part in killing our unborn child—how that all haunted him night and day. He was there to grovel."

"What did you do?"

Madison checked her watch, clearly calculating how much time she had before other parishioners arrived to join the group. "Well, Valerie, to make a long story short, eventually, I married him."

Valerie immediately pulled her hands away and pushed her chair back. She stood and stepped backward, crossing her arms over her chest in defense. "No."

"It is an unusual case. The truth is I wouldn't encourage anyone to do what I did. All I know is that when I talked to him, when he talked to me, everything about him was different. The verse in Corinthians about how we are new creatures in Christ really came home to me. He apologized, I let him talk, and then I told him never to call me again. But his words stuck with me, and I couldn't get them out of my head. Eventually, I contacted him to talk some more. We talked and talked and, a year later, we had our first date."

Valerie shook her head. "How could you just let it go so easily. What he did to you, your heart, your baby—"

"Were part of that old man who had died to sin and was reborn. Don't misunderstand me, Valerie. I'm not saying that you should run off to Savannah and start a relationship with Tyrone. What I'm saying is that I know exactly how you feel right now. Exactly. And I also know exactly how betrayed you felt by Brad, and even by me right now. What happened to you matters. What he did to you matters. Forgiving him, letting it go, it isn't going to take anything away from that. But it also isn't going to condone what he did."

Her mind swirled with thoughts and words that she couldn't even give the substance. "I have to go."

"Please come back when you feel like you can talk to me again," Madison said. "I would hate to think that the choices I made would remove you from a group you need so much."

Valerie slipped her purse over her shoulder and rushed out of the classroom.

The drive to the Dixon home took no time. She didn't even have to leave the suburb. But even as she made her way up the walk, she didn't know exactly why she'd come here.

She rang the doorbell and waited several moments, but no one answered.

Not wanting to leave, she wandered around the house to the back gate. Wondering if her old code worked, she typed in the four digits of her birth day and month on the keypad. It almost surprised her when the gate swung soundlessly open. She entered Auntie Rose's haven, following the stone path that wound through the garden. She ran her fingertips over flowers, felt leaves of bushes, breathed in the pungent smell of freshly watered earth and fertilizer. When she came up to the side of the greenhouse, she saw Rosaline's shadow through the sheer walls.

"Hi, Auntie," she called.

"Valerie!" The shadow turned in her direction. "Come on in, child."

She found her by the orchids. A straw hat hung from a ribbon tied around her neck, and mud splashed her gardening apron. Rarely did she see a hair out of place on Rosaline's head, but today sweat matted the graying hair at her temples, and wisps stuck up everywhere. "I have been out here for hours today," she said, setting down her clippers. "I thought I'd repot one plant and ended up repotting a dozen." She slipped her gloves off and grinned. "So? How are you?"

"I didn't mean to bother you," Valerie said. "I just didn't know who else to talk to about this."

The smile faded from Rosaline's face and a take-charge look replaced it. "Come on, Valerie. Let's get inside. I have some freshly made iced tea. We can have some of that and sit a spell."

Valerie sat in a little metal chair near the glass doors

leading to Rosaline's sitting room. Rosaline poured both of them tall glasses of sweetened iced tea and settled back in her chair. She took a long drink from the glass, set it on the little side table, then slapped her knee. "I feel like I should have an alarm set whenever I enter the greenhouse. It's like time stops for me in there. Half the day is gone." She stared at Valerie, her gaze direct and unmoving. "Talk to me."

Valerie told her about the letter, her conversation with Brad, and her conversation with Madison. She concluded with, "I can't believe she married him."

Rosaline nodded. "I imagine you cannot. It's hard for someone without your past to believe it. It helps us who know them now not to have known them in the past. That's the thing, isn't it? If you grow up with someone who acts a certain way, you don't really trust the changes in them if something radical happens in their lives. You have a hard time letting go of what used to be. Meet someone later, and you can hear a testimony and be impressed with the changes."

Valerie took a deep breath. "What I hear from them is that I have to forgive Tyrone."

Rosaline pressed her lips together and stared at Valerie. Finally, she said, "They aren't saying that. They're saying what they know the Bible says. But I know that neither of them will judge you if forgiving him is not something you can do right now. You have to process it. You have to work it out in your heart, with God, and in your own time. So, for them to lovingly tell you the truth is not going against you in any way, it's loving you the way they ought. If either one of them had reacted with righteous indignation on your behalf and encouraged you to continue to harbor hate and fury in your heart, then they would have been doing you a disservice." She leaned forward and took Valerie's hand. "Listen to me, daughter of my heart. You do this on your time. You don't owe anyone any explanations for that."

Strangely, she felt no tears in her eyes. She felt calm, sure. "Yes, ma'am," she whispered.

Brad sat on the step outside the apartment office. They'd cut the power to run some wire, hit a snag, and now on a late June evening in Atlanta, Georgia, the 85-degree evening with a slight breeze provided a welcome relief to the suffocating heat inside. As soon as he had the energy, he'd head to his parents' house and spend the night.

He watched Valerie's car pull into the parking lot. Briefly, he thought about how sweaty and dusty his clothes were and how he wished he'd grabbed a shower before coming outside. He didn't even have time to run in and change his shirt.

As she walked toward him, he started to stand, but she waved him down. "Sit. I can see how exhausted you are.

What have you guys been doing?"

"Digging." He scooted over and she sat next to him on the step. "Then digging some more. Oh, and crawling around in the ditch we dug. That was fun."

"How do you do this after working all day?"

He drained the water bottle he held in his hands and crushed it before putting the lid back on. "It's how I work in the office all day, knowing I can get off work and come do this work. Gets me through the day."

She leaned her shoulder against him and lightly bumped him. "I guess some men go work out in the gym, and others...."

"...dig ditches and crawl in the dirt."

He watched a line of ants that led to a dead grasshopper. They sat in silence for several minutes before she asked, "Are you upset with me?"

Surprised, he turned to look at her. The solemn look on her face, the pinched lines around her mouth, everything pointed to the seriousness of her question. "Of course not. Why would you think that?"

"Because I asked you to leave."

He turned his body, shifting so he could face her completely. She did the same thing. Reaching for her hands, he said, "I cannot put myself in your shoes. I cannot understand the things that still affect you. All I can do is love you through the hard times that rear up as a result."

She cleared her throat and stared at their hands. "But you were trying to help me, and I was just getting more and more upset."

"It was upsetting for you. You thought I'd jump to your defense. Instead, I told you the truth as I know it. I get how that's going to feel like I betrayed you, even if I didn't."

"Do you feel like I disrespected you?"

Did he? Good question. "I didn't leave your home that night feeling disrespected." He raised a hand and cupped her cheek. She looked up at him, her eyes shining in the evening light. "Listen to me. I understand what happened yesterday. I'm good. As far as I am concerned, we're good."

She closed her eyes and leaned into his hand. When she opened them again, her face had grown softer, her eyes lighter. "I don't know how you can love someone as broken as me."

His heart tugged in his chest. He thought it might just fly out. "I don't think God has given me much of a choice. It's only ever been you. It will always only be you."

Valerie shifted her body closer to his and leaned forward. Their lips met in a gentle, soft kiss that had the blood rushing in his ears and his pulse pounding. When they pulled away just enough to break contact, she opened her eyes and met his. "I think it's always been you for me, too. I just didn't remember it until you reminded me."

With a soft laugh, he said, "Until I reminded you, huh?"

Smiling in return, she nodded. "Yeah. Reminded me how much I love you and how incomplete my life has been without you."

He pressed a kiss to her forehead, closing his eyes and breathing in the scent of her shampoo, then pulled her to him, wrapping his arms around her tightly. "Glad you finally see things my way," he said, joy flooding every pore.

"Hey, Brad?"

She said his name softly, almost on a sigh. "Yes?"

Putting both hands on his stomach, she pushed and

broke contact, laughing up at him. "Why don't you go shower? I'll wait right here for you."

A bark of laughter escaped him. He leaned forward and kissed her on the tip of her nose before bounding to his feet, all physical exhaustion gone and replaced with an energy that came from deep inside. "Yes, ma'am. I'll be back."

The October sun shone down onto the garden of snapdragons, bringing out the vibrant hues of color as guests sat in rows of white chairs just on the other side of the small stream. Brad stood next to Valerie inside the gazebo, clutching her hands with both his as his brothers stood behind him, dressed in gray tuxedos. Behind Valerie, Calla Jones and Sami Jones wore burgundy colored gowns with spaghetti straps and long skirts. They carried white and orange orchids lovingly grown by Rosaline.

Valerie had chosen a simple sleeveless gown, with a heart-shaped bodice and a long, straight skirt. Around her neck, she wore her mother's pearls that Buddy had saved for this day. She'd had her hair straightened, pulled to the side, and curled in large ringlets with a white orchid nestled in the curls.

Brad could barely breathe as he watched Buddy walk Valerie down the path and over the bridge to the gazebo. Her beauty had stolen his breath. For a moment, he worried he'd do something embarrassing, like pass out. Then, once she handed Calla her flowers and placed her hands in his, his world righted and everything snapped back into order.

Danny Brown spoke, talking about love, God, marriage,

and faith. Brad let the words flow around him, hardly believing this day had finally come. He'd dreamed about it for so long. Fifteen years ago he'd written his heart's desire for this day and the lifetime that would follow on a single sheet of notebook paper and sealed it in a metal tin.

God had known all along they would end up in this place, but Brad could hardly believe it had actually happened. As they repeated their vows, he watched the emotions and expressions cross her face, knowing she loved him, knowing she longed to claim the title of his wife.

At Danny's command, he bent his head and gently kissed her lips. Their first kiss as husband and wife—the beginning of a lifetime together. She leaned into him and he cupped her cheek with his hand, wanting her to feel the intensity of his emotions, wanting that kiss to convey all the love he could never properly put into words.

As he lifted his head, he could hear the clapping from their friends and family as they celebrated this first kiss along with them. He smiled and winked down at her, then they turned to face the crowd. Calla handed Valerie her bouquet of orchids, and they walked hand-in-hand, over the bridge, and down the path to the castle.

The End

Reader's Guide: Discussion Questions

Suggested discussion questions for *Valerie's Verdict* by Hallee Bridgeman.

When asking ourselves how important the truth is to our Creator, we can look to the reason Jesus said he was born. In the book of John 18:37, Jesus explains that for this reason He was born and for this reason He came into the world. The reason? To testify to the *truth*.

In bringing those He ministered to into an understanding of the truth, Our Lord used fiction in the form of parables to illustrate very real truths. In the same way, we can minister to one another by the use of fictional characters and situations to help us to reach logical, valid, cogent, and very sound conclusions about our real lives here on earth.

While the characters and situations in *The Dixon Brothers Series* are fictional, I pray that these extended parables can help readers come to a better understanding of truth. Please prayerfully consider the questions that follow, consult scripture, and pray upon your conclusions. May the Lord of the universe richly bless you.

Uncle Buddy intentionally moved his niece Valerie away from the Dixon home so she could have "more diversity" in her life. In reality, he moved her away from the only family she ever knew and deposited her into a completely unknown environment.

1. Do you think Buddy's actions were fair for Valerie and for the Dixon brothers?
2. Do you think that disruption spurred Valerie to escape Atlanta after high school?

Acts 17:26 says: "And He has made from one blood every nation of men to dwell on all the face of the earth...."

3. Because all human beings have common ancestors in first Adam then in Noah, is it right to make decisions based on skin pigmentation or socio-economic status?

4. Phillip worried Buddy might have some personal issues with Brad and Valerie's relationship. Do you think those issues might be well-founded?

5. Women in the bathroom distinguished Valerie by her skin color in a derogatory manner. People often flippantly gossip like that. Have you ever been compelled to correct them? What kind of outcome has resulted from taking a stance?

Valerie suffers from a severe form of Post-Traumatic Stress. It brings about an obsessive-compulsiveness with her environment and causes her to experience irrational fear.

6. Do you think the anger she held onto against her attacker compounded the symptoms?

7. Do you think allowing God back into her life would ease those symptoms?

8. What kind of tools would a relationship with God give her to combat those symptoms?

Brad knows his brother, Jon, is hurting, but he doesn't know how to help him.

9. Do you think it is more helpful to push Jon for answers, or is loving him and ignoring the indicators of his pain (i.e., anger, heavy drinking, etc.) the better method to help him?

10. As the President of Dixon Brothers, Brad has taken on the mantle of leadership even among his brothers. Jon resents that, which becomes a barrier between the two. What steps can Brad take to further remove that barrier?

Tyrone indicates that he has accepted Jesus Christ as his personal Lord and Savior and has become a new creature in Christ.

11. Do you believe someone can really drastically change from such an evil abuser into a loving brother in Christ?

12. In the letter, Tyrone says that he is praying that one day Valerie will forgive him. As an act of faith, he is offering to remain in prison so that she will feel safer. Valerie has a very adverse reaction to this. Do you think she ought to forgive him?

13. Valerie is angry because Brad agrees that forgiveness should come. Despite his own initial anger toward Tyrone, Brad cites Biblical examples

to help explain why he feels Tyrone is worthy of forgiveness. Do you think he has a valid point?

14. In confiding her personal story with Valerie, Madison reveals that she actually married the man who once abused her. Do you think her husband truly changed inside?

Suggested luncheon menu for a group discussion about *Valerie's Verdict.*

Those who followed my Hallee the Homemaker website years ago know that one thing I am passionate about in life is selecting, cooking, and savoring good whole real food. A special luncheon just goes hand in hand with hospitality and ministry.

In case you're planning a discussion group luncheon surrounding this book, I offer some humble suggestions to help your special luncheon talk come off as a success. Quick as you like, you can whip up an unforgettable meal from the book that is sure to please and certain to enhance the discussion and your special time of friendship and fellowship.

Slow Roasted Beef Brisket

Valerie and Buddy share a fantastic BBQ Beef Brisket lunch together. If you'd like to make your own, here is a delicious, melt-in-your-mouth recipe.

4 pounds/lbs. beef brisket
1 $^{1}/_{2}$ cups beef stock
2 TBS salt (Kosher or sea salt is best)
1 TBS garlic powder
1 TBS onion powder
1 TBS fresh ground black pepper
2 tsp dry mustard
1 bay leaf, crushed

Preheat the oven to 350° degrees F (about 176° degrees C). Trim the fat from the brisket.

Mix the spices. Rub them all over the beef. Place in roasting pan and roast for 1 hour uncovered.

Add the beef stock to the pan. Tightly cover with foil. Lower the temperature of the oven to 300° degrees F (about 148° degrees C), and continue cooking for 3 hours (or longer as needed) until fork tender.

Kelly's BBQ Sauce

Tender meat is only as good as the sauce you serve it with. Here is a recipe that my friend Kelly the Kitchen Kop shared with me.

Mix it up and serve it with your beef.

If you want, you can optionally cover your beef with it the last 15 minutes of cooking.

1 (24 oz.) bottle of organic ketchup
Juice from 2 organic lemons
$^1/_2$ cup raisins
About $^1/_4$ cup brown sugar or pure honey
3 TBS Tamari (fermented soy sauce)
2 TBS mustard
$^1/_2$ tsp onion powder
$^1/_2$ tsp paprika
Kosher or Sea salt to taste—do not use iodized salt

NOTE:
2 TBS raw apple cider vinegar for *sweet* sauce
$^1/_2$ cup apple cider vinegar for a more *tangy* sauce

OPTIONAL:
Some readers recommend adding dash or up to TBS of your favorite hot pepper sauce to taste.
Some readers recommend adding dash of ground cayenne pepper for added heat
Other readers recommend adding 1 oz of Kentucky bourbon or (if you don't cook with any alcohol) one TBS of liquid smoke to add a light smoky flavor.

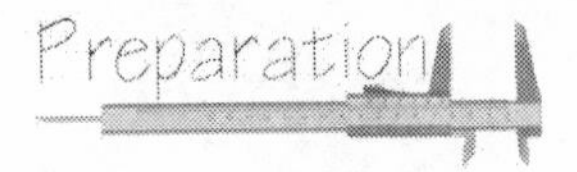

Soak the raisins in the raw apple cider vinegar in a blender. For *sweet* sauce use about 2 TBS of vinegar For a tangier sauce, use about $^1/_2$ cup vinegar.

After about 10 to 20 minutes, pulse to break them open. Don't make a paste. Let stand another 5 to 10 minutes. You are now ready to begin making the sauce.

In a blender, soak the raisins in the raw apple cider vinegar (see PREPARATION above) until ready.

Mix all ingredients EXCEPT the ketchup into the vinegar soaked raisins.

Mix about half of the ketchup last.

Blend slowly, adding the remainder of the ketchup a little at a time until the sauce is smooth.

Add salt to taste.

Add any optional ingredients (see INGREDIENTS) to taste and pulse or slowly blend until well mixed and smooth.

"Hot Potato" Salad

Because of a horrible incident in WWII involving some bad potato salad, and several resulting deaths among my grandfather's military unit, my family members have never been big potato salad eaters.

My mom insists that I made the recipe up as a child one night when she made barbecued chicken. In my memory, she always made this dish to go with barbecued chicken and it was her recipe. I honestly can't remember inventing it, and I can't remember her ever *not* making it. But I've always been very active in the kitchen, so it's possible that as a child I came up with the recipe.

Evidently, I made this recipe up because it is made and served right away, avoiding any possible spoilage issues. It is the perfect flavor accompaniment for the tangy sweet smokiness of the homemade sauce.

It's called "hot potato" salad because you make it warm and serve it warm, as a hot side dish instead of a cold salad.

6 good-sized potatoes
2 eggs
$^1/_4$ cup finely diced onion
1 large dill pickle
3 TBS mayonnaise
3 TBS yellow mustard
2 tsp Kosher salt, divided
$^1/_2$ tsp fresh ground black pepper

If you haven't already, finely dice the onion.

Also finely dice the dill pickle.

Scrub the potatoes really good—you're not going to peel them. Cut out the eyes and any "harvest" marks and discard.

Wash the eggs, too, because you're going to put them in with the potatoes.

Dice the potatoes so that 2 diced cubes comfortably fit on a spoon, about $^{1}/_{2}$ inch or a bit more than 1 cm on a side.

Put the diced potatoes in the pot. Add the eggs. Cover with cold water. Add 1 teaspoon salt. Boil until the potatoes are fork-tender, about 12 to 15 minutes. Remove from heat and drain.

Return the potatoes to the pan and fish out the eggs. Cool the eggs off with cold water just until you can handle them safely. They should still be plenty warm.

Add the diced onions and diced pickle into the pot with the potatoes. Add the mayonnaise and mustard.

Dice the eggs to cubes about half the size of the potato cubes, about $^{1}/_{4}$ inch or a bit less than 1 cm on a side. Add them to the potatoes along with 1 tsp salt and the pepper.

Stir until thoroughly combined.

Serve hot.

Coleslaw

Fresh, homemade coleslaw is a favorite dish, especially with fresh fish, barbecued chicken, or barbecued Beef Brisket!

$^{1}/_{2}$ head of green cabbage
2 carrots
$^{1}/_{2}$ cup mayonnaise
3 TBS apple cider or rice vinegar
2 TBS sugar
2 tsp Kosher or Sea salt—do not use iodized salt
1 tsp black pepper

Shred the cabbage.
Grate the carrots.

Whisk together mayonnaise, vinegar, and spices. Stir in cabbage and carrots. Mix well.

Jonathan Dixon sat in his idling truck staring at the doorway of the honky-tonk settled in the outskirts of Nashville, Tennessee. Though the place looked a little grubby from the outside, he could drive to this bar in less than twenty minutes when starting from the extended stay hotel his Atlanta team had secured for him. The next closest bar required nearly a forty-five-minute drive, and who had that kind of time?

Jon had arrived in Tennessee nearly half a year ago, assigned to the shopping mall construction project south of greater Nashville. Glancing around the parking lot, he assumed that several of the men on his team had already gone inside. He still didn't know whether he planned to go inside. So, he let the engine run and stared at the building as if it could give him some indication to assist him with that decision one way or another.

He pressed his fingertips to his temple and closed his eyes. In the six months he'd lived in that hotel, he'd stayed sober. Every single day he desired the numbing effects that the over-consumption of alcohol could offer, and every day he had managed to exercise that temptation away. But tonight, after seeing the news during dinner, he didn't feel like fighting it.

Fanatical extremists had attacked a girl's school in a village near the southern coast of the Mediterranean Sea. They'd locked the little girls inside the small schoolhouse and set it on fire with them inside. They watched it burn and killed any locals who tried to help the girls. In the end, thirty-seven girls, three teachers, and nine villagers died.

When Jon was sixteen, he went on a mission trip to Egypt. While there, he and his brothers had helped build a girls' school. Unlike the metropolitan areas near Cairo, most women in that particular region could neither read nor manage more than simple math at best. The school they helped build was the first school in that area that welcomed girls as students in more than five centuries.

Jon thought the school represented hope, that he and his team fought off prejudice and a culture that historically treated women like property, or worse. He'd felt so good about that, so right, so valorous. A year ago, he'd had the chance to go back to that country to teach and train. While there, he went to visit the school and discovered that terrorists had burned it down—just like the one last night.

A group had worked to systematically invoke terror and make sure their objections to the education of girls dominated any attempt to enlighten and elevate. Centuries old sectarian prejudice and hatred aided in the effort.

Jon closed his eyes and started to pray. "God, why? Why God? You hear me? I know I'm not perfect, but I've been willing to try to see and do things Your way my whole life. Why can't you end this hate? You made me with a heart that wants to help those in need, help those who are hurting, help those who never heard the good news that Your Son saved us from all of this. You give me that heart and then you break it over and over again? Why, God?"

Maybe it wouldn't have affected Jon so much if *he* hadn't built a school; if *he* hadn't stood there on that January morning and smelled the unforgettable odor that hung in the air over the still smoldering ruins. They had murdered seventeen little girls in a horrible, inhuman way—all because those girls had wanted to learn—and they had used the school he had helped build as the instrument of their deaths.

What good had it done to build the school in the first place? Did the cost of seventeen lives equal his individual sense of self-righteous accomplishment?

Now, another one, and even more children had died. As far as Jon understood it, this school made eleven girls' schools destroyed in the last two years. Hundreds of girls killed. Dozens of other people. All in the name of hate.

To any casual observer, Jon might have looked a little strange just sitting in that truck with the engine running, shaking his head with his eyes closed. Jon didn't care about that at the moment. "Just tell me this, God. Tell me how to make my heart stop hurting. At least tell me that. Because if you can't even do that much, then I think I can make it stop. Just tell me what I need to make my heart stop breaking. Amen."

He opened his eyes and instantly a happy couple walked out of the honky-tonk laughing. The light-haired man had his arm draped casually over the shoulder of the slim brunette at his side. In turn, she had her arm around his waist. They looked well acquainted with walking this way. Jon heard a few words between gales of laughter, something about something someone had said, and how someone else had reacted, and just how funny it all was. He looked at how happy these strangers appeared in their own private little world, in their private little bubble, as they casually headed to a pickup truck to leave for the evening. He almost felt angry toward them for their joy.

"So that's what I need?" Jon sneered, thinking of his brother Brad who had just gotten married. Brad had been in love with his wife since they were teenagers in high school. Jon had never been in love and could not, in that moment, imagine anyone ever loving him enough to even make it worth his while. "Nice try."

That settled it. Oh, he'd go in tonight. He'd go in and find a corner table and just drink. Drink away the smell of smoke in the air. Drink away hatred and ignorance on a level that brought people to commit acts of genocide in the name of their god. Drink away all the pain and poverty he'd seen in the world in his lifetime and especially drink away how it damaged his soul every single time he returned to his little world, his little bubble, his life of privilege and materialism.

He killed the engine and hopped out of the truck. He

bumped the door with his hip to make it shut all the way and latch. Last week, a bulldozer had backed into it and he just hadn't bothered to swap it out and send this one to the body shop.

He remembered how the dozer operator had stared at the truck in complete horror, absolutely certain Jon would not only fire him on the spot, but also ensure the man never had work on any other site anywhere south of the Mason-Dixon line. The ironic thing is that Jon probably could have done exactly that if he cared to do so.

Jon had his jobsite superintendent, Walter Gross, write the man up for a safety violation, and that was that. Construction work is dangerous business, and people, mostly men, get hurt and killed doing it. Safety mattered on the jobsite and could never be ignored or taken lightly. Having worked construction his entire life, Jon also recognized that accidents happen in all walks of life. Human beings make mistakes. Jon didn't feel like burning the guy to the ground over a wrinkle in his paint, but at the same time, something like that could never happen again.

In this case, Jon truly didn't care how bruised or battered his truck looked on the outside just as long as it started every time he got behind the wheel and drove him wherever he needed to go. Tonight, it brought him to this honky-tonk.

Once inside, Jon scanned the crowd. It was early, so he waved at a couple of the guys on his team then found a table in the corner exactly like he'd hoped. It was just far enough away from his crew that they could relax and not sweat the fact the boss had an eye on them. He pulled out the chair that was in the corner and tilted his ball cap back on his head. A waitress in a pair of too short denim shorts and a nearly transparent white shirt tied right under her breasts approached him. She wore her blonde hair in pigtails and had on bright pink lipstick, exactly the opposite of Jon's type, if he had a type. "Hello there. What can I get you?"

"You got a local lager on tap?"

"We do."

"Bring me a pitcher. And keep it full." He gestured around the bar. "That group there and," he looked toward the pool table, "that group there as well. On me."

"You got it, Sugar." From her reply, Jon assessed her as a lifelong local. In Atlanta, the "Sugar" would have come out as "Honey" or possibly "Hon." North of here, in Kentucky, a "Darlin'" or a "Sweetie" might have stood in for it instead. Here, the Tennessee equivalent of "Customer" was "Sugar." Jon didn't think there was a single thing about him that qualified as sugary or sweet.

As the waitress sashayed away, he monitored the door, watching people coming and going. About five minutes later, his jobsite superintendent came up to the table.

"Evening boss," Walter Gross greeted. He gestured at the chair opposite Jon's. Jon gave a slight nod of his head and the older man pulled out the chair and straddled it. His white hair was in stark contrast to his dark brown face. "Waitress just said you were buying a round for us."

"Hope that's okay with you, Walt." He straightened his chair when the waitress approached with a pitcher of beer and a stack of glasses. He handed her his personal credit card. "Thanks. Just put all these boys on my tab tonight. Sound good?"

The waitress headed back to the bar. Jon poured a glass and held it out to Walter, then poured another and leaned his chair back again, resting the glass on the top of his denim clad thigh.

Walt lifted his glass in a casual toast and took a sip of the straw-colored local brew. “It’s perfectly okay with me, boss. Much appreciated, in fact.”

Jon shrugged. “You guys have been working hard for a minute or two—more like fighting fire this week what with one thing after another. It didn’t go unnoticed. Spread the word if you see any more of our guys. I got the tab tonight.”

“I’m sure they’ll appreciate it, boss. But I think they’ll appreciate you noticing how hard they’ve been working even more.”

“You’re a good man, Walt. I’ve known that since the day I met you.” Jon scanned the room for more of his people. “I haven’t been in here before.”

Walter took his turn shrugging. “Decent for a local joint. Good place for pool and darts. Waitresses are all pretty nice. Food’s okay. Especially the burgers.”

Jon really wanted Walter to leave. Walter probably wanted nothing more than to leave. Both men knew this situation called for them to stay put and make manly chit-chat until one or the other of them finished a beer, at least. They weren’t going to talk shop, religion, or politics. It seemed unlikely they would talk about guns or fast cars. That left the only remaining topic men discussed with any amount of genuine interest.

A tall, incredibly thin woman walked in. She had on a pair of designer jeans and a silver cowboy-style shirt and carried a designer purse Jon knew retailed for over a thousand dollars. His eyes roamed down her body and he noticed the silver and black cowboy boots. “She’s certainly looking for attention," Jon remarked. "Think she's lost?"

Walter turned his head and followed Jon's gaze. "I hear she's from that big ranch just outside town. She was in here last night holding court. Watch." As he spoke, she slid into a chair at the bar. Immediately, four men surrounded her. She managed to speak to all four, giggle, place an order, and fan herself within a matter of seconds.

"Fascinating," Jon said.

Walter stood with his beer. "Not to be rude, but I'm going to excuse myself. I need to go over there and collect Ballard. That boy just got paid. He does not need to be near her right now." Walt stood, chugged down the remainder of his beer, and headed toward the bar.

While Jon watched, Walter grabbed young Cory Ballard by the back of his neck and pulled him out of the group surrounding the blonde. Cory scowled but did not go back. Instead, he found himself sitting at a table, pouting into a fresh beer. Walter sat next to him, talking low to him.

Finally alone, Jon lifted the frosty cold lager and took a long drink, swallowed three large gulps, then set the nearly empty glass back on the table in front of him. The months of forced sobriety had lowered his resistance and he immediately felt the effect of the mild dose of alcohol as it hit his system. He straightened his chair and filled his glass again, then leaned back into the corner.

He idly wondered if the Israelite slaves in Egypt drank cold beer or hot beer all those hundreds of years ago. It was an established fact that they drank beer, but had their beer been tepid or icy? If they drank it cold, how had they gotten it cold? This train of thought led him to start designing all kinds of primitive cooling systems in his imagination as he continued to drink.

About twenty minutes after the band started covering decades old country music songs, he watched a couple come through the door. The man stood tall and slender, with dirty blond hair and clothes that made Jon think of the discotheques in Europe. The woman had straight blonde hair that brushed against her chin and wore a pair of skin-tight black pants, a loose-fitting white tank top, and a tan sweater that fell off one shoulder. He knew without asking that they belonged to the woman currently holding court on the dance floor.

The couple looked around and the man pointed toward the band. Together they crossed the bar. Cory Norman, one of the jobsite foremen, immediately descended upon the blonde. She was a few steps behind the man and he kept walking. Cory had clearly had about two too many and grabbed her wrist as if he had the right. Jon stood and walked over.

At six-five, he usually stood out in a crowd. These men had worked for him for years, knew his father, knew his brothers, and knew his family. The sight of Jon walking toward him, staring right at him, made him let go of the woman and step back.

"Hey, Cory," Jon said when he reached them and could yell above the sound of the band.

"Hey there, Mr. Dixon."

Jon jerked his head in the direction of the exit. "Go on, then. I'm guessing you've had enough."

"Look, Mr. Dixon," Cory said, waving a finger in his face.

Jon didn't hesitate to grab the finger and twist it behind Cory's back, propelling him toward the door. "I said get. If you're drunk enough to be grabbing a lady who doesn't want to be grabbed, you've had one too many. If I weren't sure already, you thinking you can go wagging your finger in my face sealed it."

A group of his workmates witnessed the exchange, got to their feet, and rapidly took Cory off Jon's hands. This allowed Jon the opportunity to turn to the woman. "Awful sorry about that. You okay? He didn't hurt you, did he?"

She looked up at him with wide, almond-shaped green eyes. Despite the fact that he'd just rescued her, nothing about her screamed helpless female. Instead, she looked downright furious. "He did not. Thank you."

"That's good, then." He left it at that. The last thing he needed tonight was some doe-eyed blonde distracting him from his mission of consuming beer. He went back to his table and settled back into the corner, fresh beer on his knee. When the woman appeared beside the table, he raised an eyebrow. Slowly, he lowered his chair until all four legs contacted the ground. She just continued to stare at him. Something about her look got under Jon's skin. He gestured toward the chair Walter had vacated nearly half an hour earlier. "Take a seat?"

"Thank you." Ignoring the chair opposite him, she sat to his right and faced the dance floor. "I just had three propositions. I thought it might be safer to wait for my cousins here, if you don't mind."

He stared at her as she shifted her sweater onto both shoulders and craned her head around. He extended his hand. "Jon."

She lifted her chin in acknowledgment and placed her fingertips lightly against his calloused palm. "Alex."

For several minutes, they watched the man, Josh, argue with the woman holding court on the dance floor. "Want a beer?"

When the woman on the dance floor screeched and went after Josh's face with her fingernails, Alex nodded. "Yes. Yes, I think so." She helped herself to a fresh glass and poured from the pitcher.

Josh dragged the woman toward them, holding both her wrists with one hand. When he arrived at their table, he said, "Let's go."

"I think you need to be alone with her. I'll get a cab or something." Alex shook her head. "Besides, I'm not riding in the same car with her screeching and screaming all the way back to the ranch."

Josh gritted his teeth and said, "Alexandra."

"Sorry, cuz. She's your sister. Not mine. You have fun, now." She slowly lifted her beer and took a purposefully slow sip.

When the woman started screaming, Josh glared at Alex one more time and continued out of the bar, dragging a fighting, screeching woman behind him. After the door closed behind them, Alex took a long pull of her beer and then looked at Jon. "I need a break from those two for a little while."

"Can't say as I blame you."

The band announced a ten-minute break, and Jon silently appreciated the sudden relative quiet. It might afford him the ability to talk to someone without yelling if the need arose. He hated yelling. Only mildly curious, he asked, "What's her story?"

When Alex shrugged, the sweater fell again, revealing a

perfectly tan shoulder. "Oh, she's just kind of a hot mess." She took a long drink of beer. "Her parents sent her out here to hide from the press, if that gives you some idea. So, she decides to make a spectacle of herself as much as possible which kind of defeats the purpose of hiding out. Just bad decisions, really."

He straightened his chair and leaned his arms on the table. "What about you, Alexandra? What is your story? You hiding from the press, too?"

She ran her tongue over her teeth and smiled. "Well, Mr. Dixon, I think I'll just hold my cards close to the vest for a while if it's all the same to you."

Jon nodded. "A woman of mystery." He raised his glass in a mock toast then took a sip. Feeling the tug of attraction and the lack of inhibition that could only come from steady drinking, he tipped his hat further back on his head and grinned. "I'm pretty good at solving mysteries, and I've been known to be pretty patient in my time. I can wait."

Courting Calla

Dixon Brothers book 1

Ian knows God has chosen Calla as the woman for him, but Calla is hiding something big. Can Calla trust Ian with her secret, or will she let it destroy any possible hope for a future they may have?

Valerie's Verdict

Dixon Brothers book 2

Brad has always carried a flame for Valerie since his boyhood days. Her engagement to another man shattered his dreams. When she comes home, battered and bruised, recovering from a nearly fatal relationship, he prays God will use him to help her heal.

Alexandra's Appeal

Dixon Brothers book 3

Jon falls very quickly in love with Alex's zest for life and her perspective of the world around her. He steps off of his path to be with her. When forces move against them and rip them apart, he wants to believe God will bring them back together, but it might take a miracle.

Daisy's Decision

Dixon Brothers book 4

Ken has no idea but Daisy has had a crush on him since high school. Going on just one date can't possibly hurt, can it? Even if Daisy's just been painfully dumped by the man she planned to spend the rest of her life with and whose unborn baby she carries? Just one date?

by Hallee Bridgeman

Find the latest information and connect with Hallee on her website: www.halleebridgeman.com

FICTION BOOKS BY HALLEE

The Jewel Series:

Book 1: Sapphire Ice
Book 2: Greater Than Rubies
Book 3: Emerald Fire
Book 4: Topaz Heat
Book 5: Christmas Diamond
Book 6: Christmas Star Sapphire
Book 7: Jade's Match
Book 8: Chasing Pearl

Virtues and Valor series:

Book 1: Temperance's Trial
Book 2: Homeland's Hope
Book 3: Charity's Code
Book 4: A Parcel for Prudence
Book 5: Grace's Ground War
Book 6: Mission of Mercy
Book 7: Flight of Faith
Book 8: Valor's Vigil

The Song of Suspense Series:

Book 1: A Melody for James
Book 2: An Aria for Nick
Book 3: A Carol for Kent
Book 4: A Harmony for Steve

PARODY COOKBOOKS BY HALLEE

Vol 1: Fifty Shades of Gravy, a Christian gets Saucy!
Vol 2: The Walking Bread, the Bread Will Rise
Vol 3: Iron Skillet Man, the Stark Truth about Pepper & Pots
Vol 4: Hallee Crockpotter & the Chamber of Sacred Ingredients

www.halleebridgeman.com

With over half a million sales and more than 30 books in print, Hallee is a best-selling Christian author who writes romance and action-packed romantic suspense focusing on realistic characters who face real world problems. Her work has been described as everything from refreshingly realistic to heart-stopping exciting and edgy.

An Army brat turned Floridian, Hallee finally settled in central Kentucky with her family so she could enjoy the beautiful changing of the seasons. She enjoys the roller-coaster ride thrills that life with a National Guard husband, a daughter away at college, and two middle school aged sons delivers.

A prolific writer, when she's not penning novels, you will find her in the kitchen, which she considers the "heart of the home." Her passion for cooking spurred her to launch a whole food, real food "Parody" cookbook series. In addition to nutritious, biblically grounded recipes, readers will find that each cookbook also confronts some controversial aspect of secular pop culture.

She is a former Director for the Kentucky Christian Writers Conference (KCWC) and currently serves on the executive board. She is a Gold member of the American Christian Fiction Writers (ACFW), a past American Christian Writers (ACW) member, and Secretary of the board for Novelists, Inc. (NINC). A long-time member of the Published Author Network (PAN) and past president of the Faith, Hope, & Love chapter of Romance Writers of America (RWA) she discontinued her RWA membership in 2019.

Hallee loves coffee, campy action movies, and regular date nights with her husband. Above all else, she loves God with all of her heart, soul, mind, and strength; has been redeemed by the blood of Christ; and relies on the presence of the Holy Spirit to guide her. She prays her work here on earth is a blessing to you and would love to hear from you. You can reach Hallee via the Contact Link on her website or send an email to hallee@halleebridgeman.com.

Sign up for Hallee's monthly newsletter! When you sign up, you will get a link to download Hallee's romantic suspense novella, *On The Ropes*. In addition, every newsletter recipient is automatically entered into a monthly giveaway! The real prize is never missing updates about upcoming releases, book signings, appearances, or other events.

Newsletter Sign Up:
halleebridgeman.com/newsletter

Author Site:
halleebridgeman.com/

Facebook:
facebook.com/pages/Hallee-Bridgeman/192799110825012

Twitter:
twitter.com/halleeb

Goodreads:
goodreads.com/author/show/5815249.Hallee_Bridgeman

Homemaking Blog:
halleethehomemaker.com/Newsletter

Sign up for Hallee's monthly newsletter! When you sign up, you will get a link to download Hallee's romantic suspense novella, *On The Ropes*. In addition, every newsletter recipient is automatically entered into a monthly giveaway! The real prize is never missing updates about upcoming releases, book signings, appearances, or other events.

Hallee's Newsletter: Hallee's Happenings
http://www.halleebridgeman.com/newsletter/

Made in the
USA
Lexington, KY